RANDOM HOUSE

LARGE PRINT

The Minotaur

The Minotaur

A NOVEL

Barbara Vine

RANDOM HOUSE
LARGE PRINT

This is a work of fiction. Names, characters, places, and incidents are either the products of the author's imagination or are used fictitiously. Any resemblance to actual persons, living or dead, events, or locales is entirely coincidental.

Published in the United States of America by Random House Large Print in association with Shaye Areheart Books, New York.
Distributed by Random House, Inc., New York.

Originally published in Great Britain by Viking, a division of Penguin Books Ltd. London, in 2005.

The Library of Congress has established a Cataloging-in-Publication record for this title.

ISBN-13: 978-0-7393-2609-1
ISBN-10: 0-7393-2609-0

www.randomlargeprint.com

FIRST LARGE PRINT EDITION

10 9 8 7 6 5 4 3 2 1

This Large Print edition published in accord with the standards of the N.A.V.H.

To Jill Pitkeathley
with love

ACKNOWLEDGMENTS

I am very grateful to Lord Alderdice FRCPsych for his scrutiny of the character of John Cosway and the expert advice he gave me. My thanks are also again due to Richard, Lord Acton, a fine copy editor.

Now

ONE OF THE WOMEN BUYING AMBER WAS SO much like Mrs. Cosway that it gave me a shock to see her. She seemed shorter, but people shrink with age. Otherwise the likeness, from her curly white hair to her spindly legs and fine ankles, was almost uncanny. She was holding up a string of pale yellow beads, looking at them and smiling with that excitement you only see on the faces of women who love shopping and pretty things.

Charles has a theory that if you are in X, a distant place you have never been to before, and while there you meet or pass in the street your nearest and dearest, a spouse or lover or even your child, you won't recognize them. Not only do you not expect to see them there; you know they **can't** be there because you have certain knowledge that at this moment they are hundreds of miles away. Of course, they can be there, they are there, they have deceived you or your knowledge of their whereabouts is in fact very uncertain, but the chances are you will pass on, telling yourself this was no more than an extraordinary resemblance.

Mrs. Cosway fitted into none of the categories I have named. I hadn't even liked her, but I had certain knowledge of where she was now. She was dead. This woman looked like her but was someone else. I turned away and began to walk on. She called after me.

"Kerstin!"

If she had pronounced my name as it should be pronounced, that is as, more or less, "Shashtin," I might have turned around and gone up to her, but it wouldn't have been a shock, it wouldn't have sent a shiver through me. But she had called me "Curstin," the way the Cosways, all of them except John, invariably had done. I walked across the cobbled square and went up to her.

"You don't know me, do you? Of course I'm awfully changed, I know that. It's inevitable at my age."

The voice told me. "Ella," I said.

She nodded, pleased. "I knew **you.** You've changed too but I knew you. This is my daughter Zoë and my granddaughter Daisy. Always girls in our family, isn't it?"

Zoë was a tall dark woman in her early thirties, handsome, brown-eyed, holding a child of about six by the hand. We shook hands.

"Does she remind you of anyone?"

"Winifred," I said.

Zoë made a face. "Oh, Mother."

How often had I heard those words from Ida

when Mrs. Cosway said something particularly outrageous.

"What brings you to Riga?"

"Zoë wanted to see the art nouveau in Alberta Street. She's doing an art history course, so we thought we'd do a tour of the Baltic States." If Ella assumed I was doing the same thing, if for a different reason, she was right, but I doubt if that was why she didn't ask. The Cosways were never much interested in other people's activities. "Shall I buy this amber? You'll say it's a wicked price, I know."

"On the contrary," I said. "You'll never get it cheaper anywhere else."

Perhaps she resented this for she said rather severely, "Mother never forgave you for the diary, you know."

This wasn't the moment for argument. "It's a long time ago. What happened—is—I mean, what became of John?"

"He's still alive, if that's what you mean. Zorah took him to Tuscany with her, but he lives alone now—well, with a couple to look after him. You'll say that anyone as crazy as he is couldn't manage, but he does."

I smiled at her usage, the attributing of unlikely views to me, which once annoyed me so much.

"Buy that amber for me, Zoë, will you? Our bus will be here any minute. Oh, John, yes. He has a lovely house near Florence. Or so I'm told. Not that we ever get invited, do we, Zoë? Of course he's a rich man. The land the Hall was on was sold and they built four houses where it was. Planning! I ask you. I don't know what he does with it all. They say he never goes out and he's seventy-five now."

Their tour bus came slowly around the corner and pulled up in the square. It was nearly full. I wanted to ask her who she had married. Who was Zoë's father? They were already on the steps.

"Will you be back here tonight?" I said.

"We're due back at five, aren't we, Zoë?"

"Meet me for a drink," I said, naming my hotel. "Six-thirty okay?"

She called something back that I didn't catch. I waved as the bus moved off, and when it was out of sight, turned away. What I had heard of John Cosway made me so happy that I walked back to the hotel, to Charles and Mark and Anna, with a spring in my step.

Then

1

I AM A CARTOONIST.

We are thin on the ground, we women cartoonists; it's still thought of as a man's job, and there are even fewer of my sort who aren't English and never went to art school. Over the close-on thirty years that I have been contributing a couple of cartoons to each issue of a weekly news magazine, I have drawn Harold Wilson and Willy Brandt, Mao Zedong and Margaret Thatcher (hundreds of times), John Major, Neil Kinnock, David Beckham, and Tony Blair (nearly sixty times). People say I can catch a likeness with a few strokes and squiggles; they know who it's supposed to be before they read the caption or the balloon coming out of a character's mouth. But I was no child artist prodigy, I don't remember learning anything about art at school and for years all I ever drew was a Dog Growing for my small niece and nephew.

I'll tell you about the Dog Growing because you may want to make one for your own children. You take a sheet of paper; a letter-sized sheet, cut vertically in half, will do very well. Then you fold it in half again and fold the folded-over piece back on itself to make an inch-wide pleat. Flatten it out again and draw a dog across the folds. It's best to make it a dachshund or a basset hound because it should have a long stretch of body between forelegs and hindlegs. Then refold your paper into its pleat. The dog now has a short body but when the child opens the pleat the dog grows into a dachshund. Of course, when you get practiced at it, you can make a Giraffe's Neck Growing or a Turkey Growing into an Ostrich. Children love it and that was all I ever drew all through my teens and when I was at university.

I was going to be a nurse and then I was going to teach English. I never considered drawing as a career because you can't make a living out of a Dog Growing. It was in the late sixties when I came to England, fresh from the University of Lund and my English degree and with a fairly humble nursing qualification. I had a job lined up and a place to live, but my real motive in coming was to renew my love affair with Mark Douglas.

We had met at Lund, but when he graduated he had to go home and all his letters urged me to follow him. Get a job in London, get a room. Everyone in London, he wrote, lives in a bedsitter. I did the next best thing and got a job in Essex, near the main line from Liverpool Street to Norwich. The family who was employing me was called Cosway, and the house they lived in, Lydstep Old Hall. I had never in my life seen anything like that house.

It was very large yet it hardly looked like a house at all, more a great bush or huge piece of topiary work. When I first saw it in June it was entirely covered, from end to end and from foundation to the line of the roof, in intensely green Virginia creeper. I could see it was oblong and that its roof was almost flat but if there were architectural features such as balconies, railings, recessed columns, stonework, none showed through the mass of glossy green. Windows alone peeped out of this leafy wrapping. It was a rather windy day and, because the breeze set all the hundreds of thousands of leaves shivering, there was an illusion that the house itself moved, shrank, expanded, and subsided again.

"Be like living inside a tree," said the taxi man as I was paying him. "You'd think all that stuff would damage the brickwork. I wouldn't fancy it. Friends of yours, are they?"

"Not yet," I said.

Lydstep Old Hall was the first thing I ever drew. Apart from Dogs Growing, that is. I drew it that night, from memory as I was inside the house, and that is how I have drawn everything ever since.

Mark's sister-in-law Isabel Croft got me the job. She had been at school with the youngest Cosway girl.

"Zorah won't be living at home any longer," she said when I asked her to tell me about the family. "I don't really know who will. Ida, certainly. She housekeeps for them. Her other two sisters I never knew well. They may have married or gone to live elsewhere. The house actually belongs to John."

"The one I'm to have charge of? He's schizophrenic, is that right?"

"I don't know," she said. " 'Charge' is rather a strange word to use."

"Mrs. Cosway's," I said, "not mine."

"I never heard a name for what's wrong with John," Isabel said. "It rather puzzles me—but there, I expect Mrs. Cosway knows what she's talking about. There's a trust to administer the estate. It's a strange business, something to do with the way Mr. Cosway left things in his will. I don't suppose you want to know the details. His marriage had gone wrong, I think, and he and Mrs. Cosway hardly spoke to each other in his last years. Mrs. Cosway was always nice to me, but she is rather a difficult woman. Well, you'll see. The house is very big, but they keep some of the rooms shut up."

I asked her what she was going to say about being puzzled. She hadn't finished her sentence.

"I was going to say I wouldn't have thought John needed looking after. You've been a nurse and he didn't need a nurse when I knew him. Of course he sometimes behaved strangely, but he never did any harm. But I don't really know."

There were so many things she didn't say. Most of them she simply knew nothing about. The Cosways were good at keeping things hidden—from other people and one another.

In the novels of the nineteenth century which I had read while studying English, girls taking posts in country families are always met at the nearest station by some old retainer with a pony and trap. No such offer had been made to me. The Cosways had neither retainer nor pony and the one car they possessed was used by Ella Cosway to go to work. I took a taxi. There were always taxis outside Colchester station and still are for all I know.

The route it followed has been much built up since then and the old road has become a three-lane highway. We drove along winding lanes, some of them narrow, for part of the way following the valley of the River Colne, passing the gates of several great houses. I had read a little about the architecture of Essex and knew that the county lacked building stone. Wood, brick, chalk, and flint were the materials used and another material called pudding stone, oblong and rounded pebbles of flint, much used in the construction of churches and of some walls. But the most important material of all was timber and I gazed out of the taxi window, happy to see the information I had read of confirmed in mansions and farmhouses built of tiny Tudor bricks with weatherboarding and half-timbering. Of course it aroused my expectations of what the house I was going to would be like, for Isabel had never described it. It might have a moat, as some did, part of its roof might be thatched, its windows mullioned and its woodwork bare and unstained. And then there was the maze.

"In the grounds, do you mean?" I'd said to her. "Made of hedges?"

But she only laughed and said, "You'll see."

My excited anticipation made me ask the driver how much farther it was, and when he said two miles, I had to restrain myself from telling him to hurry up. We bypassed the village but no matter where you were within five miles of Windrose you could hardly fail to see the church, All Saints, its tall rose-red tower a landmark which drew and held your eyes. The Great Red Tower of Windrose, people called it, and some said the name of the village came from its color. Lydstep Old Hall was about half a mile farther on, at the top of a long hill. We approached it along a cart track which the taxi man called a "drive" and which had been graveled over where it opened out and the house was reached. There was no sign of a maze in this part of the grounds, only grass and ancient oak trees and holly.

The front door, of weathered oak, was of course set back, a rectangular hole deep in the green canopy. Now they were close to my eyes, I saw how large each shiny leaf was and, when one brushed my face, felt how cool it was to the touch. You can sometimes only tell an artificial houseplant from a real one by touching its leaves, and then there's no doubt. The imitation one feels stiff and dead while the real seems to breathe and yield under your fingers. The leaf that touched my cheek was like that.

I rang the bell and a woman came to the door. You may have seen her picture in the papers and on the television, though there weren't many of these and it was so long ago. None of the photographs of family members were good likenesses. The drawing I made of her was nearer, though perhaps it's vain of me to say so. At first I thought she must be an employee. She looked about fifty and wore one of those crossover overalls, the staple of sitcom dailies.

She held out her hand and said, "I am Ida Cosway. How do you do?"

The hand she gave me was hard and callused, red and work-damaged.

"Kerstin Kvist," I said and followed her into the hallway, humping my two suitcases.

No description of the inside of that house appeared in the papers and I shan't describe it now. Later on I will give some idea of how it was. I shall just say now that this hallway was the oldest part, an ancient vestige of a house which may have dated back to before Tudor times and which Ella Cosway told me had stood on this spot when the Battle of Agincourt was fought. The fine timbering I hoped to see showed on the plastered walls and low ceiling and there was some carving, vague shapes of roses and shields, half-obliterated by time and wear. Facing the front door was a great inglenook fireplace of red and black bricks.

Ida asked me if I had eaten and, when I said I had, offered me a cup of tea. Swedes drink far more coffee than tea, but I accepted because I disliked the thought of being shown to my room before I had made my situation and the terms under which I was prepared to work here clear to her (in case her mother had kept them to herself) and found out a little more about this family. She took my cases from me and placed them side by side at the foot of the staircase, rather a mean staircase for such a large house with such a noble hallway, its treads covered in linoleum and its wooden banister rail attached to the bare wall by metal struts. We went down a passage into the kitchen, very large and reasonably well appointed, but the height of its ceiling, all the pots and pans and a lantern hanging from a big black iron contraption the shape of a drying rack, made me think of a film I had seen set in the eighteenth century where food was prepared in just such a place. There were a table and a number of assorted chairs, armchairs as well as the upright kind, and a sofa covered in a blue check blanket.

"Do sit down," Ida said in her lifeless voice. "You must be tired from your journey."

"Not really," I said. "I should like to go out for a walk later."

"Goodness," she said. The monotonous tone she invariably spoke in made it unclear whether this was uttered in admiration for my hardihood or dismay at my folly. "Sugar?"

"No, thank you," and I added hastily, "and no milk either."

I had stopped her just in time. The habit of putting milk into an infusion of leaves has always struck me as bizarre. I watched with relief as she passed me a large saucerless mug of neat brown tea, clear as the water of the Colne was in those days.

"Are your mother and your brother at home?" I asked her.

"Mother is out with John." I nodded, though the day was gray and the wind rising all the time. "He insists on going out and she doesn't care for him to go alone." She managed to smile at me, a smile that aged her by sending wrinkles up her cheeks and around her eyes. "I expect that will be one of your jobs. They'll soon be back."

"Perhaps you'll tell me something of what I'll be expected to do for him. Your mother's letters said very little."

"What excellent English you speak," she said. "Really, I didn't expect it."

"All Swedes speak English." This was an exaggeration, though most do. "They wouldn't get very far if they didn't. You were telling me about your brother."

"Yes," she said. "John, yes."

I sensed she disliked the idea and was trying to avoid it, but lacked the cunning or conversational skills to do so. In the ensuing silence, I drank my tea and studied her. She was a tall woman, as tall as I am, and I, to use the system then used in England, am five feet nine. The drawing I did of her four or five weeks later shows a fine-boned face as rough and neglected as her hands, and gray-threaded hair as dull as her dark brown tweed skirt. Perhaps my cartoonist's habit of exaggerating a subject's outstanding feature came into play here, for I doubt if Ida can have been as round-shouldered as she is in my sketch. Whether I rendered the tension that seemed to grip her, I can't tell. It intensified as I pressed her to tell me more about her brother, though I tried to speak gently.

She spoke more rapidly, as if anxious to say what had to be said as fast as possible, so that pleasanter things could be discussed. "He was quite normal as a little boy. Later on he began to get—strange. My mother has her own theories as to what started it off and so does our doctor, Dr. Lombard. He treats John. He needs constant care—well, watching."

"I'm very sorry. Your mother takes care of him?"

"She and I," Ida said, "and now you. Now she's getting old—well, of course, she **is** old—it is becoming too much for her to do single-handed. My sisters and I help, but they both have jobs. It was John himself who wanted you—well, wanted someone, and of course what John wants John gets." Her dry laugh had an unpleasant sound, halfway between a cough and a gasp. I was later to learn that Mrs. Cosway and her other daughters also laughed like that, as if laughter itself was a discreet substitute for a bitter comment. "Though not as much as he used to," she said.

I had no idea what she meant.

"You said you would stay a year, I think. There won't be a great deal for you to do. And you needn't look like that"—I wasn't aware I was looking anything but interested—"there's nothing distasteful. Anyway, you've been a nurse. He can feed himself and the—the other thing, you know." She meant his excretory processes and what nurses call the waterworks, but the effort at clumsy euphemism made her blush. "You won't find it arduous. Really, it's more like babysitting, only the baby is a grown man."

She seemed to be considering whether to say more, then impulsively said, "There's madness in the family." The expression was old-fashioned then if not yet politically incorrect, but she repeated it. "Yes, madness in the family." When people say this, phrasing it in various ways, they always sound pleased about this particular genetic inheritance. Cancer or arthritis "in the family" is spoken of quite differently. "My great-grandfather was strange," she said. "He went completely insane, and his son was eccentric, to say the least."

She compressed her lips and I could tell she was feeling she had said too much. "Perhaps I could see my room now," I said.

"Of course."

We went upstairs. The passage was wide, more like a gallery, and with framed engravings on the walls. Ida showed me into a room facing the front. "This room," she said, putting the suitcase she was carrying for me on the bed, "was intended for my brother. It has its own bathroom, you see. My father was alive then and he had it put in. John didn't like it. He twice let the bath overflow and water came down through the ceiling. He doesn't like showers either—well, he doesn't much like upstairs, so now he sleeps in a room off the hall. I told you he always gets what he wants. But it's dreadful to be mad, isn't it?"

"It's very sad," I said sincerely. "I feel for you all."

"Do you?" she said wistfully, as if little sympathy for their lot had come from anyone else. "That's nice of you."

Because I like to have things straight, with everyone knowing what everyone else is doing, I asked if it would be all right for me to take a look around downstairs before I went out. At first she seemed taken aback but she rallied. "Of course. Turn right out of your room and you'll find the back stairs. They are nearer."

For a moment I was unsure if this was her rather clumsy way of telling me that now I was in the position of a servant, I must use the back stairs just as I must use the back door. But when I knew her better I understood that it was quite otherwise. She was just awkward. She had been cut off from ordinary social usage by a sheltered and reclusive life.

I unpacked one of the cases and hung my clothes in the cupboard on the dry cleaner's wire hangers provided. I mention this because these hangers epitomized perhaps more than anything the way the Cosways lived, with a mean and cheeseparing indifference to comfort. The first drawer I opened was full of pencils—well, there were probably twenty of them rattling around in it. I wondered who had left them there—the schizophrenic brother? Sometimes I think it was those pencils, hardish, soft, and very soft, that prompted me to draw and that without them, I might now be just retiring from my teaching job in Stockholm.

The other suitcase I left till later. Looking out of my window between the thin, unlined curtains of a fabric I believe was called cretonne, I saw an old lady, tall and very thin, walking slowly along in the meadow beyond the garden, with a young man. Of course John Cosway wasn't very young, he was thirty-nine, but everyone treated him as a child, including myself for a while.

The back stairs I found without trouble. They too were "linoed" in a dull gravy-brown color.

They brought me into a passage where one open door showed me the way into the back garden, flowerless but well tended, and another into a passage with many doors, all of which, I think, were locked. I say "I think" because at that time I tried only two of them. The passage was unlit, though there were bulbs in parchment lampshades hanging from the ceiling. I walked in the other direction and found a gloomy dining room. Pictures on the walls were all steel engravings of ruins in eighteenth-century Italy. Since then I have often seen engravings like these on hotel walls and marveled at why people would want to look, or be expected to want to look, at monochrome pictures of crumbling walls, broken turrets, fractured staircases, and piles of weed-grown rubble. One of those in the Cosways' dining room was of a dispirited-looking shepherd and a fat maiden reclining side by side on the topmost tier of a ruined amphitheater.

John's room, I thought, must be behind one of the doors opening off the hall. I decided it would be wrong of me to try any of those doors and went into the drawing room instead. It was large and of those slightly wrong proportions that characterize large late-Victorian chambers, for the hallway at the Hall was all that remained of an ancient building. Like the other rooms I had seen, though adequately if drearily furnished, this one was without cushions or table lamps or books. Ornaments there were but they were the kind that made me think none of the occupants of this house had chosen them; they were of the sort which friends and relatives, desperate for what to give at Christmas or birthday, bestow for the sake of giving something, no matter what. There was a paperweight in the shape of a cat and made of chromium, a green and khaki plant holder with no plant to hold, two or three small glass animals, probably Venetian, and a fretwork letter rack, designed to be on a wall but which no one had bothered to hang up.

To all this kitsch there was one exception, a geode. It was the beautiful thing in that room and much larger than these things usually are. When I first saw it I wondered where it had come from and what it was doing there, this oval stone dull as granite but showing, where it had split open, its glittering lode of amethyst quartz. I would have liked to touch it but did not quite care to. It seemed overly familiar on my first day there. There would be other occasions, I thought, and I walked back along the passage to find my way out into the garden. The interior of the house had disappointed me, but I had faith in the maze. I was sure I was about to find it.

2

How much of the lawns, shrubberies, copses, and parkland I walked over were part of the Lydstep land, I had no idea at the time. These grounds were pleasant and pretty enough, but I had been looking for a labyrinth and I hadn't found it. I was struck by the strangeness of that in itself, that a maze that by its very nature is a puzzle, should also be a puzzle to find.

As I came back, the kitchen window opened and Ida put her head out, calling to me to come in as tea was ready. I believed I had had my tea and supposed the next meal would be supper or dinner, but when I walked into the kitchen I saw bowls of tinned fruit and plates of tongue and ham, a cake and biscuits and a great many already buttered slices of bread. Frugal in many ways Mrs. Cosway might have been, but her meanness didn't extend to food. The Cosways always ate well.

"This is my mother," Ida said, and with great formality, "and this is my brother John. Mother, may I introduce Miss Kvist?"

"Kerstin Kvist," I said, giving my name its Swedish pronunciation.

Mrs. Cosway didn't get up but put out her hand. "How do you do?" She had that English upper-class voice which foreigners find forbidding and sometimes absurd. She appeared to be turning the syllables of my name over in her mind. "According to your letter your name is Kerstin," she said like an overbearing teacher, "not Shashtin. Have you changed it since you wrote?"

"K, e, r, s, t, i, n is pronounced Shashtin, Mrs. Cosway."

"What a strange idea," she said, implying by words and look that, among civilized people, only English pronunciation was admissible and that I might not know how to articulate my own name. "It must make things very awkward. Say hello to Miss Kvist, John."

My drawing of Julia Cosway shows a craggy face, the skin rough and deeply wrinkled with the same neglected look as her daughter's and her mouth set in a downward curve. I think I have caught on that ruined face the grimness and distaste it wore when she looked at her son. I had an impression of control being exercised and words she would have liked to utter, suppressed. I was too young then to know that there are women who actively dislike their own children.

Like the rest of them (as I later came to find out)

John Cosway was good-looking, with regular features and dark eyes. I had no idea then if his other sisters were tall or if he were an instance of one member of a family failing to inherit height, but when I saw him in the meadow he had seemed shorter than Mrs. Cosway. So much for the old wives' tale that a man is always taller than his mother. Of the whole family and the other Windrose people I came to know, John is the only one I never drew. It seemed wrong to try to catch the likeness of a mentally disturbed and defenseless man, as if I would be doing something unfair.

"Hello, Miss Kvist," he said in the tone of an upper-class robot.

My impression was that he spoke entirely of his own volition and not because he had been prompted. But the hand I held out to him was not so much ignored as repudiated. It wasn't quite a shrinking, more a controlled retreat.

To cover my dismay, I said, "You must call me Kerstin," and to Ida and her mother, "I'd like everyone to do that."

Mrs. Cosway had the same sort of coughing laugh as Ida, dry, cackling, and dismissive. She laughed like that then and said she would try. "But I don't know how I shall get my tongue around it."

"Shashtin," said John, with perfect enunciation. "Shashtin, Shashtin."

"Eat your tea, John." His mother spoke to this

handsome and intelligent-looking man as if he were a child of five.

Unused to digesting anything at that hour, I did my best with a slice of ham, half a round of bread, and four halves of apricot. John cut his bread and butter up into small triangles, each slice divided into four. These he spread either with jam, fish paste, Marmite, or cream cheese, each triangle different in color and flavor. Placing the plate directly in front of him, the horizontal cut through the center of the bread parallel with the table edge, he began to eat, taking care not to disarrange the other pieces when he picked up the top left-hand triangle. He seemed totally concentrated on this task, absorbed by it to the exclusion of all else.

I have already said that I prefer to get things straight and to clear up mysteries when I meet new people, for I particularly dislike being among those who expect you to know everything about them and their family, its ramifications and offshoots, without ever having been told. Such women—they are usually women—are quickly irritated and even become angry if you fail to place the child they are talking about in its proper context or are ignorant of whose wife so-and-so is or that uncle such-and-such died three years before, even though there is no possible way you could have known.

I had therefore made up my mind to ask for details of family members from Mrs. Cosway when she suddenly said, "You will need to know who everyone in the household is and where in our family they fit, Miss—er, Shashtin." She pronounced my name correctly for the first and last time.

"Yes," I said, "I will."

"My eldest daughter and my son you have already met. My daughter Zorah, that is Mrs. Todd, is not here at present. She is in London, she has a home there." Whereas now the American word for "house" is a commonplace, it was seldom used in England then. Mrs. Cosway spoke it with a kind of bitter pride. "The other two Misses Cosway, my daughters Winifred and Ella," she said, "are at present out. They seem to need constant entertainment and will later be attending a wine and cheese party, whatever that may be, in the village hall. That is the extent of our family. Is there anything you would like to ask?"

Her crisp tone and manner of one chairing a committee amused me but I took care not to let my amusement show. "Not about what you've just told me," I said, "but I would like to know what my duties are to be."

"Tea is over," she said. "We'll go into the drawing room."

John remained behind with Ida, to whom was left the task of clearing up and washing the dishes. I began to wonder if she did all the work of this house without any help from her sisters, whom their mother had made sound as if they led hectic and frivolous lives.

Now that it was close on evening the day had brightened and shafts of pale sunshine gleamed through the French windows onto the carpet, showing up the threadbare patches on its faded pink and green. Later on, a single hanging lamp, a branched wooden chandelier with two of its bulbs missing, would light this room. Mrs. Cosway had seated herself on the pink and beige sofa and with a downward patting motion of her hand, indicated to me that I was to sit in what Ida told me some time afterward was called a fireside chair, wooden-armed and with a loose seat cushion. Again I noticed that there was nothing to do in this room except watch television—no books, no record player or radio, no pictures to look at (except for a huge and very dark landscape in oils) or photographs to comment on. You could, I supposed, occupy yourself with examining the geode.

"I see you are looking at Grandfather Cosway's find."

"Yes," I said, wondering if this was the mad forebear, "it's very beautiful."

Again that dismissive laugh. It would be hard to say how I knew it was a laugh at all for no light showed in her eyes, her mouth remained downturned and the sound which came out of it was no more than a series of coughs.

"My late husband's grandfather was one of those amateur geologists. It was quite a popular thing to be in the last century. Of course they were all amateurs then, there was no such thing as a degree in these subjects and they were none the worse for that." She waited for my agreement and when none came, went on, "He was an explorer too and he found that amethyst geode while traveling to Mogador through the Atlas Mountains. On a camel, I suppose." A pause while she gave this some thought. "Do you think it would have been on a camel?"

Not realizing then—how could I have realized?—that this was the only time she would ever address a friendly casual inquiry to me, I said, "A camel or a donkey perhaps."

"A donkey isn't a dignified animal. Grandfather was very dignified, according to my husband, and corpulent, though he may not have been in his youth. He was a peculiar man but gifted. He made our library here. Did you ask me something?"

"What my duties are to be."

"Ah, yes. Really they'll consist in looking after John when I am unable to. When I'm tired, for instance." She had a disconcerting stare or, rather, one which she intended to be disconcerting. I returned it and our eyes met. "You could ask him. He wanted you. But you'll get a dusty answer." She followed this up with her cough-laugh and said unexpectedly, "I am nearly eighty years old, you know."

I don't belong to that school of thought which decrees that when someone tells you her age you should automatically reply that she doesn't look it. Mrs. Cosway looked every hour of her seventy-nine years.

"I think it will be best," she said, "for you to observe my routine with John tomorrow and perhaps the next day. Then you'll know how to take over when necessary. Once we've done that, I'd like to take a rest on my bed every afternoon after lunch for two hours and sometimes I should like to go out in the evenings." That look was again leveled at me. "One has friends in this village whom one doesn't see enough of. I would like to see them." She proceeded to tell me some of the things about John that Ida had already mentioned and some she had not. "He has medicine—well, drugs. Strictly prescribed by our doctor, of course. Without them there's a possibility he might be violent. It's a bad business, isn't it?"

I thought this a strange way of putting it. "It's very sad," I said for the second time that day, and she looked narrowly at me as if I had corrected her.

"Is there anything else?"

"I'd like you to confirm that I'm to have every other weekend off and one whole day in every week."

"Oh, yes, that was agreed."

She turned her eyes to the sunspots on the carpet. Outside, where the evening seemed to be warming and brightening all the time, Ida was putting up a washing line, taking advantage of the unexpected drying weather. John had come out with her because, it seemed, the clothes prop refused to stand erect. He took it from her, careful not to touch her hands, drove it into the ground, and stood back, nodding slightly.

Mrs. Cosway's eyes followed mine and she twisted around in her chair the better to see her son. "Strange, isn't it?" she said. "He was quite a normal child. Of course he never got on well with other boys and he used to have these tantrums. One couldn't do anything with him. But apart from that—well, what is there to say? It makes one wonder. Our doctor, a brilliant man, says his trouble is the result of a severe emotional shock."

It made me wonder, too. Ida had told me her mother had her own theories about the onset of John's schizophrenia. If she had she was clearly determined not to mention them to me—or not yet? John and Ida were pegging out the clothes now, John arranging all his pegs precisely the same distance apart regardless of the width of the pillowcase or shirt he was hanging up. Something about this surprised me, for I had never heard of obsessive compulsive behavior being part of the schizophrenia pattern.

"You may as well start tonight," Mrs. Cosway said. "He sleeps downstairs but he doesn't have his bath till the morning. I give him a sleeping pill."

She added in the sort of tone that expects argument, "Always."

"Is he a poor sleeper, then?"

She didn't answer. "He insists on the pill. He thinks it's a vitamin—well, multi-vitamins. It's better that way."

I was shocked. Of course I was. "Your doctor prescribes it?"

"Of course. 'I should tell John it's vitamins,' he said. 'Otherwise you'll find he won't take it.' "

It seemed wise to ask no more along these lines for the present. "I'd like to ask you something else. It has nothing to do with John. Are there any books in the house?"

"Books?" She said it as if I had asked whether there were any elephants.

"Yes. If you don't mind I'd like to have a look and borrow something to read. Just until I can find a library."

She seemed to be considering, weighing something or someone up. Perhaps me. Then she said, "We have a library here. We keep it locked."

I could find nothing to say.

"Yes, I daresay you find that strange. One has one's reasons. I told you my husband's grandfather made the library in this house. Let me just say that the way he made it was odd and not particularly—suitable."

This immediately made me think it must contain one of those secret Victorian collections of erotica I had read about. But all I said was, "I shall manage until I can get into Colchester and join the library."

"I didn't say we had no books. Ella has plenty. You can have a look in her room, she won't mind," Mrs. Cosway said, with the air of someone making a derogatory remark, "she's easy-going," and she laughed.

She was very old and I expected her to have some difficulty in getting up off that sofa, into which she had sunk deeply. Its seat cushions sagged and it looked as if its springs had gone. I sensed that any help I offered would be brusquely refused. But I need not have worried for she stood up as easily as a twenty-year-old and without that tell-tale movement of pushing herself upright by pressing on the seat with both hands. Once on her feet, she stood as erect as I did, her back straighter than her daughter's.

"John will want to go to bed now," she said.

It was very early, not yet seven, and an unexpectedly fine day. Ida and John were no longer on the lawn where bedlinen and shirts hung unmoving in the still air. Mrs. Cosway went off to look for him and he came back with her. Perhaps I should say that he came in and she came in, there being no sense of one having fetched the other. I saw that he moved slowly and in a dazed fashion, but there was no coercion on Mrs. Cosway's part.

Apart from mine, there appeared to be only one

bathroom in the house, though that virtually useless sanitary device, the washbasin, was to be found in every bedroom except John's. It took me a few days to appreciate my luck in having, rare in England at that time, a private shower room six feet from my bed. Where John had chosen to sleep wasn't like a bedroom at all but another drearily furnished high-ceilinged chamber with armchairs and "fireside" chairs, small tables, and an upright piano, the curtains of chenille in a color called "old gold." It was dark too, due to the Virginia creeper leaves thrusting over the edges of the window. John's bed was a convertible settee and his washing arrangements a marble-topped stand with an earthenware bowl on it and a jar for his toothbrush.

"I'll come back in ten minutes," I said, determined not to be there while this grown man undressed himself.

Mrs. Cosway gave me a look implying she hadn't expected any assertiveness from me. I said nothing and occupied myself with unpacking the rest of my clothes and setting out on a dressing table, which would serve me as a desk, the large leather-bound diary I had brought with me.

I gave them the time I had said I would, which seemed reasonable. John was in striped pajamas and a dressing gown. "Shashtin," he said, a flat utterance of my name with no apparent pride in his correct pronunciation.

"John," I said, and after that, when we greeted

each other, it was always with the simple Christian name.

Mrs. Cosway was looking at me narrowly. "I'm not sorry I was wrong but I expected someone of eighteen or nineteen. You must be several years older than that."

"I'm twenty-four," I said, feeling like Elizabeth Bennet when interrogated by Lady Catherine de Burgh.

The little staccato laugh preceded her words. "When I was young, red hair like yours was considered quite ugly."

"Luckily for me," I said, "times have changed."

"Yes." If she detected a sharp note in my response she gave no sign of it. "I expect you're thought good-looking. You have a modern face. Now get into bed, John, and I'll give you your pill."

He gave no sign of having heard her. Later I understood that apparent acquiescence from him to her instruction was really her telling him to do something he had already made up his mind to do. He wanted to go to bed, he was tired; he wanted the pill because he had been told it was vitamins. Nothing would have made him do what he disliked. It was a little while before I realized this and realized too that when he did what his mother wanted it was sometimes because he had been kept in ignorance of the true facts. But that was in the future. On my first evening there I saw John remove from the pockets of his dressing gown a ball-point pen, a pencil, a dice, a tiny green bottle with ribbed sides, a safety pin, a boiled-sugar sweet wrapped in cellophane, a tiny book perhaps measuring one inch by two, and a reel of white bandage tape. These objects he arranged in a pattern on the bedside table, several times straightening up, contemplating his achievement and moving one piece or another an infinitesimal distance away from where it had been. Mrs. Cosway waited, not very patiently, tapping one toe on the lino. At last he was satisfied. He took off his dressing gown, hung it on the door hook, and got into bed. I expected some good-night ritual, a story read or told perhaps, a hot drink brought, but Mrs. Cosway merely gave him water in a mug with a handle he could hold. She put a white tablet into a small glass dish and held it out to him. He took it, drank, and swallowed it. He was treated like a child and I half-expected his mother to kiss him. But she stepped back, careful not to touch him.

"Good night," she said, adding neither name nor endearment.

I too said good night to him and began to tidy the room, careful not to disturb the objects on his bedside table. Mrs. Cosway did nothing, but she watched me. John was asleep by the time we left the room. Only a barbiturate would work so fast, I thought, and thought too that I disapproved. Mrs. Cosway left the door ajar.

"Noise from out here won't disturb him," she said.

Nothing would have, not with phenobarbital inside him.

"You could do that if I went out, couldn't you? One must be careful not to touch him. He screams if he's touched." She looked at the watch that hung loosely on her emaciated arm. "I see it is five and twenty past seven. Supper will be in exactly one hour."

"I shan't want supper," I said. "I rather thought we had had our last meal of the day."

"Goodness, no. Ida will be cooking something and there will be cheese and a pudding." Mrs. Cosway looked me up and down critically. "You are far too thin."

I questioned whether I was as thin as she or Ida but not aloud. Ever since I had seen John given that barbiturate capsule in the guise of a vitamin pill, I had wanted to be away from her. I needed to be alone. As I had told her, I wasn't hungry and I felt that for tonight with conversation expected from me as we sat around a table, I had nothing left to say.

"Of course you must do as you wish." She said it in the tone which means you really should do as she wishes and dislikes the turn events have taken.

"If there's nothing you'd like me to do."

"Oh dear, no. Not at this hour. Here is Ella's room."

Its frivolity was a shock. I only just stopped myself gasping at its colors. Beyond a doubt, Ella Cosway's favorite color was pink, all shades of it, peach, blush, sugar-pink, rose, fuchsia, coral, and every one of them was represented here. Roses blossomed on the pale pink curtains, the covers were pink and white candy stripes, the carpet raspberry ice-cream and the cushions the color of a blonde's rouge. Even the sewing-machine cover was pink. On the striped window seat stood or sat a dozen "grown-up" dolls, each dressed in contemporary fashion, with shoes on their feet and handbags hooked over their arms. The books were in a small white bookcase by the bedhead and, judging by the dolls and the general pinkness, I feared the worst. I was wrong. My need was for a book that was quintessentially English and that gave a picture of English life in country and town, though not necessarily of the present day. After rejecting **Villette** as too sad and not in any case primarily set in this country, **Barchester Towers** because I had recently read it, and **The Egoist** because the print was tiny, I chose **Great Expectations** and carried it off with me to my bedroom.

It was not a bad room, only dull and rather bare. But the cupboard was adequate, there was a fine long mirror of the kind which I believe is called a pier glass, and a good armchair covered in the same cretonne as the curtains. I took the diary from the dressing table and settled down in the armchair to write my first entry, resolving to write something every day. Needless to say, I failed in this lofty aim, but I did write something most days. If I hadn't—well, what might have happened if I hadn't was still a long way off.

Of course there was no radiator in the room. This was England before the seventies, when central heating became the rule. In the winter it would be very cold in this house, a fire lit only in the drawing room and perhaps in the hallway fireplace, where, I'd already discovered, if you stood on the hearth and looked upward you could see the sky through the wide-open chimney. Standing there in the winter, as I did only once, I felt the powerful draft, the icy wind strong enough to lift my hair and blow it out in a horizontal stream.

That evening my thoughts kept returning to the man I always wanted to call a boy, a "poor boy," though he was fifteen years my senior, lying in a drug-induced sleep he had been deceived into. As yet I could do nothing about it, so I resolutely drove it from my mind, sat down, and began to write what had happened that day. It was about three quarters of an hour later that I heard a car come down the track. Later on I learned that inside that house you would always be aware of the arrival of a car by the noise it made grinding across the gravel.

I looked out of the leaf-bordered window, a move which involved no drawing back of the curtains as their thin fabric was very nearly transparent. At nine-thirty on that fine cool midsummer night it wasn't yet dark and I was able to see quite clearly the two people who had arrived home.

They were both women, two more daughters of the house. It was impossible for me to tell which was the elder, but I identified Ella by her cotton dress, patterned all over with large pink roses, and her high-heeled pink shoes. She had been driving, so it was her sister, the passenger, who was the first to get out of the car, a badly battered old Volvo. I may have put this in the diary, but whether I did or not, I remember that my first thought at sight of Winifred was how easy it was for a basically good-looking woman to make herself ugly with heavy makeup, a dipping hemline, and a hand-knitted droopy cardigan.

Both of them were dark-haired and tall, though Ella was shorter than her sister. Winifred looked to me like one of those women who had been told when she was young that she was growing too tall and who, accordingly, had begun to round her shoulders and stoop. It was with a stance like this that she moved toward the front door, wrapping her arms around her chest as if she was cold. I couldn't hear what they were saying to each other, though I could tell they had been quarreling. Perhaps "quarrel" is too strong a word. They must have had one of their frequent little spats, probably over some happening at the wine and cheese party.

As Winifred disappeared from my view under the porch and its canopy of leaves, Ella let out a peal of laughter. Not the cough characteristic of her mother and her sister Ida, but a silvery, ringing sound, which I'm sure was derisive, though that evening it sounded to me affectionate and sweet. Below me I heard the front door creak open and close with a soft slam.

A leaf was caught between the window lattice and its frame. I slid it out and laid it on the dressing table. Then, without thought it seems now, certainly without taking any decision, I took a soft pencil out of the drawer and began to draw the house on one of the endpapers in the diary.

3

I WAS AWAKENED BY BIRDS SINGING. IT WAS HALF-past four in the morning and the first time my sleep had ever been disturbed by birdsong. I lay there listening to these sounds which both are and are not music and seem to have tone and rhythm and a kind of outflowing of joy but with no known scale. Light came swiftly and my room filled with the song of the birds so that at six I couldn't stay there any longer but had to get up and go out.

The day before had been dull and gray until the evening, but this morning was sunny with that hazy sunshine, that mist and stillness, which herald a fine summer's day. I went outside by way of the kitchen and the several little rooms that had to be passed before I reached the garden, rooms with coats hanging up and boots standing about, with bags and sacks and drums and cans and crates—playing a game with myself to name in English all these useful objects—and finally one with unplastered brick walls that was full of flowerpots and watering cans.

Dew was on the big lawn and in the middle of

it two green birds with long beaks and red flashes on their heads were prospecting for food in the grass, vegetable or animal I didn't know any more than I knew then that these were woodpeckers. They looked up but otherwise took no notice of me as I passed along the sandy path. The clothes-line and the two posts were gone. Walking softly so as not to disturb the birds, I made my way toward the shrubberies I had only glanced at the day before. There was a little garden down there of what I called fir trees, knowing no better, though I could see their foliage was golden, red, almost white and slate-blue as well as every shade of green. It seemed an old garden, and I supposed these trees had been planted, if not by the geode-discovering explorer, perhaps by his son. The same I thought might be true of many other fine large trees down here, some with long pointed leaves, others whose foliage was broad and flat, and some which I guessed must be exotics, possibly brought here by the explorer himself.

I found a kitchen garden too, vegetables neatly planted in rows, and a rather gloomy pond, covered in lily pads and surrounded by reeds, over which overgrown trees trailed long hair-thin branches. A boat with two oars laid in their rowlocks parallel to its sides lay in the middle of this still water and its dense plant life, but it looked as if no one had sat in it or touched those oars for years and now it would be hard to shift it out of all the constricting lilies with their stems like slippery ropes.

Apart from the features of this place, the grounds of Lydstep Old Hall were dull and too tidy. The maxim of the gardener who tended them must have been, when in doubt cut down, for everywhere else trees and shrubs had been viciously chopped and paths swept with depressing neatness. Another principle of his, or perhaps a directive from Mrs. Cosway, seemed to be that flowers were in bad taste or too much trouble, for in spite of the watering cans, none were to be seen.

At first I had intended to go out into the field and take the path in the opposite direction from the way I had gone the previous afternoon, and I had reached the gate in the hedge. But now only one aim was paramount, to find the maze. I walked on over more stretches of lawn and through more shrubberies until I came to the wall which skirted the land at this point and extended parallel with the drive to the road. My only course now was to return the way I had come, but instead of going through the conifer wood and on to the woodpecker lawn, I took the path which went straight ahead beside the boundary hedge.

Nothing much was down there but for scrubby turf, currant bushes, and after a while a neglected orchard. The trees, which were probably apple, pear, and plum, looked past redemption, their trunks a bright yellow-green with lichen or gray with moss, more of their branches dead than living, and what fruit was forming on them already deformed and worm-eaten. The orchard distracted me from my search, but this hardly mattered as coming upon a maze would have immediately caught my eye and lured me away from anything else. But there was no maze. Nowhere in those grounds was there anything labyrinthine, though I couldn't go so far as to say there was nowhere a maze might once have been. It was years since Isabel had visited Lydstep, and since then she had only occasionally been in touch with the family. Wasn't it possible that in that time the maintenance of what was no more than a folly had come to seem a nuisance, involving unnecessary expense?

I tried to imagine where it might have been, but this was harder than finding excuses for its removal. I had seen no recently planted lawns or wilderness spaces where the roots of old hedges protruded through the turf, no stretches of bare weed-grown earth. Of course it occurred to me that I could ask the Cosways, some or all of whom I would meet at breakfast in an hour or so. A sudden inhibition forbade that. It would show them that I had discussed them with their old friend, and more than that. They would think me over-curious and a spy and perhaps they would be right. As it was, Ida, who was in the kitchen when I came back, eyed me with suspicion while yet having her mind set at rest. Finding the back door unbolted, she had been worrying for the past half hour that she had left it like that the night before, an unimaginably feckless thing to do.

"I'm so relieved it was only you, Kerstin."

She was wearing the same skirt and blouse with the same crossover overall, the only departure in her costume from the day before being checked carpet slippers worn over stockings rolled down around her ankles. Anxiety and stress creased her face and she looked as if at any minute she would sink down with her head in her hands. The kitchen table, a huge piece of furniture, pitted and hollowed from use and scored along its edges with knife cuts, was laden with loaves, dishes of butter, packets of cornflakes and other cereals, eggs in a bowl, pots of jam, and stacks of plates, cups and saucers.

Temporarily forgetting my resolution not to be an au pair, I asked her if I could help her.

"Oh no, thank you. I'm used to it."

After a shower and in clean trousers and shirt, I came down to the dining room an hour later. Just as I had been searching for the maze, my next objective was the phone. I had heard it ring the evening before, soon after Winifred and Ella came in, but not seen the instrument itself. The table in that bleak dining room was set for breakfast, the door left wide open, and the first thing I saw after saying good morning to John and his mother was the phone standing on the sideboard. Mrs. Cosway quickly noticed that my eyes were on it and began on a detailed list of phone rules I was to observe.

"When you make a call," she said, "you should ask the operator to time it and tell you the cost. The simplest way to keep a tally will be for you to write each sum down. You might perhaps buy a notebook for this purpose. If you are careful you won't find the cost to you prohibitive. No outgoing calls are allowed in this house after ten at night, they should be restricted to ten minutes, and none may be received after half past eight. You may have heard the telephone ring just before ten last night. That was for one of my daughters and I shall speak to them about it. I sincerely hope you will also explain to your friends not to telephone during the afternoon when I shall be resting or between seven and nine when we breakfast and one and two p.m. when we are at lunch."

I thought this, to use my husband's phrase, a bit rich. How I was going to make Mark (my Lund student friend) understand, not to mention obey, these injunctions I had no idea. But I only nodded and applied myself to a boiled egg and bread and butter. Ida, having transferred, I've no doubt single-handedly, all the food from the kitchen table to this one, had finally arrived to sit down and eat some herself.

"I hope you slept well," she said to me as if this were our first encounter of the day.

"Very well."

"My sisters Ella and Winifred will be down in a minute."

At this point Mrs. Cosway laid down her knife and said in a dry and rather unpleasant way, pronouncing my name not as I had told her was correct but as she thought best, "Kerstin wants to know everything about this family, Ida. She told me so. She likes to get things clear. Succinct sentences like the one you've just uttered won't do for **her.**"

Bewildered, as well she might be, Ida said, "I don't know what you want me to say, Mother."

"Oh, nothing, nothing. I'll do it."

Mrs. Cosway turned to me. Her son, who had finished eating, had left his crusts like a child and arranged them on the plate to form a shape like a Maltese cross. His glazed eyes were fixed not on his mother's face but at a point somewhere to the left of her left shoulder. I thought what a handsome man he would be but for the blighting of his looks and his expression by whatever it was that afflicted him.

"My daughter Ella," Mrs. Cosway said, "is a teacher at a school in Sudbury; my daughter Winifred is a cook."

"Oh, Mother," said Ida reproachfully.

"Oh, Mother, what? Winifred is a cook. She may be a very good cook, I have no idea, she has never cooked anything for me, but to my mind a cook is a servant, and I find it strange that one of my children should have a menial occupation. Someone gave her a tip the other day. She told me so herself."

John continued to sit silently, staring. He might have been in a trance, and perhaps he was. At first it looked as if he had left his boiled egg untouched but then I saw yolk on his spoon and understood he had eaten the egg and turned the shell over with its broken end inside the cup. I knew I must learn not to stare at him and luckily at that moment I heard a footstep on the stairs. Ida said quickly, "Winifred is a caterer for private dinner parties—well, all sorts of parties. She did the food for the one they both went to last night."

Before I could make any comment the two sisters came in. Their mother, possibly still brooding on the horrors of someone in her position having a hireling for a child, nodded to them but said nothing, joining her son in blank silence. It was left to Ida to introduce me.

"My sister Winifred, my sister Ella, this is Kerstin Kvist."

I was beginning to think I should have to resign myself to being the guttural and sharp-cornered Curstin for the duration of my stay instead of the Shashtin of soft sibilants. But I got up and shook hands with them.

Mrs. Cosway waited till they were seated, then said, "I suppose that telephone call last night was for one of you two." She spoke exactly as if they were sixteen and fourteen years old instead of the more probable late thirties. "I would like you to tell your correspondent that telephone calls in the middle of the night are not to be received in this house."

"Five to ten is hardly the middle of the night," said Winifred.

"Anyway," said Ella, "the call was for me. It was the head. He had something important to say about the Upper Fifth."

For a moment I was puzzled until I realized she must have meant the head teacher of her school. While she and her mother argued about this phone call—I was to learn that the daughters with each other or with their mother could sustain an argument on some trivial matter for fifteen minutes and sometimes much longer—I observed these two newcomers. As I had seen the night before, both were good-looking, Winifred particularly. But good looks are not just a matter of fine regular features, copious hair, large eyes, and a supple figure, all of which they had, but of how a woman holds herself, turns her head, smiles, her consciousness of her appearance and the air of beauty she carries with her. Neither Winifred nor Ella seemed aware of her own attractions, neither had style. Their hair was dull and in need of a wash, and Winifred's had clips in it to hold it back. Limp summer dresses and cardigans, one blue, one pink, did nothing to flatter them. Winifred was again heavily painted, especially about the eyes, her eyebrows plucked to thin lines, her mouth a scarlet gash, while Ella looked as if she had slept in last night's makeup. Their long slender hands could have been elegant but Ella's nails were bitten and Winifred's were dirty. Rather unfortunate for a cook, I thought.

It was she who said to me as Ella and her mother continued to bicker, "I don't know what you must think of us, Kerstin, going on like this in front of you. It doesn't mean anything, you know."

I have my own opinion as to family quarrels meaning nothing, but I only smiled and asked her if the party she had arranged for the evening before had been a success. It had, she said with great enthusiasm. The guests—it had been a reception to raise funds for the restoration of some part of the church—had enjoyed themselves, had eaten up all her mini-quiches, cheese and pineapple on cocktail sticks, and baby vol-au-vents.

"If there was a fly in the ointment," she said, "it was that the people there were mostly women. Mr. Dawson was there of course, he always comes. But as for the rest—it usually is like that. Men just won't come to things like this, which is a great shame as they have the money, don't they?"

My feminist soul rising in revolt (even in those days) against this sentiment, I asked her if there was much social life in Windrose.

"Oh, yes, we're a very friendly bunch. I shall be

cooking for the Midsummer Supper in a fortnight's time. And then there will be the Harvest Festival. You must come."

Still defending her right to receive phone calls at an hour "when no one, absolutely no one, would think of going to bed," Ella left the table and went off to work. The pale green Volvo, some fifteen years old, started up with a clanking and gurgling. Later in the day I saw that its hood was caved in. A considerable time before, by the look of it, someone had driven it into the vehicle ahead.

I wondered who Mr. Dawson was. A slightly embarrassed look had come into Winifred's face when she spoke his name. She appeared to have no work to go to and, in the absence of work, nothing to do. She left the clearing of the breakfast table to Ida, who did it uncomplainingly. Like her brother's, though in quite a different way, her expression never changed. While his face was blank, unaffected by mood, by frustration or anger or joy, if he felt these things, hers wore a look of patient stoicism, as if long ago she had settled into her fate and would apply herself to it till the end; not well or graciously or even mutinously—she did a poor job, leaving the table covered in crumbs and the napkins sprawled among them—but with resignation.

I spent much of the next day and the next, which was a Saturday, observing Mrs. Cosway's routine with John, and on Saturday afternoon I suggested she have her rest while I went out for a walk with him. I'd succeeded in phoning Mark and at the second attempt had spoken to him, making both calls during the permitted times. He was disbelieving when I explained Mrs. Cosway's rules to him and indignant about falling in with them. A meeting was arranged in London for the Tuesday, my first day off. I said nothing about the following weekend, reserving my expectations about that until I knew if he still attracted me the way he had done in our last months at Lund.

The village of Windrose was still unvisited, though only about half a mile away. I suggested to John that we walk there and met with the first opposition I, or anyone else as far as I had seen, had had from him. He shook his head.

"Not there," he said in his dull monotone.

When I asked him why not, he frowned and his expression became surly. It seemed wiser to leave the question for now. I was getting tired of walking around the same three fields, over the river bridge and alongside the wood, but he was determined. If he was set on following that route every afternoon, I would rebel; for the present, however, I gave in.

Accompanying him on these outings was an awkward business, consisting really in his setting off and my walking some paces behind him. In recent years I have seen Moslem women following along behind their husbands like that. It was clear John didn't want me, but his mother expected me to be there and he never said anything. The day he said he wouldn't go to Windrose was mild and dull, the sky a uniformly cloud-gray, the kind of day I have come to think of as essentially English, windless and still, the atmosphere calm and unchanging. We walked in single file ten or twelve feet apart along the kind of wide path I believe is called a ride, between low hedges, broken here and there by gates into the meadows. Blossom was out on the brambles and the elder, it was pretty and tranquil, like a painting by Constable, who had lived not far from there. Across the little valley between shallow hills, I could see Windrose, a cluster of houses, a big house a short distance away, and the red church tower rising high above paler roofs and dark thatch.

John seemed not to look around him. Perhaps it was all too familiar, and though there may have been comfort in this, there must also have been boredom. Or was he incapable of feeling bored? Who knew? I suited my pace to his, and he walked fairly slowly, his head down and his eyes on the ground. My attempts to talk to him, which I persisted in, fetched monosyllables from him at best and more often nothing. That day was the first occasion on which I said nothing. I had given up already.

We were out for about an hour. When we got back, he made his way to the kitchen, shuffling along, as he always did when inside the house, though he had walked normally along the ride. Ida, who seemed to live in that kitchen, constantly occupied at some task or other, smiled at him and said hallo. His face, usually so dull and blank, lightened a little. She made tea for him and me but made no effort to say anything more. And I saw that he was content with this, that he appeared to listen to the conversation I had with her without taking any part in it.

Ella was out somewhere, but Winifred was at home, spoiling my theory that Ida was solely responsible for the work of the household by doing the ironing. There was a great deal of it, bedlinen and table linen, underclothes, John's shirts, and the limp cotton dresses favored by all the Cosway women except their mother, who dressed invariably in black trousers and blouse or sweater. Winifred had piled it untidily on the dining table, set up the ironing board, switched on the other television (black and white and very small) and worked away slowly and in no apparent order, her eyes on the screen. It took her several hours and by the time it was done Mrs. Cosway was awake, Ida had set out the tea things, and Ella was back from wherever she had been. Seated next to me at the tea table, Winifred remarked with an air of conscious virtue that she and Ella would go to church in the morning. Would I like to come?

We Swedes are a secular lot and I hadn't been to church since I was at school, but this might be my only opportunity for some time to visit the village and I was curious too to see some of the other Windrose residents. On the other hand . . .

“May I think about it? I’ll let you know later.”

Winifred looked rather shocked, perhaps expecting me to jump at the chance. Mrs. Cosway seemed pleased rather than otherwise at my response and, bowing her head the way John did, favored the bread and butter on her plate with one of her nasty little smiles.

“Don’t be too long about it, will you?” Winifred said this as if she were arranging a bus outing for thirty or forty people to some popular London event rather than a half-mile walk to morning service. “I’m sure you’ll want to meet Mr. Dawson.”

The identity of this person I resolved to find out later, perhaps when and if I told Winifred I would go with her. Meanwhile there was John’s bedtime ritual to come and the inevitable sleeping pill. Once it had taken effect and he was bludgeoned into heavy sleep, Mrs. Cosway asked for an account of our walk. Had we followed the same route? What, if anything, had John had to say for himself? Had we met anyone? I thought this an odd question.

“We didn’t meet anyone to speak to. I saw a man on a tractor quite a long way away and when we came close to the road, some cars went by. Why do you ask?”

“You always want every detail, don’t you? Why

this, why that. I shall say to you what I used to say to the children, 'Because I say so.' "

I shrugged. "I'm sorry. But there is one thing I would like to know, if you don't mind. I suggested to John that we go to the village but he was very set against that idea. He didn't say why not and I wondered."

"As I said, you want every detail. It's very wearing, I must say. If you must know, he doesn't like going there because the people stare at him. Most of them are very ignorant. There were some children—they laughed. It was dreadful for him."

"I'm sorry," I said. "It is better I know, isn't it? So that I won't try to take him there again?"

"I suppose so. But you couldn't if he didn't want to go."

After supper, twice asked by Winifred if I had yet made up my mind, to forestall a third time, I told her I would go to church.

"I'm so glad, that's wonderful," she said, as if I had said I had come in to a fortune or bought the house of my dreams. "If it isn't raining we'll walk, shall we? It's not far. Meet down here at ten-thirty?" She turned to her mother. "You can spare Kerstin for a couple of hours, can't you?"

"I suppose so."

I was learning that this was a favorite rejoinder of Mrs. Cosway's.

Ella, changed out of her summer frock into navy blue trousers and a pink sweater with moth holes across the back, had sat in an armchair for the past hour, marking work in her pupils' exercise books. To do this she had put on a pair of large, unflattering glasses with rainbow rims, and she chain-smoked while she worked. Occasionally, Winifred (saying, "I really must give up") took a cigarette from the packet herself, but she smoked no more than one to every five got through by her sister.

Mrs. Cosway I expected to have a word or two to say on the subject of the fug Ella had caused and her unattractive hawking, but apart from removing herself to a far corner of the room, she gave no sign of disapproval. She was sewing, doing something I think may be called gros-point on a great rug-sized tapestry, whose design was hidden from me, and she took no part in the desultory conversation except to say apropos of nothing, "Zorah will be home on Wednesday."

"Yes, Mother," said Ella, "you've already told us twice."

I had set them both and their sister Ida down as inveterate spinsters, as single women were still often called in those days. This was long before there was something almost meritorious in not being married. They lived at home with their mother, were discontented, set in their ways, seemed part of the virginal sisterhood, churchy, doing good works in the parish. So it surprised me when Ida, getting up to make bedtime hot drinks for everyone, asked me if I could spare her a minute "to have a word."

I followed her into the kitchen, where she said in a low, serious tone, "I have something to tell you."

It sounded alarming, but I'm not the sort of person who, at these words, invariably thinks she must be in trouble—at least, I wasn't then, in those early days. "Yes?" I said, my voice light. "What is it?"

"Mr. Dawson and Winifred are engaged to be married."

In most circumstances, this sort of news merits congratulations and a show of joy. "That's good, isn't it? Who's Mr. Dawson?"

"My goodness, I'm so relieved you aren't cross," said Ida. "Knowing how you want everything to be open and no secrets et cetera, I thought you might be offended because no one told you the moment you came."

"Not a bit," I said, mystified.

"That's such a relief." She looked neither relieved nor at all happy. "Mr. Dawson is the rector of this parish. You'll meet him tomorrow. He will, of course, take the service. I no longer go to church myself."

"Is he a young man?" I asked, feeling like a character in a Charlotte Brontë novel, but curious to know.

"Two years older than Winifred. He's forty-two.

You'll be wondering why she doesn't wear an engagement ring."

I was not; the absence of a ring had failed to register with me. I smiled encouragingly.

"He only proposed last Wednesday."

"I see. So Winifred will be moving out to live at the vicarage."

"The rectory, yes." Ida seemed to find my innocent small-talk suspect. What she thought I meant to imply I don't know. Perhaps, knowing this family as I was beginning to, she saw me as having designs on a different, larger bedroom, though there were at least eight at Lydstep Old Hall, or else, as a single woman myself, though so much younger, envious of Winifred's coming status.

"They can't get married for a long time yet," Ida said obscurely. "Would you mind carrying this tray with the mugs on it?"

I picked up the tray and went back into the drawing room, looking at Winifred with new eyes in the light of the future awaiting her. Trying to avoid being unkind, even in my own mind and to myself, I still had to wonder what on earth Mr. Dawson saw in her to make him propose marriage. The heavy makeup she wore had been on, unrefreshed, since early morning, and was now greasy and stale. Lipstick had edged onto her teeth and leaked into the fine lines on her upper lip. Her hair hung limp and straight and her fingernails were still dirty. She must once, perhaps years before, have chosen to buy the green and yellow patterned dress of some synthetic fabric, but unless it had been very cheap or the last garment in the shop, it was hard to say why. If he could have put up with the smell of smoke which hung about her, Mr. Dawson would have done better to have picked Ella of the two sisters. But what kind of a man must he be? Did he live alone at the rectory or did he too have a presiding mother? I'd know some of the answers the next day.

Composing myself for sleep some hour or so later, I realized I'd forgotten to ask Mr. Dawson's first name. I needed it for the diary but would surely find out soon. Before I fell asleep I began thinking about the Cosways' great-grandfather and the library he had "made," whatever that meant. Collected? Amassed? Bought? For reasons not at all clear, it was kept locked. Perhaps it lay behind one of those doors in the long unlit passage.

4

THE THREE, AND FOR ALL I KNEW THEN THE four, Cosway "girls" went in for that peculiar Victorian usage of referring to Mrs. Cosway as "my mother" and to John as "my brother" as if they were not mother and brother to all of them. I saw this then and still do as indicative of the isolation in which each existed, even Winifred and Ella, who were so much together, living under the same roof from necessity rather than choice.

So, at Sunday breakfast, Winifred said, "My mother can spare you to come to church, Kerstin."

Permission was uttered in the manner of one mentioning a subject for the first time. I think Winifred said it to emphasize Mrs. Cosway's generosity in letting me go out, though there was nothing for me to do at home. John needed very little looking after, seemed not to notice whether other people were present or not, and would probably have been as content to have lived in a small flat somewhere on his own. It was at this time, so early in my stay, that I began to wonder what I was doing there. Why had John wanted someone with a nursing qualification? As I understood the matter, it was he who had asked for help for his mother. All I had seen of him so far precluded his asking for anything, certainly reasoning so far as to think additional help was needed in caring for him.

We set off for church at ten-thirty, Ella and Winifred having smartened themselves up considerably. Winifred even wore a hat, though one of the wide-brimmed, ribbon-trimmed kind generally reserved for weddings. It was the finest day since I had come to Lydstep Old Hall. The sky had cleared, the sun had come out, and it promised to be hot. A heatwave might even have been on its way, Ella said rather gloomily. She felt the heat, she told me. Her ankles would swell and she tended to come out in a rash. But at ten-thirty it was only pleasantly warm. We walked down the not very steep hill into the village, a pretty place of cottages, some of them thatched, around a triangular green with a memorial to two world wars in the center of it. There were some bigger houses too and a row of cottages, one of which, with a large plate-glass window in its roof, Ella called The Studio. This, she said, was to let.

"Again. The last tenant was only there six months."

"Artists," Winifred said in a rather contemptuous way, "are an itinerant lot. Feckless too. Don't you remember Mr. Johnston? The place was overrun with rats while he was there. Mice are all very well, but rats!"

The church stood on the sort of shallow hill that is called an eminence. It was then that Winifred, an authority on local names and north Essex lore, told me what the tower was called and that the "rose" in Windrose referred to its color. I asked her where her fiancé lived.

To my astonishment she blushed deeply, a blotchy reddening under all the pancake and rouge. "The rectory is over there." I was reminded of my reading in Victorian fiction where it was considered unwise to say too much about a young woman's engagement in case it failed to "come off" and her reputation was damaged. The facts that Winifred was forty and we were coming to the end of the 1960s seemed not to enter into it. "It's quite a fine Georgian house, isn't it?"

Not having any acquaintance with Georgian houses, I couldn't judge, but I agreed and smiled and, persisting in my embarrassing questions, asked if she intended to make any changes when she moved there.

"That's a long way off," she said in Ida's manner, her expression showing no enthusiasm for becoming Mrs. Dawson, and I couldn't help wondering if she had accepted the rector's proposal for the sake of escape from Lydstep Old Hall or even from becoming what people still called an old maid.

She was very attentive to me and took upon herself the office of a tour guide, telling me that the gate into the churchyard with the little roof over it was called a lychgate from **lic,** an Old English word for "corpse," because it served as a shelter for coffins and pallbearers on their way to a funeral. She seemed to know a great deal about ecclesiastical things, very suitable for the wife of a clergyman. I was instructed that graves should face east so that the faithful rising at the Last Day will be looking in the right direction when the Messiah returns to Jerusalem.

The church was beautiful outside and in, seven hundred years old, its stained glass smashed by Henry VIII (or was it Cromwell?) and replaced in the nineteenth century by rich red and blue depictions of saints: John the Baptist, apparently draped in a whole camel skin, a golden-haired Mary Magdalene holding a jar of what looked like Elizabeth Arden skinfood but which Winifred said was precious ointment, and Saint Paul with a beard and joined-up eyebrows. I thought these windows fine but was instructed, this time by Ella as we took our seats, that they were an unfortunate and vulgar substitute for the glories which had been there before. Both sisters, once they had laid down the prayer books they had brought with them, though at least fifty were provided on the shelf in front of us for a congregation of twenty, fell to their knees, put their heads into their hands—not easy for

Winifred in her picture hat—and, I suppose, concentrated on silent prayer.

On their way in all the members of the congregation had been chatting to one another in a lively fashion, calling out to ask friends how they were and to remark on the weather, and as soon as the service began I noticed what pride many took in not referring to their prayer books at all but reciting canticles, psalms, and responses (I may not have these names correctly) from memory. Mr. Dawson wore a white smock-like garment over a long black gown. He was a tallish man and thin, and he reminded me in looks of a professor we had at Lund, not handsome but with a pleasant, beaky face which would one day become what my mother-in-law calls "nutcrackery," nose stretching forward to meet jutting chin. The glasses he needed for reading he kept putting on and taking off, a fidgety habit I hoped Winifred would cure him of when they were married. He had a fine baritone voice in which he chanted various requests to God.

"Give us peace in our time, O Lord," rang out with a particular vigor.

Luckily, there was no one sitting immediately behind us or if there had been they had moved away, for Winifred's hat would have obstructed their view of the choir of four women sitting in the chancel, the aged men who read the lessons, and Mr. Dawson when he climbed up to the pulpit to give his sermon. I had no experience of sermons but to judge by the innumerable lectures I had heard in recent years and the many talks, I thought it good and said so to Winifred when the service was over and we were leaving the church. It had been on the subject of tolerance and not judging one's fellows when one was in possession of only limited facts about their misdeeds. Later on, at the time of the terrible events that were to come, I wondered if he had been able to put these principles into practice.

"Yes, Eric preaches well," she said, but in a lifeless tone. At last I knew the man's name and in a moment heard her address him by it.

He was standing at the church door as we filed out, shaking hands with his parishioners as we passed, telling some how nice it was to see them, asking others after the health of some relative. When it was our turn Ella went first, was asked how she was, and had her hand shaken. Rather to my surprise, having said, "Good morning, Eric," Winifred got a kiss on the cheek or the air an inch from her cheek. She introduced me and I congratulated him on his sermon. Both sisters looked rather shocked—by my presumption, I suppose, in daring to comment on the oratorical powers of a clergyman nearly twenty years my senior. But Eric Dawson smiled and thanked me.

"How kind of you to say so."

In quite a formal and ceremonious way Winifred asked him if he would come up to Lydstep Old Hall that day for supper.

"Once Evensong is over I would love to," he said. "What a charming hat, Winifred."

Again that unbecoming blush. And I felt I was back in that Victorian novel where engaged couples encountered each other only in their parents' homes, chaperoned by siblings. Did Winifred and Eric Dawson never go for solitary walks together, as I was sure other local courting couples must do? Would she never go to the rectory to be alone with him once his housekeeper who came in daily had gone home? Stay overnight? Or was this improper in the kind of world they lived in? It was all so remote from anything I had ever known that I was defeated by it and simply bewildered.

He said good-bye, that he would see us all later and that it had been nice to meet me. On the way back to Lydstep Old Hall, walking up the hill, a violent quarrel broke out between Ella and Winifred, astonishing and rather dismaying. It began with Ella asking if Eric had ever been married before.

"You know he hasn't," Winifred said, already looking put out. "Why do you ask that now?"

"It does seem strange, doesn't it? I mean, to get to the age of forty-five and never to have been married."

"Eric is forty-two." Winifred spoke with indignation as if the difference between Eric's real age and that put forward by Ella were thirty years instead of three. "He has been wise enough not to get married until he found the woman he really wanted to spend his life with."

"You, you mean? Oh, please. Do you know what they're saying?"

"I don't wish to know, thank you, Ella."

"You'll have to, just the same. You ought to know before you do anything you'll regret."

Winifred said magnificently, "I never do things I shall regret."

Ella burst out laughing, as well she might. I think they had both forgotten I was there or cared not at all. "On second thought, it may be best for me not to tell you. It will only upset you."

"Now you have gone as far as this you had better come out with it."

"Don't say you didn't ask me," said Ella in an insufferably smug way. "Well, they are saying that Eric is"—she paused for a moment to think, I suppose, what Eric was and came out with the words all in a rush—"is an **invert.** There you are. Don't say you didn't ask."

Winifred screamed out. "How dare you? How dare you? You must be mad, whoever says so is mad, sick in their minds."

"Please don't make an exhibition of yourself in the public street."

Far from a street, it was a country lane with not a soul about. In any case, Ella's words had no effect and Winifred continued to shout and scream, standing still now and stamping her foot. She took off her hat and waved it about while Ella watched, a little smile coming and going. The word she had used meant nothing to me. I had never heard it before, but of course I gathered from the context what it meant. Homosexuality was not a subject that was much discussed at that time, though more then than previously. The law which legalized sex between homosexual men in private had come into force the year before.

Ella then, in a slow, steady voice, made calmer by her sister's near-hysterics, proceeded to tell her that one rumor had it that Eric Dawson's bishop, when the gossip reached him, had advised him to marry. "I know the very words he used. 'Find some older woman, Eric,' he said, 'someone who won't be too demanding, if you understand me, and marry her to set my mind and your own at rest.' "

"You're making it up!" Winifred shouted.

"No, I'm not. I swear I'm not."

The quarrel went on all the way back to Lydstep Old Hall, all along the track and up to the front door. There both of them, by unspoken consent, became silent, each clamping her lips tightly shut as if words which must be suppressed were struggling behind them to break out. On the doorstep, Winifred said to me in bitter tones, "There now, you can't complain you're not privy to our secrets, can you?"

I began to wish I had never said that about liking to know the history and the facts of a family. It looked as if they had all had an indignant conference on the subject. Three or four hours later I was walking around those uninteresting fields, a dozen paces behind John, and because he again made no response to my attempts at conversation and didn't even lift his eyes from contemplation of the ground, I let my thoughts drift off to Eric Dawson and the rumor about him.

Very likely he was gay, not a word in vogue at the time, as far as I remember, and if he wanted to keep his job, avoid scandal and newspaper publicity, he might aim to present himself as a respectably married man. Far more experienced women than Winifred were unable to detect for a long time, sometimes years, that they had married a homosexual. But perhaps it scarcely mattered whether she knew or found out as she was certainly not marrying Eric Dawson in the expectation of passion, an assumption which was borne out by her behavior that evening when he arrived in time for supper.

I always ate very little at this meal. I had finished tea only two hours before. But when I told Mrs. Cosway that she might prefer me to go to my room while they had a guest, she looked very put out.

"I don't see that at all," she said. "You won't be in the way. I don't see you as a servant, Kerstin, but more of a companion or au pair."

The very title and function I had tried to avoid . . . Spending the evening in my room—which, whatever its shortcomings, was big and airy—with **Great Expectations** and my diary, would have been a pleasant relief, but I agreed to stay downstairs at any rate for supper. John went to bed without a fuss. "Zombie" was not a word much used then, but I had come across it and been told that it came from the Caribbean (or, as we then said, West Indian) term for the living dead. It came into my mind as I stood by, watching John arrange on his bedside table the small objects he kept in his dressing-gown pockets during the day, strictly following the requisite pattern. When I held it out to him he refused the sleeping pill with a shake of the head but took it from the little glass dish when his mother offered it. His expression never changed. Waking and asleep, it was as blank as a mummy's or a passport photograph.

I wondered if he had thoughts or if his mind, like his face, was a tabula rasa, without memory or hope or knowledge as an animal's is said to be, knowing only fear and the need for flight. I was to find out, but not then, not yet. Then, watching him as Mrs. Cosway gathered up his discarded clothes, hung up his jacket and trousers and put them away, I felt as Ida must have done when she told me about him that first day, and the tears came into my eyes. Mrs. Cosway looked at me with incomprehension, giving a little shrug. Walking downstairs behind her, I thought how, the first time she left me in charge of him at bedtime, I would take a chance and give him an aspirin instead of the barbiturate. If he would take it from me. If he would take anything from me.

Evensong ending at seven-thirty, Eric Dawson arrived half an hour later in his Ford Anglia. He had changed into ordinary clothes, including a shirt with an open neck instead of the dog collar. Again a kiss was exchanged between him and Winifred, he putting his lips to her cheek and she briefly laying the side of her face against his. He had brought the ring, explaining that he had been unsure if she would be at Matins since she had attended seven o'clock Communion four hours before. If the rumor were true and Winifred was the wrong sex for him, she was certainly devout enough. Blushing, she held out her left hand, and watched by her mother, her two sisters, and me, he put it on to her third finger. The three little diamonds, caught by a bright beam from the setting sun, made a winking rainbow pattern running up and down the wall as Winifred held out her hand for all to admire. Whether her nails had been cleaned or not was hard to say, as she had painted them the same bright pink as her mouth.

Everyone congratulated them and I asked when the wedding would be.

"It can't be soon enough for me," said Eric gallantly with a hearty chuckle.

"That depends on what you mean by soon." This was Winifred, her excitement over the ring giving way to her usual rather ill-tempered moroseness. "In about a year, I suppose. That would be the absolute soonest I could manage."

Trollope says that her engagement is the happiest time of a woman's life. It may have been so in his day, but things had changed a lot in a hundred years. Most couples who hadn't "anticipated" their marriage, as the phrase still had it, unusual as that must have been, longed with good reason for their wedding day. As for now, the people next door to us in London have been engaged for eleven years, lived together for longer, and probably will never marry. Engagement has become more important than ever, a recognized state which is almost a legal one, and a kind of second-class marriage. But it seemed that Winifred fitted most happily into the nineteenth century, with the exception of all that makeup which would have branded her fast if not a "bad woman," and would have been content to have been Eric's companion to functions, enjoying her status as his fiancée.

For supper that night we ate poached eggs on smoked haddock with mashed potatoes and spinach, a heavy dish I had never before encountered. I took no bread with it and ate nothing more. Eric, on the other hand, ate heartily. Men of his age have told me in perfect seriousness that they got married partly for love but also to have someone to cook and clean for them and do their laundry. Eric may have belonged in this category, as he probably had a lean time of it rattling around on his own in that huge rectory, and Winifred after all was well known for her cookery and organizing of meals. He had more social skills than his prospective bride, showing an interest, whether he had it or not, in my life in Sweden, the University of Lund, my parents and siblings, and what career I had in mind for myself.

"Kerstin will get married," was Mrs. Cosway's comment. She had overheard some of my phone conversation with Mark and was one of those who still, at that time, believed that the man a woman arranges a date with must be acknowledged as her likely future husband. "She has someone lined up, if what I hear is true."

Not being Winifred, I failed to blush. "Who knows?" I said in my best enigmatic tone.

"Talking of marriage," said Eric, "when is Zorah coming back?"

What the connection was between Zorah and marriage I never found out. She had certainly been married and was now a widow, but why she should have been a symbol or example of matrimony was a mystery, unless he meant she was the only one of the sisters to have had a husband.

"She seems to have been away a long time," he said.

Mrs. Cosway took this remark as criticism of her daughter. "Just three weeks," she said sharply. "And why not? It's not as if she were on a holiday. She has a home in London, as you know."

Ida, anxious to quieten things down, said that in any case Zorah was coming back on Wednesday.

"We shall be very pleased to see her," said Zorah's mother. "We have all missed her." Why did I feel this was entirely for my benefit, to deceive me? Perhaps because Mrs. Cosway's face remained grave when she said it, even sullen, as if her words were in direct opposition to her feelings.

As everyone but me began eating summer pudding, Eric, back in Victorian novel mode, said he had a piece of news for us. His eyes twinkled and I expected something on the lines of a curate offered him by the Church of England if not promotion to an archdeaconry—you can tell I knew my Trollope.

"We shall have a new neighbor," he said. "The Studio is let."

Winifred looked the most interested. Probably she was rehearsing for her future as a supportive and encouraging wife. "Do you have a name, Eric?"

"I do. I had it all from Mrs. Cusp." He said to me in an aside, "The wife of one of our churchwardens, Kerstin." Winifred was favored with an approving smile. "He is a Mr. Dunhill, an artist of some sort. Mr. Felix Dunhill."

"Felix is a cat," said Mrs. Cosway. "There was a song, I believe, something ridiculous about Felix who kept on walking."

Eric said kindly, "It was a play on words, of course, the Latin for a cat being **felis.**"

"Yes, thank you, Eric. I am not entirely uneducated. Latin was compulsory at my school."

"Really, Mother!" said Winifred, very put out. "Eric was merely being helpful."

"Is that what it was? Thank you for telling me. No doubt, he will soon tell us that Dunhill is a manufacturer of cigarettes."

Due to Eric's unfailing good humor, no more was said, and we began to talk of the forthcoming Midsummer Supper. But the significant thing about the conversation was that this was the first time they and I had heard the name of the future tenant of The Studio, all of us of course unaware that this man would have so profound an effect on the Cosways, their lives and their very existence. Yet did he? As I write these words I have to pause and take a long look at them. I think he would have liked to have that effect but I have to ask myself whether things would have been any different if he had never come to Windrose, if he was any more than a shadow passing through their lives.

5

On her way to school, Ella dropped me at Sudbury station and I caught a train to London. There resumed—or rather, at the following weekend, resumed—my love affair with Mark Douglas, a happy and delightful relationship based on a powerful mutual attraction with occasional moments of passion. He had a room in a tall house behind Ladbroke Grove, fondly called "the Grove" by the crowds of young people who were drawn to it by its almost magical magnetic powers. The sexual revolution was in full swing and we were like the girl in the song. "Those were the days, my friend/ We thought they'd never end." Mark and I made love in his hot little room where dusty trees outside the window made a permanent dusk, and afterward walked the streets hand in hand to sit outside the cafés or drink in the pubs, in that carefree state which is without fear or ambition or the deadening knowledge that things must change.

We are still friends, his wife and I, my husband and he, after all these years and six children between us. I have said how we sometimes go on holiday together. Apart from the attraction, what Mark and I shared was an enthusiasm for the study of character, fairly common in women and fairly rare in men. We still do and so does his wife, while the whole business mystifies my husband, who has no interest in what makes his friends and colleagues tick or motivates his neighbors.

At that first meeting, on a Tuesday just before midsummer, I told him about the Cosways. Unaware then that he also was a student of the mind and its emotions, I expected to see boredom lay its dulling hand across his lively face and meant to pass quickly on, but he began asking questions and analyzing character, and I knew that here was another aficionado.

It was his opinion that Mrs. Cosway ruled the household because what real money there was she possessed.

"Three things make for power," Mark said. "Money, beauty, and perseverance." Perhaps unconsciously, he paraphrased a New Testament text I had heard from Eric Dawson two days before. "And the greatest of these is money." He looked gloomy. "Horrible, isn't it? Against everything we all believe in and aim for but it's a fact."

"What about love?" I said. "It's supposed to make the world go round."

"Maybe it does. All I'm saying is that it doesn't confer power. More rubbish is talked about love than anything. Love is stronger than death, for instance. I don't know how many otherwise quite intelligent people say that."

"Of course love isn't stronger than death. I've never heard anyone say it."

"Perhaps they don't in Sweden," said Mark.

The next day we awaited the arrival home of Zorah Todd. Except for me. I had forgotten she was coming, having Mark on my mind as well as a determination to get clear with Mrs. Cosway what my duties really were. I had nothing to do except take John for his walk each afternoon, an outing which, as far as I could see, he could have managed perfectly well on his own. He never spoke, he kept his eyes on the ground, walking jerkily and doggedly like someone who does a repetitive and hated job on the assembly line he sees no way of escaping. Yet these walks were his own choice. Was I there to guard him from some unknown harm committed by him or against him? I asked Mrs. Cosway, though not quite in those words.

"Of course you're not a guard," she said. "What an idea."

She had been in a bad temper since breakfast, snapping at everyone. Oddly, though, she was better dressed and groomed than I had seen her since I arrived, the sweater changed for a diaphanous blouse, a string of pearls around her neck, and rouge on her withered cheeks. I thought she must be going out, but she was still at home at lunchtime and already talking of taking her afternoon rest.

"Of course, if you don't want to go with John on a not very long and certainly healthy walk . . ."

"It's not that I don't want to," I said with patience, "but that I don't think he wants me."

"Really, it doesn't matter whether he wants you or not, Kerstin. I can't have him going out alone and that's all there is to it. Who knows what goes on in his head?"

This sounded unpleasantly sinister to me and I decided not to pursue it. Instead, I asked her what else there was for me to do as I felt I was not earning my keep or the wage she paid me.

She shrugged, a common gesture with her. "If you feel like that, you can always give Ida a hand. I daresay she'd be grateful."

Not a very congenial idea, I thought, but still I went off to the kitchen to help with lunch preparation. None was going on or it had been done hours earlier, for Winifred had taken over the kitchen, and it was a very large kitchen, to prepare the food for the Midsummer Supper to be held in the church hall that evening. Luckily, it was a cool day for the time of year, for the fridge was far too small, as English fridges always are, to hold even a quarter of the cold meats and fish starters, salads, and elaborate puddings in process of preparation. Every surface was covered with dishes of food over which

Winifred had spread clean tablecloths while she boiled ham and baked yet another meat pie.

At the moment I walked in, she was angrily lifting up each cloth by one corner to try to find the fly that had crawled underneath and which she could hear buzzing. She lifted her head to see who had intruded into the domain she had taken over. Her face was scarlet and running with sweat, her cheeks and eyes a smudgy mess of brown and red and black like a busy artist's palette.

"What is it?" Her tone was just polite.

"I came to see if any help was needed."

"You can find the fly that's got in there if you like."

I found it crawling over slices of ham and when I lifted the cloth a wasp flew out as well. Winifred retreated into a corner of the room, flapping a tea towel and shouting, "I hate wasps. I can't bear them. It will go for me and sting me, I know it will."

Made angry by the wet towel, the wasp zoomed in on her, making her scream. I managed to steer it, not toward the open window as I had hoped, but out into the passage, and closed the door.

"Thank you for that, I loathe those things. If I get a sting it lasts for days—weeks, really."

Forbearing to say, as people do in these circumstances, that if you leave wasps alone they are unlikely to touch you, I asked her where the lunch things were so that I could lay the table.

"Don't you know?" she said, but she opened the various drawers and cupboards to show me and indicated the covered dishes lying apart from her midsummer confections.

At lunch she was calmer at first and had washed the mess off her face. Mrs. Cosway remarked that she wouldn't be going to the Midsummer Supper after all but Winifred and Ella could take me with them if they liked.

"Dr. Lombard coming around, is he, Mother?" This was Ella, her tone pert.

"That is no concern of yours," said Mrs. Cosway.

I had no idea what this was about and hoped to learn more, but Ida, to distract attention perhaps, thanked me for setting the lunch things out, and this prompted me to say that in future I would give her a hand whenever she liked. I considered myself a sufficient judge of character—I turned out to be a fool in most of my judgments but not that one—to be pretty certain she was not a woman to exploit anyone making such an offer.

About halfway through the meal, the wasp reappeared from the passage where I had driven it. Clutching her napkin and waving it about, Winifred jumped up from the table and began to shriek.

"Why doesn't someone get rid of it?" she shouted. "Why is it still in the house? Someone kill it! Kill it before it stings me! You know they always sting me."

"One did once," said her mother.

Winifred shrieked that this wasn't true. She had been stung dozens of times. Still on a high note that was almost a scream she began to enumerate all the occasions wasps had stung her. "In Colchester that time and when we were shopping in Ipswich and on the beach at Frinton and at . . ."

"Oh, be quiet!" said Mrs. Cosway.

Ida had got up and was quietly pursuing the wasp around the table as, its flight describing decreasing circles, it began circumnavigating John's head while he sat quite still, staring out of the window. Diverting from its chosen flight path, it soared quite swiftly toward Winifred, who let out a scream of pure terror and dived under the table. Ida plunged after it, flapping a newspaper that she had picked up from somewhere, and Mrs. Cosway, her patience at last gone, began demanding of everyone if they had all gone mad.

Into this mayhem, through the open door from the hallway, walked a tall, slender woman, dressed as I was sure no one in Windrose had ever been before.

"What fresh hell is this?" she said in the words of Dorothy Parker.

Calm was restored with almost lightning speed. Only John took no notice of the newcomer, returning passively to his tinned peaches and cream. Mrs. Cosway came around the table and, after a moment's hesitation, kissed the woman on the cheek. Winifred, the wasp forgotten—it had in any case disappeared—crawled out from under the table, managed a nervous smile, and said, "Hello, Zorah. How are you?"

This inquiry was ignored, as in my opinion it always should be since it means nothing, and equally rejected was Ida's suggestion that she might like something to eat. Mrs. Cosway said to me, "This is my youngest daughter, Zorah."

I held out my hand and said, "Kerstin Kvist," giving my name its correct pronunciation. It would have been difficult for me, if not impossible, to do otherwise.

"Hello." Very cool, slightly amused.

Though not what today is called a fashionista, I could assess her pale pink linen dress as by Pierre Cardin and her hair, jet black and geometrically styled, as cut by Vidal Sassoon. She was taller than her sisters but less good-looking. Let me qualify that and say that Zorah Todd's features lacked the classical proportions of Winifred's or Ida's but few would have noticed or have held to this judgment for long. Her stylishness, her charm, and something less definable, a graceful poise, the reverse of diffidence, overcame any deficiencies of appearance. The turn of her head was that of a great actress, a Garbo perhaps, and if her graceful movements had a fault it was that they looked studied. For that reason, in a deportment contest, she would have been awarded ninety-seven marks out of a possible hundred.

She went up to her sisters and kissed them, pausing to lift Winifred's left hand in hers. The ring made her smile but in a kindly way, and she congratulated her sister on her engagement as if she were genuinely pleased for her.

"I'm so happy for you, darling. Eric is a very nice man."

"Darling" was not a word I had previously heard from any Cosway. Finally, Zorah went up to her brother and knowing better than to touch him, said, "Hello, you," in a warmer, more intimate tone than I had heard any of them use. He looked at her in his bemused way, managed a half-smile. I noticed that his hands were shaking.

"Is there anyone around who can take my bags up?" she said. "I've got rather a lot of luggage."

If I had been asked I would have refused, but no one asked me. Ida said that Mrs. Lilly, the twice-weekly cleaner, would be arriving at two. She would do it. Zorah nodded. Here, and in Zorah's entrance and manner, was food for thought and something to tell Mark. Where, for instance, did this vision sleep while she was here? In one of those stark and grimly furnished bedrooms, I supposed, sharing a bathroom with four other women and her brother. It seemed impossible. To produce that exquisitely toned and polished appearance, that skin, those nails, that hair, would surely take hours of attention. Or did she go daily to Chelmsford or Colchester for professional services? That would in theory have been possible since she must have arrived by car. As I walked into my own room, preparing to take John out, I saw her car outside on the drive, parked where Ella's had been that morning. Unless, like the pumpkin in Cinderella becoming a golden coach, the battered old Volvo had been transformed into this white Lotus with red leather seats.

Zorah did not reappear that afternoon and the Lotus remained where it was. I was sorry because my curiosity about her built up to such a height that only my unwillingness to disturb Mrs. Cosway and ask the whereabouts of her room stopped me tapping on her door. The kiss she had given Winifred and her kind remark about Eric Dawson led me to believe this sister must be closer to Zorah than the others. I found Winifred in the kitchen, occupied in rotating dishes of party food from fridge to table and others from table to fridge. The refrigerator was far too small to accommodate many plates at a time and Winifred compromised by giving one set of salads and cold meats half an hour's chill, then the second set, and so on, alternating I suppose throughout the afternoon. It seemed rather unhygienic but I said nothing. Winifred had her own comment to make.

"This is very unsatisfactory but what else can I do? It gets warmer all the time, it must be up in the seventies. It makes my job very difficult."

"Will you have a bigger refrigerator at the rectory?"

She gave the Cosway laugh. "Eric's is about the size of our bread bin. I don't know how I'm going to manage. But then I don't suppose I shall have time. I shall be too busy in the parish."

It sounded a grim prospect to me. "Will your youngest sister be going to the Midsummer Supper tonight?"

"Zorah? I shouldn't think so. She never does take part in village life. Besides, when she gets home she's too cozy in her little **bower** to go out anywhere for a few days. No doubt she'll have a male visitor."

By no stretch of optimism could my room or her mother's (nor, I supposed, the other bedrooms) be called a little bower. Not caring to ask directly, still less comment on the possible visitor, I said, feeling my way, "She has made it very comfortable then?"

"You can say that again." Winifred spoke bitterly again and in a very heartfelt way. I saw that I had been wrong in assessing these two sisters as close. With one of her mother's shrugs, she shook off resentment or whatever it was and said, "I do hope you'll come."

"All right," I said, "I will."

That had not been my plan, but now I told

myself it would be a chance to learn more about Windrose and its inhabitants. I promised Winifred I would help her load the food into the Volvo and we set off, with Ella driving, at six-thirty, well in advance of the other guests. It was my first sight of an English church hall. It may differ from a village hall, but if so I have no idea how. This one was not much more than a large hut with a roof of corrugated iron. Inside it had a bare wood floor with several long trestle tables and a dais at one end which could be used as a stage. The windows were small and uncurtained, but still it was rather dark until Ella turned on the strip lighting. In the cold uncompromising light it looked a grim place.

Winifred spread cloths on the tables and we set out the food. As the plates of ham were uncovered I wondered which one had been explored by the fly and resolved to give all a miss. Perhaps because of its repeated transition from fridge to table and table to fridge, the food looked the worse for wear, the slices of meat curling at the edges and the lettuce wilting. It was hot and stuffy inside the hall, a fact immediately commented on by Eric Dawson, who was the first to arrive. He went about opening windows. After that the village trooped in, mostly elderly couples and aging single ladies. Perhaps they were younger than I remember, but then, of course, anyone over forty seemed old to me.

Clinging to Eric's arm and flashing her ring, Winifred walked about greeting people, anticipating her future as chatelaine of the rectory and parson's wife. Ella was transformed. She had dressed herself in a pink sweater and pleated skirt and washed her hair. She met a bosom friend, a woman of about her own age called Bridget Mills, and the two of them went off into a corner where the few chairs were set out and, their heads close together, began an eager conversation.

Everyone smoked and, in spite of the open windows and door, a thick blue fog built up, hanging like cumulus above people's heads. Knowing no one and with no one willing to introduce me, I went among the crowd explaining who I was and that I had been helping Winifred. They were very nice, these people, warm and friendly and welcoming. But there can be no more uncomfortable meal than a buffet supper in a place where there are twenty chairs to fifty people and few uncluttered surfaces. We juggled with a plate in one hand, a glass in the other, and in most cases a cigarette gripped between fore and middle finger of the glass-holding hand. Somewhere had to be found then to put the glass down while a fork was used on the food, and it surprised me that only one plate crashed to the ground, this being dropped by an old lady introduced to me as Miss Adams. Ella rushed over, obviously very displeased at having to leave her friend even for the two minutes it took to clear up the mess.

I learned something about village gossip that

night and, without, I hope, being unkind, the trivialities which Windrose concentrated on when any newcomer to the village was expected. For everyone talked to his or her neighbor for at least a while about the imminent arrival of a new tenant for The Studio. It was like Jane Austen but a hundred and fifty years later, long enough I would have thought for radical change. But these Windrosians were still excited by the prospect of this man's coming, and a village gathering in the church hall was the perfect venue for an exchange of information. Those who knew when he would arrive depended on others to tell them his name and those who knew his name were avid to hear his age, the precise nature of his occupation, and if he was unmarried. Perhaps, again in a Jane Austen climate, it is unnecessary to say that a bachelor of forty, as he seemed to be, was far more interesting to them than a woman of that status and age would have been. No doubt they were thinking that a single man would be in want of a wife.

A lot of the speculation seemed to be founded on wild rumors. After all, he could hardly be a painter of abstracts and a potter and a weaver of tapestries, but various people put forward with absolute conviction these and other versions of what he did. Mrs. Cusp, the churchwarden's wife, was sure she had heard of him as a Symbolist but perhaps that was someone of the same name. A retired army officer from the house next to The Studio said he hoped he wasn't "anything like Picasso."

"I hope he'll fit in," said Ella's friend.

"Maybe he'll fall in love with you, Bridget." This from an elderly female lay reader who took the service when Eric was hard pressed. Apparently she was known for her tactless frankness. "He's never been married, has he? I always think that peculiar in a man who, however you look at it, is on the verge of middle age."

This was hard on Eric, who tightened his lips, took off his glasses, and put them on again. "I look forward to meeting him, anyway," he said in a repressive way unusual with him.

Even after most of the food had been eaten I waited for young people to turn up but none came. I was the youngest there by fifteen years. It was as if a Pied Piper had come into the village some time ago and lured all the children away. I asked Eric about this.

"The young all leave," he said, fidgeting with his glasses. "There's no work for them and nothing much to do. The first thing they do when they leave school is get a car or if they're under seventeen, a motorbike, and then they're off. They go to the towns. We're getting to be a population of retired people."

The effect was depressing. I would have been glad to leave but Winifred had to stay till the end and remove all the dishes and wasted food. It seemed to me that hers was an arduous job. I hoped it was lucrative but doubted it. Her principal reward would have been the praise of approving guests. I heard someone tell Eric he was a lucky man and what an excellent wife she would make. People still said things like that in the sixties. A man's life companion was a good proposition if she could cook and clean.

One good thing about an elderly population was that they tended to leave functions early. At ten sharp couples began going home. It was a fine clear night, the sun not long set and the sky still lit and colored by it, blue and indigo feathers spread across its deep red. Because I have never been back I have no idea what that countryside is like now, but then it was all little patchwork fields, rich flowering hedges, and screens of tall trees. The elms have all gone long ago, but when I was there Dutch elm disease had not yet come to England. Few new houses had been built except for the short rows of council houses outside each village, and the cottages were almost all beautiful—if not beautiful to live in—with roofs of thatch or slate, tiny small-paned windows, and ramblers climbing their walls. Roses around the door are a calendar and Christmas card cliché but those cottages really were like that and still are, for all I know. I had seen Ida desultorily embroidering a picture of one for a firescreen.

Zorah was not at breakfast and failed to appear for lunch. This was party leftovers thriftily served up by Ida. I ate none of it, sticking to bread and cheese as did Mrs. Cosway, but I tried to keep a straight face while she wrinkled up her nose and turned her mouth down. On my way out with John I saw that the Lotus had gone. As usual he kept his head bent and eyes downcast as we walked along. I had debated with myself whether it was better to keep a matching silence to his own or to persist in talking even if I got no replies from him, and I finally decided on the latter. But there is something unnerving about an entirely one-sided conversation. Wearing and frustrating, and the speaker feels foolish. After ten minutes of what became fatuous rubbish about the weather and the scenery, I wanted to shout out, "For God's sake say something!" but of course I had to resist.

I supposed I would get used to it and come to expect a response from him no longer. This was the beginning of my speculating as to what was really wrong with him. My knowledge of mental illness was very inadequate, but I knew more than the Cosways. If he was schizophrenic, was he on any medication other than the sleeping pill Mrs. Cosway gave him every night? He acted and moved like someone heavily dosed with a tranquilizing drug, his hands trembling, his gait often unsteady. His doctor must know, I told myself, this Dr

Lombard who had come to visit Mrs. Cosway while Winifred, Ella, and I were out. Had he also seen Mrs. Cosway's son, or was John already in bed asleep?

No one had mentioned the maze. Perhaps if you had one in your grounds and had always had it, had been born to it, so to speak, and grown up with it, you had lost interest and forgotten it was there. Or was it not there? I could have asked. If I didn't it was because I felt that the Cosways' silence on the subject of something so interesting indicated it was banned as a topic of conversation. Or that, if they wanted me to know about it, they would have mentioned it by now.

This didn't stop me looking for it. I kept my eyes open while on those dreary walks with John, and whenever I went out into the grounds alone I looked, not only for a maze but for the traces of where a maze might once have been, the cut-off trunks of bushes showing through the grass, a copse of trees all of the same kind and closely planted, even a barren square of turf with no apparent purpose or use. There was nothing.

Later that week I came back from one of these explorations to find Mrs. Cosway and Zorah in the drawing room in the throes of an argument I knew instinctively that Zorah would win. She was dressed in a white suit and had pushed her sunglasses up into her black hair so that she looked like a taller version of Jacqueline Kennedy. Mrs. Cosway was holding the amethyst geode, needing both hands to do this because it was too heavy for one. Neither Ida nor Winifred was anywhere to be seen.

"Haven't you taken enough upstairs to those rooms of yours?" Mrs. Cosway was saying. "Oh, no. Now you want this. You could go and buy all these things. You could afford it. It seems to me you can afford anything."

"Just as well for you, Mother," said Zorah. "A fine mess you'd all be in if I couldn't." She turned when she heard the door. "Hello, Kerstin."

I said hello to her and, apologizing for coming in on what seemed to be a private matter, said I would go.

"No, you don't," Mrs. Cosway astonished me by saying. "Now you're here you can arbitrate." This brought one of her small Gioconda smiles to Zorah's face. "Tell me your opinion. My daughter has already removed all the prettiest ornaments from this room and not only this room. Now she wants the geode. Why? She won't say."

"Yes, I will. I rather like it."

This I thought the response of a tyrant, worthy of a dictator who can command anything or negate anything.

"What do you think, Kerstin?"

I was astonished to be asked. My opinion was certainly never again sought on any subject. "I don't know, Mrs. Cosway," I said. "It's not my business."

Zorah raised her wonderfully shaped black eyebrows. "Any judge might say that, Kerstin. Nothing that goes on in a court would be his business if he hadn't been appointed to make a decision."

"He only recommends," I said. "He has a jury."

That made Zorah laugh and as her mother allowed a small smile to widen her mouth a centimetre, Zorah reached for the geode and quickly took it out of her mother's hands. This action produced a scream of rage as Mrs. Cosway lunged at her daughter, ineffectually grabbing at the geode. It fell to the ground with a heavy thump and rolled across the floor. I heard a sound from John. He was on his feet, his hands up to his ears, his eyes bulging.

"No, no, no, no," he whimpered. "No, no . . ."

"See what you've done to your brother!" Mrs. Cosway, though crawling across the carpet, was once more frustrated by an agile Zorah grabbing the geode and holding it up high like a child with a stolen ball. "Look what a state you've got him in. You're a disgrace, you ought to be ashamed."

Zorah was smiling no longer. "Be careful what you say, Mother. You know what I mean."

That was more than I did. John had crawled into a far corner of the room where he sat with his forefingers pushed into his ears, his head bent.

Horrified as much at Mrs. Cosway's careless anger and Zorah's indifference, I watched him curl himself up on the carpet in the fetal position.

"Can I do anything?" I said, and then, "There must be something we can do."

"Just leave him." Mrs. Cosway sounded more impatient than I had ever heard her. "Leave him alone. Ignore him. He'll get up and come back eventually."

Zorah gave me an amused look. She walked over to John and said, "Never mind, old chap. You soldier on."

John stayed in his corner for about half an hour, but just as I was beginning to think this was more than I could bear, this grown man curled up on the floor, his mother reading the newspaper as if this were normal behavior, he got up and shambled back to his armchair.

The next morning Zorah invited me up to her rooms.

6

I HAD DECIDED TO GO TO LONDON THAT EVENING instead of waiting till the Saturday. Although I had settled into helping Ida in the mornings, this after breaking my firm resolve to do no housework, walking with John in the afternoon, and attending the ritual of his bedtime, I had nothing to do after that except eat and watch television with the family. I was in the dining room phoning the station for train times, when Zorah walked in.

"How are you going to get there?"

"I thought I'd go to Marks Tey because it's nearest. I'll walk. It's only a mile."

"A very long mile! I'll drive you if you like."

I accepted as I had a bag to carry, which was light enough but would become very heavy by the time Marks Tey station was reached. As I was giving Zorah the time of my train, Ida came in with a tablecloth and the knives and forks for lunch. She had been shopping in the village.

"Mr. Dunhill is moving in on Monday," she said with the pride of someone imparting a thrilling and long-awaited news item. "Mrs. Waltham told me in the post office."

In that light and slightly mocking tone I was beginning to associate with her, Zorah said, "And who may Mr. Dunhill be?"

"The artist who's moving into The Studio."

"I've never heard of him. Should I have?"

"I don't know, Zorah. I don't even know what sort of an artist he is. No one seems to know."

"Would you like me to find out?"

"Could you?" Ida spoke with the kind of admiring wistfulness I could already tell Zorah liked when it was directed at her. It implied that she was clever and that she knew the right people, a puller of strings, in the know, a spy in the corridors of power. "Could you really?"

"I expect so," said Zorah carelessly. "Leave it to me." While Ida set the table, she turned to me. "Shall I show you where I live when I'm here?"

We went upstairs. I already knew where her room must be, along the passage past Mrs. Cosway's and Ella's where I had never had reason to venture. I followed her, waiting to see another shabby chamber stacked with treasures stolen from her mother. It was not like that. She opened the door and stood back with the sort of pride I would never have expected from someone with her combination of sophistication and coolness.

"There," she said and I heard the little girl she

had once been in her voice, the spoiled child (as I thought then) which the youngest, the afterthought, often is.

Big structural changes had been made. This had probably been two rooms which she must have had combined, for there were windows at each end of it, and an arch dividing living room from bedroom. The walls were paneled and painted in ivory and pale blue in the eighteenth-century manner, and a fine cornice of swatches of ribbons and flowers separated them from the ceiling. The carpet was ivory, a vulnerable carpet which looked untrodden, and on it stood pieces of French furniture in blue and Chinese yellow as well as several deep armchairs and two sofas. I wondered if the spinet and the harp also came from downstairs rooms and, come to that, the landscapes in their slender gilt frames.

The geode stood alone in the middle of a small painted table, its pale lilac crystals glittering in the sunshine and flashing rainbows on to the white wall. Among the other ornaments, a cut-glass bowl and an alabaster lamp suggested themselves to me as also once having belonged to Mrs. Cosway. I was less sure about the jug of clouded glass which stood by itself on a tall table and I approached it curiously, gingerly laying a finger on its side.

"It's Roman," Zorah said carelessly. So might someone describe an object as coming from John Lewis's.

"Valuable, I suppose?"

"Oh, priceless, I should think. They weren't taking proper care of it downstairs so I brought it up here." Later I learned that she often referred to her mother and her sisters as "downstairs." "Lots of Roman glass and porcelain has been found in Essex, you know, but not much of it is as well preserved as that. John loves it—or he used to. He doesn't seem to care about anything anymore. If I thought he did I'd take it back."

I didn't reply. John liking any object but those he carried in his dressing-gown pockets was beyond my imagination. I expected her to say more and was disappointed when all she said was, "My bedroom is through the arch and the bathroom is next to it."

I looked at the four-poster with its white and turquoise bed curtains, the lilac and yellow and blue-green rugs and thought that, elegant as it all was and as far a cry from downstairs as you could get, it was rather like a five-star hotel. It reminded me of the Grand Hotel in Stockholm, a palatial place where a rich aunt of my mother's stayed when she came into town and where I had once been to have tea with her. But looking at the record player, the books, the television, white and neat like the radio, I could understand how Zorah might be happy spending her time up here rather than downstairs. That hardly explained why she wanted to be here at all when it appeared that she could have afforded to buy herself a house in any East Anglian village. Pretty cottages were available at that date for three or four thousand pounds and a fine house for ten.

"It's very pretty," I said.

I am not sure if my comment quite satisfied her. "I thought you'd like it."

She dismissed me by opening the door and standing back to let me pass through. Perhaps I should have reminded her she was going to drive me to the station, but I come from a family, and since that date have married into a family, where people do what they say they will and the kind of offer she made is written in stone. I attended John's bedtime ritual, still trying to think of ways I could put an end to dosing him with barbiturates. It would take me twenty-five minutes to walk to the station but less than five in a car and at that time I thought I would get a lift. I put a spare pair of jeans and a sweater into my bag and went downstairs to wait for Zorah. Something made me look out of the window and it was a good thing I did, for the Lotus was gone and Zorah with it. She had forgotten me.

I waited for ten minutes in case she meant to return and then I left, sore and angry. Although with none of that longing which is a sign of love, I was looking forward to this meeting with Mark and now I had no idea when the next train would come or when it would get to London. As it happened, it was only just over half an hour before one came, but it shuddered to a halt at every station on the line before reaching Liverpool Street an hour and ten minutes later.

Mrs. Cosway and John were always seated at the breakfast table when I came down. I tried to be up by seven, though this was hard for me, as it usually is for people of the age I was then, but it would not have been so difficult if I could have seen the need for it. There was nothing for me to do unless I manufactured chores for myself, and nothing as far as I could see to occupy Mrs. Cosway and her son. They could have stayed in bed another two hours for all they did with the time gained, but they were always up earlier than I was and always waiting for me, Mrs. Cosway pointedly looking at her watch as I came in. Needless to say, Ida had been up since God knows when to serve them their breakfast.

On the Tuesday after my weekend in London I was down earlier than usual, obviously earlier than Mrs. Cosway expected me, for as I came in I saw her give John a pill on a saucer. I might have taken no notice of this but for the start she gave.

"I didn't hear you come downstairs," she said.

My shoes had rubber soles, but they were a pair I often wore. She was beginning to lose her hearing, as I had noticed and Ella had told her, but she refused to accept it.

"I am rather early," I said.

"No need to apologize for that."

There was a ring of sarcasm in her voice implying that I might consider saying I was sorry for the many occasions I had been late but never for being in advance of my time. Ella arrived in time to hear her.

"Kerstin wasn't apologizing, Mother," she said, pouring cornflakes into a bowl. "She was explaining. There is a difference, you know."

One of their spats developed after that with Ella telling her mother that her passion for punctuality was ridiculous and it was just as bad to be too early for an appointment as too late. Mrs. Cosway denied it. If you were early you kept no one waiting, the way Ella kept everyone waiting, saving her own time but wasting theirs. How a child of hers, brought up like the others, came to have such a major character flaw she had no idea. Tempers began running high and into the midst of it walked Winifred, brilliantly made up as usual, her fingernails blood-red, to put her spoke in, as her mother said, by telling Mrs. Cosway that it hardly mattered whether she were early or late as she seldom set foot outside and never met anyone.

Ida came in with a pot of fresh tea. "Oh, please, please. I could hear you in the kitchen. Think of John. You know how he hates it."

It was true that he usually did but now he sat still and silent, his face calm as a death mask, his hands laid on the tablecloth as if about to play on an invisible instrument; I remembered the pill I had seen Mrs. Cosway give him and which, surely, had been the root cause of this quarrel. Was she drugging him by day as well as by night and if so, why?

There was no sign of Zorah. She never appeared at breakfast and I supposed she either went without or made tea and toast for herself upstairs. The evening before she had turned up for supper, a much more interesting meal than usual with a pair of cold pheasants and a game pie, all of which I guessed she had brought with her or ordered from Harrods. She said nothing about forgetting to drive me to the station and I also said nothing, recriminations being pointless. Whether it was as a result of Zorah's influence or some other unknown cause, Ella had made some improvements to her appearance during the weekend. Her face was lightly made up, her hair washed, and instead of one of her droopy prints, she wore a straight shift in red crêpe. Some man must be in the offing, I decided, for I had summed her up as a woman who would dress up when intent on attracting, and in spite of the books in her room, one who had never learned from Jane Austen that "man only can be aware of man's insensibility to a new gown."

The Cosways possessed an enormous amount of silver, and either from an oversight or because she disliked it, Zorah seemed to have purloined none of it. Coming upon Ida opening drawers and cupboards and gazing at the tarnished contents in despair, I had said I would clean it for her or at least make a start on cleaning it. I had begun, and was tackling with the silver polish and a pile of torn-up pajamas a silver tray bearing on it a cream jug, water jug, and sugar basin, when Mrs. Lilly arrived.

In the short time I had been at Lydstep Old Hall I had learned never to take on a task the cleaner might be expected to perform without offering her an explanation. This applies (and still does) to a job she would never do even if asked to, but at which, if she finds anyone else usurping it, she will take umbrage. Accordingly, when Mrs. Lilly came into the dining room, pushing a vacuum cleaner she never emptied and with a handful of dirty dusters she never washed, I said brightly, "You're always so busy when you're here, Mrs. Lilly, that I don't know when you'd make time to do this, so I thought I'd help you out."

A kind of grudging suspiciousness narrowed her eyes and wrinkled her upper lip but she accepted my explanation, though taking the rag out of my hand and showing me how to apply what she called "elbow grease." Not much time was spent on this as she had news to impart and Ida had to be called in to hear it while Mrs. Lilly trailed very slowly around the room, talking as she wiped surfaces. Her news was the arrival at The Studio of Mr.

Dunhill, her own cottage being just on the other side of the little green from his.

"He didn't have the removal people. All his stuff came in a van and I reckon it was driv"—Essex people say "driv" for "driven"—"by a pal of his on account of they both went in the Rose when they'd done the unloading. He didn't have much. A lot of books and some great big frames with cloth stretched on them and things to paint pictures on. Him and the pal had a couple of G and T's in the Rose and that's where Mr. Lilly saw them when he went in for his pint."

All this was of very little interest to me, but Ida and Winifred, who had also come in, were enthralled by it. Living in the country narrows the mind, and I wondered if I would get like them after a year of it.

"What does he look like, Mrs. Lilly?" This was Winifred, always interested in personal appearance.

"Oh, I don't know. Tall, dark, and handsome—is that what you want me to say? I'm no good at what folks look like. He's all right, about forty, got a lot of long hair. When I was a girl we used to say we'd like a handsome husband and a thousand a year. Wouldn't go far these days, would it?"

"I wonder if he goes to church," said the rector's prospective bride.

"Not by the looks of him." Mrs. Lilly gave a raunchy laugh. "I'd be surprised."

Silently but not stealthily, Zorah came in. She must have been listening outside. She wore a blue and white check dress, summertime country wear. "I can tell you exactly what he looks like, Winifred," she said. "I saw him myself yesterday."

"Why didn't you say?"

"I'm saying now, darling. I didn't imagine you'd have such a voracious appetite for the details of a bachelor's appearance." One of her crimson blushes flooded Winifred's face. "By the way, I've discovered he's a painter of abstracts," said Zorah. "He has exhibited. I don't know if he's ever sold anything. Not likely, I'd say. Whoever told you his name was Dunhill was wrong. It's Dunsford. He's about six feet tall, thin, shoulder-length black hair. Personally I don't care for long hair on a man. Some would call him good-looking." Whether or not she would, she failed to say. "Satisfied?"

"You needn't make such a song and dance of it, Zorah."

"I thought it was you doing that, darling."

"I'm going to start hoovering," said Mrs. Lilly, "so you'd best all clear off if you want to hear yourselves speak."

Ida helped me carry trayfuls of silver out to the kitchen. At a loose end now her catering was over for the time being, Winifred followed us to drift around the big room, pausing first to gaze out of the window, then opening the fridge door and pushing jars and dishes about inside.

"Zorah can be a real bitch," she remarked to the remains of cold pheasant. " 'Voracious appetite for the details of a bachelor's appearance,' indeed. She's got a nerve. When we all know she'll get hold of him. She always does."

"Oh, Winifred." Ida gave a meaning glance at me.

"Kerstin won't say anything," said Winifred. "She wouldn't be interested."

Which only went to show how little they knew me. I sat with John and Mrs. Cosway and shared with her the two newspapers they took. She read, he did nothing. Now I was beginning to see his condition as a possibly drug-induced dazed state, light was starting to dawn on other aspects of his life and habits. I asked myself—I had already asked Mrs. Cosway in vain—why she had taken me on. What was I for? Solely to accompany this poor, sluggish, zombie-like man for an hour's walk in the afternoons? And to watch him go to bed in a neglected living room with a piano in it?

My day off this week would be the Wednesday, too soon to arrange to see Isabel. I would phone her, though, and ask if I could call and see her at her home in London the following Monday. It was she who had recommended me to the Cosways and them to me, and I had a lot of things to ask her. Meanwhile, as if reading my thoughts on my uselessness at Lydstep Old Hall, Mrs. Cosway looked up from her paper and asked me if I would "supervise"

John's bedtime that evening as she, in spite of what Winifred had said at breakfast, would be going out. In the afternoon I went out with him for his walk as usual and this time I tried a different route. Seeing that he put up no resistance when, instead of opening the gate into the field, I said, "I think we'll go by the road today, John," I led him a little way down the hill and on to the public footpath which skirted the side of the meadow, went a little way into the wood and crossed a river, which must have been the Colne, by a footbridge. I hoped it would take a turn to bring us back without retracing our steps and this was what happened. We came to a lane and a signpost which pointed to Windrose in one direction and Lydstep Green in the other and turned left.

John walked obediently along, plodding like a weary horse pulling too heavy a load. It upset me just to look at him, wondering if he had been given some mind-numbing drug early that morning and possibly—though this was guesswork on my part—another later in the day. Cowardly though it was, I tried to solve this by turning my eyes away from him to gaze at the Great Red Tower of Windrose, a blunt finger pointing skyward out of the horizon, at a flock of birds which rose in formation from one of the fields and then at a cat stalking some tiny creature under the hedge. But my thoughts stayed with him and my eyes went back to his lumbering figure, round shoulders, and forward-thrusting head. Mrs. Cosway had said that it was he who had asked for me, asked for someone to help her, that is, but it seemed to me then that this was the hardest thing of all to imagine, that he might have any wishes or be capable of making any real decisions. Suppose I asked him? Would he answer? I was thinking how impossible that question would be to ask, how unlikely that there would be any reply, when without warning, John stumbled and fell over, sprawling on the ground.

Appalled, I instantly blamed myself, though nothing out of the way had happened except that we were following a different route. Though thin, I was very strong and fit and I bent down to John before remembering I mustn't touch him. He gave no more sign that he had fallen than if he had been a waxwork. Indeed, lying there, he looked like some sort of lay figure, as rigid as the stone on the road he had tripped over. Touching him would be worse than leaving him there, I thought, and I sat down on the grass verge to wait. Time goes very slowly in these circumstances and I began to wonder what to do if he stayed there for hours. He might even fall asleep, he so often seemed on the verge of it, as if sleep were always waiting beside him to pull him into its folds. But just as I was thinking I would have to leave him and go back to the house for help, he got to his feet and started to walk on without a word.

He was quite unhurt. When I told Mrs. Cosway what had happened I got an unexpected reaction. I thought she would be angry and I was prepared for that, being pretty sure that if we had followed our normal itinerary none of this would have happened. If she had said in response that as a result, she would stay in that evening instead of leaving me in charge, I wouldn't have been surprised. But she only gave one of her shrugs, a movement that conveyed indifference more perfectly than any I have ever seen.

"He's not hurt, is he?"

"I don't think so."

"He does that sometimes," she said.

And at six, home from school an hour before, Ella drove her away in the car. Mrs. Cosway's mixture of devotion and an uncaring lack of interest was beyond me. I suppose I had sentimental ideas about motherhood in those days or just my own mother as an example. An hour had passed and John shuffled off to his bedroom. I followed him after allowing him time to get undressed. When I came into the room he was in the act of arranging dice, ballpoint, plaster, green bottle and the rest on his bedside table and took no notice of me. He hadn't uttered a word, in my hearing at least, since we came back from our walk.

Mrs. Cosway had left me the barbiturate tablet ready in the glass dish. I held it out to him exactly as she did but he shook his head, turned over on his side, and pulled the quilt over him.

I said, "Your pill, John," but he didn't answer and I saw he was already asleep.

It was still broad daylight and the room was as light as it ever was. Although I knew Mrs. Cosway disliked drawn curtains, I went to the window to pull them across, but before I got there I noticed on top of the piano a framed photograph of four girls, taken perhaps twenty years before. One of them, plain-faced and spotty but just recognizable as Zorah, was in an unflattering school uniform. Ida looked much as she did today, careworn and harassed from self-imposed duties, Winifred and Ella both very pretty, brightly smiling. A middle-aged man in the picture I supposed must be the late Mr. Cosway, father of this family, handsome and with an unexpectedly sensitive face. John was not there. Could he have taken this photograph?

I drew the curtains, picked up John's discarded clothes from the floor, and went out into the hall. Zorah was standing there as if waiting for me. She looked at the shirt and socks and underwear I was holding.

"Why do you have to do that?"

"Someone has to."

"My mother will be hours. Where she's gone she won't hurry back." She was dressed to go out, her car keys in her hand, but she lingered. "John never used to be like that," she said, "like he's in a dream all the time, never saying a word, clumsy and stumbling about. What do you think is really wrong with him?"

I said I didn't know but no doubt his doctor did. She laughed. She opened the front door and slammed it behind her. The house shook. I wondered what her laughter meant and then where she was going and whom she was meeting. In spite of what her daughter had said, Mrs. Cosway came back in the Volvo half an hour later. Perceptive enough to notice that I had expected her to be out longer, Ella said, though unasked, "She only went to the doctor's."

Mrs. Cosway followed her in, opened her bag, and dropped a piece of paper on the hall table before passing on into the drawing room. Considering where she had been, for me to have kept from glancing at it would have been impossible. I had no pangs of conscience to struggle with.

It was a prescription for high-dose phenobarbital and another drug called Largactil. I had completely forgotten what Largactil was for. If I wanted to identify it I would have to find a dictionary of medicines in the public library at Colchester or Sudbury and look it up. I had decided to say nothing to Mrs. Cosway about John's refusal to take the barbiturate from me. He was asleep, would very probably stay asleep, and if he didn't and she asked me, I would admit my failure. I could see no reason for his going to bed at seven any more than I could for the afternoon walks. It was Ella who, that very evening, came to sit next to me and explain, though I hadn't asked her. This was the beginning of her overtures of friendship to me.

"You and I are nearer to each other in age than you are to the others," she said in a cozy, all-girls-together voice, though Zorah's age was nearer to mine and even then not very near. "I know you've been wondering what's the point of you going on those walks with John, and I thought I'd enlighten you.

"The fact is he wants it that way. John, I mean. He insists on that walk. You try stopping him. It's this compulsion thing he has. Just like he must arrange those things he carries about in his pocket and he must cut his bread up in patterns and turn his eggshell the other way up, so he has to go on that walk. If it's absolutely pouring and he can't go he'll make an awful fuss, you'll see."

I nodded and said I had to thank her for letting me borrow a book from her room.

"Anytime," she said and, "you're welcome," which English people hardly ever said then. "Did my mother show you the library?"

I said she had mentioned it, but I understood the door was kept locked.

"That's a lot of silly nonsense," said Ella. "I'll show it to you some time. It's quite interesting."

"A lot of rare books?"

"Well, a lot of **books.** I don't know about rare. That's not what it's interesting for, but you'll see."

Ella was fond of telling me that I would see and I usually did in time. "I've a feeling you and I are going to be friends, Kerstin. I'd like that."

Of course I had to say that I would too, and I had begun to feel kindly disposed toward this pretty woman who was so obviously insecure and self-doubting. But my thoughts were concentrated on the prescription Mrs. Cosway had brought back from the doctor, and suddenly, while Ella continued to talk, this time about her school and her problems with form Five B, the elusive definition came to me. Largactil was a preparation of a powerful drug called chlorpromazine hydrochloride and it was used to treat patients undergoing behavioral disturbances or who are psychotic. It also allayed severe anxiety. It therefore seemed quite a reasonable medication for the schizophrenic John Cosway.

7

I BECAME OBSESSED WITH THE DIARY. THE PHYSICAL part of it, the leather-bound book, had been given to me by a friend for my birthday and when it first arrived I thought it the least useful present I received. I had never kept a diary, I had never expressed a wish to keep one or regrets for not doing so. But here it was, a handsome volume, a couple of hundred pages thick inside its cover of red leather and gilt, and it found its way into my suitcase because of its looks and as something to put in the pocket on the inside of the lid.

I began to write in it only, at first, to describe the countryside and Lydstep Old Hall, having a feeling that a record of this place might be useful to me in later years. After that came descriptions of the occupants of the house, and once I had begun on their characters and conversations I was hooked. Sometimes I could hardly wait to escape from the drawing room and the company when the old black-and-white television was on, its grainy picture rippling and rolling, and Mrs. Cosway gazing at it grimly, to go upstairs, open the diary, and begin to write.

If I had been in her place or if I had been any of the others, I would have hated the very idea of it, as she did and they did when they found out. In my defense I can say I tried to be charitable and fair in what I wrote and of course I never dreamed that the time would come when I would hand this chronicle of events at Lydstep Old Hall to the police. Not the least idea of what was to come entered my mind when I committed my observations and thoughts to those pages. If anyone had warned me that they would be read by police officers and psychiatrists I wouldn't have believed it. Unless it is lent or stolen, what circumstances can there be in which a private diary is read by others? Only perhaps, as in this case, when what it records supplies evidence of a crime. I had no choice but to offer it to the police, though I have to say that there was no coercion and I gave it up to them willingly.

The first drawing I did, the one of the house, was on one of the diary's endpapers because I had no other paper. Zorah, looking like a fashion plate, was sketched in there too and for the same reason. On my day off I took the bus into Sudbury and bought paper, but using it didn't feel the same. For one thing, it wasn't the thick cream vellum of the diary but thin white stuff, and it was loose, just slippery sheets, and there was nothing in the room to rest on but the diary itself. I didn't know it then, because I had no plans for the future or ideas of what it would be, but this decision of mine to keep up my drawing and on the pages of the diary itself, formed a habit for me which some have called eccentric. When I began my cartoons I found they would only work if I did them in a notebook. Since then I have always done this, I can't make any sort of drawing (except the Dog Growing) on a loose sheet, and over the years I've torn out the page with the cartoon on it and sent it by post, then by fax, and lately have scanned them and sent them by e-mail attachment.

The next sketch I made in the diary was of Felix Dunsford.

I had no difficulty in recognizing him from Zorah's description. No one else in Windrose had shoulder-length black hair or hands quite so ostentatiously paint-stained. I had walked into the village one morning to do some shopping Ida had no inclination for and probably no time either. Windrose wasn't well endowed with shops. There was a good butcher, quite famous in north Essex, a general store that was also the post office and newsagent, and a greengrocer. The days when English villages would have either no shops at all or else a designer boutique and a hairdresser were still a long way in the future. I encountered Felix Dunsford in the general store where he was buying cigarettes and a packet of tea.

I have said that for the most part the village

people were middle-aged or elderly, so it was probably my youth which made him look me up and down in an appraising way. But it was a rude way just the same.

In a phrase I had picked up from Mark, I said, "You'll know me again."

"Sorry," he said, and, "it was only an admiring glance."

Such a remark tells you more about a man's nature than any amount of listening and observation. I went up to the counter and asked for the things Ida wanted. The eyes of the other people in the shop were on me, and disapprovingly. One woman positively scowled. I wanted to laugh but controlled myself. Holding Ida's shopping basket in one hand and a paper carrier full of vegetables in the other, I walked back to the Hall and found Winifred at the kitchen table, writing a menu and a list for a dinner party booked for the following Saturday week. When I remembered the chaos and panic of the Midsummer Supper I was glad that was my weekend off and I'd be in London.

"I've seen the painter," I said, knowing by now that retailing bits of gossip was almost a bounden duty in that household.

"What's he like?"

Zorah had already told her and so had Mrs. Lilly. "Good-looking. Long hair." Better not mention the appraising stare, I thought. "He was in the shop buying cigarettes."

"Eric is bound to pal up with him," Winifred said. "He always takes up with new people whether they go to church or not. He says it's his function, but I think he likes it."

She insisted on reading her menu to me. It seemed very elaborate for a country dinner, for this was long past the days of big house parties and before England became cuisine-aware: prawn and lobster cocktail, leek and potato soup, roast lamb, mint sauce, redcurrant jelly, duchesse potatoes, new peas, a Pavlova and a hazelnut tart, Stilton and biscuits.

"What's a Pavlova?" I said.

"A sort of meringue with raspberries and cream. Do you think it will do?"

"They'll love it. But will they get through all that?"

"Oh, yes," said Ida. "No problem out here. I suppose you'll want to take over the kitchen on Saturday. I only ask because it puts Mother in a bad temper if she doesn't get a good lunch at the weekend."

Winifred threw down her pencil. "It's my living!" she shouted. "You don't earn anything and nor does Mother and as for John—God knows he doesn't need it. What am I supposed to do if I can't have the kitchen for an hour to earn my living? It's my **job.**"

"Of course you must have the kitchen." Ida said in the tone of someone much put-upon. "Of course. I'll manage."

The previous weekend I had been in London and by the time this Sunday came around I had almost forgotten the only one I had so far spent at Lydstep.

"You'll come to church?"

Winifred's inquiry was more in the nature of a command. She had attended Holy Communion one morning in the week, so was at breakfast with us this Sunday.

"Eric will be taking Communion after Matins today."

"I'll come," I said, not revealing my vague knowledge about this appendage to the service.

John sat at the table, his toast eaten and his tea half-drunk, contemplating his folded hands which lay on the tablecloth, trembling faintly. They seemed to have an hypnotic effect on him as if they might send him into a trance or had already done so. In the light of my recovered knowledge, I questioned why a man so apparently lifeless and calm would need Largactil, but perhaps he was only lifeless **because** of the Largactil.

Isabel Croft might answer this question for me, I thought, as we set off for church. She had phoned the day before at a blameless hour to invite me, not to meet for lunch but to come and have it with her at her house. As a child Isabel had stayed at Lydstep Old Hall in her holidays and been quite close to Zorah, whom she still occasionally met. She could also tell me about the maze I had been unable to find.

Though covering the head hadn't been a rule in the Church of England for more than twenty years, Winifred insisted on wearing a hat. As a special mark of piety, I suppose, designed to impress Eric Dawson and not so very different from the habit of those Moslem girls one sees today who wear a miniskirt and low-cut top but the **hijab** tied around their heads and covering their necks.

We filed into what Ella grandly called "the Cosway pew," and the two of them fell on their knees to make their silent devotions. The organist was playing a cantata that seemed familiar, and after a moment or two I recognized the work of the Swedish composer Josef Martin Kraus. This was the music he wrote for the birthday of Gustav III, and it made me want to meet this organist and ask about his rare choice of a voluntary by a composer who hadn't even found his way into the **Oxford Companion to Music.**

The pews began to fill up, insofar as they ever did, with Cusps and Walthams, Mrs. Lilly and her husband, and several of the people who had been in the general store when I went shopping there. Ida and Zorah never went to church and Mrs. Cosway only rarely. There seemed some mystery about Ida's staying away for she had apparently once been a devout attender. Much to my surprise, when I thought the entire congregation were in their seats, Felix Dunsford came in. Instead of choosing a pew at the back, he came right up to the front and sat down on the other side of the aisle from ourselves.

His appearance caused a stir. This was partly due, I suppose, to the length of his hair. Long hair on men was common in cities then but not in the conservative countryside where the short-back-and-sides was not only de rigueur but almost a moral duty. It was soon after this that I heard Mrs. Waltham say of a teenage boy that he must be a bad lot because he had hair which covered his collar. Felix Dunsford's was much longer than that. He wore a jacket of sorts, linen and crumpled, very unlike the suits complete with waistcoats the other men had on and which filled the church with the reek of mothballs and sweat. His trousers were jeans and paint-stained at that. I judged him the sort of painter who takes pains to leave no one in ignorance for a moment of the art he practices.

Winifred was staring at him in horror. She made a move to get up and I wondered what she was going to do, but at that moment Eric appeared, went to his desk by the choir stalls, and, calling us "dearly beloved," began asking us to accompany him to the throne of the heavenly grace. Also fascinated but in a less disapproving way, Ella sneaked glances at Dunsford, pretending her eyes were on a wasp which buzzed around conveniently between his row and ours. While we sang "Dear Lord and

Father of mankind"—I thought the next line, "Forgive our foolish ways," particularly apt—she gazed past me at Dunsford and the wasp which, alighting on the hand that held **Hymns Ancient and Modern,** was crawling up his thumb toward the nail. It paused on a green paint stain it perhaps took for a leaf. Dunsford seemed undisturbed by it and continued to sing in a fine baritone voice. If it is true that staring at someone will eventually make him look at you, her gaze had that effect on Dunsford, for he turned his head and, still singing, winked. Ella abruptly jerked her head around to face Eric and the wasp flew off.

All this time Winifred, the wasp-phobic, had been trembling and shrinking, flapping her hands and sometimes shutting her eyes. She only relaxed when the insect soared off into the hammer beams above our heads. The congregation recited the "Te Deum" in the kind of sepulchral voice mourners might use at the mass funeral of everyone they held dear, and we settled down to hear Eric preach on the laudable subject of loving one's neighbor as oneself. It made me wonder if he did so and I decided he probably did. Felix Dunsford had closed his eyes and seemed to have fallen asleep.

As things were drawing to a close, Winifred whispered to me, "Have you been confirmed? You can't take Communion if you haven't."

If I was anything, I was a Lutheran as my parents were, if they were anything. I had no idea if I was confirmed or even if the Lutherans had confirmation, but I nodded to save trouble. My church visit was too enjoyable to be cut short just yet. The turmoil Felix Dunsford was causing, especially among the women in the congregation, was an unexpected treat and I wanted to see what would develop.

Eric and Mr. Cusp went through a ritual with a chalice and a silver box and people began moving out of the pews and lining up. I wish I knew the terms which were used and what the language meant, but I didn't and I'm told all is changed now. I had no understanding of Eric's meaning when he addressed us nor much of what we were doing kneeling on hassocks and waiting for the bread and the wine. Of course I was not ignorant of the significance of the ceremony but I expected a wafer on my tongue—was that the Roman Catholics?—not a cube of white bread, and I was surprised by the sweetness of the dark red wine in the chalice.

"Blood of Christ, shed for thee, preserve thy body and soul unto everlasting life. Drink this in remembrance that Christ's Blood was shed for thee and be thankful."

Everyone said Amen when it was their turn so I did too. The kind of superstitiousness of which we all have remnants brought me a stab of fear because of my probably unconfirmed state, but of course no divine retribution came down to strike me. I was hazy as to whether we were supposed to believe we were actually partaking of Christ's blood and body by a miracle of transubstantiation or if all this was a symbol. There was no one I could ask without ignominy. Felix Dunsford continued to sit in his pew with one leg crossed over the opposite knee, apparently studying the people as they went up. Most of them, when they returned to their seats, fell on their knees and buried faces in hands. I sat where I was, looking at the saints behind the altar, the Gospel makers with lion, angel, bull, and eagle, wondering if I was in a state of grace. Or was that too a Catholic concept?

Felix Dunsford grinned at me and, after a small hesitation, I smiled back. I was thinking how I could get to meet the organist. At least I could find out his name and where he lived. It was Winifred whose behavior brought me to look in Dunsford's direction again. When everyone had made their Communion, Eric recited a bit more from the Book of Common Prayer and the service was over. My husband is an Anglican and it has always amazed and amused me how quickly the transition is made in his church between an atmosphere of somber reverence and one of a community center. Even while the organist was playing—**Zadok the Priest** this time—the congregation, transformed into social club members, was chatting away, gossiping, issuing invitations, asking after missing relatives. In her future Mrs. Rector's capacity, I suppose, Winifred passed on some piece of information to her friend June Prothero, and then she went over to Felix Dunsford.

"May we have a word?" I heard her say.

"Sure." He gave her a cool but friendly grin. "Sure." He held out his hand. "Felix Dunsford at your service."

"Winifred Cosway. Mr. Dawson, our rector, is my fiancé."

"That's nice. Congratulations. I like your ring."

This wasn't at all what Winifred had expected, but she said a brief thank-you and assumed her Sunday school teacher's manner. "I just wanted to say—and you mustn't take this amiss—that your clothes aren't quite suitable for church. Not very complimentary to Mr. Dawson, do you think?"

"You want me to take them off?"

He was rewarded by one of the finest blushes he can ever have seen. It began in Winifred's cheeks and spread across her whole face, coloring her neck and the skin revealed by the V of her neckline. "Please," she said, and then, realizing what she implied, "Of course not. I meant you to wear something a little more—well, formal, next time you come."

He was laughing. "What if I haven't got anything a little more formal?"

By this time Winifred must have been wishing she had never started this. "I'm sure you have. I'm sure you can find something."

"I'll tell you what. Why don't you come around

and have a look for me? Next Sunday morning before I get dressed?" He patted her on the shoulder and walked off, still laughing.

Winifred put her hand up to where he had touched her as if she had been stung by the now-vanished wasp. "What an insufferable man."

"You asked for it," said Ella, "putting your spoke in."

We filed out past Eric, who gave Winifred a kiss on the cheek and asked if he was right in thinking he had been invited to lunch.

"Of course, darling." She sounded like Zorah.

"I liked your organist's playing," I said to him. "It was Swedish music."

"Was it now?" I could tell he had no interest in music of any sort. "Dear old Jim is sometimes too advanced for our quiet backwater."

Once he was out of earshot Ella reverted to Felix Dunsford. "Personally, I like a man to have a casual look."

"Not in church," said Winifred.

"I don't suppose he'll come again after what you said."

"You know, Ella, I think you've got your eye on him. You don't stand a chance, not once he's seen Zorah. Talk about casual. You want to take a long hard look at yourself in the mirror."

A fierce quarrel developed which only came to an enforced end when Eric's car pulled up beside us and he drove us all back to Lydstep Old Hall. John and his mother were in the living room. Eric was careful not to offer him his hand but instead dipped his head in what I believe is called a court bow. I am afraid I had put Eric down as a fool, but now my estimation of him was going up rapidly.

"How are you, old man?" he asked John.

"Fine, fine, I'm fine." The voice was the same, a robot's monotone, but the face was brighter, no longer expressionless.

The room was different. It seemed less barren and less shabby. And then I noticed the Roman vase, standing on the console table against the wall beside Mrs. Cosway's sofa. Before she left for London, Zorah had restored it to John. He sat looking at it, gazing as if meditating, his hands no longer shaking but resting quietly in his lap. At seven, apparently his bedtime of choice, he got up, shambled over to the console table, and laid his hands on the body of the vase. He held them there and then began to stroke the sleek green dimpled glass while his mother waited quite patiently for him to go into his bedroom with her.

8

WE WENT INTO ISABEL'S LIVING ROOM AND SHE poured white wine into two glasses. Of course she wanted to know how I was getting on with the Cosways and I soon saw that she looked on them with very different eyes from mine. I was her brother-in-law's girlfriend, but they were her friends, if distant ones by this time, and I knew I must be careful not to criticize.

"Mrs. Cosway was quite nice to me when I used to go there and stay. The village is pretty too, don't you think? Of course the house is strange, especially in the summer. There used to be a picture in the library of the old house as it was before their great-grandfather put a new façade on it and planted all that creeper. As you know, I haven't been there for ages, it must be ten years, but I don't suppose it's changed much."

"Maybe not," I said.

"My own father was very strict and I remember when I was a child I used to wish Mr. Cosway was my father. He was so **nice.** He always had time for the children, answered all their questions, really spent time with them, and he was patient. John becoming—well, mentally ill was something he could never quite accept."

"Do you mean he wasn't always?"

"It seems he was quite normal when he was a little boy, but something went wrong with his brain after he had some kind of a shock. Or that's what Zorah said. I don't know what it was and of course I couldn't ask. He began to have terrible tantrums and there was no doing anything with him. That was when he started hiding in cupboards and spending all day in the library. Mr. Cosway was one of those men who valued his son over any daughter and I'm afraid he thought the only career for a woman, the only happy way of life really, was marriage. But none of his girls looked like marrying. Ida got engaged to someone and that was a relief to him, but it was broken off soon after he died."

"He would have been in for disappointment," I said. "Ida and Ella both without husbands and Zorah a widow."

"Why didn't you include Winifred?"

"Oh, didn't you know? Winifred's engaged. To a man called Eric Dawson. He's the rector of Windrose."

Isabel laughed but in kindly fashion. "How like Winifred. Still, I'm glad. She'll make an excellent vicar's wife—rector's, I should say. Shall we go and have lunch?"

At this meal, a light and delicate change from

the heavy food served up at Lydstep, we talked about Isabel's husband, a civil servant in the Foreign Office, and their children, both at school that day. Unless they had both changed a lot, I found it hard to imagine Isabel and Zorah as friends, they were so different. We called people like Zorah "jet-setters" in those days, sophisticated, smart, dashing, and superficial, while Isabel was gentle and warm. You could hardly have found women who were contemporaries and of the same ethnic group who looked less alike, Zorah thin and model-ish, her black hair so geometrically cut that it looked painted on, Isabel plump and fair, the type then called an English rose.

Keeping off the subject of the Cosways was impossible for me for long. When Isabel brought us coffee I asked her when she had last seen Zorah. Surely since the ten years she had mentioned.

"Well, we both live in London, but there's a bit of a difference, isn't there? I mean, here am I in Crouch End and her house is in Green Street."

"You mean, the Green Street in the West End? In Mayfair?"

She laughed at the expression on my face. "I do mean that, yes. Zorah is very, very rich, you know. I see you didn't know. But we have met a few times. Having the children makes it difficult for me. I suppose the last time was two years ago when we had lunch. She phones and Mrs. Cosway writes—as you know."

I said bluntly, "How rich?"

"Oh, millionaire class. I'd better tell you the story. It's quite romantic in its way."

"Yes, please."

"She was very plain when she was in her teens. Huge nose and quite swarthy but awfully bright. I mean, streets ahead of anyone else in the family, not a bit like them, really. I told you Mr. Cosway had these antediluvian ideas. He thought you only bothered to educate plain girls because they'd need to earn their own livings. They wouldn't get married, you see. Zorah got a scholarship to Oxford. Everyone thought he wouldn't let her go, but he did because he thought it was her only hope. Besides, he wanted to get her out of his sight—he'd never loved her like he did the others."

"He was nice?" I said, and breaking my rule. "He doesn't sound it."

"He was of his time. Very much a Victorian. After all, he was born in the eighteen eighties. Anyway, Zorah got a first and started on a DPhil. I got the impression the others were bewildered by her brains. This would have been sometime in the late fifties. She was doing research in some obscure library which was expecting a visit from a millionaire they hoped would endow something or other. I mean, really big money was involved and Zorah was asked to show him around and look after him for the day. The next thing was he wanted to see her again and within a couple of months they were married."

"So much for Mr. Cosway's estimate of her."

"Yes," Isabel said. "You could put it like that. Raymond Todd had been married three times before and been three times divorced. The Cosways found that very hard to take, but Zorah was determined to marry him and she was of age, she was twenty-four by then."

I asked her how old Raymond Todd was.

"Getting on for sixty. He had a house in Italy and an apartment in New York and this house in Green Street. She'd been married maybe six months when Mr. Cosway died. He left a funny sort of will. I don't remember the ins and outs of it, if I ever knew, but I do know that John got everything. Mrs. Cosway has a small annuity, but none of the rest of them have any money except what Ella earns and Winifred makes cooking for people and, of course, what Zorah gives them. She's been amazing—I mean, very, very generous."

"Is that why she spends so much time there? She's got those houses and so on, yet she apparently spends weeks at Lydstep. I've wondered why, but perhaps it's so that she can be on hand to help them."

"Perhaps." Isabel looked dubious. "I suppose she likes it."

That mystery remained unsolved, as far as I was

concerned. It seemed to me that Zorah could have given her family financial support just as well from London, or Italy, come to that, as from a bedroom in her mother's house. I asked when her husband died.

"Oh, not long after Mr. Cosway. He left Zorah all he had. He had no children from any of his marriages, you see, so she got the lot." Isabel laughed. "Do you know the first thing she did? She had her nose done."

"Plastic surgery, d'you mean?"

"Absolutely. She's got a neat little nose now. You have a look at it next time you see her."

"I wish you could remember," I said, "the details of Mr. Cosway's will."

"I don't think it's a matter of remembering. I don't think I ever knew."

"Perhaps he didn't have much money," I said, "but he had the house."

"And the land. Don't forget that. Several hundred acres and it's all let out to farmers. Besides, I think there was quite a lot of money. He was a stockbroker, you know, and doing very well after the war, my mother said. She said John's trouble was a shocking blow to him. He adored John, he was enormously proud of him, because he was clever you know in a curious sort of way, but he sort of couldn't realize his intelligence, if you understand what I mean. It was there, he'd do algebra puzzles and that sort of thing, but he couldn't put it to practical use."

"What exactly was he like when you knew him?" I asked her.

She considered. "There was always something peculiar about him. He never seemed to have any feelings for people and he was totally undemonstrative, hated to be touched, for instance. I saw some relative, an aunt I think it was, try to kiss him and he just screamed out loud. His own family knew better than to try that. There were all sorts of other things he did, like hiding and doing violent things, breaking things, throwing them around. I was last there for Zorah's wedding ten years ago. Eleven actually by now."

"Was John normally dull and lethargic?"

"I don't think so. No, he wasn't. He did puzzles, played word and number games, you know the sort of thing. Of course he could never work and there was no question of university. For one thing he would never answer questions and never ask them. I think they'd say now that he'd lost his hold on reality if he ever had any and he never showed the least emotion. Is he like that now?"

"Not really," I said. "No, he's not like that now. He's—well, nothing now."

She showed me some photographs, two of her and Zorah as teenagers, Zorah's hooked nose and spots the way they were in the picture on the piano, then one of a thinner and livelier-looking John with Zorah and Ella, but they told me nothing I didn't already know.

The album was put away and I said, "Now tell me what happened to the maze."

"What do you mean, what happened to it?"

"Where is it? What is it?"

"I'm amazed they haven't told you. It's in that wing of the house that leads off to the right from the hall."

I asked her if she meant it was inside the house.

She laughed. "It's the library. The door's at the end of that passage and it's the biggest room in the house."

Double doors faced me. First looking over my shoulder in a guilty way, I tried the handles, but both doors were locked. Through the empty key-hole, I could see nothing except a kind of uneven darkness. I turned away and went out into the sun-shine, noticing for the first time that the windows at that end of the house were entirely overgrown by Virginia creeper. Someone, perhaps the gardener, had cleared the others but the ones I thought must be those of the labyrinth library were hidden under blinds of shiny green leaves. Even close observers would think they were looking at windowless walls.

But the doors were locked. It wouldn't have been beyond my ingenuity to find the key. After all, it surely wasn't a dark secret. The motive for locking it up must have been that in the 1960s the books were of no possible interest to anyone. If it were opened, it would have to be cleaned, as would the other locked rooms along the passage. Mrs. Lilly already grumbled enough about the work expected of her. Therefore, I thought it unlikely I would be refused a key provided I guaranteed to lock the door again after I had seen the place. But something stopped me asking. These "somethings" were coming to me quite a lot, warning voices really, telling me, "Better not" and "Leave it for now," though I had never before experienced premonitory cautioning with no apparent reason for it.

My hope of entry lay with Ella. Along with her overtures of friendship, she had said she would show me the library "sometime," yet had looked suspicious when I showed enthusiasm. I decided to try to let the suggestion come from her, perhaps in reply to a request for more books, as I would soon have exhausted her small collection.

Eric paid us a visit in the evening, driving Winifred home from wherever she had been. Sherry was brought out in his honor and, longing for the privacy of my room, the diary, and **The Woman in White** which I had just begun reading, I said I would leave them, but Mrs. Cosway, for some reason, insisted I stay. Winifred, who had been presiding at something called the Women's Prayer Group, was in a highly nervous state about the dinner she was to prepare the following weekend. She wished she had never undertaken to do it and it was now impossible to get out of. Eric, true to the form she had claimed for him and having forgotten this engagement of hers, had invited Felix Dunsford to the rectory for what he modestly called "a simple evening meal" on the same night. He had been relying on Winifred to do the cooking and hence her dilemma. Moreover she said she disliked Felix, his appearance, his manner, and his attitude to herself. What on earth had possessed Eric to invite him?

"I rather like him," said mild Eric. "Besides, he comes to church, which is more than you can say for most people."

"You mean he's been once," said Winifred. "He came to mock."

"I'm sure you're wrong there, my dear. He knew the liturgy, he sang the hymns. I do notice these things, you know."

"You couldn't help it, the way he planted himself in a front pew. And, you know, that isn't done in country churches."

"I don't in the least mind its being done in mine. It's most unfortunate you can't be there when he comes. You'll prepare something for us in advance, won't you?"

This gave rise to a small explosion. Surely she had enough worries with this dinner preying on her mind? Why could a man not learn to cook? It was very hard on her having so much to do. He should remember the catering she did was **earning her living.**

"I shall console myself," said Eric, "with the thought that once we are married you won't have to earn your living."

A much larger explosion this time. I doubt if the term "sexist" had been invented then but that was the word Winifred would have used if it had. "What makes you think I'm going to give up my profession when I'm married? I never said so. You've never mentioned it before."

"I took it for granted. Any man would."

"I know dozens of men who wouldn't, hundreds. A lot of men would be delighted their wives work. I can't get things ready for you on that day and that's flat. You'll have to take him into Sudbury or somewhere to a restaurant."

At this point Mrs. Cosway, who looked as if she was enjoying all of it, poured Eric more sherry without asking him if he wanted it. I suppose she thought he needed refueling. Ella had so far listened in silence, with a little smile on her face.

"Why not bring Mr. Dunsford here?" she said.

"That means Ida has to do it." I had never known Winifred showing any consideration for her elder sister before.

"Not at all," Ella said. "I will. I can cook, though no one seems to know it."

"Be thankful they don't." Ida spoke with unusual bitterness. "You might have to take on my job."

"I? I'm a breadwinner in case you haven't noticed. **I** have a real and very valuable career. I'm not messing about cooking fancy dishes for stockbrokers."

One of their acrimonious rows developed, Winifred insisting almost tearfully that she could only do what she was trained for and Ella saying it was such a drawback to have no "real" qualifications. But when she had vanquished Winifred she repeated her offer and Eric accepted.

"I quite like the look of Felix Dunsford," she said with that irritating little smile.

"If that means you're after him," said Winifred, "you want to be careful. I see him as a dangerous man."

This led to Eric, presumably trying to calm things down, quoting tediously from Shakespeare a passage about someone thinking too much and therefore being very dangerous. Winifred shook her head slowly, Ella smiled, while Mrs. Cosway had closed her eyes and appeared to be asleep. Going up to my room and the diary, I wondered why Eric wanted to marry Winifred, why he would want to marry at all; and since she very obviously was not in love, why she wanted to marry him. Since then I have learned that people marry for status, for security, for escape, because they have got into it and would find it very awkward and embarrassing to get out of, and of course for money. Besides, there was always the bishop's cautionary advice to Eric, as relayed by Ella, that he should find himself a wife.

What happened later would possibly have happened whether Felix Dunsford had been asked to Lydstep or not. Yet I am not sure. They could have met him in church. The kind of functions and meetings Winifred and Ella attended were shunned by him, the pub and a shady club outside Sudbury being the kind of places he preferred. So would they have met him again? Or would Winifred's encounter with him when she told him off about his clothes have been the only one?

Both are possible. They would have spoken in the street or "passed the time of day" as the English curiously put it, bumped into him at a drinks party after Winifred was safely married. Engaging herself to Eric Dawson had made not knowing him better impossible. Eric always took up new people. I think it was partly the clergyman's proselytizing need to add to his flock, partly an aversion to solitariness, and quite a lot of just wanting to be kind. It seemed to extend to anyone and everyone, for in the year I was at Lydstep he made friends not only with Felix Dunsford but also with other newcomers, an architect and his wife and an old man who had moved into a Memorial Green cottage when he was widowed.

Eric always began, apparently, by inviting the new friend to the rectory for a meal. Winifred had prepared these dinners or suppers herself in the past in her capacity as itinerant cook. It was through her asparagus soup, roast lamb, and **tarte Tatin** served up to Peter Johnston, previous tenant of The Studio, that she and Eric had first discovered that, in his words, they were "made for each other."

"Before that everyone thought he was keen on Ida," said Ella, who had followed me upstairs.

I hastily hid the diary. "Ida?"

"She used to do the flowers in the church when Mr. Clare was the rector, and when Eric came she kept on with it. This will be four or five years ago." Ella had produced a bottle of rosé and two glasses. "I've told you how Eric takes up every new person who comes to Windrose. I meant men, of course. My sister was the only **old** person, so to speak, he got pally with, and the only woman."

"You mean he and Ida went about together?"

"Not exactly. It was more that she'd go to the rectory on some pretext—or no pretext, I expect—and she'd make tea for herself and him and they'd chat, that sort of thing. I don't know what happened but nothing came of it."

I said it didn't sound like a grand passion.

"No, it wouldn't suit me, but I expect you'll say that's what he's got with Winifred." Ella was fond of telling me what I would say in almost any given situation and she was always off the mark. She gave me a conspiratorial smile. "Not everyone feels things with the same intensity as you and I do, Kerstin."

Cautiously I steered us to the subject of the library without mentioning it, only saying that when **The Woman in White** was finished I would have nothing to read.

"Yes, I promised to take you into the library, didn't I? But I don't know if you'll find anything you fancy." She looked over her shoulder, then leaned nearer to me. "My mother doesn't like people going in there, you know. She's afraid the door will be left unlocked and John will get in, though the state he's in these days I don't suppose he even knows where it is anymore."

I waited, unwilling to say anything that would betray my increasing desire to see behind that door.

"I doubt if anyone's been in there for five years," she said. "The key's in a secret place, but I expect I can find it."

Not that evening, though. She settled herself in my armchair for a cozy chat.

9

HE WAS EVERY HERO OF GOTHIC ROMANCE, every lady novelist and dramatist's creation of the kind of man attractive to naïve women. He was the forties film star who looks best in knee breeches. I am not saying this was apparent to me at once, but I had an inkling of it as Felix Dunsford slung himself into an armchair and lounged as if exhausted from enterprises such as dueling, making love, climbing mountains in a storm, and swimming the Bosporus. He was dark, almost swarthy, and in those days when for a man to be unshaven was as bad as wearing earrings, showing a day or two's growth of beard. His long black hair was greasy but his open-necked white shirt was clean. Shaking hands rather reluctantly, Mrs. Cosway looked at him as if she had never before seen a man without a tie.

I think it's worth saying here—though of course I didn't realize it immediately—that he must have studied the Byronic hero. The way he behaved can't have been natural. It was too stereotyped, too **fictional.** This was how he wanted to be, no doubt because he found it paid dividends. I never saw him act out of character and this was one reason why he always appeared dull to me. I could predict what he would answer or say next, and if at first this amused me, after a while it became tedious. Even then, that first evening, I knew he would habitually drink too much, have little or no means of support, live dangerously, chase women and misuse them, and when things became too hot to hold him, disappear.

Felix wasn't the only dinner guest. I had been hoping it wouldn't be too long before I saw Dr. Lombard, the doctor Mrs. Cosway had visited that evening when I had been left in charge of John. She addressed him as "Selwyn" and he her as "Julia." This would hardly be noticed now when everyone calls everyone else by their given names, but it meant something then. Selwyn Lombard and Julia Cosway were friends of long standing. The portrait I made of him, taking up a whole page of the diary, was of an old man, though a few years younger than his friend, tall, his hair still dark. His face would have been handsome but for the big hooked nose. A greater contrast in dress to Felix, whose picture faces him on the opposite page, could hardly be found, for the doctor was wearing a black pin-striped suit with waistcoat and a gray tie like shiny pewter.

Knowing that he prescribed for John, I expected him to ask after him, but nothing was said. Like the Cosway women and Eric, the doctor took it for granted John wouldn't be there and, either by a conspiracy with Mrs. Cosway or because he gave the matter no thought, kept silent on an awkward subject. Eric Dawson turned out to be one of those people who can't be in the presence of a doctor of medicine without consulting him. He had met Dr. Lombard before and this time was scarcely in his company for five minutes before he was pointing out some problem with, of all things, his fingernails. Sitting next to the doctor while our drinks were dispensed by Ida, he spread both hands out on the little table between them and asked why his nails were splitting and scaling. Had he a fungus? It was embarrassing when he was baptizing babies.

"I think you'd better come over to my office when you have a moment, Rector," said Dr. Lombard, barely suppressing a smile. "Here and now won't really do, will it?"

Eric seemed rather taken aback and was putting on and taking off his glasses when Felix Dunsford said in his languid Byronic voice, "That reminds me of the woman in the restaurant who saw her dentist at a table on the other side of the room. She rushes over, opening her mouth and sticking her fingers inside, and tells him about her toothache. 'Madam,' says he, 'I'm thankful I'm not your gynecologist.' "

This made Dr. Lombard roar with laughter and Ella managed a sort of giggle. But the effect on the others was to stun them with shock. It seemed that nothing of this enormity had ever before been uttered in the drawing room at Lydstep Old Hall. Mrs. Cosway closed her eyes and shook her head slowly from side to side. Glancing at Eric, Ida as rapidly looked away. The look on the rector's face was (as the English say) enough to curdle milk. Felix produced a squashed Capstan Extra Strong packet from his trouser pocket and offered it to Ella.

"Cigarette?"

"Oh, no, you must smoke ours," Ida intervened in a hostessy way, handing around cigarettes from a box. "They are rather milder than yours, but perhaps you won't mind."

"I won't mind," said Felix. "Never look a gift horse in the mouth, that's me."

His anecdote I used years later as the subject for a cartoon. Several readers of the magazine wrote in to say it was disgusting and they were surprised at me. The shock and outrage in these letters brought back the Cosways and Eric, all but Ella deeply embarrassed. Soon afterward she went to the kitchen to see to her dinner. Her appearance was much improved that evening, rather obviously as I thought, since everyone knew she "had her eye" on Felix Dunsford, as Winifred had put it. The red suit that was her best flattered her more than anything I had ever seen her wear. When she had makeup on, as she did that evening, she applied it with a surer and less lavish hand than Winifred's. Felix's eyes followed her as she left the room, but naturally, because he was a laid-back ladykiller modeled on movie pirates and highwaymen, he gave no sign beyond a lazy smile that she attracted him.

Mrs. Cosway, determined from the start to dislike him, inquired what kind of things he painted and asked rather rudely if he could make a living at it. He was the kind of man it is impossible to offend and he gave the impression of being impervious to hurt, but this too may have been assumed. Eric might have told us, quoting as he liked to do, that he was one of those who when "moving others are themselves as stone" and that they "rightly do inherit heaven's graces," if he had ever seen Felix in any light but as a pleasant newcomer to the village. There were a lot of heaven's graces about Felix, I could see that, though I never felt the attraction he had for the Cosway women, and I think this was because, apart from his dullness, he was old. Not old as Dr. Lombard was but, if considered as a possible lover, well over the hill for me. Would he have been impervious to that if he had known it?

Mrs. Cosway began to come around at the point when he answered her question, telling her that painters hardly ever did make enough to live on.

"There are other jobs around," he said, favoring her with his lazy smile, "if you're not proud. I'm not proud, am I, Eric?" He appealed to the rector of Windrose as if they were bosom friends, as if he had known him since their schooldays, instead of only having met him a week before. "I can work a bar." I don't think Mrs. Cosway knew what he meant. "I can clean flats. I'm thinking of doing a spot of sign-painting. You know the sort of thing: 'Beware of the dog, no hawkers or circulars.' Americans say, 'no solicitors' but they don't mean what we do."

Ella, who had come back to announce dinner, giggled hysterically. "Please do come and eat," she said.

She was a better cook than Ida, possibly better than Winifred, who of course was away somewhere, preparing dinner for other people. I don't remember much of what we ate and for some reason I didn't put it in the diary. Perhaps, unlike the sundial, I counted not the sunny hours but only the dark or boring ones. An excellent bread-and-butter pudding with sherry and cream in it I do remember. If the way to Felix Dunsford's heart was through his stomach, Ella was more than halfway there.

After we had finished and Ida was clearing away—Ella's culinary efforts didn't include washing up afterward—Winifred came in. She seemed breathless as if she had been running instead of driving the old Volvo, and she began apologizing to Felix for being out. Considering he was only there **because** she had to be out, he looked puzzled.

Dr. Lombard suddenly said, apropos of nothing that had gone before, "The galleries in the Hermitage in Saint Petersburg"—it was the sixties, so he said Leningrad—"if laid to end to end, would be six miles long, the same length as the Nevsky Prospekt."

I was later to learn that he often came up with non sequiturs of this kind, though I had no idea of it then. But this one rather interested me and I would have liked to know more. Apart from Mrs. Cosway who said, "That's fascinating, Selwyn," the others ignored it with the indifference of those who have heard it all before. Dr. Lombard got up and said it was time he went home, he was too old for late nights. No one seemed surprised and I supposed—rightly as it happened—that the Hermitage remark was a cue, as were others of a similar kind, for his departure.

Standing in the doorway, making some future engagement with Mrs. Cosway, he reminded me in profile of someone I knew, though I couldn't think who it was. Was there anyone I knew with a nose like his? Or was it some other aspect of his face that suggested another face to me, the line of his jaw, jowly now with age, or the set of his dark eyes?

Soon after he went, Ida settled down to knitting and Zorah appeared. We heard the roar of the Lotus, a door slamming, and then she walked in.

"What have you all been up to?" We might have been children caught raiding the fridge.

"Eric brought Mr. Dunsford to dinner, Zorah," said her mother. "I don't think you've met him."

Felix was sitting next to Ella. This was because she had positioned herself beside him, not he beside her. He got up when Zorah approached him, but his movements seemed to suggest that he found irksome anything which interrupted his desultory conversation with Ella and Ida. Such indifference, I thought, must be unusual for Zorah in her white dress and high white sandals, bringing scents of patchouli and sandalwood with her into the room.

"Would you like a drink?" The tone in Mrs. Cosway's voice when speaking to her youngest daughter, placatory, anxious, almost wheedling, I had never heard her use to anyone else. "Eric is going to have a whiskey."

It seemed to be with an effort that Zorah managed not to shudder. She shook her head. But when the whiskey was produced by Ida, she beckoned her over. Beckoning was a favorite gesture of hers, though this was the first time I had seen it. She looked closely at the bottle.

"A single malt, I see," she said. "Very expensive."

This breathtakingly rude remark didn't deter Eric, as I suppose was intended. He let Ida pour him the usual measure and said to Felix, "Won't you change your mind?"

It took very little to change Felix's mind when it came to accepting a drink he had just refused.

"Why not?" He gave Zorah a snide sideways glance which seemed to say, "So much for you."

She lit a cigarette which she put into a long red holder, turned to her mother and said, "Where is my amethyst thing, darling?"

Only Eric and Felix were unaware of what she meant. The Cosway women were not only aware but somehow galvanized by what she had asked. It seemed to me that they were sitting on the edge of their chairs, holding their breath, with the exception, that is, of Ida who, still on her feet, was turned to stone, the whiskey bottle raised up in her hand.

Mrs. Cosway was the first to speak. "I put it in the library."

That alerted me. With the drink and the warmth I had been feeling sleepy, but suddenly I was wide awake.

"But, darling," Zorah said, "no one goes in there from one year's end to the next. What's the point of putting it there?"

"It isn't **your** amethyst thing. It's a geode and it belongs to Mother." Winifred's voice was shrill with nerves. "She can put it where she likes."

Zorah nodded. "I'll take it back when I go upstairs."

I expected protest. None came. Ida gave a deep and heavy sigh. "Would anyone like more coffee? Mr. Dunsford? Eric?"

No one wanted more. I wondered how bitter Ida felt and whether Eric had given her reason to think he cared for her or if he was quite innocent and had merely been friendly toward a woman he liked. Their faces gave nothing away. Felix Dunsford reclined in his chair, his right leg crossed at the knee over his left, the whiskey glass so loosely held in his long thin hand that it looked as if it must at any minute fall to the ground. He might have been settled there for the night, might drop asleep before much more time had passed. I began thinking of what Zorah had said about taking the geode with her when she went upstairs, the geode which was in the library. She would know where the key was.

Utterly defeated in the matter of this chunk of Atlas mountain rock, Winifred lapsed into sulks. No doubt to change the subject utterly, Eric asked Felix if what he had said about sign-painting to earn his living was seriously meant. Felix looked up languidly.

"Sure. Why? Do you want a sign painted?"

He made it sound like a faintly absurd thing to wish for. It was Winifred who answered him, still sullen.

"I expect Eric meant that there's nothing to tell people that the rectory is the rectory."

Whatever he had meant, Eric said, "Everyone knows it is. They don't need to be told."

"Visitors do. Don't you think it would be nice to

have a beautiful sign lettered 'The Rectory'? Or even 'Saint John's Rectory'?"

Felix laughed. "You don't know it would be beautiful. You've never seen anything I've done."

"If I come and call," Winifred said, "will you show me?"

All this was unexpected. If it had been Ella who had asked for a sign for Lydstep Old Hall I wouldn't have been surprised. She was the one marked out for his attention that evening. She was the unattached one—Ida hardly counted, she never did, evidently never had with Eric—the single "girl" available to be courted. Zorah was a curious law unto herself. Winifred was spoken for.

But now Ella intervened. There was a winsome note in her voice which she perhaps thought attractive to men. "May I come too? I'd love to see your **real** paintings."

"I'm not used to all this popularity." But Felix sounded as if he was very used to it, as if it was his way of life.

"Shall we make a date then?" Winifred's smile and sparkling eyes suggested she thought this was contemporary slang, as perhaps it was. "One afternoon next week? Say Tuesday at half past two?"

Ella's wail was a little too piteous. "Then I can't come! I'll be at school. Some of us have to work, you know."

"Oh, just drop in, why don't you?" Felix was getting bored with this and Eric was looking at his watch. "I'm always there and if I'm not you'll find me in the pub."

Zorah said, "Good night, darlings," and floated away.

Now or never, I thought, and careless of whether my abrupt departure was rude, I followed her. Truthfulness seemed the only course to take, and when Zorah came out of the dining room, where the key must have been kept, I told her I would like to see the library when she went in to fetch the geode.

"For the books," she said, "or the maze?"

"For both."

My answer seemed to please her, for she nodded. "I hope my sisters aren't going to make fools of themselves over that man."

I would have preferred to say nothing, but she was looking as if she expected a reply. "Winifred is engaged," I said.

That made her laugh. She switched on the rather dim light that lit the passage, we walked to the end of it, and she unlocked the door.

The walls were lined with bookshelves, unglazed, and at first sight the books in them, jacketless and all bound in somber colors, looked mostly dark red, but there were green as well and blue and brown. Those that I could see, that is, the ones that filled the shelves on the right-hand side, for ahead of me, facing them, was a free-standing bookcase of the same height, forming a passage so narrow that a fat person couldn't have squeezed along it. At the corners, on the end of each bookcase, stood a bust in marble of some luminary of the past, statesman, philosopher, or scientist. The lighting, like everywhere else in Lydstep Old Hall, was dim, inadequate to read much by, and the stone faces seemed to hover in the half-dark, frowning or deep in thought.

Zorah stood watching me as I made my way along this passage, my feet leaving shiny marks in the dust on the floorboards, turning to the left at the end of it, the only possible route. She followed me. Having made this right angle, I was confronted with a choice, either to turn left again into a parallel passage or to proceed straight ahead where the space between the wall and the freestanding case was a little wider. The easily recognizable faces of Balzac and Frederick the Great eyed me with distaste. The books which surrounded me gave off that curious, rather sour smell old paper has, especially dusty old paper that is shut up for long periods in an airless space.

It seemed natural here to go on tiptoe. I took the left turn, found the wall of books on my right was broken halfway along, offering me another choice, to go on or turn right. At first I had rather resented Zorah's accompanying me, but then I felt glad of her presence. This place was so bizarre, the old, somehow Victorian, stench of paper and ink and leather so overpowering, that I felt intimidated. If I had been claustrophobic I should have had to turn back. As it was, with her behind me and the delicate, very modern scent of her perfume so at odds with the stronger smell, I went on, taking turn after turn and short passage after short passage without any thought of a plan or making any attempt to memorize the course I had taken. I may have noticed the titles of volumes as I passed them, but I could remember none of them later that night. Only the faces stayed in my memory and I was afraid they might visit me in dreams.

Why is it that sculpted or carved faces, when seen by night in a half-lit place, have a frightening effect, while effigies of animals or artifacts do not? No one expects the lion on a tomb to raise its head or stretch out its paws but everyone of an imaginative turn of mind fears that the human head in stone may turn, the lips part or twist into a snarl. Those heads never did come back to me in nightmares but nor did they ever cease to make me uneasy, though I went into the library several times after that, and always the faces seemed to follow me with their sightless, pupil-less eyes.

"Next time you come, darling," said Zorah with a soft laugh, "you must be like Theseus in the Minotaur's lair and play out a thread behind you. A ball of Ida's wool will do."

As she spoke I stepped into a wider space, a square formed of bookcases. In the middle of it stood a lectern of bronze, made in the shape of a young man holding a book spread out on his outstretched hands. At his sandaled feet, also in bronze, lay two discarded volumes, one with Homer engraved on it, the other with Plato. The book in his hands, however, was real, paper and ink and leather, and when I approached I saw it was the Bible, open at the Book of Wisdom in the Apocrypha.

"Great-grandfather Cosway made the maze and put that monstrosity there," said Zorah. "God knows why but the young chap is supposed to be Longinus, the one who wrote about the sublime, not the one who put his spear into Christ's side. He's rejecting Homer and Plato in favor of Holy Writ. He was no relation of mine, I'm glad to say."

I thought she must mean she was no relation of Longinus's. Looking at the page at which the book was open, I read, "The souls of the righteous are in the hand of God and there shall no torment touch them."

The bronze hand felt cold to my touch. Longinus wore the tunic and breastplate of a Roman soldier and his hair fell in long curls to his shoulders. With his delicate profile, rather like that of Michelangelo's David, his short skirt and long bare legs, he looked in the dimness more like a girl than a man-at-arms. The lights in this place were low and his shadow long, falling across the entrance to two more passages.

"Shall I get you out?" said Zorah. "You could wander around for hours. Some have."

I wanted to ask her if the only reason the labyrinth library was kept locked was to keep John out and if so why. What would he do? I didn't ask. Ella would be more approachable if less intelligent. Turning around corners, taking passages I was sure I had not been along before, I saw the picture Isabel had mentioned hanging on a bookcase end, a mezzotint of a house I took on trust was Lydstep Old Hall, for I would never have guessed it. Zorah found the geode on a shelf full of Victorian geography books. She lifted it down, holding the heavy thing in both hands.

"I'd like to come in here again," I said as we left the library.

She hesitated, then said, "No reason why not. Most of the keys live in a drawer in the dining room but not this one. I'll show you where you can find it."

I went with her into the dining room and watched her open the door to a cavity in the wall. The door was the picture of the couple in the amphitheater. "There was once a safe behind here," she said. "No use any longer. They've nothing to keep in it." She laughed, then said, "Better not," and stopped.

Better not what? She put the key back. The table

was still littered with the debris of dinner and I began clearing it on to a large tray Ida had left behind. Zorah watched me with an expression largely blank, slightly amused.

"Good night," she said and went away, carrying the geode.

10

SITTING ON THE FLAT ROOF OUTSIDE HIS ROOM on that warm Saturday night, over a bottle of Riesling—Chardonnay as the default tipple was a long way in the future—Mark and I discussed the Cosways, he being by this time almost as interested in their doings as I was. I had asked him why he thought Zorah behaved as she did. Why did she, who could live anywhere, choose to spend so much time at Lydstep, a shabby house in a pretty enough but remote part of north Essex? What was the battle for the geode about?

"It's for power," he said. "It's power she wants and she's got it. Don't ask me why because I don't know. I don't want power and I don't know why anyone else does. But they do."

I told him what Isabel had said to me about Zorah's wealth and how it was far greater than I had thought at first.

"From what you say about her comments on the whiskey, she doesn't just give them an income over and above what they've got, she likes to remind them of it. She sounds a real bitch."

"I don't know. I wonder if she has some motive for doing this, dating back to her childhood. She's taken every pretty ornament out of her mother's house upstairs to those rooms of hers. And that's what I don't understand. She could buy anything she wanted, she could have far more valuable things."

"That's not the point, is it? Those are **their** things, things that have memories attached to them for Julia. Old people are like that. They look at some old vase or whatever and it reminds them of visiting Auntie in Broadstairs in nineteen-fifteen. Or else they had it as a wedding present. Taking those things upstairs must really hurt Julia whereas stuff Zorah bought, even very valuable stuff, wouldn't mean anything at all to her. And, incidentally, do you know what her name means?"

"Whose name? Zorah?"

"I looked it up when you first told me. I'd never heard it before." No Internet in those days, no easy reference. Mark had traced it through the Proper Names section of a Bible with a subject index and concordance he had found in Kensington Public Library. "It's not a woman's name at all. It means 'a place of hornets,' " he said. "Book of Joshua, chapter nineteen."

"Why would you call your little girl after a place of hornets?"

"People just like the sound," said Mark. "Look at all those parents who call a boy Gideon. They don't know it means 'a lame man' and if they did I don't suppose they'd care. Shall we have another bottle of wine?"

For power. The thought of it brought a shiver down my spine. Perhaps power always does and in that lies its appeal. And there are no two ways about power, no gray area but all black or white. If you want it you want it all, as much as you can get and where you can get it, but if you don't want it you are indifferent to the whole thing and simply fail to see the point.

It was an ugly picture, this girl with an offensive name which, once you knew what it meant, could only be seen as a reflection on her character, moving back once she was rich into the family home where she had perhaps been neglected, and exerting a kind of tyranny over those who remained there. But why had the Cosways so little money? Fairly obviously it was because Lydstep Old Hall cost a lot to run. They could surely have moved away, sold the house for a hotel or residential home, but they stayed. So what happened to the rents from the farmers who leased the land? What became of the money Mr. Cosway left? Isabel had said there was a trust and perhaps it obliged them to stay.

Wills have to be published, no matter whose they are. Only the Royal Family are exempt. But I knew nothing of that until Mark told me and it was a while before I asked him. Back at Lydstep, I found Zorah had gone. It seemed that she and I had been in London at the same time, though in very different parts of it. Winifred was in the kitchen making coffee for Eric, who had brought her back after Evensong. She immediately began telling me how Felix was going to paint a sign for the rectory gate and she was to call on him and see his work. I thought it kinder not to remind her that I had been there when the arrangement was made.

Eric had to wait a long time for his drink. As soon as Winifred had started on the subject of Felix Dunsford she was unable to let it go. He was so charming, such an interesting man. She had been quite wrong about him. Of course he was eccentric, he was bohemian, but that was only to be expected from an artist.

"I was wrong when I said he came to mock, you know. He was at Matins this morning **again.** But he was much more discreet about where he sat. I think he realized it was pushing it to sit in the front pew."

It was rare for her to attend Evensong and I wondered if she had been only in the hope of his turning up again.

"I'm quite excited at the prospect of seeing his work," she said. "I have a sort of intuitive feeling that he's good. We have so little real culture in this place, you know, Kerstin. It's a refreshing change to have someone like Mr. Dunsford living among us. Would you like some coffee?"

"No, thanks," I said. "It keeps me awake."

But I went into the drawing room to say hello to Eric. I expect it was my imagination that made me think he looked forlorn, reading the Sunday paper there in that barren place which might have been the lounge of a middle-grade Swedish country hotel. There was a brownness and a fawnness about it, a general shabbiness, not a book, not a cushion, only the seldom emptied ashtrays, which made it hard to believe this was the living room of a county family. Poor Eric was not unsuited to it. Handsome as Winifred was pretty in a worn, unrealized sort of way, he too had a rather shabby air. I hoped she would iron his shirts and press his trousers; no one appeared to be doing it now. She brought his coffee and his glum face brightened. I wouldn't have believed that now she was with him she could go on talking about Felix Dunsford, but she did.

"Yes, he's a pleasant chap," was all Eric said, but it was enough to stimulate her to further eulogies. Now it was to enthuse over the ease with which he had "got on" with everyone at Lydstep, his graceful manners and, once more, his charm. Having had enough, I said good night and went off upstairs to the diary.

A few days later I expected more excesses from Winifred for I had seen her come back from the village from John's bedroom while he was getting into bed. But she was strangely quiet, not only on the subject of Felix Dunsford and his works, but on any other. She sat by the French windows in the drawing room, apparently reading a cookery book, but spending most of the time, as far as I could tell, gazing into the garden and at the low hills and woods of north Essex beyond. Ella came home far later than usual from school. It was as if, unable to join Winifred at The Studio, she had decided to stay away as long as reasonably possible, perhaps to avoid hearing how her sister had enjoyed herself. But Winifred was unwilling to be drawn and answered her questions in monosyllables.

"What do you mean by 'Yes' when I ask you if his pictures are any good? How are they good? Are they abstracts? Representational? You don't know, do you? You know nothing about art."

"I never claimed to," said Winifred.

"But you know what you like? Is that it? The trouble is that no one in this house is educated. Oh well, you are, I suppose, Kerstin, and Zorah is, for what that's worth, but you know what I mean."

No one knew. I doubt if Ella did herself. She was angry and jealous and lashing out at whoever happened to be there, as was her way. "I shall go and see for myself, that's all. He said to drop in, so I will." She seemed to lose her nerve and said, as if I were a suitable chaperone, "You can come with me, Kerstin."

"I can't spare Kerstin for that kind of thing," said Mrs. Cosway.

I kept silent, while inwardly amused. That rather pleasant inner laughter died when Ella said, "I tell you what I'm going to do now, Mother, and don't try to stop me. I'm going to go up to Zorah's—place, and go in and take back **your** geode. And while I'm there I'm going to get the lamp and the watercolors and—and the harp and everything else she's pinched."

"Her door will be locked," said Mrs. Cosway coldly.

"I have a key." Ella did not specify how she had come by it or elucidate at all.

"There'll be trouble," warned Ida.

"There's always trouble," said Ella. "It seems to come naturally to this family."

Mrs. Cosway cast up her eyes. "I suppose it comes to all families. We are no different."

Ella's answer to this was a burst of laughter, harsh and unamused.

In the event I did go with Ella to The Studio. I am sorry to have to say it but I went, according to the diary, not because I sympathized with her feelings or liked Felix Dunsford or to see his paintings (though I was curious about them), but because I wanted to watch her behavior with him and his with her. It was a Saturday. She wanted to get there by two, but I reminded her that the pub stayed open until half-past. Three seemed a wiser time.

Though dressed in her usual weekend clothes at lunchtime, baggy trousers, sandals, and a blouse, the way I judged Felix would probably like to see a woman, she changed afterward. Mrs. Cosway had agreed, at Ella's behest, not mine, to take John for his walk, and as soon as she was out of the house and Winifred occupied in the kitchen baking cakes for the Mothers' Union coffee morning after Matins next day, Ella rushed upstairs. Coming down a quarter of an hour later in a dress never before seen by me, she asked if her appearance would do.

"Is this frock too smart? Now tell me honestly."

I rather liked the striped pink and white cotton, the tightly belted waist and low neckline. Ella had a very good figure, and with discreet makeup, not plastered on like Winifred's, she looked pretty and young. Still, all she needed was a big hat to go to a royal garden party. In the high-heeled sandals she had put on, walking at even a reasonable speed was impossible. At the rate we were going we would be lucky to get there by three-fifteen.

"What did you think of Selwyn Lombard?" Ella said once we had set out.

I said, more or less truthfully, that I had not thought much about him. In my ignorance I added nothing about his reminding me of someone I knew because it seemed impossible that she would help me. "That was the first time I've seen him."

"It won't be the last," she said with a little laugh. "He and my mother are **very** good friends."

Though this, uttered in a loaded voice, could only mean one thing, I put it down to jealousy or resentment on Ella's part. These people were so old, to me then so impossibly ancient, that to think of any sexual tie between them was grotesque. Now, although I am twenty years younger than they were then, love and sexual relations between the elderly no longer seem ridiculous. I have heard of too many cases of passion among septuagenarians to feel that. But at twenty-four I dismissed Ella's confidence as hysterical rubbish.

She said no more. Her feet were hurting. She lit a cigarette and drew hard on it. At Felix Dunsford's gate she turned to me and whispered, "I feel quite nervous. Silly, isn't it?"

Against my own wishes, I said, "Would you rather I wasn't with you? I can always go and sit on a seat on the green."

"Oh, God, no, Kerstin. I'd never go in at all without you."

It looked at first as if going in would be impossible. There was no doorbell. We used the knocker to no effect. I offered to go around the back and look for him in the garden.

"We'll both go," said Ella.

The back garden was a narrow, weed-grown strip planted with plum and apple trees that looked as if they had never borne fruit and never would. In a deckchair under one of them sat Felix, smoking a cigar. An old table which had apparently been used in a workshop, it was so scored with saw cuts, held a full ashtray and a half-empty bottle of red wine.

He looked up, and in true Rhett Butler–Maxim de Winter style, gave no greeting and no sign of surprise at seeing us. "Some guy in the Rose gave me this," he said, waving the cigar. "Very kind, I thought. I don't know what you're going to sit on."

"Oh, we can sit on the ground," said Ella gaily, "can't we, Kerstin?"

"I suppose I'd better give one of you my chair."

He spoke in a wondering tone as if this example of good manners on a man's part had been learned eons ago at school or his mother's knee but was now almost lost in the mists of time. Slowly he got up. Ella sat in his chair, blushing, though not so unbecomingly as Winifred.

"We thought you would show us your paintings," she said.

"Maybe," he said, "later. Do you want any wine?"

We shook our heads. What made this woman and her sister call him charming? Sexy, yes, maybe. (Did anyone use the word then? Certainly not in the sense of being exciting in a nonsexual sense.) He was sexually attractive if that was all you wanted and all those Gothic hero or antihero qualities were present. But wasn't he also trivial and shallow? I was a prig, I suppose, I was young and I thought Ella should have known better. I thought she should have got up, told him not to bother, she was sorry to have disturbed him, and we would go. Of course she said none of that.

Men like Felix Dunsford are very difficult to talk to. I have met more of them since then. They trade on their mesmeric power, that which makes women enthralled by them, and which renders conversation beyond the merest innuendo unnecessary. Perhaps they talk to men. Women they despise and won't waste conversation on them, and this, horribly, is at the root of their attractiveness. It may be that Felix could have talked by the hour about Rouault and Kokoschka or the latest art movements or the Italian Renaissance, but I was too ignorant of these things to broach them. (Not having been to art school and thinking of myself even now as an amateur, I still am.) I'm sure Ella was too. Nervous and awkward, she tried asking him about sign-painting. She knew enough—I suppose that as a teacher, she would—to inquire if he had taken a lettering course at art school. He grinned and nodded, said something about the Slade where he had apparently been, and asked if either of us had any cigarettes as he had run out. By this time the cigar was a stub on top of a mountain of cigarette butts in the ashtray.

Ella fell over herself to offer him a cigarette from a new packet she had in her handbag. He took two, put both in his mouth, and performed the old seducer's trick of lighting them and handing one of them to her. Somehow he had assumed I was a nonsmoker, and it was true I got through fewer cigarettes than the Cosways, forced to ration myself on cost grounds.

"Better go in and show you my daubs," he said.

Possibly stimulated by a rush of nicotine to the brain, Ella said in bright tones, "I warn you, I shall be strictly honest. If I don't think they're any good I shall say so."

"Do you know anything about painting?" He sounded, at last, deadly serious. "Because if not I'd rather you didn't comment. If you mean you'll tell me if you like them, that's another thing."

Flustered by this as anyone would be, Ella flushed again. I wondered if these sisters' tendency to blush, like madness, could be genetic. "I don't mean to offend," she said in a small voice.

That made him laugh. He patted her shoulder, a bare shoulder in that sleeveless dress, and she shivered. We went into the house, one bedsitter and a kitchen that doubled as a bathroom downstairs, furnished by a landlord not generous with domestic comforts and occupied by a man who never washed dishes or put anything away. A ladder went up through a square hole in the floor above to the studio proper.

"I can't bring them down," he said. "Can you climb up in those shoes?"

"I can take them off."

Ella managed to sound as if she would take anything off, strip herself naked if necessary, for the sake of seeing his pictures. She took off her shoes and suddenly ceased to be a tall woman, barely reaching to his shoulder. He seemed to like that, for smiling down at her, he said, "Here, let me carry those."

Why she needed shoes upstairs was not clear. Perhaps he wanted to demonstrate his prowess at shinning up a steep ladder with widely spaced steps, a pair of white strappy sandals hanging from two of his fingers. He glanced at them, smiling, as some women look at babies. By this time it seemed to me that seeing the paintings themselves, ostensibly the purpose of our visit, had become irrelevant. But none of us was going to say this. We stepped off the ladder into a big room with a ceiling window, a broad sheet of glass that I suppose gave a north light. I was obviously not in need of help to step off the ladder, but Felix put his hand out to Ella, who took it tentatively yet with a kind of gravity, so that it seemed symbolic of a much more significant contract than an accepted offer to prevent her falling.

Canvases were everywhere, some turned away toward the wall, some in a transition stage, and there were stacks of hardboard sheets for painting on with acrylic. His finished work he brought out as one canvas after another and placed them on the two easels. Studying his face, I hoped to see there some sign of emotion at thus displaying to comparative strangers what must surely be the most important achievements of his life. But it had become as blank as John Cosway's and I wondered if this assumption of a deadpan glaze was his way of defending himself against Ella's "strict honesty" and what he saw as my indifference. Within seconds expression had returned and he was turning on Ella his habitual highwayman's grin.

"I think they're lovely!" Whether she was as enraptured as she sounded or putting on a very good show of it, I don't know. "I love this one." She had chosen an abstract—but they were all abstracts—in blues, grays, and the pink of her dress. "Wouldn't it look marvelous in a room with a blue carpet, Kerstin? What is it called?"

"Ocular Orgasm," he said.

No one talked much about orgasms in those days. "Climax" was the word more often used if it was used at all. Ella surprised me, and him too perhaps, by saying coolly, "Oh, yes, we had to read Reich while I was in college."

We went down and Ella put on her shoes, Felix holding one after the other up to her on the palm of his hand like Prince Charming with the glass slipper. Leaving, I went down the path ahead of her, she lingering to be whispered to by him, and when she caught me up, flushed and giggling, she told me he had asked her out.

"I'm to have a drink with him in the Rose on Monday evening, Kerstin."

That was nice, I said, while wondering if he ever took women anywhere but to the nearest pub. Not many village locals served anything more than a pie or a sandwich then, and I thought Ella might have to wait a long time before she got taken out to dinner.

"I was afraid he'd ask **you,**" she said confidingly. "You're quite good-looking really and much younger than I am."

"There was no chance of that," I said.

"What do you think Winifred will say? She's got so **pompous** since she landed Eric." My impatience with her changed abruptly to pity as she said, "I'll have to stop biting my nails. I'll have to **grow** them." She looked into my face. "I'd like to get married, Kerstin. Do you think it's awful of me to confess that? Women aren't supposed to."

I said that of course I didn't think it was awful. Most women wanted to be married sometime or other.

"Do they? Winifred always used to say she didn't care—till Eric asked her, that is."

There is something frightening about being aware that a friend is heading in the completely wrong direction and knowing too that warning them will be useless and only offend. I knew, as surely as I knew any fact, that Felix Dunsford would never marry Ella, that he would probably not marry for years and when he did his choice would be to marry money. It was impossible for me to say this to her, a woman thirteen years older than myself. Even if I could she would have ignored it and been angry as people always are when warned off someone else.

I drew her that evening. She too had a whole page to herself in her pink striped dress and the shoes Felix had carried upstairs for her. My sketch pleased me and I thought I was getting better at it. I resisted a sudden impulse to draw a balloon coming out of her mouth. I couldn't think of anything for her to say.

11

Hoping to see more of the Dunsford drama unfold, I decided to go to church in the morning. Several surprises awaited me. The geode was back on the table where I had first seen it, though Ella had apparently lost heart when it came to restoring the watercolors. In the hallway I found Mrs. Cosway with Winifred, her shapeless trousers and jumper changed for a pin-striped suit and a small felt hat.

"You're coming to church, are you, Kerstin? It's just as well Ida says she will take care of John then, isn't it?"

Mrs. Cosway had a way of making blameless, even virtuous, behavior sound self-indulgent. "I'll stay here if you like," I said. I had too little to do in this house as it was and had left her to accompany John on the previous day. But it was she who had told me to go with Ella and she who in the usual course of things never went to church. "I really don't have to go."

"No, no. You must go if you want to. Ida has volunteered."

She said it with a sigh as if my destination were a night club. Because she was with us we had to go in the car and as a result got to church very early. Ella had maintained her elegance, though the torturous sandals had been abandoned. We walked around the churchyard, looking at tombs. It was a warm sunny day and the flowers people had placed on relatives' graves were wilting in the heat. The others stopped in front of one on which a pink marble slab was engraved with the name John Henry Cosway and the dates 1830–1907. I was told that he was the discoverer of the geode but no one said anything about his being the founder of the labyrinth library.

Eric arrived in a rush, his cassock billowing and his face shiny with sweat. He paused to kiss Winifred on the cheek and I noticed that she wiped her face afterward on her handkerchief, smearing it with brown and pink makeup. Her hair newly washed and glossy, her nails painted a silvery pink—to prevent further biting?—Ella watched her sister with a small superior smile.

As it happened, Felix failed to turn up. Events too intensely anticipated often fail to come off. Probably he felt he had exhausted the possibilities of church. Of the only pretty women he had encountered there, one was engaged and he had already begun his onslaught on the other. Dr. Lombard arrived instead. He came in soon after we did. I was sitting in the aisle seat, Winifred next to me, Ella next to her, and Mrs. Cosway at the end. Perhaps they had arranged things that way for Dr. Lombard to slip in next to his friend. A whispered conversation began between them, neither of them being among those who dropped to their knees for silent prayer, and when the service began they remained seated, their heads bowed and their eyes closed. On our way out, presumably because we were inside a place of worship, Dr. Lombard told me that wedding cakes were shaped in pillared tiers like Saint Bride's, Fleet Street, because, long ago, a baker had made one which was a small replica of the church for a marriage reception and created a precedent.

Eric came back to Lydstep with us, bringing Winifred in his car. I wrote in the diary that night that looking at the house as we approached, I thought of how it would be transformed when the leaves fell from the Virginia creeper. Then, instead of cloaked in trembling green, its brickwork would be covered in some sort of web, formed by myriads of tendrils. Gray, green, or brown? All such thoughts were banished by the sight of a white-faced Ida running down the front steps when she heard the cars.

"What's the matter?" Mrs. Cosway struggled out of the car, needing Ella's hand to help her get on to her feet. "What's wrong?"

"It's John. He's had a fit."

We hurried in, I at least having no idea what

form this sort of fit might have taken. John was nowhere to be seen. Ida looked at her mother, then at the great heavy sofa, its arms and the frame of its back of carved wood, its upholstery a gingery-brown corduroy. This, it seemed, was familiar territory to Mrs. Cosway.

"Give me a hand, would you, Kerstin?"

For a woman of her age she was very strong. I had helped her move the sofa a little way away from the wall before I fully realized what she was doing. When I saw John I stepped back, and I think she saw from my face that I would refuse to expose him further to Eric's aghast gaze and that of his sisters. He was sitting on the floor in the triangle made by the slope of the sofa back and the wall, and he must have squeezed with difficulty but perhaps in extreme stress into this narrow gap. His arms were wrapped around his knees, his head laid on them but turned toward us, and his face was white and wet with tears. I have never seen a face, not even a child's, so drenched with tears, so dripping with water from his red and swollen eyes.

"What did you do to him?" Mrs. Cosway spoke in a thin, tired voice.

Ida shrugged. "I touched him. I didn't mean to. I must have been mad. He suddenly said out of the blue that he'd like to do a crossword puzzle, the one in the paper. I was so **pleased.** I thought how he hadn't said anything like that for ages and I—oh, I took hold of his hands and squeezed them and he screamed and got in there and—oh, I must have been mad."

"As you say, you must have been. It's too late now. I don't know why you said 'a fit.' He hasn't had a fit."

"The only thing to do, Eric," said Winifred, as if he had asked, "is just to leave him there until he comes out in his own good time."

"But he's weeping." I thought it strange that Eric said "weeping" instead of "crying." A biblical usage perhaps?

"Yes, well, he does."

"Hadn't we better put the sofa back?" I said.

Eric helped me and we shoved it back to where it had been before. John made no sound at all. Suddenly recalling her omission, Mrs. Cosway said, ruefully but not with much distress, "I suppose I forgot to give him his tablet. It's happened once or twice before. But I'm glad you've seen it, Kerstin. Perhaps this will cure you of thinking you know better than I where John's medicine is concerned."

I was taken aback. It was only once that I had ventured to dispute the need for giving him a pill, and that had been a barbiturate, not the Largactil. Had there been something in my face to show her, when she handed him the sleep drug in the evenings, that I disapproved? Had she read my "thinking" in my expression?

John would have no walk that day. We ate our lunch without him. He remained where he was for hours, Mrs. Cosway remarking as she went off to her afternoon sleep that he had no sense of time. While I helped Ida with the dishes, an operation conducted in almost total silence, Winifred and Eric went outside and sat in deckchairs under the mulberry tree, he with a corner-knotted handkerchief spread over his face, she reading, like an elderly couple on the beach.

Ella said to me, "Come into my room, I've something to tell you."

I hoped for great things, though scarcely of so sensational a nature, and I went very willingly up into Ella's pink bedroom with its frills and its doll inhabitants. The first time I had seen them I had been alone with Mrs. Cosway. Now seemed the time to comment on them.

"You dressed all these yourself?"

"Well, yes. Do you like them?"

"They're beautifully done," I said diplomatically.

"You might not think me keen on fashion, the way I slop around at weekends, but I actually love it when there's someone to notice. Now I'll open the window, it's really hot today, isn't it, and we'll make ourselves comfy and have a nice drink and a cigarette."

She produced a bottle of rosé, a very fashionable drink and her favorite. I expected it to be warm but she had kept it in a cold dark cupboard and it was pleasantly cool. We lit cigarettes.

"You must be wondering what I'm going to say."

I smiled encouragingly.

"Oh, don't worry," she said. "It won't affect you in any way. It's our **cross.** I mean, the cross we have to bear. Not Winifred much longer, of course, and maybe not me either. Who knows?"

She must have meant rescue by Felix. An English proverb exists about counting one's chickens before they are hatched. I think there should be one about sterile eggs and no chickens ever coming out of them.

But, "It's about my father's will," she said.

I had intended to ask Mark next time I was in London how I could discover that will's contents. Now I might hardly need to.

"You'll be wondering how it can concern you and why I should want to tell you family secrets. Well, a will isn't private, it has to be published"—thank you, Ella, I thought—"so a secret it's not. We do have those"—she laughed a little hysterically—"but this isn't one of them. It's just that I imagine you must find a lot of things here rather—well, odd. I thought they ought to be cleared up."

I assumed an interested expression, though not one as avid and fascinated as I felt. It is unwise in these circumstances to look greedy.

"My father and mother weren't on very good terms. That's making it sound better than it was.

They were on very bad terms and had been for some time. I don't know why unless it was something to do with Dr. Lombard." She changed tack abruptly. "John was quite a normal little boy, or so they say. He's two years older than I am. He had mumps when he was five and I think that's what changed him. Dr. Lombard says no, but he doesn't know everything, though he thinks he does. Whatever happened, it didn't make him stupid. He could do amazing algebra problems and that kind of thing.

"Well, Daddy had made a will, leaving everything including the house to Mother, but something happened to make him change it. He made a completely new will in which he left Mother an annuity and everything else including the house to John. Mother has a life interest in the house, but it belongs to John, so neither of them can sell it."

"What about the rest of you?" I said.

"He thought we'd all get married. That was what he expected women to do and the only real career for them. Zorah **was** married. He couldn't understand it, that the plainest and youngest of us got married first. Of course what Raymond Todd—that was her husband—liked about her was her brain and her style. All his wives had been clever. The second one was quite a distinguished physicist.

"As I say, he thought we'd get married and our husbands would keep us." Ella gave the Cosway coughing laugh. "Ida's engagement was broken off within weeks of his death. I had a chap, but there was no chance of him marrying, and the one after him was married already. I expect you thought I was a virgin."

I said not quite truthfully that I hadn't thought about it.

"Well, I'm not. I suppose Winifred is, but I daresay Eric is too. My God, but that'll be some wedding night. I'm digressing, aren't I? I was telling you about the will. Daddy left everything to John on—well, certain conditions. That would mean we'd have to ask **him** for what we wanted—I think he meant we'd have to treat him properly—and in point of fact that means asking the trustees. Daddy set up a trust for John, you see. If he wants something he has to ask the trustees, they're Daddy's nephew Adam, who's a heart specialist, and Daddy's solicitor, Mr. Salt, and the son of an old friend of his called Jerome Prance. And Mother. Mr. Salt insisted he include Mother, but the others always outvote her, so her being there isn't much use.

"John asked for money to spend on impossible things. A sports car, for instance, and then he wanted a boat. The trustees let him have the car and he crashed it into a wall in Great Cornard. I said there were conditions. Daddy thought John would die young, so the will says that if he dies before Mother or if he has to be committed to an institution the house goes to her for her lifetime and the money between those of us who remain unmarried. But only if it's some outside authority that commits him, not if it's Mother. Everything goes to John if she dies first—unless he's in an institution, that is—and passes to us on his death or our children if we're dead. I shouldn't think there'd be any children, would you?"

"Money must be provided for John's upkeep," I said.

"Oh, yes, for all our upkeep really. Mother has to send our food bills to the trustees and bills for Ida's clothes—Ida has literally nothing and Winifred only what she gets paid for cooking that stuff for people—and plumbers' and electricians' bills. There aren't any extras, though. We never have holidays—how could we with John? I suppose Eric and Winifred will go to the seaside for a fortnight every year now. Of course Zorah's got her house in Italy and she goes all over the world as well.

"John doesn't like being touched and he freaks out, goes crazy, if anyone tries to kiss him. That's a disaster. And he's had fits, real fits. About five years ago Mother started drugging him to keep him quiet. He used to shut himself in the downstairs lavatory for hours on end. It was worse when he shut himself in the library. He **loves** the library but he'd throw the books about. Mother got it into her head he'd set the house on fire, though he'd never shown the least inclination to that sort of thing.

But that was when she and Dr. Lombard started the drugs. She gets them from Dr. Lombard, it's all aboveboard, they're prescribed for schizophrenics."

"Those drugs have been continuous for **five years?**"

"There have been times when she's—well, withdrawn them. I may as well tell you why. Zorah's very fond of John, she said it was wrong what Mother was doing. If John needed that kind of dosage he ought to be in a proper mental hospital under supervision."

"And Mrs. Cosway did what Zorah told her? Just like that?"

"My mother wouldn't cross Zorah. Zorah—gives her things. Well, money mostly. All the drink in the house comes from her and all the decent food. She pays for Mrs. Lilly. The trust wouldn't, not with four women in the house already, they said. She's promised to buy me a new car—well, us a new car—and she will but in her own good time. I suppose she likes keeping us in suspense. Anyway, you can see why Mother wouldn't go against her. Not while she's here, that is."

"Does she pay me?" I said, thinking that if she did I would be obliged to go. I could hardly stay and be party to this bribe and threat game.

But Ella shook her head. She produced a mother-of-pearl inlaid box full of colored "cocktail" cigarettes. I fancied a black one, she, of course, pink.

"John pays you. That is, the trust does. Zorah told Mother to lay off the drugs again and see what happened, try an experiment. It actually worked for a few days, he was quite lucid and ordinary, doing his maths again and reading the papers. He told my mother she ought to have help and that's when he got Ida to apply to the trust for—well, for you. I don't think Mother was keen, but there wasn't much she could do. John got bad again soon after that, having tantrums and locking himself in the downstairs loo. You'll say Mother and Dr. Lombard could have him committed and that would solve a lot of problems."

I interrupted her to say with perfect truth and indignation that **I** wouldn't say it.

"Oh, well, most people would. Daddy was too cunning for that. As I said, my mother only gets the house and the money if John's committed to a mental hospital by an outside authority. That means two doctors and one of them has to be a psychiatrist."

The prospect of human villainy shocked me in those days. I'm sorry to say that it seldom does now. By the time you get to my age, you have seen too much of it to feel anything but sad. But at that time I was very shockable and showed it with a stare and an exclamation.

"My God, Ella!"

She had a greater capacity for getting the wrong

end of the stick than anyone I have ever known. "Yes, it's tough on Mother, isn't it? I try to remember that when she's being nasty. She's got a lot to put up with."

Long after this, my husband, who is a lawyer, though not a solicitor, told me that he doubted if this will would ever stand up in court in the event of anyone contesting it. More than that, he said he wondered what kind of a solicitor this Mr. Salt was that he could draw up such a will. It seemed to me at the time only that the Cosways were subject to some very shady advisers, first Dr. Lombard and then this Mr. Salt, who had also managed to get himself made a trustee.

Still, it wasn't for me to say any of this to Ella. It would have done no good and caused great offense. I asked instead about the library. And since she had offered to take me in there, I could confess that I had already been in with Zorah. When I did she made a face, poured us more wine.

"John used to spend hours in there, moving the books and rearranging them. It got too much for Mother. He started taking books out and piling them on the floor so you had to step over them to move around and sometimes you couldn't because he'd built a wall of them. And he didn't like the Bible being there—you know, the one Longinus is holding—and he'd take it down and replace it with something he did like. Once it was Bertrand Russell's **Principia Mathematica.** He said he was a militant atheist."

"John?" I said, thinking of the poor zombie downstairs.

"Yes, John. Honestly. Look, Mother's asleep, Ida's in the kitchen, and Winifred won't care. Why don't we go down to the library now?"

Now the shock of it was past, I could look at the books the library contained. It was full of treasures, enough desirable books to last me the whole year. Victorian novels by such obscure (to me) authors as Sabine Baring Gould and Mrs. Henry Wood filled a whole wall in that passage I had taken to enter the central square. There was **The Origin of Species** in what may have been a first edition, Paley's **Evidences,** Gosse's **Omphale,** and Newman's **Apologia Pro Vita Sua.** There were thousands I had never heard of before and have never come across since.

Another wall, this one in a passage I was nearly sure I had not passed along before, was devoted to the works of philosophers, and one at a right angle to it, to mathematics. Though fairly quick at mental arithmetic, I am hopeless at maths but I know enough to be sure these were not the intellectual recourse of Mrs. Cosway or her daughters. Trying not to look at the nightmare face of a stone Milton, I took down Euclid's **Elements,** brushed, then blew the thick dust off its cover, and brought it under one of the dim lights. **John Cosway, his book, 1938** was written in a strong but strange hand on the flyleaf. As I turned the (to me) incomprehensible pages a folded sheet of yellowing paper fell out. In the same handwriting it was headed **Euclidean Algorithm** and underneath John had written, it was undoubtedly John, **the technique used to find the largest natural number that divides (with zero remainder) two given natural numbers. Repeated use of the division algorithm finds this number, called the greatest common divisor.**

Now I don't know if there is anything particularly intellectually challenging about this, only that it was so to me, but evidently not to John, who had written underneath a series of numbers and finally one which he called this greatest common divisor. If this paper was written at the same date as his name was put in the book he was nine years old at the time.

I could only think that there must be a mistake somewhere, but speculation when one is in possession of so few facts is useless. My companion this time wore the look of a woman gleeful at bringing a delightful surprise to someone else, quite different from Zorah's supercilious expression.

"It's amazing," I said, pleasing her.

Dante, I seemed to remember, was conducted by Virgil around the infernal regions, and I wondered if his guide enjoyed himself as much as Ella seemed to enjoy taking me around the labyrinth library.

"If you come on your own," she said, "you'll have to bring a ball of wool and unravel it behind you like what's-his-name in that place in Crete."

Did they all say that when they brought in a visitor? Still, it must happen seldom. She had told me so much, yet so little. So few mysteries had been solved. There seemed to me then to be a life going on in this family and this house underneath the existence they presented to the world and me, a secret force like that which Eric had described that morning as the workings by which God subdues all things to himself.

We made our way back to the double doors, along the narrow and tortuous passages where books themselves were the bricks and mortar forming the walls. That dust itself has a smell was a discovery I made that afternoon. I learned too how claustrophobia may suddenly come into being in someone who has never known it before. Without being exactly difficult, breathing became something of an effort and panic fluttered under the mind's surface. Coming out of there and into the hot sunshine of the garden was more than relief, it was like stepping into another world.

Ella had gone to put the key back behind the amphitheater engraving. I was alone, breathing deeply, relishing the light and the warmth, the grass and the green branches swaying in the breeze.

12

Ella was out a long time. She had left to meet Felix Dunsford at six. I refused to take part in the discussion that started at ten as to why she was still out. One after the other, at five-minute intervals, the Cosways remarked that four hours was a very long time to spend in the White Rose, Mrs. Cosway adding that she couldn't understand why anyone would go in there at all. I alone, it seemed, supposed that a good part of it had been spent elsewhere, most likely at The Studio.

We were watching television when Ella came in. Or the television was on and Mrs. Cosway was watching it. Without looking around, she said sourly, "You have missed the only good program we've had this year."

"No doubt you had something better to amuse you," said Winifred.

"I had something different."

Ella looked pensive. She was unusually silent, though she kept glancing at me and I expected to be asked to come to her room with her. Since her campaign of making me her friend had begun, she also increasingly made me her confidante. The revelations about the will had been followed a day later by a detailed account of her affair with the married man and there had been a drive around the villages, undertaken, I think, to point out to me the "close" of modern houses where he lived. But that evening the invitation I expected never came and it was the end of the week and August before she asked me in a mysterious voice, loaded with suspense, to come and sit in the garden with her. Apparently she had run out of rosé, for she brought out a tray with coffee in a pot and two cups and set it on the table under the mulberry tree. The gardener was mowing one of the distant grassy areas, an endless task in summer when the lawns are extensive and one has only a small hand-mower.

"I know it's your favorite," Ella said. "I got it specially," and it was true I had expressed a preference for coffee over tea. "We won't be disturbed down here."

The garden was tended twice a week by a morose and silent man called Cox, a relative of Mrs. Waltham the postmistress, and so it had a far less neglected look than the house. His services of course were paid for out of the trust as were mine. With dreadfully inadequate tools, he kept the grass mown and the hedges trimmed and if there were no flowers to be seen, perhaps the color they would have brought was not to be associated with Lydstep Old Hall. It was a close, humid day without much sun, the sky overcast but not really threatening rain or any change in the dull weather. Coffee in the garden was a good idea but not the place Ella had chosen. In August mulberry trees drop their moist dark purple fruits which, when they flop on to a hard surface, look like coagulating blood. Even on grass its stains are unpleasant and there were plenty of these around the table. My own jeans and shirt were black and liable to come to no harm but Ella wore her stripy frock and I dreaded the effect on her of a mulberry splitting open on her skirt.

Balkan Sobranie cigarettes were produced and our cups filled. "We ought to keep silkworms," said Ella with one of her giggles. "All these mulberry leaves just go to waste. I wonder if there's any profit in it. We could do with an increase to our income." I had no opinion to offer on silk production, so only smiled. "I've got something to tell you," she went on unsurprisingly. "I wonder what you'll think of me. Of course, being Scandinavian, you won't be shocked."

I don't much like being lumped together with Danes, Norwegians, and Finns as if we were all a single tribe, looking and feeling the same, holding to the same principles or lack of them, spending our time reading Hans Andersen and going to plays by Ibsen, all gloomy and suicidal alcoholics and all of us leading sexual lives like characters in **I Am Curious,** a daring set of films of the time. But I said nothing.

"Well, here goes then." She looked up at me, then away. "I've slept with him. We didn't waste much time, did we? Oh, not that first time, not that evening I came home and Mother said I'd missed some TV program, not then. Two days later, actually. That first evening—well, we didn't **go all the way.** You'll say I shouldn't be telling you this." I interrupted to assure her I wouldn't. "Really?" she said. "It's funny but it's easier telling you things like this because English isn't your mother tongue, is it? So I don't feel words have the—well, the **resonance** they'd have with Zorah, say—God forbid!—or Winifred. Do you know what I mean?"

"Of course," I said, hoping very much that her assessment of my grasp of the English language would not lead her into clinical detail or a run-down on what he said to her and she said to him.

"Because we are friends, aren't we, Kerstin? We can tell each other things we wouldn't tell other people?"

I was strangely moved by this. She was thirty-seven but she talked like a fifteen-year-old and an insecure one at that. "You can be sure I won't tell anyone, Ella," I said. And I meant it and stuck to it—while this was possible. Neither of us could have foreseen what was to come when the diary became an important piece of evidence and I would have to speak and tell everything I knew. But not for the life of me could I think of anything more to say to her or ask her. I could smile, I could look attentive and drink my coffee—and a great deal better than Ida's it was.

"He's a very good lover," she said, lighting a cigarette.

That comment has always embarrassed me as do all such words as "performance" and "technique" in this connection. They seem to reduce love-making to a stage production or display and to herald that clinical detail I feared. Perhaps something in my expression warned her of my distaste for she quickly changed tack, saying, "He wants me to spend the whole weekend with him. I'd have to lie to Mother and Ida if not to Winifred, I couldn't tell them what I was really doing. And Felix feels the same. He wants us to be discreet. For the sake of my reputation, I suppose. To protect me."

Or to protect himself, I thought. Not for the sake of his reputation but to leave his freedom unthreatened.

"Then he said something funny. He said, 'I don't want you to go out with me, I want you to stay in with me.' Wasn't that funny? I could sneak out after dark on Sunday night and no one would see, he said."

"You could, I suppose."

It wasn't for me to ask her if she really wanted to be the female actor in this back-to-the-village-you scenario or what she thought was the point in the late 1960s of a single man keeping a by then quite permissible relationship with a single woman a dark secret. It looked as if this would develop into the kind of affair a man like Felix Dunsford has with women who have no money. Once he has begun the process of enslavement, he can stop even taking them to the pub. If they want a drink they can bring it with them. He won't mind providing a cup of tea. A man of this sort will go on for months or even years like that. With rich women it is quite different. They have luxurious homes for him to go to with ample drink laid on, they can pay for expensive hotels, weekends away, he won't even have to give them tea or waste heat and electricity on them. But Ella was one of the poor women—in more senses than one.

"Zorah is cruising round the Aegean on someone's yacht," she told me, leaving the subject of Felix. "A man with a title, I can't remember his name. Mother is afraid she'll marry one of them and then she'll—well, stop the benefits."

She might also stop squirreling away Mrs. Cosway's property, I thought but didn't say. Lighting yet another cigarette, Ella asked me what I thought of Dr. Lombard. I said I didn't know, I hadn't thought much about him.

"He's coming over this evening. You can **study** him. I'd love to know what you really think. It's all very well Mother worrying about Zorah remarrying. Winifred and I thought for years she'd marry Selwyn Lombard."

"Your mother, do you mean?"

"Of course. Did you think I meant Zorah? The trouble is, or the good thing is, it turns out he's got a wife alive somewhere or did have a couple of years ago."

We went in when Dr. Lombard arrived and I was sent for. I don't know why I was, as he went into John's bedroom and once I had opened the door for him and closed it behind him, I was banished and told to help Ida with the dinner.

"He's a good doctor," Ida said. Her attitude to him was very different from Ella's. "Prescribing that Largactil for John has made a great difference to all our lives. Before that you could say John ruled this household, we were all slaves to his whims and moods."

This aroused in me an enormous distaste and disapproval, though I should have found it hard to say why. Perhaps it was better for John to be drugged into a kind of somnolent apathy, his eyes glazed, his feet stumbling and his hands shaking, than to be subject to fits and locking himself up in bathrooms. I said nothing, only listened while she continued to sing Lombard's praises and her mother's reliance on him until she had gone a long way toward convincing me that he and Mrs. Cosway were lovers of long standing.

He came into the drawing room after a while,

told me Mrs. Cosway was "seeing to" John and, calling me "young lady," said she would not require my services that evening.

"Give Dr. Lombard a drink, would you, Kerstin?" said Ida.

He chose that kind of sweet pale sherry which to me is the worst drink in the world, and sat sipping it, nursing the glass in his hands. I was at a loss with him, finding nothing to say and waiting in vain for him to speak. After a few minutes, he put the glass down and picked up the newspaper. Something he read made him laugh quite raucously. To my relief, Winifred came in and, almost immediately after her, Mrs. Cosway. He struggled to his feet, took Winifred's left hand in his, smiling at her engagement ring, but her mother got a warm kiss on her cheek close to her mouth.

"You left your doctor's bag in John's room, Selwyn. Don't forget and go home without it."

Someone was using the phone in the dining room. I passed the door which was slightly ajar and heard Ella's voice say, "Will you take a message to him? Say it's Tamara."

I had never heard the name before. It sounded Russian to me or from Central Asia. I was to hear it several times in the future. As I went on toward the kitchen, I looked back and saw Ella come out of the dining room.

"I suppose you heard that."

"Yes," I said. "Yes, I did."

"He hasn't got a phone and anyway I wouldn't want him to phone me here. I mean, anyone might answer the phone. So we have an arrangement. I phone the pub and ask them to give him a message. He says to say it's Tamara, then he'll know."

Come to that, he would have known if she had said it was Ella.

"I'll have dinner and then I'll go down there. That will give him a chance to have a few drinks and see his friends. I won't go into the pub. He'll go home a few minutes before I'm due. I'll think of something to tell Mother."

I said, because I could stand no more, but I said it gently, "You're not committing adultery, Ella."

She laughed uneasily and ran upstairs, coming down for dinner dressed up in pink flowered cotton and high-heeled shoes. Picking at her food, clock-watching, she was in a fever of impatience. I tried to put myself in Felix Dunsford's shoes, asking myself how I would feel as a man confronted by this combination of frenetic eagerness with a passionate desire to please. Ella would be a heavy burden. The moment Ida took away our dessert plates, she was on her feet, eyes on her watch.

"Where are you going to, my pretty maid?" said Dr. Lombard.

"Oh, just down to the village to see my friend Bridget."

"Having a party, is she?"

This was Winifred, speaking in a very dry voice. Ella gave her a venomous look but said nothing. Two minutes later we heard the car start up and move off down the drive.

"What it is to be young," said Dr. Lombard and told the quite famous story about Augustine's astonishment when he came upon Saint Ambrose reading to himself silently instead of aloud, something apparently very rare at the time. He got up, said he was an old man and needed his "beauty sleep."

"Now don't forget your bag," said Mrs. Cosway. "I told you it was in John's room." Having eaten and drunk very well, he was obviously unwilling to move far. "Kerstin will fetch it for you."

I went, not too pleased at being sent on errands, but attempting a pleasant smile. After all, I was their employee. John was fast asleep, deeply and heavily asleep, spreadeagled on his back. I pulled the eiderdown over him, though he was quite adequately covered. What made me glance at the photograph? I took it to the window where just enough light remained for me to see it. I had seen it before. I saw it, when I bothered to look, every time I assisted at John's going to bed. This time I looked at it with new eyes. There in the group was Zorah some years before she had had her nose reshaped. When she was a teenager it was a large hooked nose, a replica of the one which had been facing me across the dinner table.

There could be no doubt. I picked up the doctor's bag which belonged to her father and took it downstairs to give to him.

13

IT IS SUPPOSED TO BE A GREAT HONOR TO BE asked, but I WAS rather taken aback when Winifred invited me to be her bridesmaid. I imagined Mark's laughter if I told him I had accepted, I imagined the weary business of fittings for dresses and, worse, the tripping up the aisle, and I said no, trying to be as nice and grateful-sounding about it as I knew how. Her asking me seemed to point to a lack of friends. Had June Prothero been asked and had she refused? Though I tried not to show disapproval or even criticism, I found it strange that a woman of forty would want bridesmaids and I wondered if this wedding was to be a frothy and girlish affair of long white gown, bridal veil, bouquets, and beribboned cars.

It appeared that it was. The dress was to be made by a woman in the village who did such things and the cake ordered from a shop in Sudbury which specialized in weddings. I wondered if it was to be a cake like the one in Dr. Lombard's anecdote, tier upon tier supported by white pillars. Winifred, though busily involved, showed as far as I could see no enthusiasm for these preparations. To look at her and listen to her, one would have thought she was preparing for the marriage of someone else and someone to whom she owed a duty but didn't much like. That may have been how she felt about herself. There were changes in her too, in her appearance for one thing. Thinner and paler, she looked better for the slight hollowing of her cheeks and the fining down of waist and hips. I wondered if it was my imagination that her hair looked cleaner—her nails certainly were—as if washing it took place every other day instead of once a week. The makeup too had been modified. She looked both more like Ella and much prettier. Often, catching sight of her when she was unaware of it, I saw how near she had come to being a beautiful woman.

Eric too had noticed it. From being surely the dullest wooer in all Essex, he was becoming gallant, he was paying compliments, and the lifeless kiss planted on Winifred's cheek had livened and moved to her mouth. No doubt it was pleasanter when the lipstick was pale and less sticky. Another change was in her attitude to what she had called her "profession." She appeared to have retired, perhaps at Eric's request or perhaps it was by her own decision. By the middle of September we heard no more of her needing to earn her living.

About this time the invitations arrived from the Colchester printing firm and Ida was delegated to fill them in, she having in everyone's opinion the most legible handwriting. Winifred had drawn up the list without, as far as I know, consulting anyone else.

"I'd awfully appreciate it if you'd ask Felix," Ella said in a far humbler tone than she usually used to Winifred. Thanks to the painter's guarded behavior and wish for secrecy, their affair, or "relationship" as she called it, was still largely unknown. "I'd really love him to be there."

To my surprise Winifred said, "I've already asked him."

"You have?"

Winifred responded by showing her the list. One of those fine Cosway blushes spread across Ella's face—from pleasure or resentment? While she was reading the list Zorah came in, took it from her, and scrutinized it as if it were a legal document, a contract perhaps or a deed. She had been back from the Aegean cruise for about a week and during that time the promised car, a yellow Hillman, had been bought and the geode restored to her own rooms. This happened on the evening of her return. She must have guessed who had entered her domain for she said to Ella within an hour of her arrival, "I congratulate you on your skill as a burglar."

Thinking of the car, no doubt, which had already been spoken of though had not yet materialized, Ella said she was sorry but it was unfair on Mother taking her things.

"Unfair!" Her word made Zorah laugh. "Oh, really, what an absurd word to use of anything **I** could do to this family after what has been done to me."

She said no more, but the next day a man arrived from some company which fitted locks opened by keys with registered numbers that could never be copied except on the owner's application. He was upstairs a long time, operating on Zorah's front door, and it was dark by the time he left.

The guest list in her hand, Zorah said, "One of you has been a fast worker in getting to know Dunsford. I see his name up among all the relatives and someone I take to be Eric's sister."

" 'Fast worker' is a very vulgar expression, Zorah," said Winifred. "Mr. Dunsford has become quite a friend of Eric's."

"Oh, **Eric**'s. I see. That explains it."

"Felix is a very good friend of mine too." Ella said it bravely, giving Zorah a defiant look. By this time she would have very much liked the affair to be known and the two of them regarded as a couple.

It is perhaps strange that I should talk about bravery in connection with a woman of thirty-seven talking to her sister of thirty-five. But courage was needed by those sisters in standing up to Zorah and I could see why. Money and power and what I understood was her burning desire for revenge had created her personality and made her frightening. Besides, though the car had come, other benefits derived from Zorah that everyone (except John) would be afraid to lose: money itself, food and drink, and generous gifts, as I was soon to realize.

"You may as well tell me," she said, "what you want for a wedding present."

At that time gift lists were already being registered with department stores, but unfashionable people living in the country hadn't noticed this new development. Winifred hesitated, and said at last, "I was saying to Kerstin the other day that Eric's fridge is about the size of a biscuit tin."

"So you want a fridge, do you? I've always thought it peculiar that the British call a refrigerator a fridge and the Americans, who love abbreviations and acronyms and all that, call it a refrigerator."

"That's the sort of thing I'd expect Selwyn Lombard to say."

Ella laughed. I could tell she hadn't thought about what she was saying. The words had just rattled out of her.

The change in Zorah was frightening. She became very still and pale, as if she had suddenly been struck by a chill, and yet there was something snakelike about her. She had grown fangs and would strike. I understood then that she knew Dr. Lombard was her father and hated the knowledge, that she had possibly changed the shape of her nose not only for enhancement of her looks but to make the resemblance less marked. She said to Ella in a voice as clear and hard as glass, "I hope you'll take care of that car and not batter it about like you did the last one. It's simply a matter of learning to drive properly, you know." Her manner was that of an unkind aunt to a small niece. Without comment, she watched Ella get up and leave the room. "So I am to buy you a fridge, am I, Winifred?"

"That would be very generous," Winifred said.

"It would. Still, I don't have a sister married every day. In fact, I hardly ever have one married at all. You had better go and choose a fridge tomorrow but not more than three hundred pounds, mind."

As it happened, I went with Winifred into Colchester to choose the refrigerator. I was amused by her choice, not so much because it was the largest and best equipped in the store but on account of her rejection of the one she preferred. The big one was more expensive, costing at £299 19s. 11d. just a penny less than the top price specified by Zorah.

"Actually, that's the one I really like best," she said, pointing to the refrigerator she had decided not to have. "I think it might fit into the rectory kitchen better and I prefer the door fittings. But

Zorah said up to three hundred so I may as well have the big one."

That made me wonder if Zorah had also set a ceiling on the car price and Ella had been careful to come only just within it. The youngest of Mrs. Cosway's daughters might have her power and take her pleasure in the family's obsequiousness, but they had learned how to take the maximum advantage of her.

On the way back we stopped outside the rectory gates and Winifred asked me if I would like to see inside it. What interested me was finding out if she had a key to the house, but whether she did I never discovered, for Eric saw us from the window and opened the front door. We walked into a large, square, and shabby hallway and on into a larger, oblong, and shabbier living room. Rectories and vicarages all over England were like that then, though I didn't know it at the time. I didn't know that incumbents of parishes were expected to live in vast "gentlemen's" houses, once occupied by clergymen with private incomes or with horribly disproportionate stipends, some of them as little as fifty pounds a year, some of a thousand. And this in the days when you paid your servants a few shillings a year to keep these mansions clean. I thought all that had died away with the passing of the nineteenth century.

Now, of course, a vicar looks after three or four parishes and lives in a little purpose-built vicarage (of the same design all over the country, though executed in the local building materials). When Eric occupied Windrose Rectory, a house of ten bedrooms and four "reception" rooms, he had a cleaning woman from the village come in each morning, do some desultory sweeping up, and prepare a sketchy evening meal for him.

Men in the sixties were unable to do much about the house and never considered learning how to clean and cook. I doubt if Eric could have wielded a vacuum cleaner or boiled an egg. Perhaps he was capable of boiling a kettle but that was something else I never found out, for Winifred said to sit down and she would make tea. Lydstep Old Hall, dreary as its carpets and furnishings were, had an interior out of **House and Garden** compared with what was to be Winifred's home. The living room, where Eric and I sat on a long sofa of scuffed brown leather in front of a grim steel-gray metal and marble fireplace, was a large, echoing chamber, its walls painted many years before a dirty cream. A chandelier of wooden branches and parchment lampshades had a branch broken and a lampshade missing. The velvet curtains were dust-colored and the carpet olive green with a just discernible pattern of dark brown. Outside the window I could see a wilderness of weeds, tall and tired at that time of the year, all of them overgrown by rampant brambles. I was sorry to find that my face had shown how I felt.

"It needs a woman's touch," Eric said sadly.

"It will get one." If he thought anyone from Lydstep, but particularly Winifred, capable of transforming this place he must have been very unobservant.

"Yes." He added naively but engagingly, "I'm looking forward to being married."

His prospective bride called me to come and look at the kitchen. It too was big and gloomy, though apparently refitted not long before, perhaps when Eric's incumbency began. The refrigerator was larger than a biscuit tin but not very much.

"I must tell Eric about the new one," she said.

This she proceeded to do over tea, frankly telling him that she had chosen the most expensive refrigerator because Zorah had "plenty of money and could have spent twice as much without noticing."

Eric said something feeble about its being very kind of Zorah. "But that's your province, my dear." His eyes began twinkling, a feat he achieved by looking up and down under lowered lids. "I shall not have occasion to pay many visits to the refrigerator, I'm sure."

I expected Winifred to rise to this, as she normally would have. But she said nothing for a moment or two while Eric talked to me about the kind of people who would have lived in this house a hundred years before, a household consisting of parents, four or five children, a nanny, perhaps a governess, two housemaids, a parlormaid, and a cook.

"The living was a good one and in proportion the parson was getting five times what I get."

Winifred looked up and asked him abruptly if he ever heard confessions. It was news to me that any clergyman in what I thought of as a Protestant Church—Eric always corrected me, saying Anglicans were Catholics but not **Roman** Catholics—was allowed to hear confessions or, come to that, would wish to.

He looked surprised but said, "I have to if I'm asked."

"But have you ever?"

"Once or twice," he said, "when I was in my last parish. It's usually very devout ladies who want it. I asked them to come around to the vicarage and I heard their confessions in my study."

"I don't suppose they were very sensational."

"Now, my dear, I couldn't possibly discuss the content."

"I didn't ask you to."

He saw that he had offended her, not a difficult thing to do, and became placatory, smiling and putting out his hand to cover hers. "There haven't been any since I came here." I saw that he thought she was jealous, resentful of the very devout ladies who contrived to be alone with him. "I don't suppose there will be. I believe Tom Trewith at

Bishop's Colne hears them on quite a regular basis."

"Really?"

Whether Winifred ever went to open her heart to the Reverend Mr. Trewith I never heard. Presumably, she told no one if she did. But I wondered, as I wrote in the diary that evening, what she had to confess. A kiss from some predecessor of Eric's? Some teenage fumbling? Since she was a "very devout lady" herself, possibly she would consider this worth confessing to someone who could absolve her.

When I had finished writing I drew a little picture of Eric on the facing page. It isn't a bad likeness and I was quite pleased with it. Eric is sitting in his study and a woman who looks a lot like Lily, the barmaid at the White Rose, kneels at his feet with a balloon coming out of her mouth that says, "Bless me, Mr. Dawson, for I have sinned."

It was the first cartoon I ever did.

14

THERE MUST HAVE BEEN MANY PEOPLE THEN, though very few now, who went to church as I did; not because I was in the slightest degree devout, not because I could even have called myself an agnostic, but solely because I enjoyed it. I liked the words, the prose of the Book of Common Prayer, the music, the hymns (even though, or perhaps because, some of the verses were ridiculous), the lessons, and the beautiful place in which we sat. I even rather missed it on those Sundays I spent in London, something I never dared tell Mark.

So it was no hardship to me to walk down to Saint John's with Winifred and Ella, always asking Mrs. Cosway's permission and always being told that she supposed so. A newcomer to the village was in church one Sunday morning in late September. Since she was young, female, and very good-looking, she was unlikely to be one of those taken up by Eric and made his friend. Felix homed in on her in a way which terrified Ella. She clutched my hand.

"Who's that?"

"I've no idea, Ella."

"Ask Mrs. Cusp."

The wife of the People's Warden was sitting just behind me. I turned to her with my question, to be told the newcomer was married to the architect who had just moved into a newish house by the Memorial Green.

"Married, then?"

Ella's panic was subsiding. She lived in a world which hadn't moved with the times, which hadn't noticed the sexual revolution and the rising ascendancy of youth. A married woman was still inviolable, still sacrosanct. Felix had taken no notice of Ella. Our pew might have been empty for all the significance it had for him. As carelessly dressed as usual—Winifred's admonition had brought about no change in his clothes—he was pointing out to the architect's wife the hymns we should be having as they appeared on Eric's numbers board and finding them for her in **Hymns Ancient and Modern.**

But I had other things to think about at Matins, for the organist whose playing had pleased me some weeks back was once more at the organ and once more playing Kraus. Knowing that British universities go back in early October after the long summer vacation, I saw that this was probably my last chance for weeks to speak to him. He wouldn't be here to play the wedding march for Winifred in November. As it happened, this was another morning of coffee and cakes being provided by her after the service and as I stood there with my cup of coffee and my custard cream biscuit, Ella introduced me to the man who had just walked down the aisle from the vestry.

"Kerstin, this is James Trintowel."

We talked about the music and about King Gustav III, architect of the Swedish Enlightenment who was assassinated while attending a masquerade at the opera. James said he had Kraus's **Proserpin** on records (two LPs in those days) and I should come up to their house on Saturday for a meal with them and he would play some of it. His mother and father would be delighted. It happened that I should be in Lydstep that Saturday, Mark being home at a family wedding in Shropshire, so I accepted.

Winifred, Ella, and I had walked down and intended to get a lift back from Eric, but Ella left us at The Studio gate. She was going to wait for Felix to come back from church. I had seen him walking the architect's wife home while I was eating my biscuit, but I saw no point in telling her that. Winifred said nastily that chasing men was always a mistake, and Ella, unable to think of a retort, turned away in silence. We walked part of the way up the hill, waiting for Eric to pick us up. Winifred was silent for a while, then began brightly talking about fittings for her wedding dress, how Ella was making her own dress and June Prothero's, and whether their bouquets should be mauve or pink chrysanthemums. Abruptly, after a pause, she asked me what I thought of Felix.

"Does it matter what I think, Winifred?"

"It does to me." She spoke in a sad, serious voice.

"I don't think he's a very interesting man," I said.

"What on earth do you mean?"

"Well, since you ask, he has no conversation. He may know a lot about art but he knows nothing about anything else. All he does is lounge about looking lazy. His manners are awful and he has no charm, though he thinks he has lots. He's vain. He's treating your sister badly."

This pleased her. "What do you mean?"

I saw no reason to protect Felix Dunsford's dubious interest. "You must know she's in love with him. He never takes her out except to the pub and I don't think he does that anymore. He's her lover"—she winced—"but he barely acknowledges her in company. He pretends their affair has to be a secret, but there's no reason why it should be. She's not married and as far as I know he's not."

"Of course he's not married, Kerstin. I had no idea things had gone so far between them." I could tell she was lying. "But how can you say he's not interesting? I think he's fascinating."

"It's not the same thing," I said and then Eric's car drew up alongside us.

The Virginia creeper was taking on its autumn

color. There was something much more remarkable about a house clothed in red leaves than in green. From a distance it looked like a great hedge of bright flowers, but its strangeness really only struck home when we were upon it, almost underneath it, and the rippling wind set those scarlet leaves quivering and trembling. We went into the house and a fallen leaf was blown in with us.

Rain began soon after we had finished lunch. It started as a thin drizzle. Confident that John and I would be able to go for our walk as usual, Mrs. Cosway went upstairs for her rest. Within minutes it was pouring. I decided to act on my own initiative and abandon all thoughts of going out.

"We'll stay in this afternoon, John," I said, noticing to my continuing disquiet that I was still talking to him as if he were nine years old, the mental age Ida once told me she and his mother had set for him. Every time I caught myself doing this I resolved to stop, but so far I had failed.

"I shall go out," he said.

"It's raining, John. It will be nasty"—I changed this child's word—"unpleasant."

Giving no sign he had heard me, he said nothing but stared at the table where the Roman vase stood. He could gaze at a point in the middle distance for very long periods of time, hours sometimes. Observing him—with interest and I hope with great pity—I often wondered if this staring was symptomatic of his condition or the result of the Largactil Mrs. Cosway gave him daily. And what was that condition? This occupied my mind a lot. I wished I had studied more psychiatry, I wished I had real experience in nursing psychiatric patients. None of those few I remembered had been particularly intelligent. I mean by that, of course, that they had been sick in their minds and often their bodies but those minds hadn't been capable of intellectual feats. Was John's?

"I shall go out now," he said.

It had begun to pour.

Crossing him could result in his behaving like he had done that day in the summer when he hid behind the sofa. Mrs. Cosway would blame me if that happened, and though I would like to say I wouldn't have cared if she did, this wasn't quite true. She made plain her dislike of me being there at all by a cold yet curiously indifferent harping on characteristics of mine (largely invented by herself) and by comments on my alleged inquisitiveness, accompanied by that chilling cough of a laugh. I was in danger of being driven by her into a nervous condition of doing almost anything to avoid more of it.

"I'm sorry, John," I said, "but you can't go out in this. Look for yourself."

Ida caught my eye and made a little movement of

her head, designed I suppose to indicate that he was incapable of this. But John did rouse himself up, his hands shaking more than I had ever seen them shake, and go sluggishly to the window, where he stood staring into the garden, or as much of it as he could see, a green and brown blur through the lashing rain which streamed down the panes. To my surprise, and certainly to Ida's, he turned around and came back to his seat. There he picked part of the Sunday paper off the table where the geode had been and seemed to make an attempt to read it, falling asleep after a moment or two from weariness or frustration or the drug.

John always took his bath in the mornings, usually when he first got up but sometimes later, if there were difficulties with the hot water supply, which happened quite often. To bathe was his only reason for ever going upstairs, a part of the house I had been told he disliked, though not of course told by him. He never objected to going up there for his bath, as far as I could see. That Monday there was no hot water at six in the morning but after much stoking of the kitchen boiler by Ida and feeding it with a new supply of "anthracite nuts," Mrs. Cosway decided that John could take his bath at ten. She went upstairs with him.

Free for half an hour, having helped Ida with the table-clearing and dish-washing, I took the key from behind the amphitheater picture and went back into the library to search for more books which might have been John's. My luck was in. I had to climb the library steps to reach the top shelves. Each one held two rows of books, one in front of the other. It was impossible not to feel, as I did when I had taken down the Arnold Bennett and H. G. Wells novels from the front row, that those behind had been deliberately hidden. They were philosophical works by Kant, by Kierkegaard and Hume among others, and a daunting book on quantum physics. Back in my room I found inside this one a sheet of paper covered with incomprehensible (to me) hieroglyphics which, as far as I could make out, were equations indicating how to measure radiation variants. The date on the flyleaf was 1950 and I thought the paper might have been John's.

This of course was quite a long time before he fell into the hands of Mrs. Cosway and Selwyn Lombard. His father was still alive and I supposed he had been much under his father's care and protection. There would surely have been no mind-numbing medication in Mr. Cosway's time. I decided that I would like to know more about John Cosway the elder, where he thought this myth of John's mental age came from and what was wrong with his son.

Once again, I asked myself the same question. Not schizophrenia, I was sure, not a manic-depressive condition. In no sense of the word was he "mad." What made him the way he was seemed to me to have happened when he was a child, as Isabel had hinted at, or was still in the womb, or through a gene passed on down the Cosway family. There might be instances of ancestors who had behaved strangely, hiding, hating raised voices, maintaining long periods of silence, violent when asked to do something feared, phobic when touched, but highly intelligent, particularly in the areas of mathematics and physics. Somehow I felt that in Victorian times and earlier, such people might have been better treated, looked on as no more than eccentrics. Were there any such among John's forebears?

Outside the rain continued to fall, and although I could see nothing from inside the library, I could hear its drumming and sometimes hear sheets of water dashed across the glass by the rising wind. It was rather strange in there, claustrophobic, enclosed, twilit, yet with the constant sound of falling water in the background. Nothing else could be heard. It might have been any time of the day or night. I thought this was perhaps why John liked it. It must have been peculiarly suited to someone who wanted to be alone, eschewed human contact, appeared only to love inanimate objects, needed books, puzzles, conundrums, more than any companionship. Perhaps he liked the stone faces which so intimidated me. They were not real, as he would know they were not, and unable to assume the expressions of rage or exasperation or despair he daily saw in the living faces around him.

At that moment I saw locking the library up to keep him out as particularly cruel, and I was starting to think what I could do to put an end to this embargo, when a kind of howl, half scream, half groan, broke the near silence. I had thought nothing but the swish of falling water would be audible in the library, which seemed hermetically sealed, but I heard that sound.

Growing familiar by this time with ways in and out, I twisted around corners and down short passages, flung open the door, and came out into the passage. A hubbub of voices reached me from the hall. Winifred and Ida were there, Mrs. Cosway lying on the floor at the foot of the stairs, not unconscious, already struggling to sit up. I saw her wince with pain as she tried to move her left leg. All around her on the floor were the bits and pieces she had been carrying downstairs and which must have contributed to her fall, a glass of water—broken and the contents splashed everywhere—John's pajamas, sheets of newspaper, and her knitted cardigan.

"Don't try to move," Ida said. "I'll phone Dr. Lombard."

"He won't be able to get me up off this floor." She sounded angry rather than hurt, but when she lifted her hands I saw that the left wrist was crooked. "I think my leg's broken too. How did it happen? Did someone give me a push?"

"Mother," said Winifred, "what are you saying?"

Mrs. Cosway waved her good wrist at the stairs. On the first landing John stood, holding the banisters, looking down.

"If Eric were here," Winifred said brightly, "I'm sure he could lift you."

"Well, he's not, so what's the use of that?"

Ida came back to say Dr. Lombard would be there in five minutes. "Now, I wonder if John might possibly . . ."

"I don't want him near me," her mother snapped back.

John began to come downstairs. He paused at the foot and stood looking at his mother. Then he went into the downstairs lavatory and locked himself in. I heard the key turn. Trying to treat him like the rational adult I was becoming sure he was, I asked him if he was all right. His mother had fallen down the stairs, but she was well if injured. He was on the other side of the door, but he made no answer when I told him this. He made no sound at all.

"He'll be in there for hours," Ida said.

"I know you think I'm making it up," said Mrs. Cosway from the floor, "though why I should invent such a thing about my own son, I can't imagine, but I have a very strong feeling I was pushed."

No one said anything. I knew John was incapable of touching, still less pushing, anyone. Winifred shrugged and cast up her eyes. I heard Dr. Lombard's car and within seconds he was in the hallway. To me, before this, he had simply been an old man, pompous, given to strange irrelevant anecdotes, any character he might have blanked out by my new knowledge that he was Zorah's father. That morning, I suddenly recognized that he was a very strong old man, thin and muscular, his fitness revealed by sweater and flannel trousers. He knelt down with ease—I had been wrong about the reason for his failure to kneel in church—and spoke to Mrs. Cosway. Hearing him call her "darling" almost shocked me.

"Are you in pain, darling?"

"My leg hurts," she said. She lifted up her right hand, now beginning to swell. "I don't know what I've done to my wrist."

"I'm going to take you to the hospital."

Mrs. Cosway had doubted that he would be able to get her off the floor, but he did so with ease, slipping his arms under her and lifting her up, rising from his kneeling position with only the faintest sign of strain and no sign that he had hurt her. She looked into his face and he smiled at her, an exchange of tenderness between them which made Winifred purse her lips and frown.

"I said you wouldn't be able to get me off the floor, Selwyn, but I was so wrong."

"Then I'm glad I can still surprise you after so long."

"Where are you going to take her?" Winifred's voice was abrupt and sharp.

"The cottage hospital."

Dr. Lombard bent his head, touched Mrs. Cosway's cheek with his lips, and carried her out of the house. Over his shoulder he said, "I'll call on my way back and tell you what's happening."

Once the front door closed Winifred made the noise the Victorians rendered as "Pshaw!"

"He means well," said Ida.

"The road to hell must be so well paved it never needs maintenance."

This was the only mildly witty thing I ever heard Winifred say. Years later I tried to use it for a cartoon but the circumstances were never right and I abandoned the idea. Winifred went into the dining room to phone Eric. Moral support was what she wanted him for, I suppose, but I wondered if there had ever been or ever would be the kind of shared tenderness, sympathy, and enduring love between those two as I had just seen in the faces of that old couple.

Mrs. Cosway's accident and departure for the hospital rather eclipsed the interest there might have been in Zorah's arrival from London in the Lotus. "Where's John?"

Ida didn't answer. "Mother's fallen downstairs and Dr. Lombard's taken her to the cottage hospital."

"I asked where John was."

A while afterward, when I began to know Ida's true nature, I wouldn't have been surprised by her failure to tell Zorah that Dr. Lombard was expected at any minute. She knew very well Zorah's hatred of Selwyn Lombard, the hatred any child might feel for the parent who has both fathered her and also wrecked the family life of the home she was to grow up in. If she had known he was coming she would surely have gone up to her own rooms, and Ida was aware of this. Yet she said nothing and it was left to Winifred to tell Zorah that John had shut himself in the lavatory.

"Why did he?"

"Why does he do anything, Zorah?"

"Do you know, I think much of what he does is very reasonable and logical."

"Mother," said Ida, "has got it into her head that John—well, I don't say pushed her downstairs but gave her a push. Perhaps it was a joke."

"That is a foul slander and John doesn't joke, as you well know."

The doorbell rang, Winifred answered it and Dr. Lombard walked in. "Hello, everyone. Sorry to have kept you in suspense so long. Poor Julia has a Potts fracture of the right ankle but her wrist is only sprained. She may be a week in the hospital or only a few days."

Zorah picked up the newspaper just before he came in and began to read it as if he had never arrived, as if she, Winifred, Ida, and I were alone. Apart from the nose, which in her case of course had been altered and was small and tip-tilted, she and Dr. Lombard I could now see were very much alike, so similar that anyone seeing them together—Mrs. Cosway's husband?—could have had no doubt as to her parentage. He had turned his eyes on her and I thought I could see in his look regret that she ignored him and a wish for a reconciliation, now the man legally her father was dead.

"She'll need clothes, I suppose," said practical Ida, already making lists and plans in her mind. "I'll go in tomorrow."

"So will I, of course, I shall be so anxious." Whether Winifred would have said this if Eric hadn't arrived in Dr. Lombard's wake, for she was always keen to make an impression of virtue on him, I hardly know. "She'll want things to read too. And I expect the food is awful, isn't it?"

"She said she'd like some biscuits and orange juice," Dr. Lombard said.

Why these innocuous words should have been the trigger to send Zorah to her feet and depart for her rooms upstairs, who can tell? Perhaps her exit had nothing to do with the words but only with the voice which uttered them and its possessor. Dr. Lombard watched her leave with the same rueful expression.

"How long will she be—er, incapacitated?"

It took Eric to ask this question. Perhaps the others had not quite liked to. Dr. Lombard said it was hard to tell. Mrs. Cosway was no longer, as he put it, in her first youth.

"Nor her second," said Eric as if delivering a profound philosophical principle.

"It may be a couple of months before she can walk without crutches."

"We're getting married in just under five weeks."

"It's quite obvious," Winifred said, "that the wedding will have to be postponed. I can't get married without Mother being there."

She might have disguised her delight a little. She sounded triumphant and Eric seemed to notice how exultant she was, for he frowned and gave her a puzzled look. Even intelligent clergymen, I have noticed since then, need breezy platitudes and comforting sweet nothings among their stock-in-trade, and Eric now brought one of these out for the cheering-up of the company.

"What a blessing you have Kerstin here! There must be so many little tasks performed by Mrs. Cosway she can take over now she knows the ropes."

Did I know the ropes? Perhaps, but that was not

to say I liked them. I could see I was faced with several dilemmas, one of them major. Some rejoinder was probably expected from me, but I said nothing. Ida looked at her watch and, keeping to her inevitable eternal role, said she would get tea for everyone. I offered to help her and followed her out to the kitchen.

Rain was still streaming down the windows and although the clocks wouldn't go back for a month, it was dark enough in the middle of the afternoon to have lights on. Ida started on a low murmured catalog of all the things Mrs. Cosway used to do and would be unable to do now, of the folly, however understandable, of carrying too many articles in one's hands when walking downstairs at the age of seventy-nine, and when and if her injuries would ever at her age fully mend.

I paid very little attention to this. My mind was occupied with John, still locked away and still silent, responding not at all to Dr. Lombard's efforts outside the door to cajole him out and Eric's exhortations to him to be "a good chap." Knowing he would come out eventually, I would have left him alone. I was far more troubled by Mrs. Cosway's accusation. No, not troubled, angered. John, I knew, would never push her or anyone, and this would not be due to morality or love for her or fear of consequences but simply because to push you have to touch. And you have to care enough to hate. Why had she accused him? I knew she couldn't have believed it herself. The motive she might have had, the desire to be rid of him, was too dreadful to be thought of.

Eric went away at last and Dr. Lombard went. I don't know when John came out, but early in the evening I came upon him in the drawing room, gently stroking the Roman vase as if it were a pet animal.

15

THE RAIN FELL ALL EVENING AND THE WIND, RISing to a gale, tore off the first of the red leaves to fall that autumn. A lake of water, quite deep in places and whipped by the wind into little waves, had spread across the drive in front of the house by the time John went to bed. This was at eight rather than at seven, the first departure from his routine.

He seemed to take a longer time than usual arranging the ballpoint, the plaster, the dice, and the rest at his bedside. The pattern, always precisely the same, slowly took shape. It was like someone setting out counters on a board for a table game. Satisfied, he shed his dressing gown and got into bed. I wondered why I—or anyone—had to be there. To prevent him doing something dangerous or harmful? Perhaps, though he showed no sign of diverging from his rigid routine.

I knew he would refuse the phenobarbital. He had refused to take it from me the evening his mother went to fetch his prescription and he would again. I didn't attempt to give it to him. But after he was asleep and throughout that evening I kept asking myself what right I had to find prescribed drugs unnecessary. Unattractive as the prospect was, I would have to ask Dr. Lombard. I would have to go to his office and consult him.

As it happened, he came to Lydstep Old Hall to speak to me.

This meeting seemed even more urgent in the morning. Uncertain what to do about getting John up, I went into his bedroom at about seven, but he was gone. On his own, he had gone upstairs to run his bath. I noticed too that the objects from the bedside table were gone; back, I supposed, in his dressing-gown pockets.

Ida was of course up, a draggled sight, her hair fastened back with an elastic band, her tweed skirt fastened at the waist with a safety pin, and her bare feet in the kind of carpet slippers my grandfather used to wear. When she saw me she said, as if it were eleven in the morning, "I thought you were never coming. Have you forgotten we have to give John his tablet?"

The Largactil. She must have taken it from Mrs. Cosway's medicine chest the previous evening. Now she handed the bottle to me and said, "You have to put it on his plate and let him pick it up himself. He won't want it if you've touched it."

John was watching me. He followed with his eyes the progress of tablet from bottle to spoon to plate where it rolled a little before coming to rest. Then he looked hard at me and said, "No."

Ida said, "Why not, John? You know Kerstin. You like her, don't you?" There was no response to this, no sign in his expression that he had even heard. "Suppose I do it, then. I know, why don't I pick up your pill like this? In a different spoon and put it on a different plate? How's that?"

A slow horror was breaking over me as I heard her speaking in this tone to a middle-aged man who had been a child prodigy and was obviously very clever still. But there was nothing I could do and nothing John **would** do. He was determined not to touch that pill.

"Try a glass dish like the one he has in his room," I said.

Showing more weariness than she ever did in her mother's presence, Ida sighed, opened the sideboard, and found a small glass dish. The white tablet was dropped into it and the cajoling began again in much the same words. Exasperated beyond patience, John picked up the glass dish with the pill in it and, while his sister waited in breathless anticipation of his finally swallowing it, hurled both across the room where the dish hit the wall and broke in pieces and the pill disappeared behind the sideboard.

I thought Ida was going to tell him he was a naughty boy. "There's nothing we can do," I said quickly. "We have to leave it."

She set up a sort of wail. With a look of angry bitterness at John, she got on to her knees and began scrabbling about under the sideboard, cutting her fingers on broken glass, a prefiguring of things to come, almost an omen. There she discovered two other pills, one white but a different shape, and one red, a number of needles and hair clips and a lens from a pair of glasses, but not the Largactil. I said nothing and she took my silence for disapproval, which is what I suppose it was.

"They are very expensive, you know. They can't just be written off like that."

Surely Mrs. Cosway obtained them on the National Health Service? I thought it wiser not to ask. Winifred and Ella came downstairs together, as they often did, though on no less prickly terms than they usually were. Hospitals had quite rigid visiting hours in those days and Ella wanted to know when these were. No one could tell her, Winifred reminding her that finding out this sort of thing was what the phone was for. Ida cut into the ensuing argument by telling them of John's failure to take his pill.

"It's useless telling me," said Ella. "I know nothing about it."

"You don't suppose I do, do you?" Winifred gave her elder sister a bleak look. "That sort of thing isn't my province. I am nearly out of my mind with worry about my mother, which doesn't seem to concern the rest of you at all."

Eventually it was she who discovered from the hospital that visiting was from six-thirty to eight every evening except Sundays. Mrs. Cosway was "quite comfortable." While they argued about who should go to see her that evening and whether taking Eric along would be too much for her, I made bread and marmalade triangles for John. He took them and said, to my astonishment, "I could do that myself, Shashtin."

His sisters looked at him as if he had committed some social solecism.

"All right," I said. "You can do it tomorrow."

Dr. Lombard's morning office hours ended at ten and I was about to leave the house and walk down to see him, when he arrived. His last patient had gone and no more were expected.

"Ah, the very one I wanted to see," he said when I opened the door to him. "I'd like a word with you, young lady."

He seemed tired and it occurred to me that he was a very old man to be still running a GP's practice but perhaps he had a partner. Either Ida or Winifred had told me he was a few years younger than Mrs. Cosway, so probably he was getting on for seventy-five. I realized he looked younger than he was because, as it does in some rare cases, his hair had remained copious and dark, scarcely touched with gray. The great hooked nose gave him the look of an old eagle, predatory and irritable.

He knew better than to attempt touching John's hand. Most of the things I wanted to say and ask could hardly be brought out in John's presence and

Selwyn Lombard seemed to know this too, for after greeting him and asking him if he was all right, he led me with a proprietorial air into the dining room.

"Now Mrs. Cosway is temporarily away," he began, seating himself in a chair at the table, "I should like to give you some instructions regarding John's tablets. Sit down, sit down."

I sat.

"The tablets labeled phenobarbital you will find in Mrs. Cosway's medicine chest—in her bedroom, that is—are administered to him one at a time at bedtime. The Largactil or chlorpromazine are the ones I believe Mrs. Cosway gave you. Exactly seven, one for each day she expects to be in hospital. If she should be there longer I will come and allot you any further tablets you need. Now is that clear, young lady?"

"It's perfectly clear." You wouldn't like me to call you "old gentleman," I thought. "My name is Shashtin, Dr. Lombard."

"Yes, yes," he said. "Kerstin, as you say."

I had expected him to object to my correcting him, but he showed no sign of offense. "Dr. Lombard?"

"Yes, yo—Kerstin?"

"What exactly is wrong with John?"

"Ah. It started with something we call childhood schizophrenia, the result of brain damage brought about by a shock. An emotional shock, that is."

I looked inquiring, but he had evidently decided not to enlighten me on the nature of this shock. "Since then, it has developed into a full-blown psychosis. The result is that he may be violent, harming himself and others. No doubt, he hears voices telling him how to react against his nearest and dearest. It is likely he suffers from all kinds of delusions as to who he is and who they are and possibly from hallucinations. There, does that satisfy you?"

I nodded, though it didn't. Later on I found that in every respect Selwyn Lombard's diagnosis and catalog of symptoms were wrong and his recommended palliatives ill-judged and harmful. Even then I recognized obvious inaccuracies, but I was no farther toward understanding what was wrong with John.

"Swedish, aren't you?" Dr. Lombard said suddenly.

"That's right."

"Descartes spent a long time with Queen Christina of Sweden. René Descartes. He was a French philosopher, you know. Well, there's no reason to think you do know, is there? He felt the cold up there, poor thing, spent most of his time in an airing cupboard."

This was the first anecdote I ever heard him tell that was apropos of something under discussion. Inevitably, I knew what would come next and it did. " 'I think, therefore I am,' " he said. "A bit above your head, I expect. I must be off. Don't hesitate to phone me if you have any problems with John."

I thought of the problem Ida and I had already had. Should I tell him? Perhaps wrongly I decided not to. But I had an unpleasant feeling, possibly quite unfounded, that he might try to force that Largactil down John's throat. I saw him to the door and because the sun was shining and the day was milder than of late, I went outside with him, avoiding the puddles which were all that remained of the previous evening's deluge, and stood for a moment in the sunshine. Together we looked back at the house and its covering of crimson leaves.

"Extraordinary sight," he said. "They'll all drop off, you know, and a fine mess they make."

For the rest of that day I watched John to see if he suffered any adverse effects from being deprived of his chlorpromazine, but there seemed to be none. Beneficial effects there were in that he was more alert and while out with me seemed to enjoy his walk, taking an interest in his surroundings, though speaking no more than usual. He prepared his tea in his usual way, covering each quarter slice of bread with a different spread, and, to my surprise when I handed him his teacup, he said, "Thank you very much, Shashtin," pronouncing my name correctly as he invariably did.

From what I had seen since my arrival at Lydstep Old Hall, I had decided that Ida was Mrs. Cosway's favorite child. Apart from the fact that she was the eldest by several years, I had no idea why this should be. Winifred and Ella looked more like their mother and talked more like her, both in their ways having a similar ruthless attitude to life, a talent for snapping, and a rude manner when they chose to show it. Ida's was a much weaker character. She was dull and never had much to say for herself, her reproofs seldom going beyond an "Oh, Mother!" She was untidy in her person and, I suspected, none too clean, but Mrs. Cosway loved her best—if she loved anyone apart from Dr. Lombard. Still, it was Winifred and Ella who went most often to see Mrs. Cosway, coming back with stories about the ghastliness of the food, the awful hospital smell, and the "lower-class" people with whom their mother had to share the small ward.

"I wonder if she would like to see Eric," said Winifred. "It might be a comfort to her."

Ella sniffed but said nothing. While they were out and I was with John, in his bedroom, Zorah had appeared and was sitting in the drawing room, her expression one of acute boredom.

"I suppose you'll go in tomorrow," said Ella, supposing no such thing.

"I've had flowers sent."

Once I knew Zorah's story, it was interesting to observe the enjoyment she apparently took in being as rude and provocative as she liked while knowing that offending other members of this household could harm her not at all. I imagined her feelings on her husband's death, if not before, when she must have realized that the people who had treated her with dislike and contempt were now in her power. She had judged that their greed would overcome any principles they might once have had about taking charity or flattering her for the largesse she could give them. Watching their faces and hearing them wheedle must have been like a stimulating drug to her, particularly when she heard and saw Winifred's reaction to the offer of three hundred pounds' worth of kitchen equipment.

I wondered what was in the note which must have accompanied the flowers sent to her mother. No doubt it had been coolly and subtly offensive. It was only when in the presence of Selwyn Lombard that she lost her sangfroid.

John could never be violent, I had been sure of that, no matter what Dr. Lombard said, no matter what absurd accusations his mother made, but I was wrong. It had never occurred to me that there would be an argument over the administering of the Largactil at breakfast time. It wouldn't be administered, that was all. John had been fine the day before, brighter if not more talkative, and I could see no reason not to forget about the drug once more. Ida thought otherwise. I suppose she was afraid of her mother. She was waiting at the table for John when I came down, and the tablet was already in a glass dish identical to the one he had upstairs, a glass of water at the ready.

He took his seat, ignoring her, and reached for his egg. Usually someone else sliced the top off for him but that morning he did it himself and very expertly too. Ida said, "Your pill, John. Better take it before you start to eat."

"No," he said.

"Now come on, you always have your pill."

Those words, for some reason, started a train of thought as I remembered reading somewhere that Largactil should not be given over a long period. One of its effects could be a tremor in the hands and difficulties of movement. What was a long period? I took my coffee, keeping my eyes on John. He seemed to be ignoring Ida but when she repeated what she had just said, he laid down his spoon and said in a much louder than usual voice, "I am not taking it, so you can give up."

It was the longest sentence I had ever heard him utter.

"Suppose Kerstin gives it to you?"

It cost Ida something to say this. Like her whole family, she wouldn't have cared for anyone to be preferred over herself. But she desperately wanted John to take that pill and if she paid the price of rejection for it, so be it.

"I don't think so," I said.

Ida shrugged, looking determined, and stupidly she spooned up the pill and thrust it an inch from his face. Quick as a flash he lashed out at her with his right arm, bending it toward his chest at the elbow, flinging it wide and hard, and striking her across the face. She jumped up with a cry. She put both hands up to cover and hold her mouth where he had hit her.

I was frightened. John was mad, everyone else said so, and we fear the mad. I did my best not to show fear, telling Ida in a voice I tried to keep from shaking that she should leave the room, go upstairs, anywhere for the time being. She went, scurrying, carpet slippers flapping. After taking two or three deep breaths, I forced myself to go on eating. John, who had gone momentarily bright red in the face, was now continuing calmly with his breakfast.

Though uninjured, Ida was much upset by the incident. She sat at the kitchen table for hours, her head bent and sometimes held in her hands. It made me think of one of those servants I had read of who, though they have a bedroom of their own, look on the kitchen as their natural habitat, a place in which to live and move and have their being. I wouldn't have been surprised to learn that Ida secretly undressed and got into her nightgown there, washing hands and face at the sink. I made her a cup of tea in the middle of the morning; Winifred, having changed her mind about giving up work, had gone out to cook for someone's luncheon party and Ella of course was at school.

"Why did he do that?" she kept saying. "Why did he hit me?"

He was simply exasperated, I wanted to say but did not.

"Of course we all know really that he's quite mad. Stark, staring mad. I don't care what my father said, it's my belief he was mad from birth. Well, from being a little kid. You can get that way from a shock."

"How long has John been given Largactil?" I asked, though I knew the answer.

"Oh, years. Four years? Five? He has to have it. Well, look what happens when he doesn't. I shall never dare tell Mother. And now two of those pills have got lost. Today's one's gone missing as well. I don't know what's become of it."

It was supposed to be my day off, a fact of which I reminded Winifred after John and I came back from our walk and she, exhausted from preparing and serving lunch to a party of bridge-playing ladies, was lying down on the sofa.

"You aren't going out, are you?"

"Yes, I am," I said firmly. "I'm taking the bus into Sudbury."

There, in the public library, I looked up Largactil in a medical dictionary. This, somewhat condensed, is what it said:

A proprietary preparation of the powerful phenothiazine drug chlorpromazine hydrochlo-

ride, used as a major tranquilizer to treat patients with behavioral disturbances, such as schizophrenia. Available only on prescription, Largactil is produced in the form of tablets, syrup, and a suspension, in three strengths.

It should not be administered to patients with certain forms of glaucoma, whose blood-cell formation by the bone marrow is reduced, and only with caution to those with lung disease, cardiovascular disease, epilepsy, Parkinsonism, abnormalities of the adrenal glands, impaired liver or kidney function, hyperthyroidism, enlargement of the prostate, or any form of acute infection, who are pregnant or lactating or who are elderly. Prolonged use may result in motor difficulties, a shuffling gait, and tremor in the hands, all of which may become permanent.

Withdrawal of treatment should be gradual.

All this was even worse than I supposed. I sat for a long time in that Victorian library, once a corn exchange, thinking of the consequences which might result from continuous use of Largactil. Were checks ever made on John's movement disorders? I had no idea, but I guessed not. It seemed to me that a drug he didn't need but which was brutally administered to him, was crippling his limbs and giving him something like Parkinson's disease. Leaving the library to catch my bus, I also thought of how he was refusing to take his drug, which meant it was cut off completely instead of gradually withdrawn as the book recommended.

When I got back to Lydstep Old Hall I found John trying to read the newspaper. He had his glasses on but they were inadequate for his needs and he was using a magnifying glass procured from somewhere to help him. I guessed he hadn't had his eyes tested for years and now at nearly forty, his sight was beginning its nearly always inevitable deterioration. As far as I could tell, the magnifying glass didn't help him much, for when he saw me he laid it down, took off his glasses, and smiled. It wasn't the first time he had smiled at me, but I don't think it had happened more than once or twice before. I asked him how he was feeling, using precisely the tone I would to any other man of his age.

"I'm fine," he said.

The first time I saw him, back in June when he was having tea in the kitchen with his mother and Ida, I had thought him a handsome man, his looks marred by the blankness of his face. Now that this dull mask had begun to lift, I saw once more how good-looking he was, his face the legacy of two people with fine classical features, his hair dark and thick and his eyes the clear dark blue of Winifred's. Recovered from the exhaustion of her day, she was looking at him too, but with distaste.

16

LITTLE IF ANYTHING WAS SAID ABOUT OSTEOporosis in those days, so I don't know whether Mrs. Cosway's bones were brittle. At her age, they probably were. But the fracture of her ankle was a straightforward break; no one seemed much worried about it and Eric was beginning to say that he had been premature in postponing his wedding. Why had no one thought of taking his future mother-in-law to the church in a wheelchair? But the ceremony was now fixed for mid-January.

I told no one what I had discovered about the nature of Largactil, for I was sure the Cosway sisters would be uninterested and Dr. Lombard take no notice or, more likely, be angry at my interference. I knew myself that I was being presumptuous, unlearned as I was in medical matters. Still, I watched John very closely, noting as one could hardly help doing that he was far more alert than usual, more **human,** occasionally speaking, trying hard to read, and at mealtimes arranging his own potatoes and carrots in patterns and slicing the tops off his eggs himself. I asked Ida about his sight—

the other sisters never wanted to talk about John—but she looked unconcerned.

"He can't see very well and his glasses aren't strong enough for him. Even if he puts them on you can tell he can't read the paper unless he uses a magnifying glass as well."

This confirmed what I had seen myself. I lay awake a long time that night telling myself I must speak to Dr. Lombard, whatever the consequences. The worst that could happen was that he would abuse me as a lay person presuming to teach a medical man his business, but surely I could bear that. In the end, however, I never contacted him. I am afraid I eventually told myself that at least John was not taking the drug at present, perhaps would not even after Mrs. Cosway came home if she were still incapacitated. She might even assume Ida or I was taking on this duty. So I said nothing and wondered many times afterward if I should have, if my speaking out might have altered events. But I doubt it. I doubted it then and I do now. Only if John had made a miraculous recovery from his disease or disability or whatever it was, if he had suddenly got better and taken himself away, would he not have been involved.

I went to see Mrs. Cosway once while she was in the cottage hospital, accompanying Ella one evening. She seemed less than pleased to see us, which I attributed to Dr. Lombard's being at her bedside. Without letting go of her hand, which he had been holding when we came in, he began telling us, though no one had asked, the origin of his name.

"Lombard comes from the Italian 'Longibardi,' the long-bearded, but I'm afraid you young ladies are in for a disappointment if you expect me to wear a long beard."

Behind their backs, Ella cast up her eyes, but I think she liked being included with me as a young lady. I have no more idea if his explanation for his name was true than I have for the accuracy of any of his strange irrelevancies. Leaving, he told us never to eat the liver of a polar bear, an eventuality possible only if one lived in the Arctic. The amount of vitamin A it contained was enough to poison us. Mrs. Cosway said, "You know so much, Selwyn!" and put up her face to be kissed.

On the way back to Lydstep Old Hall, Ella opened her heart to me. "I told Felix I'd come and see him this evening. After all, it's only eight. He said I could come if I liked and give the place a clean. He'd be in the pub. To be fair, I had offered to do some cleaning, it's in an awful state."

"Why can't he take you to the pub?"

"He says I'll cramp his style. But this doesn't upset me as much as you might think, Kerstin, because I know he's beginning to depend on me. And he talks about the future, about me being there. I mean, he says things like he may go away for Christmas and it'll be good to know I'll be there to keep an eye on the place. The same if he goes to Spain next summer, as he sometimes does. He sees me as a permanency, you see."

"I do see," I said, marveling at the man's effrontery and her acquiescence.

"I would love to stay the night sometimes. Women always want that when they're in love, don't they? Just to lie side by side with him all night would be so wonderful. He says no, he can't share a bed with anyone."

I had been invited to the Trintowels' for the following day. It was my weekend off, but in the circumstances everyone conveniently forgot this and I couldn't be bothered to remind them. I would take the next one instead when Mark would be back from his family wedding. I had much to tell him.

Going to White Lodge and spending the evening there showed me as perhaps nothing else could have what an ordinary English middle-class family was like by contrast with the Cosways. Not quite ordinary, of course, for the Trintowels' was a big house, though not half the size of Lydstep Old Hall; they were obviously well off and both parents professional people. But they had about them what the Cosways, for all their efforts, so conspicuously lacked, a country Englishness, so that they had flowers in their garden, heating in their house, comfortable furniture, a kitchen modernized since the 1920s, a sense of humor, friends, and good manners.

Mrs. Trintowel asked me to call her Jane. I did so and continued to do so up until her death thirteen years ago. She was warm and kindly without being effusive, a great talker and benevolent gossip, "a woman of a few words, a few hundred thousand words," as her elder son, my husband, used to say of her. She was also bossy, a trait which didn't show itself to me until later. Her warmth put me at my ease immediately. I am not shy, but at White Lodge I was not even diffident after the first few minutes. James's father made me laugh by saying as soon as we had shaken hands, "My wife is dying to hear all about the Cosways and so, I admit, am I," though it was the Trintowels who told me about them.

I had never realized—there was no reason why I should—the degree of curiosity with which the village regarded the occupants of Lydstep Old Hall or how bizarre the Windrosians found them. The Trintowels enlightened me. Everyone knew of the long love affair between Julia Cosway and Selwyn Lombard and vague threats were made ("he said she said he was going to report him") of alerting the General Medical Council to what was going on. Eventually Mrs. Cosway left Dr. Lombard's list and went to a doctor in Great Cornard, but the rest of the family remained in his care. The resemblance to him of the youngest child had not passed unnoticed, the unfortunate nose being the giveaway.

"Everyone knew, though no one talked about it much," Jane said, "for the child's sake."

Ida had been engaged. She broke things off when it was discovered the man had a criminal record.

"Robbery with violence and indecent assault, my dear."

I said it seemed a curious combination, which made Gerald Trintowel laugh.

"Julia Cosway found out. She put private detectives on to him; the man showed no outward sign of being anything but law-abiding. We met him, didn't we, Gerry? Can you believe it?"

I tried to be careful not to be indiscreet, always difficult with someone like Jane Trintowel. Reminding myself that these people were my employers and I lived among them, I thought I owed them some loyalty, at least not to disclose things I had seen and heard which could only be known by an insider and confidante. Perhaps I shouldn't even have listened. To avoid doing so in the company of these kind and hospitable people, about to give me dinner, was beyond me.

"Ella is rather sweet, I've always liked her. She has tried so desperately hard to get married, coming on strong with one man after another . . ."

"Come on, Ma," said James, "you can't possibly know that."

She ignored him. "And then it's Winifred who finally gets engaged. Eric Dawson is fearfully dull, but a parson ought to be dull, don't you think? He's nice as well. I hope they'll be happy."

"Kerstin is probably deeply embarrassed by you expecting her to betray her employers' secrets, you know." This was Gerald, shaking his head in half-hearted disapproval of his wife. "I've noticed if you haven't that she listens but doesn't say much."

"She's just not a talkative person, are you, Kerstin? I mean, who talks as much as I do?"

I had to speak then, or be set down as impossibly standoffish. "John," I said, "how about John?"

Both Trintowels had lived in Windrose only since the 1950s, but White Lodge had belonged to Gerald's parents and he had lived there as a child. He was older than John and remembered him as a small boy.

"He was the kind of child that everyone says they can't do anything with. Julia used to bring him and Ella down to the village, and if there was something he didn't want to do he'd lie on the ground and scream. He ran away too. Twice, I think. The first time he was found fast asleep in a barn. The second was more serious. He was gone for a couple of days, I think. He must have been about ten by then."

"Tell her what Julia said to your mother."

"She doesn't want to hear that, Jane. Repeating things like that is the worst kind of tittle-tattle."

"Well, if you won't tell her I will. Julia met Gerry's mother in Dr. Lombard's waiting room, of all places. She'd got Ella with her, come in for some injection or other. She was about six months pregnant with Zorah—wanted to let the doctor listen to his daughter's heartbeat, I daresay . . ."

"Oh, **Ma.**"

Jane took no notice of him. "Anyway, Gerry's mother asked her if there was any news of John and she said, 'I wouldn't care if he never came back, not with another one on the way. Good riddance.' "

"She didn't mean it, Jane. She was overwrought. The funny thing is that John seemed all right when he was a little kid. I remember Julia bringing him to the house for tea. Winifred too, she was a bit older. He was quiet and well-behaved, used to sit there with a picture book, but he'd eat a very hearty tea. Then he got ill with something. Whooping cough? Mumps? One of those and it was after that there was no doing anything with him."

As for Zorah, no one had much to say. Jane, of course, contributed what there was. She had been sent away to school when she was seven, was at boarding school for eleven years, then at university. Even in the holidays she seldom showed herself in the village or other people's houses.

"I'm sure Julia dreaded her being seen with Lombard and the resemblance picked up on, though everyone knew. John—her husband, I mean—he knew. He found out. Zorah had tonsillitis or something when she was six and Lombard came up to the Hall. John Cosway saw them together and that was enough. That was the reason Zorah was packed off to school."

"You can't possibly know that, Jane."

"Yes, I can. Your mother told me."

We had dinner—a very good dinner—and more Cosway talk was punctuated by James saying plaintively that he was planning to carry me off to his room to hear Kraus. This was my original reason for coming.

"Never mind that," his mother said, plying me with an autumn version of summer pudding and whipped cream. "She can take the records away and play them up at the House of Usher."

"I'm afraid I can't," I said, laughing. "They haven't a record player."

The extreme oddity of this was commented on at some length. I felt that on the whole I had managed to learn a lot without giving over-much into the temptation to talk about all the things I had seen, heard, and intuited and which they had no idea of. Then, dinner over and coffee refused on the grounds that it would keep me awake, I followed James upstairs to hear the first act of **Proserpin.**

It was later, as I was about to leave, given a lift home by Gerald Trintowel, that my eye was caught by the photograph among many on a hall table of a man in his twenties with bright eyes and a wry smile.

"Is that your brother?" I asked James.

"Yes, that's Charles. He'll be here for the weekend in a couple of weeks' time."

Hospital patients never come home on the day they think they will or the hospital says they will. It is always a day earlier or a day or two later. I would have supposed no hospital would like the bother of sending someone home on a Sunday, especially in those days when Sunday still meant something, when everything was closed and skeleton staffs were kept. It is just one of those mysteries, peculiarly associated with a clinical situation, another being why the food which surely should be more nutritious and "healthy" than in any other circumstances is so appalling, and why it is necessary—or was then—to make sick people wake up at six in the morning.

Expected on Monday, Mrs. Cosway was brought home on Sunday morning by Ella, who missed church to fetch her. She looked thin and seemed weak, her ankle in a cast and her wrist strapped up. One of the nurses had signed her name on the cast and drawn a smiling face next to the signature.

"I tried to stop her," Mrs. Cosway said, "but in my weakness I gave in. Stupid nonsense. I don't know what gets into people."

Ida was in a dilemma. Should she tell her mother John had refused the Largactil or remove the number he would have taken and say nothing? As it was, there were only twelve left in the bottle.

"I think I'll just not mention it," she said, putting five tablets into the wastebin. "She can just start again in the morning. She won't see much change in him, do you think?"

I could see a change. Ida simply found it easier not to do so. After his attack on her, and he had been provoked, there had been no more violence. But on the rare occasions John spoke his speech was clearer and the things he said more coherent. His rituals remained unchanged, the favored objects still set out on his bedside table by night and kept in his dressing-gown pocket by day, his food still arranged in patterns. Still, his walks obviously brought him some enjoyment; they were no longer the dogged tramping with head down and eyes fixed on the ground that they had been. Above all, I had noticed, if Ida had not, how much more alert he seemed, as if he was at last deriving energy from somewhere and leaving the zombie state behind.

Start again in the morning, as Ida had hoped, Mrs. Cosway could not. Her early rising, she said, was a thing of the past. I must supervise John's getting up and let her sleep. "One of the girls" would have to help her out of bed when the time came, get her on to her crutch, and help dress her. All this took a long time and John's breakfast was over and he settled in his armchair by the time she came down. Not that she had forgotten the tablet she regarded as essential he took.

"You will have to carry on giving it to him," she said to me, "or Ida will. I see we've only a week's supply in the bottle. Remind me to ask Selwyn for a prescription when he comes."

He was expected at ten when his morning office hours were at an end and he was punctual. I happened to open the door to him and he greeted me typically.

"How are you this morning, young lady?"

In expansive and jovial mood, he must have been looking forward to seeing his old love again, and she managed one of her rare smiles when he came into the drawing room. She lifted her face to him and he kissed her on the lips. If I had been the only other person present, I would have gone and left them alone together, but naturally John stayed and neither Ida nor Winifred showed any signs of going.

"I shall never walk properly again," Mrs. Cosway said. "It's only to be expected at my age. My left leg will be shorter than my right, I heard them muttering about that in the hospital, they thought I couldn't hear. I shall be left with a limp and heaven knows whether I shall ever be able to use my right hand again, I doubt it. There was a nerve twisted inside there, I'm sure of it."

Like Eric, Dr. Lombard was one of those men

who twinkle when in a good mood. He would purse up his mouth, open his eyes wide, and turn them this way and that to rather ferocious effect above his eagle's nose. "Let your words be sweet and tasty, Julia," he said, "for tomorrow you may have to eat them."

She smiled slightly at this. I think Dr. Lombard expected some sort of congratulation from one of the others on his wit but none was forthcoming. He went on to reassure Mrs. Cosway about her arm and her ankle, citing all sorts of cases he had known of people a decade older than she was who had recovered full function from worse injuries than hers and, in one instance, gained enhanced flexibility. These days she would have been expected to attend physiotherapy sessions, but if that was so then, it hadn't reached the cottage hospital.

Ida, always apparently greedy for more domestic tasks, went off to make coffee. I noticed she had failed to remind her mother about the prescription and I decided I wouldn't. We all listened to a recital of anecdotes from Mrs. Cosway of hospital dramas, capped by others even more improbable from Dr. Lombard, and then the coffee came. I understood soon afterward that there was to be no reminder from Ida as she got up and excused herself on the grounds of needing to make a meat pie for lunch.

Dr. Lombard told an irrelevant vignette, the one about spaghetti owing its origin to the noodles Marco Polo brought back from China, kissed Mrs.

Cosway, and said he would look in again on Wednesday—why do doctors, and no one else, say they will look in again? I went to the door with him, out of politeness.

"She's very frail," he said when out of earshot.

I nodded. There seemed nothing to say.

Halfway toward his car, he turned and said, "Those leaves will be falling soon. They should have cut that stuff back but if they had I daresay the house would have fallen down. You look skeptical, young lady, but I tell you it's all those millions of tendrils are holding the place up."

He got into his car and drove off. I never saw him again.

17

I WALKED INTO THE DRAWING ROOM AT ABOUT TEN on the Wednesday morning to find John wearing his glasses and with the newspaper held close up against his face.

"Would you find the big magnifying glass for me, Shashtin?" he said.

His diction was perfect, as was his pronunciation of my name. Excited because he wanted to read, because at last he wanted to do something, I rummaged through drawers full of rubbish other people would have discarded. There was no one about to ask and Ida wasn't interested. Eventually, I found the glass, a large heavy one, washed it under the kitchen tap, and brought it back to him. He experimented with holding it close against the print, then farther away, with his glasses on and without them, but no result seemed satisfactory and he flung glass and paper down in disappointment. Mrs. Cosway was brought in soon afterward by Winifred and settled in an armchair.

"Where's Dr. Lombard?" were her first words.

"He didn't say a time," I said, "only that he would come."

"He knows I'd expect him early. Do you all realize Zorah came last night? Not that she has been to see me. That would be too much to expect."

"She's awfully upset, Mother," Ida said. "She came down here on purpose to see you."

Using a very old-fashioned expression I had read in books but never before heard, Mrs. Cosway said, "You can tell that to the Marines."

John, who had been staring into his lap, lifted his head and turned his eyes on his mother. He said in a slow, deliberate voice, "I want to see a proper specialist. About the way my hands shake and I stumble when I walk. A specialist in London, a Harley Street man will be best."

Mrs. Cosway was astounded as well she might have been. She was silenced but only for a moment. "No, you don't, John. Dr. Lombard sees to all that."

John, naturally, ignored her. "My sight is worse. I need new glasses."

"Yes, well, we'll take you to the optician in Sudbury and you can have your eyes tested."

He held up his shaking hands. "I need an expert. I want you to tell the trust."

"All this is nonsense," Mrs. Cosway cried. "Who has put you up to this?" She looked at me, but I had done nothing, unless thought has power.

"They won't let you have it on the Health Service, you know. You'd have to pay."

"That's what I said. You must ask the trust to pay."

"No, John, it's not necessary."

I expected Ida or Winifred to intervene, but I should have known better. They said nothing.

"I'm going to get the money out of the trust."

"I've said no. The answer is no and that's all there is to it. One of the girls will drive you to see the optician."

John stood up. He turned his back, dropped to the floor, and lay flat on the carpet, making no sound at first, then starting to thrash about and shout. As he paused to draw breath the doorbell rang. Everyone thought, of course, that it must be Dr. Lombard.

"Thank God," said Mrs. Cosway, "that must be Selwyn at last."

I went to the door. It was Eric. He came in, looking grave, but his expression changed to incredulity when he heard John's yells.

"What on earth is that?"

"John. He's lying on the floor making that noise."

"Good heavens." Eric cleared his throat and put on an expression of immense seriousness. "I am the bearer of bad news. Oh, not to you, Kerstin."

"What is it?"

"Dr. Lombard passed away this morning. He had a heart attack during his office hours. An ambulance came and they took him to the hospital, but it was too late. His housekeeper came over to the rectory and told me. I'd better go in there and tell them."

"Break it gently to Mrs. Cosway," I said.

He had called her frail but she was alive and he was dead. The front door was still open. As I went to close it I noticed Zorah's Lotus on the driveway, half-hidden by Eric's modest Ford.

They all moved out of the drawing room, Mrs. Cosway hanging on to the arms of her two daughters, leaving John to thrash and scream. But the noise he was making lessened, and when I went back in there about twenty minutes later he was in the fetal position, his fingers covering his eyes. That was the most distressing sight of him I had ever had, though not would ever have.

Mrs. Cosway had taken the news with the calm of utter shock. Winifred and Ida, it was easy to see, had no idea how to cope with her. It would have been different if this had been some close relative who had died. The death of an old lover, even the great love of her life, as I suppose she saw him, could hardly be treated as a legitimate and honorable cause of grief. Embarrassment must be associated with it. The pretense must be kept up that this was just a family friend who would be missed but whose passing would certainly not cause any profound sorrow.

"In the midst of life we are in death," said Winifred who, as befitted a clergyman's betrothed, had begun introducing biblical snippets into conversation. "He'd had his allotted span, his threescore years and ten. Four or five years more, actually."

"And man is born to trouble as the sparks fly upward," said Zorah, coming into the room. "Has anyone else a wise saw to contribute? May I know who is dead?"

The recollection of what Selwyn Lombard had been to Zorah, and that owing to this peculiar circumstance she ought to be told at once, must have come into everyone's mind simultaneously, with the exception, that is, of Eric's. Innocently he looked around at our embarrassed faces and said, "Unfortunately, Dr. Lombard passed away this morning."

Zorah approached him, staring into his face. "You mean he's dropped off his perch at last?"

An awful silence answered her.

"Well, good riddance," she said. "Let me know where they're burying him and I'll come and dance on his grave."

This last word was cut off by Mrs. Cosway's scream. She made the same sounds as her son, shouting wordlessly, her head thrown back, her feet drumming on the floor, the plaster making muffled bangs as it struck the carpet. Zorah left the room, looking pleased with herself. A point had been reached when I felt I had had enough. This was the first occasion on which I thought I could no longer stand it. I must find Ida and tell her to forget about my undertaking to stay a year. I had had enough and must go. I could no longer stand this family—dysfunctional before the word was invented.

The thought that if I left I would have to separate myself from Mark and go back to Sweden stopped me. I went back into the drawing room. John had got up off the floor and gone, or so it appeared until I looked around, shifted the sofa, and found him hunched up behind it like a fugitive or a frightened child.

A lover has no status. Mrs. Cosway was regarded by Dr. Lombard's middle-aged children and teenage grandchildren as no more than a friend and erstwhile patient. Still, I am sure she would have gone to the funeral if she had been able-bodied. Alone of the Cosway family, Winifred attended. But there was nothing unusual in this. Since becoming engaged to Eric, who of course conducted the services, she had taken it upon herself to attend every funeral, though there had only been four since the ring was on her finger. Mrs. Cosway waited at home, anxious to hear all about it the moment Winifred returned. Who was there? Did she speak to his son and daughter? What about the flowers, the address, and the tributes? The funeral was timed for two in the afternoon and Winifred might reasonably be expected back by three-thirty, but when John and I returned from our walk she was still not home. Mrs. Cosway may have rested but not slept.

There was nothing unusual in her wearing mourning. She had always dressed in black, but now it seemed deeper and more like widow's weeds, due perhaps to the addition of a long black scarf or stole she had rooted out from somewhere. By contrast Zorah, who occasionally appeared downstairs to make some cheerful or optimistic remark, dressed herself up in fashion-model clothes, quite unsuitable for the country. She had had a party up in her "apartment" to which about a dozen smart-looking people turned up in cars. One was a Rolls whose driver sat out there at the wheel, smoking and reading magazines until his employer came out at midnight. I was invited, but only Ella of family members. She went, though I didn't, and had a bad hangover next day which luckily for her was a Saturday. She told me the party was to celebrate Dr. Lombard's death. I doubt if most of the guests knew this or cared.

What Mrs. Cosway thought about it I have no idea. She spoke to me very little at that time. We sat in silence together with John, waiting for

Winifred to come back. Four o'clock went by and five. Ida got tea and Ella came home.

"I couldn't eat a thing," Mrs. Cosway said. "I suppose Eric will bring her back."

Ella had been fidgety and nervous ever since she was told what her mother was waiting for. This remark of hers was obviously expecting the answer yes, but that was not what she got from Ida, the only one of us who appeared to know.

"No, he can't. She told me he was going straight to his appointment with the Archdeacon after the funeral."

As we all moved into the dining room for tea, Mrs. Cosway limping along with the aid of her crutch and Ida's arm, Ella pulled me aside into a doorway.

"She's with Felix."

I must have stared at her.

"I tell you, she's with Felix. She'll have gone to him as soon as the funeral was over. Eric would be out of the way, you see. She says they're just friends, but is it likely? I don't think Felix could be just friends with any woman under seventy."

She spoke with such extreme bitterness that it had brought the color fiercely into her face.

"We'd better go and have tea," I said.

Winifred came in at twenty to six.

"You've been so long," said Mrs. Cosway, "it has nearly killed me. You've been hours and hours."

"Serena Lombard invited me back to the house, so of course I couldn't say no. I can't imagine why you were so worried."

"Mother wasn't worried about you," said Ella. "It's just so thoughtless partying with these people when Mother was waiting for you to tell her about the service."

"Partying, indeed! I had a cup of tea and a piece of fruit cake."

She sat down next to Mrs. Cosway and began telling her about flowers and hymns and tributes to Dr. Lombard. Could it be true, this story about her and Felix Dunsford? I thought about the postponed wedding and the rectory sign but still disbelieved what Ella had told me. Her affair with him was still going on and more passionately, if what she said was true. Yet he hadn't gone with her to Zorah's party, though invited at her special request. I could see that he was willing to do nothing which might show him to the world as Ella's accredited lover, a man she could with reason have called her boyfriend, but that was not to say he was making love to Winifred as well.

She was older than Ella and though basically better-looking, had something churchy in her appearance, some suggestion that her proper sphere was behind a stall at a bring-and-buy sale. The dowdiness of her clothes contributed to this as did, oddly enough, the thick makeup she wore, all of which gave her the air of a Sunday school teacher sprucing herself up to visit a rich London relative. But was it possible Felix saw the fine features under the powder and lipstick and, come to that, the voluptuous shape under the floral dresses and jersey suits? Perhaps he found something titillating in the idea of breaking down her goody-two-shoes manner. And what of Eric? Winifred wanted to be married as much as Ella did and was far nearer to her goal. Would she give it up for an adventure with Felix? On the whole, I thought not.

It was my weekend in London and I was looking forward to being with Mark again. That morning, before catching the train to London, I went into the village to shop for the weekend. This was usually one of Ida's many jobs, but currently she had so much more to do than usual, her mother still needing to be helped everywhere she went after the wearisome business of getting her up, washed, and dressed. Bags would be heavy to carry so she made me take Mrs. Cosway's old shopping trolley, a kind of basket on wheels made of a tartan waterproof material.

It was this contraption which prompted Felix's remarks when he met me pushing it across the Memorial Green.

"A beautiful girl like you shouldn't be seen with an old lady's pushcart."

"Don't look then," I said.

"But seriously, Kerstin, what's the idea?"

"Seriously, Mr. Dunsford, I don't want to carry two heavy bags of groceries up the hill."

"Felix. Now, if you'll come into The Studio and have a glass of something with me I will carry your bags up the hill and we can chuck that monstrosity on the village dump."

There was no village dump, as far as I knew. I said no, thank you, I hadn't time, and he said to make time, and we argued amicably enough along these lines, walking along together by then, inevitably in the direction of The Studio because it was also in the direction of the butcher and the greengrocer.

"Are you scared of what might happen?" he asked me.

"Why? What might happen?"

Instead of answering he said, "So you don't mind wasting your youth doing household chores? Come on, we're at the door. You know you want to. You're too young to resist, aren't you, Miss Kvist?"

His effrontery, his vanity, made me rude. "You're too old to persuade me, Mr. Dunsford," I said.

I was rewarded by a look of fury, which pleased me, but something miserable too which didn't. I knew I had just made an enemy but cared not at all for that and walked away from him into the greengrocer's. I might reasonably have given him that joke response, "You say that to all the girls," if I even knew it at that time, for it seemed clear to me that he tried to make love to any woman of a fair standard of attractiveness. Why not Winifred? But would she?

Back at Lydstep, an argument had begun again about John's physical condition, Mrs. Cosway continuing to refuse his request to ask the trust for money for a specialist and Ida and Winifred backing her up.

"I shall ask Zorah," he said. "Zorah will help me."

Mrs. Cosway seemed more shattered by his using so long and so reasonable a sentence than by its content. She turned on Ida, speaking as if he was somewhere else.

"What's happened to him that he's talking like this? He wasn't like this when I went to the hospital." A thought struck her, though not apparently the one Ida dreaded. "We must be running out of his tranquilizer. Have we run out?"

"Almost," Ida said.

Could there be a greater irony than this woman lamenting the fact that her psychotic son's condition was improving? "You'll have to get another prescription from—yes, Selwyn's partner."

She grew silent, hanging her head. Those words had perhaps brought back memories of Dr. Lombard. On the other hand, I believe these were never far from her mind, she thought about him and remembered him all the time. It was more likely that she had just realized the possible difficulties that lay ahead.

"How many tablets are there left?"

Ida could answer this question truthfully because she had given John no more since he struck her and by then that was ten days before.

"Seven."

"As many as that? Are you sure?"

"I can show you, Mother."

"No, I'll take your word for it, but I would have thought there were fewer."

In a week's time someone would have to go to Dr. Lombard's partner, a young man with, I had been told, progressive ideas, and ask for a prescription for Largactil. We shall see, I thought, and went to catch the train for London.

18

I DON'T KNOW IF IT WAS THE LARGACTIL WHICH damaged John Cosway's sight or if it had just deteriorated as he approached his forties, as it sometimes can. He already had glasses for reading, and if they were inadequate for the purpose this may only have been because they were the same pair as he had had five years before and he simply needed his eyes tested again. I don't know.

I half-guessed what was wrong with him, though my conjecture was full of doubts, not least the one about my own inadequacy at making any sort of diagnosis. I had no qualifications except an English degree and my humble nursing diploma. How would I know from reading medical books without direction or supervision? Perhaps it was a case of telling myself, "I always knew that's what it was," rather than feeling a quiet satisfaction when the specialist gave the verdict which confirmed my guesswork.

Everyone knows about autism now. Everyone has heard of it. Hardly a week goes by without some article about it in a newspaper. Not then, though it had been described and named twenty-five years before. A society for sufferers and their parents was in existence. But it was not accepted as a legitimate disturbance of the psyche with a probable physical cause. The word wasn't in the **Oxford Dictionary** and most people, if told it, would have had no idea what it meant. Doctors—Lombard had been one of them—called it "childhood schizophrenia" and attributed it, as he had done, to emotional trauma.

It is thought autism can result from childhood infectious diseases. And one theory might be that John, who was very ill with mumps when he was a child, developed his at that time. Maybe and maybe not. Boys are affected more than girls. A Swedish study of Asperger's, the type I believe John had, found a ratio of four boys to one girl, and it is harder to detect in women, perhaps because their social instincts are stronger than men's. Asperger himself, whose syndrome is less severe than Kanner's, suggested that his might be the extreme end of the continuum of the normal male personality, a startling claim. It implies that men with an excessive degree of maleness would be, or are, selfish, lacking emotion, taking what they want when they want it, knowing no altruism, tactless and blunt, and liable to rages when they fail to get their own way. A conundrum for some Ph.D. seeker? Or a wild exaggeration?

Such people speak little or not at all. They lack

social skills, appear to be without affection, are restless, and are often destructive, compulsive, and routine-driven. Some will lie on the floor and scream when frustrated. Egocentric, they have no idea that other people have thoughts or feelings. If one of the definitions of the schizophrenic is to be unreasonable, the Asperger subject can be said to be too reasonable. He never lies but utters what he thinks and feels without tact or appropriateness, does what he chooses and runs away from what he dislikes.

I read about Asperger's in a scientific journal I came upon among other medical literature in the library—yes, **the** library, the labyrinth at Lydstep Old Hall. They were not very old, these journals. Someone must have put them there. John himself before Lombard and Mrs. Cosway went to work on him? It was more likely to be Zorah, attempting to discover for herself what was wrong with her brother, but when she saw his decline, giving up in despair.

When John said he would ask Zorah, I had assumed he meant to ask her for the money which consulting a psychiatrist or specialist in diseases of the central nervous system would cost. She was rich. A consultation would only be the beginning, there might be second opinions sought, surgery carried out and hospitalization. But Zorah was rich and could afford it almost without noticing the amount. However, that was not what he meant. A few days after I got back, while John was having his tea in the kitchen with Ida, Zorah walked into the drawing room and said that she intended to inform the trust that John wanted to see "a top man about his tremors and his unsteady movements."

"I know just the man," she said. Zorah always knew everyone. "He helped a friend of mine who had Parkinson's. It was almost miraculous. When the time comes I shall drive John to London myself."

"Then you can pay for it," said Mrs. Cosway.

"Now wait a minute. Your husband set up the trust for just that purpose, to take care of John." It was a shock to hear her refer to John's father like that, reminding us all that he was no relation of hers. "He could hardly have foreseen that you and that lover of yours would conspire to make a zombie out of John. He couldn't tell you'd fix things so that he was an imbecile with no use for money. Well, he has a use for money now and I'm going to see he gets it. From its proper source. From the money he has a right to."

Mrs. Cosway addressed the ceiling to which she cast up her eyes. "I would never have believed my own child could speak to me like that."

Whatever it did to Mrs. Cosway, using such terms to her mother must have taken it out of Zorah. I had thought her tough and invulnerable, a woman of iron, but I had misassessed her, for she had gone paper-white and I noticed that her long and elegant hands, which hung down by her sides, were shaking the way John's still did sometimes. She turned without another word and went back upstairs. There she must have done what packing was needful, very little I imagine, and gone straight out, for I heard her say to Winifred in the hall that she was off to London and might be away for several weeks. But there she would remember what she had said, as her first act when she reached her house would be to write to the trust.

The Lotus had hardly disappeared down the drive when Ella, who had slipped out of the drawing room when Zorah came in, reappeared, triumphantly holding up the geode in both hands. Coming down to make her announcement, Zorah must have been, as I had supposed, in quite a state, keyed up to an unusual defiance, and had forgotten to lock her door. How Ella guessed she would I had no idea unless she checked every time her sister appeared downstairs. This possibility brought me a feeling of powerful distaste. I had preferred Ella to anyone else in that household and sympathized with her over Felix, but the idea that she might study and plan in this way to outwit Zorah chilled me. I watched with a revulsion I tried to disguise as she pranced across the room, the geode held aloft like a trophy, and finally set it down on the table where it had once been a permanency. I had lost count of the number of times that lump of rock had been carried downstairs, taken up again, and brought down once more. Ella let out a prolonged peal of Cosway laughter.

"How about that?" she said. "Never say I don't have your interests at heart, Mother."

Mrs. Cosway said nothing. She made a sour face, signifying disapproval or mild congratulation. It was hard to say. Zorah's declaration had turned the latest capturing of the geode into an anticlimax.

"I've got the harp too but I'll need someone to help me downstairs with it." Ella turned to me. "Kerstin? Come and help me and then we'll have a drink."

"Kerstin has to get John to bed," said Mrs. Cosway.

"Not yet, surely? I thought he was going to bed later these days? He isn't tired at seven, Mother. He's not a baby."

It was true that since Mrs. Cosway's accident John's bedtime had subtly moved toward half-past seven, towards eight, then nine. It was all part of his slow improvement, his gradual progress toward becoming a human being.

"Everything I say is overruled these days," said Mrs. Cosway. "It has happened since I fell downstairs. Who would have thought an accident happening through no fault of one's own would change a whole family's attitude toward one? Who would have thought my children would decide to turn me into a senile old woman with softening of the brain?"

"Don't be absurd, Mother." This was Winifred who had been fidgeting about for the past half-hour, looking at her watch and apparently listening for something she might miss if she failed to concentrate.

"No one thinks that I have been bereaved. If one of you had died I should receive boundless sympathy." Mrs. Cosway looked her daughters up and down as if such sympathy would have been misplaced. "But the fact that I've lost the only man I ever loved means nothing to any of you."

Winifred pulled her soon-to-be-rector's-spouse face. "You shouldn't talk about it. You should keep it to yourself. It's not—not seemly."

"What would you know? You and that fiancé of yours. Now there **is** an old woman."

It has always struck me as strange that the people who make this remark are usually old women themselves. What Winifred might have said in reply was never uttered. The phone began to ring in the dining room. It first made her jump, then run out of the room, calling, "I'll get it, I'll get it," as she went.

I went upstairs with Ella, who was carrying a bucket of ice she had fetched from the kitchen. Into this went a bottle of her favorite rosé, cooling while she broke a large bar of fruit-and-nut milk chocolate into squares, a curious choice to go with wine. We lugged the heavy gilded harp downstairs but left it in the hall, where it brightened things up a good deal. Back in her bedroom, the dolls in their fashionable clothes seemed to be staring at us, possibly warning us, to judge by their stick-thin figures, of the dangers of consuming chocolate. I had half forgotten how feminine the room was, how many yards of frills it contained, how many ribbons and artificial flowers. The nightdress case on the bed, a pale blue satin heart with pink and white appliqué roses, I was sure I had never seen before.

Ella poured us each a glass of wine. "I'm thinking of getting sloshed this evening. Now don't look like that, it's not something I make a habit of. But Felix is meeting an old schoolfriend in Colchester, so we can't see each other." She took a big gulp of her wine. "That's better. Isn't Mother impossible sometimes? And Zorah! I don't know what you must think of us." Correctly receiving my smile as meaning my thoughts could be of no consequence, she changed tack entirely. "I don't think I ever told you how I came to dress the dolls, did I?"

"No, you never did."

"Well, I thought those peasant dresses they were in were too impossibly old-hat—sorry about the pun—for words, but it took a bit of a nerve stripping them off." She giggled. "Everyone knows everything that goes on in this house, you see—well, you **must** know—and I thought Mother would make a frightful fuss, but I was all prepared to say to her, no one wears those clothes anymore, not in the countries they come from they don't. I started making the clothes for them. I copied them from pictures in magazines. I spent a fortune on **Vogue,** you wouldn't believe. And when they were all done I was really proud of them. Winifred came in here and so did Mother and, would you believe it, **they never noticed a thing.**"

I laughed appropriately, asked her because it seemed a question she would like, how she was getting on with making her bridesmaid's dress.

Her face clouded. "I haven't even got the material yet and the wedding's in about eight weeks. Of course I can do it in that time, but Winifred hasn't made up her mind about the color. And I'm doing June Prothero's too, you know."

Having no idea how long it would take to make a dress, a task beyond the skills of anyone I knew, I couldn't offer an opinion. She refilled her glass, admonished me for drinking so slowly, and said, "I have to tell you something. I don't think Felix is the marrying kind. You'll say that doesn't matter so long as he loves me."

I was tired of denying these comments attributed to me. "I suppose it may matter to you," I said.

"Do have some more wine. I'm on my third glass. As for mattering, I tell myself love's better without marriage, it lasts longer. Look at Mother and Dr. Lombard. I mean, that was immoral and cruel to Dad and a scandal and everything, but it **was** love and it **did** last."

An interesting sidelight on sex education, I thought, when a mother teaches her daughter to prefer illicit love to marriage and teaches her by her own example.

"I really do love him, Kerstin. He's 'the very eyes of me' like that poem, I don't know who wrote it. I adore him."

And I could see she did, her pretty face held up to the light, flushed rose with the rosé, a look in her eyes of yearning and need. Then she said, leaving the subject completely, "I've been meaning to tell you something ever since this improvement to John. You know the way they're always talking about this mental trouble of his starting with an emotional shock? Well, they haven't told you what the emotional shock was, have they?"

I agreed that they hadn't.

"When he was a little boy he wandered into Mother's bedroom in the middle of the afternoon. She thought he was asleep. But he wasn't and what he saw was her and Dr. Lombard in bed together. How about that for the primal scene?"

Though I tried to look suitably impressed, I didn't believe that what John had seen would have had much effect on him. Autism, they were saying even then, always had a physical cause.

"Ida told me. John went running to his big

sister—that's how she put it—and told her what he'd seen. She said she didn't believe him but she did later on. I don't know if Mother knew—I mean, if she saw John—but I'm sure Lombard didn't or he wouldn't have gone on talking about emotional shocks. He'd have kept quiet on that one."

I left her to the rest of the wine. John and Mrs. Cosway were alone in the drawing room. She seemed to be asleep, lying on the sofa with the leg cast propped up on one of the arms. If I had not known such behavior was impossible for John, I would have thought his determined attempts to read the telephone directory purposely staged to annoy his mother, and also perhaps to hasten a consultation with a specialist. But Asperger's people never behave like this, they have no involvement with others' emotions, and although I then had no name for his condition, I knew its manifestations. John tried to read because, after his long drug-induced stupor, he was waking up to a desire for knowledge and a need to use his failing sight. His mother came into it not at all. As far as he was concerned, she was there as we all were, because we were there. Like the furniture but inferior to the Roman vase.

"Time for bed, John," I said.

He looked up at me. "No," he said.

I thought this would be sure to wake Mrs. Cosway, but she slept on. I doubted that I could encourage John to get up by any words and certainly not by any physical move. Touching him was always out of the question. He laid down the paper and said, "Library."

Why attempt to stop him? It seemed to me that the more alert he became, the more "normal," the better things would be for everyone. I went with him to the dining room to find the key, daringly showing him where it was kept, then to the library, where I left him, searching out those mathematics and science books which had once been a source of pleasure to him. Somehow I knew the intricacies of the library plan would hold no mystery for him. He would be able to find his way to its center and back blindfold. And if he threw books on the floor and replaced the Bible in Longinus's hands with some work from the classics? Wait till it actually happens, I thought.

Returning to the drawing room, I met Winifred coming down the stairs into the hall. She stopped at the foot, stared at the harp's golden shimmer in its dark corner, and smiled. My first thought was that I had never seen her look so nice. She had used a lighter hand than usual with the makeup, her hair was clean and shining, and, instead of a floral dress and cardigan, she had put on trousers and a new blue sweater. This was not the way she dressed for Eric and church business. She put her head around the drawing-room door but Mrs. Cosway was evidently still asleep, for she withdrew it quickly.

"Tell Mother I've gone out, will you, Kerstin? I'm going to take the car—no, on second thought, better not. I'll walk."

For some reason this made her laugh rather hysterically. She took a coat out of the hall cupboard, huddled herself into it, and started to walk. A powerful draft came into the house with the opening and closing of the front door. It was November and growing cold, the only heating provided at Lydstep Old Hall coming from an open fire in the drawing room. I had gone back there to put on more logs when Ella appeared. She stood in the doorway.

"Your mother's asleep," I said.

"Come out here."

She had drunk the best part of a bottle of wine and she was unsteady on her feet. "Where has Winifred gone?"

"She didn't say," I said.

"I saw her go. I thought she'd take the car, but I know why she didn't. She didn't want it to be seen outside The Studio."

It took me a moment or two to understand her. "What do you mean, Ella?"

"She's gone to Felix."

"I'm sure you're wrong. You said he was meeting a friend in Colchester."

"**He** said he was. He'll tell any lie. Oh, what shall I do?" She threw herself into my arms and began to cry. "What shall I do? What will become of me? I love him so, I wish I'd never met him, I don't know what to do."

I still thought it more likely Winifred was with Eric or at some church meeting. Then I remembered the trousers. She would never go to anything connected with the church in trousers.

"Ella, if you're right," I said, "it only means she's gone to get him to do some work for her. Paint a sign or something. Be reasonable, she's getting married to Eric in two months' time." I spoke my thought aloud. "What could he see in her? Aren't that churchy look and manner very off-putting?"

"You're wrong there," Ella said with extreme bitterness. "He'd see that as a challenge. That would be something for him to break down and overcome. It would excite him—it has to be that. What else has she got, for God's sake?"

Impossible to answer her. The more she said the more I began to see she might be right. "I've started biting my nails again," she said. "I'm going back to my room and I'm going to open another bottle and drink it **all.** It will stupefy me and I'll feel like hell tomorrow but I don't care!"

It was very dark by then, lights on everywhere in the house but still not making it light enough. The air held an icy chill. A powerful scent of roasting meat came from Ida's kitchen. In the drawing room Mrs. Cosway was waking up, concentrating, as she had to, on moving her cramped fingers and swinging her injured leg and foot down on to the carpet.

I gave her the crutch and my arm and we made our slow way into the dining room, where Ida had switched on a tiny electric heater. It was windy and leaves fluttered down outside the window, one of them, soaked by intermittent rain, pasting itself flat against the glass like a forbidding hand.

"Where are my other daughters?"

"Winifred said to tell you she's gone out, Ella is upstairs." I made what is called an intelligent guess. "She doesn't want any dinner. Zorah . . ."

"I know where Zorah is, thank you." Mrs. Cosway picked up her soup spoon. "This is the time of day when I most miss Selwyn, though oddly enough, I seldom saw him in the evening of late. I am bereft without him."

"Oh, Mother," said Ida.

"Oh, Mother, nothing. What do you know?"

The rest of the meal was eaten in silence, broken occasionally by Ida's small-talk. It had been very cold that day, was there a chance of a white Christmas, there were still a number of potential guests who had not yet replied to Winifred's wedding invitations. Mrs. Cosway said nothing. Without waiting for dessert (which she called "pudding" even if it was fruit salad), she held her arm up to me to be helped from the room. In the drawing room she sat in front of the television, unseeing and unhearing I am sure, for she can't have been interested in a pop concert.

A log fell off the fire and rolled a little way across

the glazed tiles. Ida said, "We need a fender," and came back into the room with a kind of metal wall, about six inches high and shaped like an E without the central bar. This she put around the tiles. It was the wrong size and its color clashed with the brown glaze, but the Cosways never worried much about things like that.

Ella never reappeared that evening and Winifred had not returned by ten-thirty, the time I thought of going upstairs to the diary. It was then, noticing the light on at the end of the passage where the library was, that I realized we had forgotten all about John. That is, I had, for Mrs. Cosway and Ida no doubt thought I had put him to bed hours before. I found him in the library fast asleep over a book of square roots, the magnifying glass fallen out of his fingers on to the floor. I would have to wake him, get him into his bedroom, and face Mrs. Cosway's anger. That was something I hadn't cared about when first I came, but now the thought of it cowed me a little. I spoke to John, trying in vain to wake him; and telling myself that I could always leave, I was not obliged to stay in this uncongenial house, I left him to sleep among his books.

The wind had become a gale by morning, ripping the dark red burnt-looking leaves off the creeper and whirling them in a wild dance before letting them drop to the ground. By this time they were sparse on the house and lying in heaps across the flowerbeds, each leaf much bigger than I had supposed when I first saw them, some of them as large as plates but shaped like those on a grape vine. Stripped off, they left behind a network of tendrils, thousand upon thousand of them, like the web of a giant spider, which veiled without hiding the brickwork. And this was not red or brown as I had supposed, but composed of those bricks called "white" which are really a light yellowish-gray and come from over the border in Suffolk. Small decorative tiles in red and black above the windows and around the porch also emerged with the falling of the leaves, and the house which I had thought must be ugly without its covering appeared rather handsome.

Ella felt too ill to eat breakfast. She had done as she threatened and had that second bottle. She drank black coffee standing up in the kitchen, moaning softly, before leaving in the car for school. Winifred was looking beautiful. Felix Dunsford seemed to have that effect on women, at least when he began with them. Later on he made them ill. But I was still disbelieving. She might look like that, smile like that, and have such happy laughing eyes because she had had a good night's sleep or received a bold compliment from Eric.

Ida I thought the quietest of the sisters and the least characterful. She was a housewife without being a wife, one of those country housewives of the time who were still living in a domestic setting of twenty years before, house-cleaning a religion, literally so, for she never went to church. She cooked, she swept and dusted, washed and shopped, with a martyred look sometimes but without verbal complaint. I never saw her read a book or even look at the newspaper. Television she would watch but in a dull, preoccupied way, and since she could never sit still for even half an hour, she would be up and off to the kitchen every few minutes to make tea or stoke the boiler or turn on the oven. While sitting down she was usually sewing something or knitting. She was the first to get up in the morning and, as far as I knew, the last to go to bed at night. It wouldn't have surprised me to have found out that she got up several times in the night and came downstairs to check she hadn't left the gas on or a tap dripping.

Angry I would have said she could never be, any more than ecstatic or grief-stricken, but she was angry when she came home from Dr. Barker without the prescription she had been to ask for. Indignant perhaps describes her reaction better, for she neither became excited nor ranted. With a glance at John, who had come out of the library sometime in the small hours, she helped Mrs. Cosway out of earshot into the dining room, whispering to me to come too.

"He wouldn't let me have it. I told him Dr. Lombard had been prescribing Largactil as a matter of course and do you know what he said? 'Well, he was wrong there,' he said."

"I have never heard a medical man criticize another medical man," said Mrs. Cosway, who had overheard in spite of Ida's efforts. "How dared he find fault with Selwyn?"

"I was—well, taken aback. I felt really cross but what could I do? Dr. Barker wanted to know if John was violent or—well, noisy, and I had to say he wasn't." She didn't say if she had told him about the blow John struck her when she had provoked him.

"He will be without his medicine."

Ida must have known differently, but saying so would have revealed that several weeks had passed without the Largactil being given. "He said he would write a letter to some psychiatrist—I don't remember the name—and I was to make an appointment for John to see this man and take the letter." So Dr. Barker was prescribing just what John and Zorah wanted, I thought. "The psychiatrist was the right person to decide what treatment John should have," she said. "Dr. Barker said he wouldn't be responsible for prescribing a powerful drug like chlorpro—oh, I can't pronounce it—to someone he hadn't even seen. I was very angry, but what could I do?"

"I suppose I shall have to go and see him," said Mrs. Cosway. "We can't be expected to live here with a mad person who's not restrained in any way."

This was her own son she was speaking of, and I suppose my shock showed in my face.

"You needn't look like that, Kerstin. You have no idea what life would be like with him, absolute hell. Oh, why did Selwyn have to die? I need him so."

"Don't, Mother," said Ida.

"I shall go down to see him myself. Kerstin can drive me." She looked sourly at me. "I suppose you can drive?"

"I can drive," I said.

"Sometimes I think my whole world is falling apart. The only man I ever loved is dead. My mad son is going to spend thousands of his father's money on unnecessary treatment while he's denied the drug which is really necessary by a jumped-up, officious little general practitioner. I wonder if things could be worse."

Unusually talkative, Ida said to me in the kitchen that she wouldn't mind things being worse so long as they were different. I looked at her in consternation. Complaining about her lot was rare with her, even rarer any sign on her part that she found her dreary routine at Lydstep burdensome.

"Sometimes I think I'd do anything for a change," she said.

19

One of the first cartoons I ever did shows the Prime Minister of the day, a very unpopular politician, standing on the balcony of Buckingham Palace while an anti-government demonstration goes past, and saying to the Queen, "Why do they hate me so, ma'am? I never did them any good."

This of course is an old joke—of Jewish origin, I think. It isn't really funny. It appeals because it ought to be a flagrant untruth, but when people think about it and its implications, they know it's sound. John had never done his mother or his sisters any good, had done nothing to them, good or bad, but I think they all disliked him deeply. Felix did nothing but harm to Ella and Winifred and they both loved him.

In a rare moment of openness, Ida told me her mother had purposely infected John with mumps when he was five years old. Two children in the Prothero family, June and her brother, had the disease and Mrs. Cosway invited herself, Winifred, and John to tea. She knew, having read somewhere or been told so by Dr. Lombard, that a boy should have mumps early in his life because if he gets it when he is in his teens the effects of it may be to make him sterile. She meant well.

He was very ill. I don't know why Ida told me about it unless it was to show that good intentions can be misplaced.

"She had his welfare at heart," she said. "She meant to do the best for him. And she had to pay the price, of course, nursing him for week after week. He was a dreadful patient. I was fourteen and I remember it well. There weren't any long-term effects, though."

Weren't there? I don't know. As I mentioned before, medical opinion now is that autism results from some physical cause. Mrs. Cosway had no idea of this. More to the point, Lombard had none either or refused to accept it. Whatever Ella said, I believe Mrs. Cosway knew that John had been in her bedroom and knew what he had seen. The irony was that she secretly blamed this for his disability while exonerating herself for manufacturing the true cause. She was guilty where she had no need to be and guiltless where she had been dreadfully at fault. But I don't know and I never shall.

Geodes were seldom seen at that time except as exhibits in geology museums, but only a few years later they had become almost requisite furnishings of shops selling alternative remedies and beauticians' salons offering distillations of flowers picked at certain phases of the moon. The Cosways' geode fascinated me when I first came to Lydstep Old Hall, partly by its size but much more by the lavishness, the brilliance, and the color of the amethysts encrusted inside its wide-open mouth. I suppose they were only amethyst quartz but they were of such a rich violet that they looked to me like the precious stone itself.

Once I had seen the Roman vase, the geode became for me what it had really always been, a lump of rock with a curious kind of purple lining. The mountain regions of Africa and Asia were rich in such things. But the Roman vase, or jug as I suppose it should be called as it had a lip and a handle, was not only a man-made thing of great beauty but almost infinitely precious, a priceless object almost two thousand years old.

The glass of which it was made was a cloudy green, the color of pale jade, but stained with a darker shade, so that its surface was like a map of islands, large and small, on some unknown sea. Its base was the same deep green as were its mouth and its handle, this being twisted like a rope. Precious as it was and made of a vulnerable material, it hadn't a fragile look but seemed solid—confident, if an inanimate object can be so. I valued it so much more, I thought, than its owners did (with the exception of John) because I marveled at the miracle of its survival over those long centuries.

I still have a fragment of it which I keep in a little jeweler's box in my bedroom. Its edges are razor-sharp. There is no doubt I shouldn't have it, for when I found it under a corner of the drawing-room carpet I should have sent it at once to join the hundred or so other pieces of green glass, though there was no question of the vase being repaired. It was far beyond that.

The two sisters were barely on speaking terms that weekend. Ella had confronted Winifred with accusations that she was trying to take Felix away from her, to which Winifred responded by telling her she was making a fool of herself. After that they passed in the house without a word and studiously avoided speaking to each other at table, Winifred wearing a smug expression and Ella made ugly with resentment. On the Sunday evening Eric came up to Lydstep Old Hall, bringing Felix with him.

John was there when they arrived. It was seven-thirty, but he was there. No longer stupefied with drugs, he was beginning to do as he liked and do it after the fashion of high-functioning autistics, that is without regard for the feelings or wishes of others. I inwardly applauded him. When Eric came into the drawing room with Felix, John was sitting in his usual armchair, and being John, he neither got up nor extended his hand but looked at them and said to Felix, "Who are you?"

It was the first time I had seen Felix taken aback.

To be fair to him, he had never seen John before, very likely had no knowledge of him—both sisters were good at pretending he didn't exist—and was surprised to see him there. "Hello," he said. "I'm Felix. Felix Dunsford."

"Dunsford," said John and repeated it. "Sounds like a place in the Midlands."

Mrs. Cosway was still a long way from learning what had happened and what the future might hold. "Time for bed, John," she said.

He ignored her. It was plain to the rest of us that he meant to stay up for dinner. Ida brought drinks, but in this John had no interest. He moved ahead of everyone into the dining room and when the rest of us eventually went in, there he was sitting at the table examining cutlery as if he had never seen any of it before.

I could almost admire Felix's skill at being in Ella's company without giving the slightest sign that they were more to each other than acquaintances. And I don't mean he did this, as secret lovers famously do, by a studied indifference and off-handedness. He behaved exactly as he would have done if she were the future sister-in-law of his friend and they had met two or three times. He was pleasant to her, easy, he even gave a hint of perfectly proper flirtatiousness. I couldn't fault him, but I could tell his expertise came from long practice. Or he might be rehearsing for the way he intended to behave in front of her husband after he had seduced the architect's wife. As for Ella, she kept up her resentfulness until Eric delivered his news, and after that she was watchful and tense.

"Felix has kindly agreed to paint Winifred's portrait." What was kind about it I don't know since he was presumably being paid. "I've told him there's to be none of his abstracts." Eric was in his twinkling mood, a mischievous smile on his lips. "He's agreed this will be a conventional portrait. We envisage something in the manner of Sir Joshua Reynolds, don't we, dear?"

I felt almost sorry for Felix, who whatever its merit, took his art seriously, being obliged to fit his style into this prescribed mold. Lounging at the table with his elbows on it in the way Mrs. Cosway loathed, he nodded idly. I could guess what was going on in Ella's mind. Was this the reason for Winifred's evening visit of the week before? Was there no more to it than that? Or had this been dreamed up to deceive Eric and perhaps everyone else? She looked the picture of nervous wretchedness. No one had told her of Felix's imminent arrival—did anyone but Winifred know?—and she had taken no pains with her appearance. A woman who dressed up and made up for men and occasionally for other valued company, she had seen no reason to change out of her scruffy trousers and tired sweater for her sisters and Eric. Now she plainly felt at a disadvantage and had sneaked out of the drawing room to pass a lipstick over her mouth and rush a comb through her hair without much obvious improvement.

John said not a word throughout dinner and, when it was over, pushed back his chair and left the room. Any manners he might once seem to have had depended on the stupefying effect of the drug which made him too sleepy and dull ever to exert himself. His stillness (albeit with trembling hands) had passed for politeness and his inertia for acquiescence and obedience.

These were conditions Mrs. Cosway wanted back again, and wanted them to the extent of leaving the house the next morning for the first time since she came home from the hospital. I drove her down to the small purpose-built medical center where Dr. Barker had his office.

The practice nurse had to be fetched to help me get Mrs. Cosway out of the car. She winced and groaned and complained but finally made it into the waiting room. Three people were before us, a young woman with a sleeping baby, an old man with a cough, and Jane Trintowel. This brought back to me Jane's story of her own mother-in-law meeting the much younger Julia in just this place thirty-five years ago. Of course she knew from me about the fractured ankle, so she showed less shock than she might have done over Mrs. Cosway's changed appearance, her wasted face and by then skeletal body. The strong, resonant voice that came from those pinched lips may have surprised her.

To her greeting of, "How are you, Julia? I hear you've had an accident," Mrs. Cosway replied that Jane could presumably see she had had an accident, she didn't hobble about with a crutch for fun.

"I can see you're still the same old Julia."

Jane turned to me, asking me when I would be free to come to White Lodge again. James was back in Bristol until the middle of December but her elder son came down every other weekend. While we were discussing dates and possibilities, the young mother went in to see Dr. Barker, was in there only a few minutes, and the old man went in.

"You take my turn, Julia," Jane said when we had fixed on a Friday I would take as my day off. "It can't be comfortable for you having to sit about on a hard chair."

"It's not." Mrs. Cosway didn't thank her. "But my whole life is uncomfortable. I am used to it."

A girl who had come in and sat down next to Jane giggled, perhaps from embarrassment. The nurse came back to tell Mrs. Cosway Dr. Barker was ready for her, and the two of us took her to his office door. There I finally decided not to go in with her. She would expect me to support her, even say that John was impossible without the Largactil, and that I couldn't do.

"I'll be in the waiting room when you're ready," I said.

"You've wasted no time making friends, have

you? I suppose you can't wait to get back to gossiping with the Trintowel woman."

It was the nurse's turn to be embarrassed. She cast up her eyes. I went back to Jane.

"She looks **awful.**"

"I know, but she's very strong. She's not ill."

"And John?"

"Better. He still shuffles a bit and his hands shake, but I think he's a lot better without the drug Dr. Lombard gave him."

And he was destined to continue without it, for Dr. Barker refused a prescription to Mrs. Cosway just as he had to Ida, saying as adamantly that John should be seen by a psychiatrist for his needs to be evaluated. He would gladly find a suitable one at a Colchester hospital, say, write this man a letter, and make an appointment for a consultation.

"I told him it was all unnecessary," Mrs. Cosway said in the car on the way home. "One ought to know one's own son. He's schizophrenic and he needs tranquilizing or he'll be impossible to manage. It was your duty to come in there with me and support me, but no, you preferred chatting with your friend."

"It would have made no difference," I said, and again thinking that I could always leave, I didn't have to stay there. I screwed up my courage. "Why not let John see the Colchester man? It probably wouldn't cost anything." While keeping my eyes on the road, I could sense her staring at me. I made myself go on. "I don't suppose you're interested in what I think, but in my opinion John's all right as he is. He's better than he was. Why can't he be allowed to go on living the way he is now?"

"You're right in one respect. I don't care what you think. I suppose you've been discussing me and my private affairs with Jane Trintowel."

"I can tell you exactly what we said if you like."

"Thank you but I don't wish to know."

Dr. Barker's second refusal to supply the longed-for prescription seemed to affect Ida and Winifred as badly as their mother, Ella to a lesser extent. She was too preoccupied by a gnawing anxiety over Felix to show concern for John, saying only that she wondered how they were going to cope with his hiding in cupboards and screaming on the floor. It was a week since Felix had been in touch with her, for she said she couldn't count the occasion of his coming to dinner. There was no phone at The Studio, not particularly unusual in country places at that period, and at the start of their affair he had always phoned her (ignoring the proscribed times) from the call box outside the post office. He had told her that if she needed him she should phone the pub and leave a message as from "Tamara."

"I don't know why, Kerstin. You know what he's like. I sometimes think he tells any woman he's going about with to say she's Tamara." I struggled not to smile. She gave the Cosway laugh. "It's funny, isn't it? Mike the landlord must think he's such a faithful lover, getting all these calls from this one woman."

"You don't know that he's not."

"A faithful lover? I'm not a fool. Oh, what shall I do? I expect Winifred is with him now, sitting for him. And when that's done she'll be lying down for him. You'll see. I phoned the pub yesterday and said to tell him Tamara phoned. Come to that, I phoned the day before yesterday. I lie awake at night listening for the phone. I know he's capable of phoning anytime up till midnight. When he came up here for dinner he **shook hands with me.** He'd think that funny. He has broken my heart."

At this point the phone rang. She ran off to the dining room to answer it, came back to say it was June Prothero for Winifred. "She said she'd try the rectory. I had to laugh."

But Ella settled down to her regular evening task, the making of the bridesmaids' dresses. The real dislike and jealousy she now felt for Winifred did nothing to hinder her willingness to do this and I suppose the pleasure she got came from knowing she would get a free dress out of it. The material had been expensive, a watered silk in a bright shade of orchid pink, a bad color and too thin for a January wedding. Velvet in a neutral shade would have been better but Ella anticipated getting a garment out of the pink silk she could afterward wear to summer garden parties. She even put aside the pieces left after the cutting out so that she could make a doll's dress out of them.

"I shall redo the blond one from Poland," she said. "I've never liked that suit I've put her into. She can have a new pink frock. I don't know what I'd do without my hobbies, Kerstin, they're what keep me sane."

She had set up her sewing machine in the drawing room. Mrs. Cosway was displeased and Ida irritable at what she called "the mess." She was always picking up pins and bits of thread from the floor. The machine was old and noisy, making it hard for her mother to hear the television. John ignored it. He went to bed when he liked these days and had again spent a whole night in the library. The walks too were no longer regular events. From insisting on them, he changed his mind and decided to go only occasionally. When Mrs. Cosway told him he needed exercise and fresh air and told me to get ready and put my coat on, he went into the lavatory and locked himself in.

Ella was at school and it was Winifred who tried to get hold of the key by poking it through the lock from the outside with a knitting needle. We heard it fall to the floor. She had a kitchen implement which I believe is called a fish slice at the ready to insert under the door and draw the key out but John got there first, picking it up just as Winifred's scoop went in. He sat in there for five hours, occasionally running one of the taps above the basin.

Mrs. Cosway was sure he meant to flood the place, but nothing happened as he always turned off the tap after a few seconds.

Walking as an activity essential for his health was forgotten after that episode, but John seemed to bear a grudge against Winifred, I assume because she was the one who did most to get that door unlocked. If he was incapable of affection, he appeared to be able to dislike. But I don't know. Maybe what he felt was simple fear. He shrank away if she came near him. Everyone knew that it was unwise and perhaps cruel to touch John, but Winifred had only to pass within a few feet of his chair for him to pull himself away and hunch his shoulders.

This new behavior, which Mrs. Cosway called "defiance," she constantly complained about as the result of the refusal of Dr. Barker to prescribe Largactil or, as she put it, "John not being allowed to have his drug." A further addition to her troubles came when Zorah turned up with news of the appointment she had made for John to be seen by an eminent consultant in Harley Street. She would take him. Before that she would drive him into Sudbury for an eye test.

I saw her glance at the harp and nod slightly, but if she noticed the removal of the geode from her rooms she said nothing about it and did nothing. The trust had replied to her letter that any consultancy fees would be paid. John's appointment was for a date soon after Christmas and a week before Winifred's wedding.

Christmas is a feast of great importance to Swedes, but I hadn't yet decided whether to go home for it. Very indecisively, I kept saying to myself that I could always go home permanently, I could leave, go home for Christmas, and not come back. Why was I staying when no one appeared to need me? Mrs. Cosway was due to have the plaster cast removed from her leg in the coming week and would soon be back to normal. Her hand was completely healed and she had once more taken up her tapestry work. I provided a certain companionship to Ella which I thought she could do very well without, and as for helping Ida, she often seemed to prefer doing the tasks I did herself. I had spent a pleasant Friday evening with the Trintowels, met Charles, and been invited there for Christmas. Perhaps it was the immediate attraction of Charles which made me accept or just the conviction that I should certainly leave by February or March and go home then.

If John had become more lively and alert (defiant), Winifred went about in a dream, quiet, preoccupied, and sometimes gazing at objects with that compulsive stare which is unseeing because the mind is occupied elsewhere. She showed no interest in wedding acceptances and refusals—it was I who noticed Isabel's writing on one acceptance card—and was indifferent to the bridesmaids' dresses Ella was making, while the hymns to be sung at the ceremony, once so important to her, had lost their significance. What apparently absorbed her were the sittings for her portrait, though she never spoke of them beyond saying as she left the house that she would be going to The Studio.

In the early evening, now John needed no attention from me and wanted none from his mother, I helped Ida and was in and out of the dining room, switching on the electric heater well in advance of dinner, drawing the curtains on the damp starless night, and laying the table. Believing no one was in there, I walked in one evening with a handful of silver to see Winifred on the phone and hear the end of her sentence.

". . . Tamara phoned."

Remembering what Ella had told me, it was easy to reconstruct the earlier part. "Would you take a message and tell Felix Tamara phoned?"

She put down the receiver with a sharp bang. I took no notice of her, said nothing, but I knew then. The phone call told me Ella had been right. There was no possibility of Winifred's using that code name for any reason except that she was having an affair with Felix. She hadn't been phoning him to say that she could or could not sit for him the next morning but to make, or most reluctantly unmake, an assignation. Where did that leave Eric?

Or their wedding? Was this a last—and first too—fling? It went deeper than that, I thought. With her it would be either nothing or a whole-hearted passion.

While we were finishing dinner the phone rang. Ella was nearest to it and she twisted around quickly to grab the receiver, to the loud complaints of her mother.

"Oh, really, it's too bad. No one is to telephone here at this hour."

Ella was waving a silencing hand at her, saying into the phone, "Of course I'll come. In half an hour. Of **course.**"

Winifred had turned him down for some reason, so he sent for Ella. It was simple. She had flushed and pushed away her plate.

"Please don't ever flap at me again, Ella," said Mrs. Cosway. "It's dreadfully rude. It's disrespectful, though that counts for nothing with you."

"I couldn't hear what was being said." Ella had discovered the virtues of the passive voice, an invaluable aid to subterfuge in the English language. "Please, Mother," she said in the tone of a ten-year-old, "may I leave the table?"

Mrs. Cosway made a sound of disgust, flapping her uninjured hand in the way she had found so irritating when Ella did it. A silence fell, broken by the arrival of Eric, who had come for coffee after his meeting of the parochial church council. The reason for Winifred's disguising herself as "Tamara" to call the White Rose was revealed.

"I passed Ella driving down the hill," he said. "I'm afraid she was breaking the speed limit." He took his glasses off and put them on again for no apparent reason, as was always the case with him.

20

WITHOUT CENTRAL HEATING, LYDSTEP OLD Hall was an uncomfortable place to be that cold winter. John, who had borne it presumably without complaint during the drugged years, now began to show his discomfort in his own peculiar way. He never said more than, "It's cold" or "I'm cold," but he would wrap himself up like someone with limited resources preparing to spend a month in the open air of the Arctic. First of all his winter-weight dressing gown went on over his clothes—the pockets full of his ritual objects—then he would bring the eiderdown off his own bed downstairs, and if he decided this was inadequate, a couple of blankets would be fetched from the airing cupboard and, often, a sweater or two put on under the dressing gown. Those were the days before duvets and tracksuits and padded coats, so he had to manage as best he could. One day, particularly cold with flurries of snow, he went upstairs, diverging from his rule about only doing so for baths, got inside the airing cupboard, and sat there on the lowest shelf, having pushed Winifred's laboriously ironed sheets and pillowcases onto the floor.

For half an hour or so no one knew where he had got to. Mrs. Cosway, by this time free of her cast, her ankle still swollen, was loud in her lamentations on the results of the absent drug. I found John myself and seeing him there, was reminded of Dr. Lombard's story of Descartes in Queen Christina's airing cupboard.

His desperate quest for warmth prompted him to make another move toward seeking the help of the trust. Using his ancient reading glasses and the extra-powerful magnifying glass he had got Ella to buy him in Sudbury, he spent a lot of time scanning central heating advertisements in the newspapers. Finding a system he liked the look of, he announced in his very abbreviated way that the trust must produce the money to have it put in at Lydstep Old Hall.

"Nonsense," said Mrs. Cosway. "I won't ask them. It would be a shocking extravagance. We live in a temperate climate, especially in this corner of England."

As she was speaking, an easterly gale Ella said felt like Force Ten was tearing past the windows, carrying with it the last of the autumn leaves. From under his mounds of down quilt, blankets, and a shawl he had found somewhere, John said, "Zorah will."

At this, Mrs. Cosway screamed aloud and as the sound died away the doorbell rang. It was Dr. Barker, come to "take a look at" John, though no one had invited him. John, who had never previously met him, refused to comply, and when Dr. Barker made inept attempts to persuade him, huddled himself first into a corner, then departed into the lavatory, where we heard him lock the door.

"I told you to take the key away," Mrs. Cosway said to Ida.

Outside the door, Dr. Barker began cajoling him to come out or let him come in. John maintained silence until the nagging became too much for him and he let out a yell so bloodcurdling that we all jumped and Dr. Barker said, "I am afraid I am going to have to wash my hands of this, Mrs. Cosway, for the present at least."

"Wash whatever you like," she said. "I didn't ask you to come here upsetting everyone." And after that, whenever she mentioned him, she called him Pontius Pilate.

It was another five hours before John came out. By that time most of us felt we could no longer stand these interruptions and I was again on the point of deciding to pack my bags. However, it did result in Winifred writing to the trust and asking for central heating to be installed. It never was, of course. There was no time and after what happened, no need or wish. But for obvious reasons Winifred was feeling so elated these days that she would have done almost anything John or anyone else asked. A point had been reached at which she was Felix Dunsford's favored lover, almost the **maîtresse en titre,** while Ella was relegated to the girl from the village, called upon when the favorite was not available.

It must have been tiring for Winifred. Since then I have seen others play it, this game of a woman juggling two men, one the husband or accredited fiancé, the other the illicit and secret lover. Most of them do it very well, but it surprised me that Winifred should be so expert, she who seemed scarcely to have had a boyfriend before Eric came on the scene. With absolute ease she fell in with the Tamara ploy, concealed as best she could her excitement, and succeeded in keeping Eric in a state of calm ignorance. Nor do I know what she thought would happen when Christmas was past and her wedding date approached. She was seizing the day, and the day—nearly every day, it seemed—brought Felix, sitting for the portrait and, no doubt, making love with the portrait painter afterward.

Never talkative, Ida became almost silent as Christmas approached. I sometimes saw her look wonderingly at Winifred as if she suspected what was going on but couldn't quite believe it. Perhaps she had noticed that her sister, recently such a fanatical churchgoer, no longer attended Holy Communion or any services apart from Sunday Matins. In December, I was told, Ida would normally have been even busier than usual making preparations for Christmas, but this year Winifred was to do everything. This was her wish. It would be the last time, she said, as the following year she would be having Christmas at the rectory.

Ida looked bewildered when she said that, seemed about to speak but did not. Perhaps her thoughts were the same as Ella's and mine, that in spite of everything, Winifred still intended to get married in three weeks' time. And continue with the affair afterward? It certainly suited her. The flush on her cheeks, the brightness of her eyes, and the gloss on her hair were almost indecent if you knew what had caused them. Ella invited me up to her bedroom to tell me she was thinking of telling Eric.

"What good would that do?"

"It would bring it out into the open. He'd break off the engagement and maybe think he'd had a lucky escape."

"Surely it would make him very unhappy," I said. "She's his fiancée, but don't forget Felix is his friend, or Eric thinks he is. Wouldn't it be better for them to marry and then for Winifred to forget Felix?"

"Like I have?"

"I suppose that means you haven't."

"I still phone him. If he wants me I go to him. You think that's humiliating?"

I shook my head and from pity did something unusual with me. I put my arms around her and hugged her. She began to cry, sobbing against my shoulder. As for Felix, he treated Winifred much as he had Ella, apparently expecting her to keep their affair secret, phoning her at Lydstep, but if anyone else answered, either putting down the receiver or asking for her without giving his name. On those occasions I think he disguised his voice, for several times when I answered, it was a man who asked for Winifred in an unfamiliar voice, but it was not till long afterward that I realized the light tenor tone and slight Scots accent must have been Felix. He was a good actor. No doubt he had had plenty of rehearsals. He and she were never seen about together and his excuse this time would have been to save Eric from discovering their association. The two men were often seen in public together, Felix dropping in for tea at the rectory or having drinks bought for him by Eric in the White Rose.

Winifred was not welcome in the pub and was never taken out for a meal. Again the explanation would have been that Eric must never know. Did she mind? I don't think so. While Ella had wanted the whole world to know she and Felix were lovers, it was in Winifred's interest even more than his to keep things secret. She was plainly enjoying herself, discovering the joys of sex rather late in the day. I believe her mother and June Prothero and the church people attributed her improved looks to her impending wedding and perhaps to her love for Eric, soon to have its consummation. For there was no doubt that at that time she meant to get married and on the appointed day. She had had a final fitting for her wedding dress, the flowers were ordered, and a "going away" suit and coat had been bought from Colchester's top dress shop.

Mrs. Cosway thought, and loudly said, that for people in her and Eric's "position" to have a wedding rehearsal was ridiculous. Like royalty or film stars, she said. In accordance with her current mood, Ida had no comment to make. She broke her near-silence only to say to me while we were preparing dinner one evening, "I should like to see Eric Dawson happy," her use of both his Christian and surnames adding solemnity to her remark. "He's a good man."

For a moment I thought she was indicating that she knew about Winifred and Felix, but I soon realized I was wrong. "I used to go to church," she said, "but I stopped. I never really believed."

What did this mean? She said no more, relapsing into her sad silence.

Winifred was a very different woman from Ella. Not for her confiding in someone years younger than herself or indeed in anyone, for I don't suppose she whispered secrets to June or Mrs. Cusp. She had an elevated idea of her own importance and also of her virtuous and upright character. This must of course have been severely put to the test by the Felix affair, carried on while she was engaged to another man, but I have no doubt she made solid excuses to herself for her behavior. Eric was a husband, not a lover. She would be unflinchingly faithful to him once they were married. He would never know. She would make it up to him in appropriate ways. This was her Indian summer, soon to end.

Once or twice more, as Christmas approached, Felix came up to Lydstep Old Hall for drinks or coffee or dinner. As far as I know, he never made an offer of reciprocation. He always came with Eric, never on his own. With his reputation for making friends with any newcomer to the village—the men, that is, for he was too proper ever to have been seen about with any woman but Winifred—Eric organized "chaps' days out" when he and two or three others would go off for lunch in a hotel somewhere and spend the afternoon in Brightlingsea or Frinton. Felix may already have been on such a group outing. The fairly heavy drinking which went on would have suited him, though not the absence of female company.

As with Ella, he behaved as if there was nothing between him and Winifred, neither glancing at her too much nor too little. He even talked about the coming wedding which he meant to attend, although, as he said in a rueful tone with a lazy grin at Mrs. Cosway, "The bride's mother hasn't invited me, but my pal here says I can come."

His "pal here" said in rather a flustered way that he was sure this was an oversight as Felix would be very welcome. Compressing her lips, Mrs. Cosway still managed to stretch them into a tight smile. The first invitations which went out had included him but it seemed that she had changed her mind when Ida was sending out the second lot. She loathed Felix, as she never missed a chance to say as soon as he had left.

"Of course if your husband-to-be brings him here, what is there to say? It isn't my house. It belongs to John."

What John thought of him no one knew. The probability is that he never thought of him at all. John was unaffected by people who took no steps to cross him or ignored him as he ignored them. Encountered by me in the passage on his way back from the lavatory, Felix asked me what was wrong "with the silent guy."

"I don't know." What I half-guessed hadn't yet been confirmed. "Ask Winifred," I said.

He was an excellent actor. His face betrayed nothing. "D'you know, I never knew he existed until the last time I was here. Is that peculiar or just the way they behave in this creepy house?"

"How's the portrait coming on?"

He grinned. “Ask Winifred,” he said. That was the only hint of their affair he ever gave.

I found myself hoping Eric would never know, that Felix would maintain his discretion, whatever its purpose, whatever the main chance he kept his eye on, until they were married and across the years to come. I liked Eric. He wasn’t my kind of man, but he was kind and unselfish, cheerful and pleasant. I felt sure he would rarely tell a lie and then only a white one, and never break a promise. Full of good intentions, Mrs. Cosway had said of him, adding that we knew what those led to. Eric himself once preached a sermon about the intention amounting to the same thing as the deed, quoting something about a man who lusts after a woman having already committed adultery with her in his heart. If that is so, meaning well ought to be the same as doing well. But I don’t know. I only know that he deserved better than the treatment his fiancée and his friend had meted out to him.

Within minutes of their driving away, Zorah arrived. They must have passed on the Windrose road. It was after ten-thirty, and usually when she came at that time she went straight upstairs, but that evening she walked into the drawing room where Mrs. Cosway was still sitting with John and two of her daughters while Ida and I cleared away glasses and emptied ashtrays. She seldom sat down when she entered a family gathering but wandered the room, “as a roaring lion, seeking what she may devour, like it says in the Bible," Winifred once said.

John was the first one Zorah spoke to. It was always so. "Hello, you." He didn't shift his gaze from the Roman vase. Ella's eyes had turned guiltily toward the geode, a glance Zorah didn't miss. "You can keep that thing if you want," she said. "It's no use to me."

"That's a new departure," said Ella.

"As you say. But I intend to depart, you see. Leave, go, shake the dust of this place off my feet. It's no good looking like that, Mother. I know what you're thinking. The answer to your next question is, no, I shall be leaving the vase behind too. Mind you look after it. You can have the spinet and the harp too—I see you've already helped yourself to it. Incidentally, those geodes are in all the crystal shops in London now, they're two a penny."

"Do you mean you're moving out?"

"That's what I mean, Ida, yes. Sometime after Christmas. After John's appointment with the specialist. Are you still getting married in January, Winifred?"

"Of course I am!"

"No of course about it. You were going to get married in November but you didn't."

I asked myself if Zorah could possibly know about Felix. Surely not. How could she?

"You will do very well out of my going, Mother," she said. "You'll get my rooms and another bathroom all beautifully decorated. What more do you want?"

They were all thinking, all of them but John, that with Zorah's departure the gifts would go too, the wine, the food, the cash presents. I could read Ella's thought that thank God she had already got the car out of her.

"I may have Christmas here with you all. I haven't decided yet. In any case you can take it I'll provide the turkey and the booze."

In the drawing room next morning, I went over to the console table and laid my hands on the Roman vase. It was the first time I had ever touched it. I ran my fingers over its surface, feeling its smoothness, which at the same time was faintly dimpled. It was cool but not cold to the touch, jade-colored but not opaque as jade is, reflecting light but not images from its rounded surface. A strange and unlikely urge to possess it made me lift it up with extreme care, but I put it down almost at once, unwilling to be found handling it by a Cosway.

I had no idea then and have none now as to its value. Did it in fact even belong to the Cosways? Some ancestor of theirs had found it buried in the grounds, miraculously intact. Waste dumps have always been rich sources of treasure because householders tend to throw away their rubbish on the same site as that used by the generation immediately before them, while that previous generation favors the site used by his forebears and so on back for centuries. So it is quite possible that excavating a Victorian rubbish heap may lead you on down and down to Tudor and even medieval detritus. I have never heard of Roman remains being found under later waste repositories, but I suppose it is possible. This, at any rate, was what Ida told me was the burial place of the Roman vase, long since become the neglected orchard.

It was not quite intact, there being a tiny chip out of its base. Perhaps this was the reason for its being thrown away, though "thrown" was hardly the word as, again according to Ida, it had been found encased in a great earthenware jar. What became of the jar I have no idea.

Apart from the house itself, the Roman vase was the only inanimate thing I drew in the diary. I tried to draw it from memory but found, sitting in my bedroom, that I had forgotten the precise configuration of its mouth and the twist pattern of its handle. Everyone had gone to bed except John, who was in the library and likely to stay there for hours. I went downstairs to imprint on my mind those details of the vase.

The harp glowed dimly in the darkened hall. A faint light showed under the double doors to the library. I imagined John in there, sitting on the floor, I supposed, with his back resting against Longinus's plinth, surrounded by tumbled books, amid dim light and deep shadows, and I felt happy for him.

The house was as silent as only houses which stand alone in countryside can be by night. I studied the vase, its shape, its texture, the sugarstick twist of its curved handle. No one came in, though I was afraid all the time that they would, and ask what I was doing there.

Switching off the lights, I went upstairs again, treading softly. Before I went to bed I drew the vase in the diary and was quite pleased with the result. The fears I had experienced downstairs, creeping on tiptoe, afraid to turn on lights, made me marvel at myself. I who had used to be determined, robust, and cheerful was gradually becoming—as I saw it—mouselike and diffident. It was Mrs. Cosway who was grinding me down, changing me into the submissive creature she would probably have liked me to be when I first arrived.

Why did I draw the vase when it never crossed my mind to draw the geode or the hall fireplace or the harp or the library itself? Why draw the vase and not the mulberry tree or the boat floating on the pond or Ella's room with the frills and the dolls? Why not the orchard with its withered trees or the piano in John's gloomy bedroom? I flatter myself if I say it was because of my foresight and because I knew its long ancient life was not to last much longer. I had no such reason. I drew it only because it was the most beautiful thing in Lydstep Old Hall.

21

IN THE FIRST HALF OF DECEMBER I HAD TWO PROposals. They were the only proposals I ever had, for I have no memory of my husband ever asking me to marry him. We just knew that one day we should be married because it seemed the logical next step in our shared life.

Mark was the first to ask me. I was in London for the weekend and we had been talking about my vacillations over whether to leave Lydstep or to stay. I knew I shouldn't burden poor Mark with all this, but I suppose I had no one else on whom to unload my troubles, and usually, as soon as I arrived, although I tried not to, I would begin on a catalog of Cosway horrors and my own general feelings of uselessness. Mostly, he had no solution to offer. He would only tell me to put up with it a little longer, to stay until after Winifred's wedding, or else, probably exasperated, would say there were only two choices before me. If I disliked it so much I might as well leave now.

"I meant to stay a year," I said. "At least, I meant to stay till you go to America."

Mark was committed to a postgraduate course at a university in New Hampshire and intended to go there in August for two years. We had known that from the beginning and accepted it. Once he had gone we might never see each other again. No doubt we would correspond but we would regard ourselves as free and not in any way committed. It seemed that he was beginning to see things differently.

"You could leave and still stay in this country," he said.

I said I couldn't afford it. I might find other work but I had nowhere to live.

"Move in with me."

I said nothing. I looked at him and he took my hand.

"Move in with me and come with me when I go to America."

These arrangements, recognized relationships, as they might be called, were far from being accepted then. The United States, I felt and said, would have been still less likely to tolerate a graduate student living on campus with his girlfriend, even if this were possible.

"You could marry me," he said, and seeing my shocked face, "that was brutal of me, I shouldn't have put it like that. I should say, will you marry me, Kerstin? I should like it very much."

I didn't want to be married, but nothing would have made me put it in those words. For some reason, saying no upset me terribly. I don't think I actually did say it. I shook my head, muttered something like, "I can't, I can't," and began to cry. He held me and I cried against his chest, making his sweater all wet. That was the first and only time he ever saw me in tears, and I had to tell him truthfully that I didn't know why I was crying. Perhaps it had something to do with thinking it a great honor to be proposed to by this nice, kind, good-looking, and clever man whom I liked so much but didn't love at all, and knowing that marrying him would make us both unhappy for maybe the rest of our lives.

The weekend was spoiled, as I sensed it might be when my tears started. And the rest of our weekends were spoiled too, for Mark, who had never previously been in love with me, now fell in as into a fast-flowing river which carried him helplessly along. Once the idea of marriage had come to him, he couldn't let it go and his unhappiness and frustration began the following day. He who had been so light-hearted and funny and interested in everything grew silent and miserable. I left him sadly, feeling wretched in his company in a way I never had before. Instead of keeping to our old arrangement of my phoning him once or twice in the next couple of weeks to say when I would next be in London, he promised as if I had asked for this, that he would ring me every day.

Going back to Marks Tey in the train, I imagined the effect this would have on Mrs. Cosway, for I was sure the phone calls would be made at forbidden times. Perhaps I would finally be driven to leave by Mark's calls and Mrs. Cosway's wrath, and I would be forced to take refuge with him for at least a while. In that way phoning me might have something approaching the effect he wanted.

I was on the last train, and the last taxi bore away the passenger who had been just ahead of me in the line. The night was mild for December and I decided to walk. It was less than two miles but a very long way in the dark for someone carrying a backpack. Today, I think, I should have been afraid. Perhaps we grow more apprehensive as we get older or else there is genuinely more reason for fear than there was. Certainly I felt far less nervous as I walked through the lanes and along a footpath that skirted the hedges than I often did in the drawing room at Lydstep Old Hall with Mrs. Cosway, yet my path was lit only by a damp-looking moon. My head was full of Mark and his disappointment and my own hurt that I had hurt him.

At first, when I came into the house at a little after midnight, I thought all the lights were out and everyone had gone to bed. Then, glancing down the passage on my way to the stairs, I saw the line of light under the library doors I had seen on the night I drew the vase. I knew it must be John in there yet I opened the right-hand door and went in. The lamps in the library were all of low wattage and a kind of dismal twilight pervaded the place, some of those tortuous passages and the walls, heavy with books, being in the darkness of long, deep shadows. The stone faces, Greek and Roman and medieval and eighteenth-century, with clustering curls or laurel wreaths or Voltairean caps or periwigs, stared at me with blank, sightless eyes. No sculptor has yet found a way of making eyes look lifelike. I had no string to pay out behind me, but I knew my way without difficulty to the center by this time and there I found John, sitting on the floor at Longinus's feet, reading, or trying to read, with the aid of his magnifying glass and a flashlight propped up on a stack of textbooks, a thick leather-bound volume.

He didn't look up. He knew who it was, for he recognized my tread, and this failure to give any sign that he knew I was there, which in another man would seem like gross rudeness, I took as a compliment. With me he felt no need to be guarded, to withdraw into himself, or take the extreme step of hiding. You could say he trusted me, though this may be a concept alien to those with his affliction. At least he felt no need to be afraid of me. After a few moments he looked up but without acknowledging me, and stared expressionlessly into my face. I saw that the book he had been puzzling over was **The Shorter Oxford Dictionary.**

The silence in the library was so deep that I hesitated to break it. I had nothing to say, for whatever his mother and sisters might have done, I had no intention of trying to dislodge John from the library, warn him not to strain his eyes or chivvy him into going to bed. But we often talk when we have nothing to say, simply to fill a silent void, perhaps because the absence of sound frightens us. I moved a little away from him, to his relief I think, because he returned to his dictionary, adjusting the flashlight, which had slipped when he turned around to me. As usual when he was in here, he had removed the Bible from Longinus's grasp and replaced it with a great tome of Locke's political philosophy. Someone must go in there after John's occupancy and put that Bible back. Winifred, I guessed it would be.

There was a chiming clock somewhere in the labyrinth. One of the family, John himself most likely, had set it going again, and now it tolled out a single sonorous note. It was one hour past midnight. The clock having broken the silence, I felt less apprehensive about doing so and I said good night to John in an even tone.

To my surprise he said, "Good night, Shashtin." He didn't look up.

I went to bed, leaving any entry I might make in the diary until the next day.

Along with the rest of us, John was invited by Eric to The Studio to view the finished portrait of

Winifred. Mrs. Cosway refused for him, saying that someone must stay at home with him—why?—and it had better be her since no one else was willing.

"I don't want to go anyway," she said. "The last thing one wants is to see the inside of that man's house."

My previous visit to Felix's home had been back in the summer. Since then large quantities of rubbish had accumulated, mostly in the shape of old newspapers and magazines and empty bottles. Whatever Ella and Winifred did on their visits there, it wasn't cleaning. The place was seriously filthy, a state of affairs which Eric and Winifred seemed to regard as not only normal in a painter or "artist," as they called him, but quite admirable. I doubt if they would have found a like untidiness attractive in me, but I was careful, especially in the vicinity of Felix, to give no hint of my own sketches.

When not a single glass or mug could be found, Eric said that looking for a reasonable standard of hygiene from someone with Felix's gifts would be like expecting housewifely skills from Gauguin. It was in the style of Gauguin rather than Reynolds, which Eric had said he would have preferred, that Winifred's likeness had been painted. She was in raptures, blushing crimson when the dirty piece of cloth—an old curtain?—was drawn aside by Felix and the work revealed.

Perhaps to avoid having to join in the delighted praise, Ella had removed herself to the sink where she was rinsing out all the cups and mugs she could find under the cold tap, there being no hot water, and showing an intimate knowledge of the household arrangements as she did so. After she had dried them on the only available teacloth, apparently the fellow to the curtain which had been used to cover the portrait, Eric filled the various vessels from the wine bottles he had brought. I would have been very surprised if Felix himself had provided anything for his guests to drink. We drank a toast to the painter, then to the engaged couple, Eric being in his element while all this was going on, finally raising his "glass," a paint-stained mug with a picture of the infant Prince Charles and Princess Anne on its side, to "my beautiful bride."

The portrait, still unframed, was carried back to the rectory by Eric and Ida, where a check in an envelope was handed over. I went too, curious to see it hung. The sign Felix had painted had at last been put up by the gate. His lettering was impeccable. That evening I wrote in the diary that providing this painted signboard was the only good thing Felix Dunsford had done since coming to Windrose and in any case he had been paid for it.

The picture was to be hung over the fireplace in the room Eric called the "lounge," a word which conjured up to me places of cream tweed sofas and cut-glass ashtrays, nothing at all like the rectory's shabby living room. The portrait, in ivory and reds and purples, brought the only color. I thought it a poor likeness. It's not to my credit that I never recognized what a good painter Felix was.

"Shall you like having your own face staring down at everyone when you have guests?" Ella spoke in dry, almost sarcastic tones. "It would embarrass **me.**"

"Possibly," said Winifred, "but it's not your portrait and you're not going to live here."

I remembered what Ella had said about telling Eric and for a moment I thought she meant to say something which would make the situation clear. But she only continued to stare at her sister. Eric announced that since "the sun was over the yard-arm" we should all have a drink, though what little sun there was had been nowhere near the yard-arm when we had the wine in The Studio. Winifred seemed far less familiar with the arrangements at the rectory than with those at Felix's and it was Ida who fetched a tray laden with bottles and took glasses out of a gloomy heavily carved sideboard. Meanwhile, Winifred stood in front of the portrait, which was balanced on the brown marble mantelpiece, staring at her own face with doting narcissism.

It was the day after that when the snow began. I was used to snow. We in Sweden seldom passed a winter without it and sometimes it fell for months on end. In England, it seemed to me, everyone hoped to get through the winter without snow, but if it must come, let it be at Christmas. A white Christmas was what they wanted. After that it could go away until next year. Things seldom worked out like that but this year they did, at least as far as the snow at Christmas went.

There is a belief, almost universal, that the temperature rises when it snows. This is a myth, as one of my children doing a meteorology course told me. I believe it got colder with the snow that year. At Lydstep Old Hall fires were lit in fireplaces which had held no coal or wood for decades. Ella drove into Sudbury and, with grudging consent from Mrs. Cosway, bought electric heaters. Wrapped in blankets and eiderdowns, wearing woolen gloves, John did his Descartes act and sat in the airing cupboard day after day. Lydstep Old Hall had become a gray house with a white roof, desolate and sad to look at, its windows glassy black eyes. It was hard to tell if Zorah was there or not. To protect the shining bodywork of the Lotus, she put it away in one of the barns no one had used for half a century.

"She's ended it," Ella said to me. "Winifred, I mean. When the portrait was finished, that was the end. I expect she said so. I expect she told him that with the **last brush stroke** that was the last time. I shall never forgive her, never. But she looks miserable, doesn't she?"

I found it hard to agree. To me she looked much the same as usual. Nor did I believe Ella. I saw no reason to think Winifred had ended anything.

"She knows she's got to marry Eric. It's her fate. Besides, if she doesn't she thinks Ida would."

"Surely Eric himself would have some say in it."

She shrugged. "What do you think of the doll?"

It was in the pink silk of the bridesmaids' dresses and holding a bouquet of tiny artificial rosebuds. I said it was very nice, but I must have sounded vague. I was thinking of Ida and Eric. Eric and Ida—how much more suitable that would have been than the present arrangement.

My second proposal came in the following week. It was from John Cosway.

If the cold had continued he might never have made it for he was always in the airing cupboard or otherwise directing his energies to keeping himself warm. But mildness returned with heavy rain and Winifred went about saying it was more like August than December, a wet August. When John emerged he began to spend long hours in the library, perhaps making the best of the warmer weather before the cold that was sure to come drove him back upstairs again. But in the late afternoon he usually returned to his chair in the drawing room where Mrs. Cosway always was and where Ida, still aproned and harassed, would drop onto the sofa for occasional ten-minute breaks before rushing off back to housework.

Whatever Winifred had said, the temperature was far from anything this country saw in August and Ida had always lit a fire in this room. One of the advantages of central heating is that one can spend time in any room one chooses, while in its absence there is no alternative to sitting as close as possible to the only fire in the house. I had been helping Ida sort out two large cardboard boxes full of sadly shabby Christmas decorations, deciding which could be used again and which disposed of, but this more or less done, both of us were in the drawing room, Mrs. Cosway was lying on the sofa, and John was standing at the end of it, in front of the console table, with his gloved hands on the rounded body of the Roman vase. His mother watched him in a fretful way as if she feared he would break it. Winifred had just come in. She was brimming with excitement, the result no doubt of an afternoon with Felix, and I had a sudden fear that she wouldn't be able to contain herself but would break out into some wild exhilarated confession.

Nothing like that happened. Ida got up to make the tea, I said I would help, and as I got to my feet, John said, "Will you marry me, Shashtin?"

As a high-functioning autistic, he had simply expressed a desire, as he always did, and because he knew nothing of tact or discretion or that this request is always made in private, was without normal inhibitions, had no shyness or care for the usages of the world, he had expressed it in the presence of three other people. At that time, I had never had a shock like it. I don't know that I have since. I was simply dumbstruck. The awful silence was broken by Winifred, whose pent-up excitement burst out of her in a shriek of laughter and the worst question she could have asked.

"Marry you? Are you mad?"

They thought he was. Mrs. Cosway said, "Ignore it. The best thing to do is ignore it," and she turned on me eyes full of anger.

I thought then and wrote in the diary that evening that if I did what she asked I would have to live with this cowardice for the rest of my life, I would never forget it, I would never get over it. In a voice that I am sure sounded strangled, I said, "Thank you very much, John, but I'm afraid the answer is no."

He said nothing. Whether there was some peculiarity in me which brought tears into my eyes when I am proposed to, I don't know, but again I felt like crying. I could do that in Mark's room but not here, and I made an enormous effort to control myself, clenching my fists and driving my nails into the palms of my hands.

I could see no change in John's expression, no danger there of his feeling a similar distress to my own. Mrs. Cosway now turned and addressed her daughters.

"That's why he wanted her. I always suspected it. What other reason could there be for his asking for a young woman to help me? **Ostensibly** to help me. Anyone would have done, of course." She turned to me. "I don't know how you've been making up to him. I don't want to know. You may care to hear it would have made no difference. He was obviously set on this from the start."

Was he? Had he really only asked the trust for help for his mother in order to have a girl in the house to marry? Perhaps. I would never know. His motive in wishing to marry anyone was hard to imagine, unless he saw marriage as a way of escape from this place. He wasn't mad, even then I was quite certain of that, but there was no doubt he was very different from other men of his age. Could he love? **Did** he love anything or anyone but that vase and perhaps Zorah? And if so, was it remotely possible he loved me?

All this passed through my mind, though not till later. After the things Mrs. Cosway had said, gross insults and intended as such, I walked out of the room and went into the kitchen. There I busied myself with putting the kettle on, setting cups and saucers out on a tray, and finding a cake and some biscuits. It was still too cold to use the dining room until the electric heater had warmed it for an hour or two. After a blankness in my head which lasted a full minute, I began to ask myself what John thought marriage was. What did anyone who screamed when he was touched think marriage was? Was I only to be his silent companion and servant or did he believe our coming together would unlock in him reserves of self-expression and social interaction? But I realized I was attributing to him thoughts and feelings he could never have had. Possibly he believed he wanted to be married because there was so much talk of marriage with Winifred's wedding only a month away. Then there came back into my mind the dreadful question she had asked him.

"Are you mad?"

I sat down at the table and when Ida came scurrying in, the hated tears had begun. She looked at me and shrugged.

"Goodness knows what all that was about."

"I don't want any tea," I said and I went upstairs to my room, wondering how I was going to face John later and, come to that, the rest of them.

22

But for Mark's proposal and my refusal, I would have left Lydstep Old Hall that very evening. I couldn't go to the man I had said no to and tell him I had changed my mind and would he take me in. And there was another reason for staying. Along with my refusal of John, I had found myself feeling tender toward him in a way I had never been before. Though I could do nothing for him while I was there except respect him and his wishes, I felt there would be a kind of betrayal in deserting him just when what he had asked me seemed to indicate a need I had never before suspected.

So I forced myself to come down that evening and the next day and the next and try to behave as if nothing had happened. This was hard because Mrs. Cosway seemed to blame me for John's behavior, while several times I caught Winifred staring at me in wonder as if she was amazed by her brother's choice or was speculating as to what I had done to deserve it. Perhaps she, like her mother, thought my red hair a grave disadvantage in the attraction stakes. Ella had heard, probably from her, about John's very public proposal and was so enthralled by the whole idea that she wanted to talk about it all the time, trying to lure me with offers of rosé and chocolates to her room, where I was expected to analyze John's feelings and my own. I resisted most of it, but the very act of resistance made me tired and exasperated.

The cold weather came back and we had a heavy snowfall. Driving was impossible until the snowplows came out and cleared the roads. I was used to snow at home and had brought a pair of padded waterproof boots with me, new to English eyes and pronounced by Winifred to be "not very elegant." These boots enabled me to get down into Windrose and do the shopping, which I brought up from the village on an old toboggan I found in one of the outbuildings and dragged up the hill behind me. Apart from the kitchen boiler, the open fire in the drawing room, and the two new electric heaters, Lydstep Old Hall was now to be heated by paraffin stoves, fetched by Ida from the "boot room." I had never before seen anything like these black cylinders that Mrs. Cosway called "lamps" and which were fueled by paraffin. This was among the items I was asked to bring back from the village, told by Ida to buy the kind which was colored pink because blue paraffin smelled. The pink smelled quite strong enough to me. Its powerful chemical reek, even less pleasant than the smell of petrol, spread through the whole house with no chance of escape as all the windows were kept firmly shut against the cold. Mrs. Cosway switched off the "electric fires," as she called them, whenever she was near one, on the principle that using them would overload the system and cause the house to catch fire.

No one else went out. In a way I thought opposed to all her usual habits, Mrs. Cosway built up her strength by flexing the foot she had injured and describing circles with both feet. It was a kind of physiotherapy formulated by herself and it seemed to work. She had always been thin and upright. Now her strength was coming back. She told Winifred this was a regimen for getting herself fit for the wedding. Winifred received all such remarks and good wishes with indifference, barely smiling. If anyone pressed the point she said, "Let's get Christmas over first."

A lot of people I encountered on my shopping trips to Windrose talked like this, making the feast which I had always loved into a burden and speaking about it as if it were an ordeal to get through before the business of normal living could resume. Only Ella spoke of Christmas with a childlike thrill in her voice. As the cold intensified and, after a brief thaw, nightly frosts closed in on us, John sought refuge in the airing cupboard or, with two paraffin heaters in the drawing room and the fire built up high, huddled himself inside a sleeping bag Ella had found in one of those rooms off the kitchen I had passed through on my first morning there. He never again referred to his proposal. He took no more or less notice of me than he had ever done. This didn't stop Mrs. Cosway taking up a station by his chair when her pacing was over for the day. She brought an upright chair for herself and sat there, stitching at the tapestry, as if protecting him from some onslaught I might make.

One evening when I went into the dining room to switch on the electric heater half an hour before dinner, Winifred was in there making a phone call. I left the room at once but not before I had seen from her guilty look and darting eyes that Ella was wrong and she had been telling Mike at the Rose that this was Tamara with a message for Felix. Zorah too stayed at home, though scarcely showing herself. A male friend of hers appeared, turning up in a jeep-like vehicle high above the snow. She must have given him a key to the house for though I saw him arrive, the front-door bell never rang and no one came to let him in. Late that evening, when I went up to bed, I heard laughter from behind her door and the sound of music. There was a heavy fall of snow that night and the visitor's car, buried in a drift, became an igloo by morning. After staying up there with Zorah for another twenty-four hours, he finally dug his car out on Christmas Eve and drove away.

This evening had always been Christmas to me,

as it is in much of the continent of Europe, and it came as a surprise, and not a pleasant one, to find that in England it was nothing more than the eve of the Great Feast. A time of last-minute preparations, cooking, present-wrapping, cake-decorating, table-laying, but not of festivity. Eric came, bringing Felix with him, and the two of them joined Winifred in the kitchen to drink sherry while she mixed stuffing, iced the cake, and made crumbs from a white loaf for bread sauce. I went out there at one point to fetch a hot drink for Mrs. Cosway and found Winifred flushed and laughing, obviously excited at being the focus of attention for not one but two men, she who until quite recently had been on the shelf and heading for old maidhood.

"The silent guy," as Felix always referred to John, had begun to treat him with antagonism. This would have mattered not at all but for Winifred's determination that her brother and her lover must like each other. I have noticed this phenomenon since in families, when a woman is so besotted with a boyfriend that she expects all her relations and everyone she knows to admire him as she does. But with a man like John, certainly not insane but suffering from a peculiar mental condition, she ought to have known better. She had no more chance of success with John than she had with her mother. At least Mrs. Cosway was coldly polite to Felix. John could only express his true feelings, egocentric, indifferent to others' sensibilities, insensitive, isolationist, for this was Asperger's unchangeable nature. I believe Winifred still thought, as I once had, that now the medication was in the past, he would gradually become like everyone else.

This would never happen, and when the men came into the drawing room, each holding a newly refilled sherry glass, John, who had been working out some mathematical puzzle with paper, pencil, and magnifying glass, looked up and said to Felix, "You're drunk."

Winifred, inheritor of her mother's short fuse, screamed at him to shut up—how dared he speak like that? I half expected Felix to laugh, but his vanity had been hurt and perhaps he was aware that the accusation was not far off the truth. He scowled and said, "Thank you very much. You don't pull your punches."

While Eric was muttering, "Oh, dear, oh, dear, how very unfortunate," Winifred began playing the difficult game of apologizing to Felix and scolding John at the same time, managing a sweet smile in one direction and a ferocious frown in the other, rather like the masks of comedy and tragedy you see in theaters.

"There's no use making a fuss about it," Mrs. Cosway said. "It's been said and now you might as well forget it." She addressed Eric. "If only Pontius Pilate had given us the tablets Selwyn Lombard prescribed none of this would have happened."

"It isn't too late, you know," Winifred said to her brother. "There are other doctors. You could be back on it next week and it won't be up to you. It will be Mother's decision." She turned to Felix and said in a scathing tone, "Asking Kerstin to marry him! That's the kind of thing that happens when he's deprived of his medicine."

I didn't like this, but there was nothing I could do. Throughout it all John had been half-buried as he always was these days in sleeping bag, quilts, and blankets. Trailing them behind him, hitching them up as he went, and still clutching the magnifying glass, he shuffled across to the high-backed sofa and crawled into the three-sided cave between it and the wall. A pink satin eiderdown effectively blocked the opening behind him. Everyone but Felix knew he would be there for hours, possibly all night.

Mark had gone to his parents in Shropshire. We hadn't met since that weekend when he proposed to me, but this was as much due to the snow as to any awkwardness between us. The next morning I was due at White Lodge to spend a day and a night and a day with the Trintowels. Determined not to dwell morbidly on Winifred's remark, I fiercely pushed her words out of my mind. But what took its place wasn't much improvement. I went to bed early, thinking how absurd it was that I, who was quite without any religious faith, should be feeling melancholy and lonely because for once I was deprived of a Christmas Eve celebration with my parents and my brother and sister. I found it hard to sleep and I was still awake when Eric brought Winifred back from the midnight service of lessons and carols.

I had bought small gifts for Jane and Gerald Trintowel but nothing for the Cosways, and I was surprised when Ella knocked on my door at eight in the morning with a present for me.

"No one can sleep properly the night before Christmas, can they?" she said. "So I didn't think you'd mind me bringing this bright and early."

Not to be outdone and thinking fast, I gave her the gift of soap and perfume which was an extra I had wrapped up for Jane in addition to their wine and chocolates. Years later I told Jane. She smiled and said it was just as well as she had always disliked that particular scent.

"I want to laugh," she said, "but I can't when it's anything to do with that family. It seems wrong to think of them in any way but tragic."

Ella gave me a doll. It was smaller than those in her bedroom, an eight-inch-tall blonde of the Barbie type in a short yellow dress and knee boots.

"It's a Courrèges copy. I must say I'm rather proud of her boots. I made them out of the fingers of Mother's gloves. I'm keeping my fingers crossed she won't decide she needs them."

I still have that doll. It is ugly and absurd and I

would never have dreamed of putting it on show in any home of mine, but somehow I can't throw it away. My daughter found it when she was a little girl and wanted to play with it. I refused—not because I ever treasured it, but because of where it came from and the dreadful events associated with it. Thirty-five years later it is as clean and its clothes are as exquisitely made as when Ella gave it to me in my bedroom at Lydstep Old Hall, as the sun coming up over Windrose colored the fields of snow with her favorite pink.

With his bedclothes and his magnifying glass, John had buried himself behind the sofa for eighteen hours. Twice he had come out to go to the lavatory and on each occasion, she told me, Ida had been worried that he would lock himself in and carry on his vigil or strike or whatever it was from there.

"There is nothing to be done, I suppose," she said. "If I take the key away it's going to be so embarrassing for guests not being able to lock themselves in. Did you have a good time at the Trintowels'?"

I said it had been very nice, thank you.

"They've got two sons, haven't they? The younger one used to play the organ in church in the days when I went. I met the older one once. D'you know, Kerstin, I'd have thought he'd be just your type."

She was right, but of course I didn't say so, if I even knew it then. "I've got a boyfriend," I said.

The question of the hour—of several days to come in fact—was who was to give Winifred away. Apparently, in the absence of her father, some male relative of the bride or family friend had to do this, and Winifred might have fixed on an uncle or the nephew who was one of the John Cosway Trust trustees. But the Lydstep Old Hall people, with the exception of Zorah, had fallen out with them, and relations were now confined entirely to business.

"Of course John ought to do it," Winifred had remarked during Christmas lunch while her brother was still behind the sofa. "He could have done if he'd still had his medicine. He'd have bumbled through it all right."

Her mother told her not to be silly and Eric was very shocked. Ella, who told me about it, said, "So Mother said she assumed she was going to do it. It was surely possible for a woman to give her daughter away, and Eric said, yes, it was, and it would be quite suitable. And then what do you think happened? You'd never guess in a million years. Winifred said, 'Why shouldn't Felix give me away? He's a family friend and he's Eric's friend. I thought it would be nice for him to be Eric's best man, but George Cusp is up for that, so why shouldn't he give me away?' Well, Mother was absolutely furious, she said she'd never heard of anything so preposterous and if that happened she wouldn't even go to the wedding."

I asked Ella what the person who gave away the bride would have to do and say.

"He isn't supposed to say anything. He goes with the bride to the church and takes her arm up the aisle—you see how John couldn't possibly have done it. The parson—it'll be the Archdeacon—says, 'Who giveth this woman to be married to this man?' and he doesn't say anything, just stands there, but most get it wrong and say, 'I do,' and then he walks away and sits down and the bridegroom says that bit about taking thee to my wedded wife. Well, Winifred got quite excited at her idea and when we'd finished the Christmas pudding and Ida was handing around chocolates, she got the Prayer Book and she and Felix started going through it together, their heads touching if you can believe it, and laughing and reading bits out. I don't know what Eric thought, but he didn't say anything. Felix read out the bit about the minister 'receiving the woman at her father's or friend's hand' and said that was clear enough. It meant he was more suitable than Mother because there was nothing about the minister receiving Winifred at her mother's hands."

"So what happened in the end?"

"Well, nothing really. Eric said it wasn't necessary to have anyone to give a bride away and it was time to change the subject. He seemed a bit uneasy by that time."

I asked her why Winifred wanted Felix.

"I see it as a symbol," said Ella. "It means she's giving him up to get married. He's giving her up to another man. You'll say it's in very bad taste and I'd agree, but it's what a father does in a sort of way."

"In a sort of way," I said.

Zorah hadn't been with them at lunch but appeared in the afternoon, beautifully dressed, her hair done in a new way and wearing a pair of high-heeled shoes "I'd have given years off my life for," said Ella. Having put away a "vast amount" of the sherry, burgundy, and brandy, all of it provided by Zorah, Felix had fallen asleep, sprawled out in the armchair where John usually sat. Mrs. Cosway was also asleep, Eric was dozing, and Winifred was lying back with closed eyes, fairly typical it seemed for any English family on Christmas afternoon. Zorah looked carefully at Felix, walking around him and putting her head on one side, like someone studying an unusual specimen of wildlife.

Though she said very little, John must have heard her voice for he came out at last, dragging his bedclothes with him.

"Felix was asleep in his chair and that made John angry," said Ella. "He stood over him, staring. It was awful. I thought he was going to hit him, but Felix woke up. John said, 'You're in my chair. Get up,' and Felix did, very quickly. Winifred told John never to behave like that again, which was absurd, you know, because it's always useless saying anything like that to him. Zorah started laughing when John said what he said and then she told him not to forget she'd be driving him to London in the middle of next week to see the specialist. Then Mother said, 'Let's see if **he** puts you back on your Largactil.'

"Felix left soon after that. He hadn't taken offense, I don't mean that. He said he'd enjoy the walk home, it would clear his head. But I know him and I think he was going straight to the pub. They'd just opened. But I think Winifred is giving him up," said Ella, "or he's giving her up. After the wedding Felix will just be Eric's best friend until some new person comes to Windrose." She hesitated. "Do you think he'll come back to me?"

"Surely you wouldn't want him?" I should have known better.

"Oh, yes, I would, Kerstin. I'm not proud. I know he's a drunk and faithless and he'll never be successful but I love him."

Zorah had taken John to Sudbury for an eye test a week before Christmas and he was promised new glasses. The day before he was due to go to London with her I too went there and spent the afternoon and evening with Mark, returning on the last train.

He looked very serious when I told him of the latest Cosway troubles. "I think you ought to leave," he said. "It sounds as if something nasty is going to happen."

"What sort of something nasty?"

"I don't know and I may be quite wrong. I don't understand why you want to stay on."

"Don't you?" I said.

"If you mean because of what I asked you, you can still come and share this room. If you don't want me to I'll never mention marriage again. I'm in love with you, but I won't mention that either."

On the way back in the train I thought about taking up his offer. I could wait until Zorah had taken John to London, Ella was at her sewing, Winifred at the rectory—or The Studio?—and Ida being a housewife, and then break the news to Mrs. Cosway. Only one doesn't break good news and I was sure she would be pleased. It would be a relief. It meant nothing to her that I took half the work off Ida's shoulders. Ida could manage on her own. She always had before I came.

Things would be better, I thought (and wrote down when I got back to Lydstep) after Winifred had gone. The constant sparring between her and Ella would be over and Felix would no longer come there; I was sure Ella was wrong and he wouldn't return to her, not that when he was "hers" he had ever made that plain in public. No, he would become, for a while, a frequent visitor at the rectory, neither he nor Winifred betraying by a glance or a catching of eyes or exchanged half smiles that they had ever been more to each other than friendly acquaintances. So I was thinking as the train came to a stop at Marks Tey, and because rain was falling, washing away the snow, I was obliged to take an expensive taxi back to Lydstep.

There was one week to go before the wedding. Winifred asked me if I would like to hear her banns called for "the third time of asking." I had no idea what banns were or what asking meant in this context; she explained and told me too that Eric wouldn't be calling his own banns (perhaps this wasn't allowed, I don't know) but the vicar of the next parish would do it as he had done on the two previous occasions. In the event, I, Mrs. Cosway, Ella, and Winifred all went to church, while Ida stayed at home to be with John, happier with his new glasses and able to dispense with the magnifying glass.

I read in the paper the other day, thirty-five years later, that the publishing of banns of marriage is likely to disappear along with other Church "reforms." I don't know why and maybe there is no good reason. It was pleasing to hear the ancient formula spoken by Mr. Moxon from Saint John's, Lydstel le Grand, as he asked us, all thirty or so of us, if we knew "cause, or any just impediment, why these two persons should not be joined together in holy matrimony." It made me think of Jane Eyre and Mr. Rochester's wedding and the first wife's brother speaking up to tell of the impediment, but Eric had no first wife and the bride having a lover is no cause for refusing to join two persons together in matrimony. Felix was there, sitting where he had sat that Sunday in summer when Winifred had reproved him for his clothes, and when the organist, who wasn't a patch on James Trintowel, struck up "Praise, my soul, the King of Heaven," sang as lustily as he had done before.

I thought of John and his proposal. He was a single man, a "bachelor of this parish," and I was a single woman. We were free and there was no impediment to stop us marrying. If it was what John wanted he could have spoken the responses, said the words. Recalling the terms of Mr. Cosway's will, I could see why Mrs. Cosway was worried and why she sat close by John to protect him from his predatory caregiver.

The Church of England fascinated me then. Now it only disappoints me. In those days I used to marvel at an institution dedicated to a religion where no one seemed to believe in God and everyone believed passionately in ritual and rubric. It was my first visit for some weeks and I watched, rapt, as some knelt, some remained sitting, all closed their eyes in prayer, some crossed themselves while others witnessed the crossing disapprovingly, some sang "Hallelujah!," others "Alleluia!" and all gave a kind of court bow, dipping their heads, when the Creed was said and the words "Jesus Christ, His only Son, Our Lord" were reached. I don't know why. I didn't then and I don't know now. Were their minds devoutly full of Christ's passion, his suffering, his descent into hell, and his mystical resurrection? Or did they think of the roasting joint and whether their neighbors would be coming back after church for sherry?

Eric was to come to the Hall for lunch. This had been the usual arrangement for weeks by then, but this time Felix wouldn't be with him. There was something formal, I thought, almost ceremonial in the way he said good-bye to Winifred, taking both her hands in his and, to everyone's surprise, not least her own, kissing her cheek. In the days of Ella's ascendancy there had been nothing like this, and as I watched them, the puzzle of why Felix seemed to prefer the older sister was solved. For all her prissy ways, her apparent devoutness, and her Sunday school-teacherish way of talking, Winifred gave off a charge of sexual energy entirely absent from Ella. I felt it then, a powerful sexiness in the way she breathed and the gaze of her eyes and the parting of her painted lips. If I could feel it, how much more must Felix? He had awakened this in her, he must have done, for I am sure it wasn't there before.

She wanted him to come back to the Hall with her. Without him her day was spoiled. She had only Eric, an encumbrance and a nuisance as well, a stumbling block to any plans she might make, but an inescapable and in some ways desired fate.

She had to have a husband. Without a husband, she was no better than Ida or Ella, an old maid, a spinster. But did she have to give up Felix?

Because I wouldn't be at the wedding, I was to be shown Winifred's dress, a special treat. It was a classic bridal gown, of white silk and having about it those special wedding-dress features you never seem to see in connection with any other kind of costume, points on the long sleeves that extend over the hand, a stand-up collar like a calla lily, a train which would be carried up the aisle by Ella or June Prothero and which would make the dress unwearable on any subsequent occasion. The headdress which went with it was rather like those worn in portraits by Elizabethan ladies and which always seemed to be shaped like a gable on the front of a house. A veil would be attached to float down Winifred's back.

It was absurd, of course, all of it was, not least because this kind of regalia was once designed for a young virgin being delivered from her father's hands into her husband's. Winifred would be forty-one a week after the wedding and a man who was not her future husband had recently been her lover. And it was true that a few months before, in the heavy makeup and the dirty fingernails days, these clothes would have seemed grotesquely unsuitable for her. She would have been taking a risk in wearing them lest she set off giggling in the church. Not so by the time I saw them. Her natural good looks had come into their own, she had shed years off her age, and there was a spring in her step. She had become young, six or seven years older than I was; through love or sex or something of that sort, she had regained her youth. She would no longer disgrace that gown and it would no longer show her up for a fool without taste or judgment.

Winifred had been abroad very little so she was excited, or seemed to be, about the prospect of her unknown honeymoon destination. For once Eric was doing the romantic thing and taking her away to a holiday place he refused to reveal.

"You can tell me," said Mrs. Cosway. "I won't give the secret away."

"It will be much easier for you not to if you don't know," said Eric.

"If I guess right I shall be able to tell from your face."

"I doubt that, Mater," said Eric.

This was the sobriquet he had finally decided on, having rejected "Mother-in-Law," "Julia," "Mamma," and Felix's facetious suggestion, the awful "Winsmum." I don't think Mrs. Cosway liked "Mater," though she probably thought it the best of the bunch.

She began naming cities and holiday resorts in European countries in the hope of detecting their destination from his expression—"Paris, Rome, the South of France, one of those costas, Crete, Lake Garda"—until he came the nearest to losing his temper I had ever seen him.

"Oh, Southend," he said. "Where else?"

For a long time, ever since the wedding was postponed from November till January, I had been sure they would never get married, but once Christmas was past and the days went by quietly, I began to think it would happen. Things had reached a stage when cancellation or even further postponement would cause so much trouble and be so expensive as to be untenable. The clothes were ready, the honeymoon was booked, the rehearsal was about to happen, and the cake was delivered. Wedding presents had begun arriving.

We all went down to the church, where Mr. Cusp deputized for the Archdeacon. It had at last been decided that Mrs. Cosway should give Winifred away but in her absence, Ida performed this function. Stony-faced, she walked Winifred up the aisle and when Mr. Cusp asked who was to give her away, handed her to him, stepped back, and sat down at the end of the front pew. She kept her eyes off Eric, gazing straight ahead of her into the chancel.

Ella's expression was supercilious, as if she thought the whole thing as absurd as the wedding itself would be, while June Prothero smiled with earnest cheerfulness, occasionally making arch remarks about how pretty Winifred was looking and what a wonderful man Eric was. I half expected Felix to be there, but there was no sign of him. His presence wasn't necessary, I am sure he hadn't been invited, but this would hardly have stopped him coming if he had wanted to. As we left the church and came out into the cold dark of a country night, drifts of dirty frozen snow lying on the verges, I thought how, with the coming of the New Year, he seemed to have been abandoned. Winifred had left him behind as she went forward into her new life. Eric, no doubt, had other things to think about and would pick him up again when he returned from his mysterious destination. So I thought.

We drove past the White Rose, brightly lit, Christmas decorations still in the lighted windows, holly wreaths still hanging on the doors. I saw Ella turn to look as we went by, hoping for a sight of Felix perhaps or still so besotted that a place he frequented continued to hold a compelling magic for her. Winifred, on the other hand, at the wheel, kept her eyes on the road, and Ida, sitting beside her in the passenger seat, kept the silence she had maintained since before she escorted the future bride up the aisle.

That winter she had aged. I remembered when I had first seen her, when she admitted me to the house in early June, how I had thought her good-looking, though her appearance was neglected, and had guessed her age at about fifty when she was in fact forty-eight. Since then she had had a birthday but it looked as if it had brought her to the verge of sixty instead of forty-nine. A few minutes after we were back in the house I went into the kitchen to give her a hand.

"Will you be going in May?" she said as I began peeling vegetables. "I mean, at the end of May when your year is up?"

"As you say, my year will be up," I said.

"So you'll leave? You won't stay on for another six months?"

"I haven't been asked to do that." I might as well give a warning hint, I thought. "I'd better tell you, Ida, I've thought of leaving before May."

"Only thought?"

"Let's put it this way. I was employed here in a nursing capacity to help care for someone I thought was mentally ill."

"He **is.** He is mentally ill."

"He doesn't need a nurse, does he? I'm left with nothing to do except help you and before I came I made up my mind that what I wouldn't be was an au pair."

I dried my hands, took the tablecloth from one drawer and the cutlery from another. She said nothing. The water in the large saucepan she had set on the electric burner began to boil and she slowly tipped in the cauliflower florets. I went to the dining room and found the door I had left open closed against me. As I opened it Winifred's voice said, "Tell him Tamara is on her way, will you?"

An intake of breath behind me made me turn my head. I looked around at Ida but couldn't tell from her face if she had heard.

23

Reading the diary after all these years, I have been thinking how different things would be today. Impossible, for instance, for The Studio not to have a phone. Winifred wouldn't be dependent on a land line without extensions in a house the size of Lydstep Old Hall but would have her own mobile which she could use in the privacy of her bedroom. I doubt there would be all this elaborate cooking and table-laying. Mrs. Cosway was old and had been ill. Today she would still have her meals prepared but they would be brought to her on a tray while the rest of the family, even John, would be left to forage for themselves. But what am I saying? Isn't it even more unthinkable that all these middle-aged people would still be living at home with a parent? I don't know what level of sexual morality is expected from a Church of England clergyman thirty-five years later, but it seems unlikely to me that a man and a woman of Eric and Winifred's ages—or any ages, come to that—would contemplate marriage without living together first for a while.

As for John, now his Asperger's would be recognized for what it was. No one would call him schizophrenic and no doctor would prescribe for him a powerful tranquilizer like chlorpromazine hydrochloride. Afflicted only by Asperger's, he would never be classified as mentally ill but only as "different" and, as a child, as having "special needs." But all this happened thirty-five years ago.

Winifred had no dinner with the rest of us that evening. What she told her mother and sisters I don't know, but the prevailing opinion seemed to be that she had gone to the rectory. It was a grim meal. John, of course, never did anything to please. It was not in his nature, it was impossible, something his mother and sisters never began to understand. And when he got up from the table after eating his first course and disappeared, Mrs. Cosway began on a whining monologue about his selfishness and how it had only begun to show itself when the drug was withdrawn. In this she had the support of Ella, who rattled on about how leaving him without tranquilizers was bad for him and everyone else, and suggested that "this specialist of Zorah's" might well put him back on them.

He had gone into the drawing room where we found him, holding the Roman vase. He hadn't lifted it off the cabinet but was standing in front of it with his hands around its bulbous lower part and when I came in with Mrs. Cosway, he took the left hand away and lightly touched the spiral handle with his forefinger. It was impossible to tell from his blank expression if he admired it or was astonished by it or even found it repulsive.

Mrs. Cosway, whose only remarks ever made to him were to admonish him, now asked in a snapping tone if he intended to break the vase. What did he think he was doing, touching it at all? Being John, he took no notice of her, he didn't even turn his head, but began running his hands down the sides of the vase, gently stroking it, feeling I suppose its smooth, though dimpled, surface.

He never broke things through carelessness but only because he meant to break them, as in the case of the glass dish when Ida tried to give him the Largactil. Mrs. Cosway must have known this, but she chose to ignore or forget it, went over to him, and laid one finger not on him but on the vase. Quickly he took his hands away from that finger's proximity, returned to his chair, picked up his blanket and eiderdown, and left the room. I knew he was on his way to the library and once again meant to spend the night there.

Ida had uttered no word since, after following me to the dining room for no apparent reason except perhaps to continue the discussion about whether I was leaving or not, she had overheard Winifred sending her cryptic message to Felix. Apparently she had understood it as well as I had, though how I didn't know. She, certainly, had never been in thrall to Felix, but somehow the code-name was known to her and she had realized its significance. With only two more days to go until her wedding, Winifred was at The Studio with a man Ida loathed, deceiving a man Ida loved and would have liked to marry.

She came into the drawing room and sat down, grim-faced, with "the mending," a basket full of woolen clothes moths had attacked, and various items of underwear and nightclothes which had broken straps or torn flounces. I believe the custom of darning socks and sewing hems which had come down was out of date even then. Probably the arrival of synthetics put an end to it. But Ida still darned and mended and hemmed, possibly in the interests of economy but more likely because she saw it as a housewife's duty. It would have pleased Eric, I was sure. What a wife he had lost when he rejected her and picked Winifred.

Her head bent over a hole in one of John's socks, Ida looked in a state of suppressed distress. She said nothing, perhaps because she was afraid of crying and betraying herself. Mrs. Cosway, of course, had turned on the television and she and Ida sat side by side, watching it. The program was one of those serials the BBC used to do so well. I was frightening myself with a collection of Victorian ghost stories I had found in the library and I wasn't sorry when Mrs. Cosway fetched me from the book with a reproof, though I could have preferred her to do it in a pleasanter way.

"I suppose the television isn't good enough for you, Kerstin. Oh, no, you have to show your superiority with something more intellectual. To my mind, one doesn't read a book when others are present. A newspaper or a magazine perhaps, but not a book."

When I first came to Lydstep I had been so strong and bold, so able to hold out against her and assert myself. No longer. She had beaten me down and taught me to take the line of least resistance. My parents and my brother and sister wouldn't have recognized the girl who closed her book without protest and said she was sorry, she hadn't meant to be rude.

So I watched television with them, browbeaten into wishing Ella would reappear. She and I had very little in common, but we could talk to each other amicably. To the others I felt I had nothing to say and if I were left alone with either of them and without television to resort to, we should be utterly silent. But Ella stayed up in her room with the dolls and the rosé and the chocolates, putting the finishing touches to the bridesmaids' dresses, as she told me next day.

It was impossible for Ida to stay still for more than a few minutes. She laid her mending aside, left the room for some reason to do with clearing up or making hot drinks or general useless bustling, came back, and watched another two or three minutes of the serial before she was off again.

Mrs. Cosway took absolutely no notice of these comings and goings. Another sign of my almost broken spirit showed itself in my fear of being caught glancing at the clock or, worse, looking at my watch. It was the television which told me, when the episode came to an end, that it was ten-thirty. I was getting up, about to say I was going to bed, when Mrs. Cosway remembered John.

"He'll have to come out of there and go to bed," she said.

Since John had been going into the library most evenings the door was no longer ever locked. He might have lost the key. At any rate, it couldn't be found. Mrs. Cosway had made a tremendous fuss about this, but a useless fuss just the same. What happened that evening I never knew for sure because she told me curtly that she would "see to it" and my assistance wasn't necessary.

There was a huge crash, as of a hundred heavy objects falling on to the floor, a woman's thin scream, and the cries John typically made when he was frustrated. I ran to the library with Ida behind me. We managed the short passages in the usual half-dark, I going too fast and bumping my head on one of the corner bookshelves, dislodging precariously balanced volumes, to find a welter of heavy books piled on the floor, Mrs. Cosway sprawled on top of them, and John crouched down, yelling and waving his arms. The Bible Longinus had been holding teetered on top of the pile while the saint held out his empty hands as if begging for mercy.

With Ida's help, Mrs. Cosway struggled to her feet. She wasn't hurt.

"I tried to make him come out and go to bed," she said. "One gets so sick of this behavior. I used to think he'd do anything I asked, but that's all changed."

"Did you touch him?"

"Well, of course I did, Ida. I had to if I was going to get him out of here. He got into a state and threw all those books about. I don't care anymore. I'm going to leave him and go to bed. Let him get on with it."

It was a futile exercise, this. Many times that I remembered each of them had accused the other of touching John while knowing how he hated it, each had reprimanded the other while surely being aware of doing the same thing herself. He always cringed and screamed but they seemed never to learn.

We went to bed. I could hear John's shouting for a long time and when it stopped the silence seemed deeper than I had ever known. He would be lying on the library floor, wrapped in his quilts and surrounded by the books he had swept from the shelves. It was cold but there were worse places to spend the night and he had done it before. Yet I thought of how alone we were out here in the midst of nowhere, in the darkness, surrounded by empty fields. The purplish-blue sky was covered with stars. Without a breath of wind, yet very cold, the air was utterly still and the garden was still spotted with old snow in shaded places. Unable to sleep, I had wrapped my eiderdown around me and sat at the window looking out. I hadn't heard her come in, but I assumed Winifred was long back from what was perhaps her last meeting with Felix, that she had put the car away and was now fast asleep in her bedroom along the passage.

So I was surprised when I heard a car coming. The engine sounded loud and clear in the still cold air. Winifred parked and got out. With no coat over her thin blouse, and flimsy high-heeled shoes on her feet, she stood on the crumbling concrete steps and stretched her arms up to the sky, throwing back her head and smiling at the stars. She seemed to be in a kind of ecstasy. A white moon, nearly at the full, showed her to me in clear detail, her breasts lifted, her fingers stretched out, her arms embracing the night.

It is like this that I remember her best. Not as the fussy, churchy moralist, the doer of good works in the parish, the rector's fiancée, the bad-tempered, embittered sister with no real role in the family, the "professional" cook, but as this beautiful woman, transfigured by passion and exulting in the man she loved. This is how I thought of her when, meeting Ella and her daughter in Riga and asked who Zoë reminded me of, I said, "Winifred."

24

My drawing of Winifred was the last one I ever did in the diary. Now, as I turn its pages, I see that everyone in the household had a place there, even Mrs. Lilly, but not John and not Cox the gardener, who never while I was there showed his face indoors. Mrs. Cosway appears twice and as a caricature, I am afraid, her frown and glare exaggerated, her thinness stick-like. Among her dolls, Ella looks pretty, and I doubt if she would have had much objection to this sketch if she had ever seen it. Ida appears as a drudge, a Mrs. Mopp character with a broom and curlers in her hair, and I don't even know if she would have minded. As for Zorah, she couldn't fail to be flattered.

The Roman vase is like an illustration in a book about archaeology. I think the police were pleased to see it just as they must have been pleased by my drawing of Winifred, for by the time they saw the diary, both woman and vase were gone. Of one, nothing remains but her niece's resemblance to her; of the other, the small sharp fragment I still possess.

I remember very clearly where we all were and what we were doing the day before Winifred's wedding. Everyone got married on a Saturday then, it was taken for granted that your wedding would be a Saturday, so Friday must have been the day it happened. A cold day but without snow, a dark day, the sky like a gray blanket spread low across the countryside.

Lunch was a makeshift affair of cold leftovers. The English are proud of serving inadequate and unappetizing meals the day before any sort of feast. Tomorrow they would have lunch at a Sudbury hotel so today we must fast on scraps of tinned ham and pickles found in the bottoms of jars. All of us were there for this meal which was taken at the kitchen table under that great iron rack I was always afraid might drop down onto my head. John was supposed to sit next to his mother, but he wasn't having any of that and had moved himself to the far end of the table where he rearranged his cutlery and cut his bread and butter into very small triangles. Ida had a seat next to me, but she was seldom in it, taking the chance while she was actually in the kitchen to bob up and down, fetching things out of cupboards and putting plates in the sink. Opposite me Mrs. Cosway and Winifred sat side by side while Ella was at the head of the table, facing her brother. All the time I was in that house, Zorah only once ate with the rest of the family, and it wasn't on that Friday. She had driven away in the morning with no intention of coming back.

"I've given you a very expensive wedding present," I heard her say to Winifred. "You can't expect me to be there as well."

But for the fridge, which was at the rectory, the presents were all over the dining room, the reason for our eating in the kitchen. Isabel had sent an electric mixer. It looked rather incongruous in that room with its dreadful dust-colored curtains and the lithograph of the youth and the maiden in the amphitheater. A check from Mrs. Cosway remained discreetly in its envelope, Ella had given them the very unlikely present of a secondhand set of the **Encyclopaedia Britannica,** and Ida a firescreen for which she had embroidered a peacock perched on a branch of cherry blossom. This wasn't the only picture among the gifts. Felix's small oil of lovers on a bed was as unlike the amphitheater engraving as could be, being poised between the erotic and the pornographic. The idea of it hanging in the rectory made me smile—surely my last smile of that day. When lunch was over John set off for his walk without telling anyone he was going. I knew because I caught sight of him on the lawn, making his way toward a gate in the perimeter wall, and I caught up with him as he reached the path through the shrubbery.

"No, Shashtin," he said, and, "not you."

I asked him why not, but when I got another

"no" I obeyed him. I was afraid he might lie down on the frost-whitened paving and begin to scream or curl himself up behind a bush. Indoors again, I thought of telling Mrs. Cosway. Once I wouldn't have hesitated, but now, in my subdued state, prepared to do or leave undone a great deal in the cause of avoiding a row, I decided against it. The consequences would be noisy and furious and would change nothing.

His walk was far shorter than usual. He was back after half an hour. It was very cold outside. A white mist had descended on the garden and hung there, utterly still. The drawing room was the warmest place in the house, with a big coal fire burning, an electric heater on, and two oil stoves in corners of the room. As she sometimes did, Mrs. Cosway was taking her afternoon rest on the sofa and had covered herself with a blanket in Black Watch tartan, the kind of thing which had been put over one's knees in the days before cars had heaters. When I went into the room to check that John was warm enough, I found her sleeping deeply and John for once without the eiderdown in which he usually wrapped himself. It was covering his armchair but not himself and he had evidently just slipped it off because for the first time I ever remembered, he was too warm. At only four, it was already dusk, the mist darkening, giving a claustrophobic feel to the house as if going outside would be impossible, as if the thick gray stuff would press against the doors, forcing you back. As usual, the curtains were wide open—Mrs. Cosway resisted all attempts to close them and keep the heat in—showing nothing outside but an almost opaque screen of fog.

So that Ida could knit and Winifred read her book, **Anglicans in the Nineteenth Century,** all the lights were on and these were reflected in the bulbous side of the Roman vase, curved yellow shapes on its green translucency. Mrs. Cosway slept, Winifred turned another page, Ida finished a row and began on the next one. The wool she was using was thick and ash-gray and the finished work, hanging down past her knees, looked like a scarf, but the paper pattern on her lap had a picture on it of a pretty woman wearing a red sweater. Everyone was around the fire. John was gazing at the vase, as rapt as someone watching a long-desired television program, the world absent, other people nowhere.

The phone rang at about a quarter past four. I was on my feet, so I went toward the door to answer it, but Winifred almost pushed me aside in her effort to get there first.

"I'll get it, Kerstin."

It can't be, I thought, not today, she can't go to him today, but I wasn't tempted to listen. I was tired of it and I went upstairs. To my bedroom to read Disraeli's **Sybil** in front of the heater Ella had sneaked in, telling me "not to say a word to Mother."

Ella was in her own room, with a similar heater, or she had been when I passed her door, for I could hear the murmur of her radio. **Sybil** I found very heavy-going and I have never read beyond the third chapter. In the circumstances, I don't think I would have if it had been the most exciting book in the world. Its title, an innocuous if not very attractive English Christian name, has the same effect on me as "Tamara," on the rare occasions I have heard either of them since. I don't shiver, but the names give me pause in whatever I am doing and for a moment holds me still.

Before the noises came from downstairs, a few minutes before, I heard Ella's door open and her feet tap down those uncarpeted stairs. I had been sitting by the window but moved away. An icy breath could be felt between glass and window bars even though outside it was still and windless. With no Mrs. Cosway to hinder me, I drew the thin curtains and sat on the bed. I expected at any moment to hear the front door open and close, the Hillman start up and Winifred drive away for her last time alone with Felix. But there was silence, as thick and heavy as it can only be in winter.

The worst sound in the world broke that silence, not a scream but rather a long-drawn-out cry between a groan and a howl. No words, nothing human about it except that I knew it was human, the sound the tortured must make or those who have received the ultimate bad news. I got off the bed and listened to what followed it, a jumble of voices, all of them on the edge of terror, no words distinguishable. The door to Ella's room was wide open but the room was empty. I came to the top of the stairs. The sounds had died now to groans and a kind of soft wailing.

I was dreadfully afraid. What I would have liked to do was throw a blanket around me and plunge out into the fog, run down the hill to people who were cheerful and ordinary and who chattered and laughed. But I had to go down. I descended slowly, feeling the blood drain out of my face, feeling my hands begin to shake. Ella was in the hall, as white-faced as I must have been, her eyes huge and staring. The drawing-room door was closed. I opened it and saw what I had come down to see. I went in first, she following me. At the sight which met me I thought I would fall but somehow I stood my ground.

Blood was everywhere. The room itself was so dingy, every color muted, its browns and fawns and pinks dulled, and the blood was so bright, splashed on the muddy carpet, sprayed scarlet on clothes and skin. John lay on the floor, his arms upraised as if to clutch at someone to hold and clasp against himself, an impossible happening. The wailing, horribly pathetic and sad, came from him. On the sofa, Mrs. Cosway crouched as if she had been standing up on its cushions but had lost her balance. Like a record stuck in a certain groove, she was repeating over and over, "What have you done? What have you done?"

Unbelievably, Ida crawled on the carpet, picking up bloody shards of green glass, her hands covered in blood, tears streaming down her face. A hundred or more fragments of green glass, some of them bloodied, were scattered about, and among them, between Ida and her mother, lay Winifred. I looked at her and at her head and face and then I looked away, covering my mouth. I shut my eyes, opened them, and, determined not to retch, dropped onto my knees and felt for a pulse in her neck and at her wrist. There was nothing. She had her coat on, a scarf around her neck.

"Is she dead?" This was Mrs. Cosway and her voice was a squeak.

"Yes." I wanted to tell her to get down from there, but I couldn't. "She's dead."

"John did it." This was Ida, lifting her head, her voice on the edge of becoming a scream, her raised hand full of broken glass. "He did it. He picked up the vase and did it."

"He went for her," Mrs. Cosway said. "I don't know why." She looked down at her son, now rolling silently on the carpet. It was then that I noticed that his hands were clean and free of blood. "I suppose it's what mad people do."

I said I was going to phone the police. It was too late for an ambulance. In the icy dining room I found Ella was already on the phone, showing more coolness and nerve than I would have expected from her. Blood was on her pink sweater and on the phone receiver where she had touched it. It was then that I remembered Mrs. Cosway accusing John of pushing her when she fell downstairs. She was doing it again now.

"They're coming," Ella said in a lifeless tone.

"What happened?"

"I didn't see. I'd come down, it was so cold upstairs, and I came in here to look at the wedding presents. I hadn't really looked at them before. I came out after a bit and there was Winifred in the hall putting her coat on. She went into the drawing room but left the door open. I heard her tell Mother and Ida she was going out to see June. I couldn't stand it, Kerstin. I went in and I said, 'She's not, she's going to Felix Dunsford. Ask her if she's not.' I didn't wait to hear what happened. I was shaking all over."

I told her she would have to tell the police all that.

"I'm going to have some brandy. D'you want some?"

"No, thanks," I said.

She looked at her bloodstained hands. "Do you know what I keep thinking, Kerstin? I keep thinking he won't want to know us now, not any of us, not after this."

This shocked me. I thought I was beyond being astonished by anything the Cosways did but obviously this wasn't so. To keep myself from shouting at her I went back into the drawing room. My hands and my voice shaking by then, my legs unsteady, I saw Mrs. Cosway on the floor, creeping toward Winifred's body. Her hands were bloody, but I couldn't see if the skin was broken. Ida's was and badly, a sliver of glass dangling from a cut on her thumb. She had abandoned her task of picking up the glass, a housewife even at the edge of doom, and was back in the chair where she had been before I went upstairs. Sobbing and moaning, she stared at her wounded hands as the blood dripped onto her gray knitting.

When she saw me she managed to speak. Her voice came out in a thin hoarse squeak. "Someone had better tell Eric what John has done."

"That can keep for half an hour." Mrs. Cosway knelt over Winifred's body, ignoring John.

He rolled himself up when he saw me, got on to his knees, and seemed about to hide behind the sofa. Something deflected him, perhaps the confrontation at his own level with Winifred. All expression had been wiped from his face. He got to his feet, lumbered slowly out of the room and down the passage. I went after him, but I was too late. He went into the library and I heard him turn the key in the lock. He must have kept it about him ever since it appeared to be missing, perhaps in his dressing-gown pocket with the bandage tape and the ballpoint, the dice, the bottle, and all the rest.

I had become tongue-tied. Instead of going back into the drawing room I sat down on one of the upright chairs which were ranged against the walls in the hall. A fire had been lit the day before in the great old fireplace, but the remains had never been cleared away. I sat there, looking at the ashes. An icy draft was blowing down that wide-open chimney, so strong that the lightly poised harp quivered. Ella had told me that if you stood on the hearth and looked up the chimney on moonlit nights and positioned yourself correctly you could see the moon up there in a square of sky. I closed my eyes, willing my hands to stop shaking. I kept saying to myself, it's not true, John has done nothing, and then that I wished I had left when I said I would and gone home.

The police were slow in coming. This was due to the fog. It took them three quarters of an hour to get to Lydstep. There were two of them and later many more but just two at first. I don't remember their names because I never wrote them down and it is thirty-five years ago, but I know they were ordinary, quite common names, Wilson and Smith or Brown and Johnson or others of that sort, the sort thousands of English people have, just as thousands of Swedes are called Andersson and Svensson. The middle-aged one was a chief inspector, I think, and the young one was a sergeant, or that may have been later. And there was a doctor, a pathologist, I think. But I don't know. What they looked like I have also quite forgotten. I let them into the house and took them to the drawing room.

Mrs. Cosway was quite calm by this time, chillingly so. Without waiting to be asked, she said to the older policeman, "My son did this. He is mentally ill, he is schizophrenic."

"I see." The older one was kneeling down, looking at Winifred. "You saw this?"

"Of course. We were here."

"You were here, madam?" he said to Ida.

She nodded. "My brother killed her with that thing."

"Yes, why he had to destroy a priceless vase," said Mrs. Cosway, "I never will know."

The sergeant gave her the sort of look I once did when she said something more than usually outrageous. He said, "Is there some other room we can go to?" And then, "Where is Mr. Cosway now?"

That was the first time I had ever heard John called that. It seemed to make him into a different person and lift him out of the two roles, child and murderer, imposed on him. I told them he had locked himself in the library and went with them down the passage. I knelt down by the library door and looked through the keyhole. The key was in the lock. Poking it through wouldn't have retrieved it from this side for the bottom of the doors were flush to the wooden flange at their foot. The older policeman told the sergeant to break the doors down but he could see this was impossible; they were heavy and made of oak.

Ella had joined us by then. "Some of the keys fit more than one door," she said. "We could try others in the lock."

She and I went into the dining room. Ida and Mrs. Cosway were sitting on opposite sides of the table, not looking at each other but past each other at opposite walls. I hadn't noticed till then that they both had blood splashes on their clothes but nowhere on their skin. There was a powerful smell of the carbolic soap Ida used in the kitchen. They had washed their hands and Mrs. Cosway's showed cuts to her thumbs and fingertips and palms. No one spoke. I looked in the sideboard drawer. The left-hand division of it was full of keys, some with labels tied on them with string, and among them was a small white tablet of Largactil. The drawer must have been slightly open when John threw away the pill Ida was trying to give him. Ella picked out possible keys, maybe ten or twelve of them, and we had started back when Mrs. Cosway spoke.

"When they have got him out of there they must take him away. We cannot live in this house with a homicidal maniac."

"Oh, Mother."

Ida had made her usual rejoinder to shocking remarks from that source and Mrs. Cosway hers to this reproof, "Oh, Mother, nothing."

After the key John had used had been pushed through the lock, Ella tried one after another of those we had brought from the dining room. Almost the last one she tried—it was labeled **bedroom five**—unlocked the door. I saw the interior of the library with new eyes, the policemen's eyes, the way I had seen it the first time I went in there. They were even more astonished by it than I had been. At least I knew from the first that a library and a labyrinth both existed in this place. They stepped over the threshold to be faced by a wall of books and were led by Ella along tortuous passages, expressionless marble faces looming above their heads, every turning leading to more laden shelves, every narrow defile apparently a dead end until a side passage suddenly opened where it had seemed there was only paper and vellum and that smell of ancient printer's ink. The sergeant's face showed half-angry bewilderment as the last angle was past and we were all crowded together in the central space. John was there but no one went near him.

Someone—Ida, I suppose—had replaced all the books he had pulled off the shelves last time he was there. He was sitting on the floor, his back propped against Longinus's plinth, and he had been writing or drawing something in a notebook. The two strange men he had never seen before disquieted him, that was obvious from his expression, but he didn't speak. He put the notebook and pencil on the floor and got to his feet. There was blood on him, but not much, and it was on his clothes, not his skin. His hands were intact, not a cut to be seen. His eyes moved from one policeman to the other, to me, to Ella, then, quite quickly for the slow mover he usually was, he stepped into the passage behind him and was gone. He had disappeared into that part of the library where I had never ventured, a wilderness of bends and angles, all lined with the ten thousand books Zorah had told me were in there.

"Can you get him to come out?" The sergeant addressed Ella in an exasperated voice.

"I shouldn't think so. You mustn't touch him, you see. He goes mad if he's touched."

"He's mad already," said the chief inspector.

No one attempted to follow John. I picked up the notebook he had been writing in. It was clean of blood, unmarked by anything but the pencil he had used. He had been drawing and proving the theorem of Pythagoras.

Looking at it, Ella said, "He used to do that a lot when things were bad for him and he was troubled. Pythagoras comforted him."

The policemen were uninterested. Conferring, they seemed to decide to send for "people who can deal with this sort of thing," and asked Ella if they could use the phone. What Mrs. Cosway thought of their summoning what people usually call "men in white coats" I don't know, but she must have overheard them. Still half-disbelieving it had happened, I had a desperate desire to run away, to go anywhere out of this dreadful place, and I said to the sergeant, he being the more approachable of the two, "I should go to Windrose and tell Mr. Dawson. They were to be married tomorrow."

"We'll do that," he said. "We'd prefer you to stay here."

With my chance of even a brief escape gone, I went back into the dining room where Mrs. Cosway told me to make everyone tea. Her outburst about homicidal maniacs seemed to have restored her, for she looked much better. Though she had addressed me, Ida got up. Ida always did get up when anything needed doing. It was as well she did, for though I could make good coffee, the brewing of tea defeated me. I could never quite appreciate the need for the water to be on the boil and can't really to this day. Her hands bandaged in dishcloths, Ida made the tea while I set out cups and poured milk for those who wanted it.

Everyone had their tea and had begun drinking it when the people who had come for John arrived. I heard the van they came in but I didn't see them.

Their going into the library seemed to me like a kind of desecration. By that time I was close to thinking of it as John's place, somewhere he might have spent the greater part of his time if this had been allowed, almost have lived in there among the ten thousand books, pulling those he disliked off the shelves, reading his Euclid, solving his number puzzles, and been happy. Only it hadn't been allowed.

They hunted the poor Minotaur and brought him out. I saw none of this. Ida told me. Whether they charged him with Winifred's murder before they took him away, I don't know. Of this sort of procedure I know nothing. I believe the inspector left the house a bewildered man. Apparently, he expected insanity, as he called it, and mathematical ability to be mutually exclusive. In other words, if someone was mentally disturbed he must also be stupid. Anything else he couldn't understand but he didn't dismiss it, he was genuinely puzzled.

More police had arrived by this time and concentrated their efforts on the drawing room. What they did in there I don't know but it took a long time. They must have measured things and taken photographs but it would have been less thorough than it would be today. One of them came out and said he would like all the clothes we had been wearing that day for forensic examination. The inspector came back at about seven, told us Eric "had been informed" and he would appreciate it if none of us went anywhere that evening. With a sharp look at me, he said we must not on any account go far, definitely not leave the country, and were to notify the police if we intended to leave Windrose.

"I don't know about anyone else," said Mrs. Cosway, a remark which might have served as an epitaph for her, "but I should like dinner."

"Oh, Mother," said Ida, but she got up as usual.

I expected Eric to make some sign, to come or phone. Perhaps he had gone to Felix or asked Felix to come to him. I had no idea if he had loved Winifred or just wanted a suitable wife and, though he was wrong, he had thought her suitable. Neither he nor Felix appeared. No one in that house, as far as I could tell, showed the least grief over Winifred. Shock, yes, a certain amount of fear, but I saw no sorrow.

The fog lifted as a little wind got up. Into the clearing sky, dark blue between the shreds of whitish cloud, the moon sailed. As they left, the police were talking to each other about the fog lifting and driving back being easier than coming here. We had all had to change our clothes and let them take away the ones we had been wearing. Mrs. Cosway laid herself face downward on the sofa, Ida disappeared into the kitchen, and Ella to her bedroom. John was gone. All this I have remembered as best I could because I wrote nothing in the diary that night.

25

I don't know if a psychiatrist saw John, I don't know what was said or done to him or where he was kept. Mrs. Cosway must have known the answers to these questions and probably Ida too, for different police came the next day and talked to them for a long time. Ella too was closeted with the police, though she said to me afterward that they had told her nothing. On that day Mrs. Cosway's attitude toward me changed.

It was much worse than it had been up till then, verging on violence. It began in the kitchen at breakfast, a meal which, it seemed, was to be taken in silence, no one eating much but everyone drinking more tea and coffee than usual. Mrs. Cosway was the first to speak and then not until Ida was collecting plates and cups and putting them on a tray.

"John doing what he did," she said, "just goes to show how criminally negligent Pontius Pilate was in refusing me his drug. He was never aggressive while he had it, he never did any of those things he'd been doing like striking Ida and destroying books. It culminated in murder and all because that wicked man kept his drug from him." She turned to me. "Why are you looking like that? What does that look mean?"

Shock must have shown in my face. I said I was sorry but I wasn't aware of looking any different than usual.

"You did look different, very different. You need to remember that all this is no business of yours. You're an employee, not a family friend."

"Yes, she is," said Ella. "She's my friend."

I gave her a grateful smile. That had been kind. I said nothing to Mrs. Cosway, but she had not yet said as much as she wanted to.

"The police will be back today and they'll want to talk some more to Ida and me. I don't want you there, Kerstin. Do you understand? You have no business to judge us. I don't want you sitting there disapproving in your holier-than-thou way. Is that clear?"

Ida, who might have intervened on my behalf, continued to take our breakfast things off the table. I said it was perfectly clear and got up. The police themselves would decide who should be present when they continued with their questioning, and Mrs. Cosway must have known this. She simply wanted an excuse to exclude me. I don't think I had ever been holier-than-thou, but I had disapproved of her, in her attitude to John particularly, and I was young enough to have shown it.

This provided a good reason for me to hand in my notice and go, but I remembered what the inspector had said to us the day before about staying where we were. I especially had been singled out as not to leave the country. Almost automatically piling plates and cups on the draining board, I looked at Ida where she stood with her back to me, staring out into the garden which was once again lying under a blanket of snow. Backs can be as eloquent as faces and hers, round-shouldered, slack under the floral cotton overall and moth-holed gray sweater, the muscles giving one nervous twitch, told me she had nothing to say to me and would welcome my departure. Her stance and her attitude showed me more than anything else had how close she and her mother were, almost of one mind. I don't know how long it was before she turned around and began on her unending tasks, for I left her and went into the library.

The drawing room was out of bounds, its door taped shut. Our bedrooms were our refuge or, in my case, the library. I rediscovered it that morning, learning to guide my footsteps by the kind of books which were the various walls of the maze, English literature in one, science in another, ancient German and Danish dictionaries in Gothic script on the shelves Longinus faced and encyclopedias in one wall of the passage John had run down to escape. I went down it and after rounding two corners (ghosts and the occult, fine arts and travel) I saw signs of a struggle where the people who came for him must have hunted him down. I expect my distaste showed in my face then, but there was no one to see it.

Books had fallen or been pulled out of the shelves, most of them classical literature; Ovid's **Metamorphoses** and Tacitus's **Annals** lay face downward, their pages creased. I didn't want to imagine John's capture here or the carelessness of those who came for him and who had no more interest in the volumes their struggles had displaced than they had in his fear. I knelt down and picked up the books, smoothing out the thin fine paper and blowing dust off spines.

Back in the open space where John had been sitting, I too sat on the floor and looked at his notebook, at Pythagoras, drawn with exquisite precision, on other pages at algebraic equations I was unable to understand, and strange propositions presented, all of them, it seemed to me, beginning on the lines of letting something squared equal a and something else to the power of five equal b. I picked up the English–Swedish **Esselte Studium** dictionary and diverted myself by looking up long English words whose meanings I didn't know, but diversion was not what I found. I was too wretched for that and too angry. For a moment, no more, I asked myself if John could possibly have killed his sister, if he would have wanted to, for no more reason than that she had touched him or said something he found unacceptable. For a moment—then I was back at my firm conviction that it was impossible, an invention of Mrs. Cosway's or of Ida's.

True, he had struck Ida, but that had been from exasperation. To my mind, I might say to my knowledge, the violent emotions which would be a preliminary to such a deed were not in his makeup. Put more simply, he wouldn't have **wanted** to do it. I could almost have said he wouldn't be interested. Winifred deceiving Eric with another man wouldn't have concerned him, would have meant nothing. If she had made him angry or upset he would have run away to hide himself. All that meant nothing to them. They wanted him charged with murder and found not to be responsible for his actions. That way they could be rid of an encumbrance.

I heard the police arrive and someone inadvertently slam the front door. I heard Ella say, "If you want me I'll be upstairs in my room."

Probably I should have been upstairs in mine. Before leaving the library I walked around it once more, learning its intricacies. The time passed very slowly. I had been in there only half an hour. Ella tapped on the door after I had been in my room no more than five minutes. I had been writing in the diary and she spotted it at once, unmistakably what it was in its dark red leather binding, lying face downward on my bed.

"Oh, a diary! May I look?"

Thinking of the drawings, I said I'd rather she didn't, but I was too late. She looked at the one of Lydstep Old Hall under its summer leaves, but failed to comment on it and turned to the first page. The entries were in Swedish.

"Silly me, I should have known. Now tell me, Kerstin, am I intruding?"

Relieved that she had stopped before coming to the drawing of herself and her dolls, I said truthfully that she was not. I was glad to see her but had nothing in my room to offer her.

"That doesn't matter. I couldn't eat a thing. I just picked at my breakfast. Isn't everything absolutely **awful?** I feel I ought to apologize to you on Mother's behalf, she was so rude and unkind, but of course she's under a great strain. We all are. Mind you, I think that in a way it's a blessing in disguise."

I thought perhaps I had misheard. English colloquialisms sometimes eluded me at that time and I wasn't even sure what "blessing" meant, though it was a word I had heard often enough on Eric's lips. She couldn't have meant the killing of Winifred had some sort of good aspect—could she?

"Well, look at it this way, Kerstin. You and I are friends, aren't we, so I think I can speak frankly. Winifred was behaving terribly badly. She'd have made poor Eric a hopeless wife and in my opinion she was using Felix unforgivably. Honestly, is she that much of a loss?"

I said nothing. Starting to wonder if others among the Cosways were not madder than John, I picked up the diary, closed it, and put it out of Ella's reach. She had a groomed appearance that morning as if the whole of her, hair, hands, clothes, and her skin itself, had been brushed and smoothed. I soon saw why.

"Now I want your advice, Kerstin. Tell me honestly what you feel. Do you think it's too early for me to—well, resume my relationship with Felix? I mean, should I ring up the pub and leave him a message?"

She took my silence and blank look for encouragement.

"Of course, you'll say that at first he may just want to talk. He'll have no one to talk all this over with. I mean, he can hardly discuss it with Eric, can he? Wouldn't he welcome the chance to meet me and be alone with me and have a real heart-to-heart? And after that things should go back to their old footing."

The last thing she really wanted was my honest opinion. I would, anyway, have been afraid to give it; it was too violent and condemnatory. Holier-than-thou it might well have been and Mrs. Cosway would have been justified. At that moment it seemed to me that almost anyone would have been holier than Ella, but at the same time I felt I was dealing with someone far younger than myself, more a child than a woman. I said, carefully restraining myself, "It would be wiser to wait a week or two. I would let him make the first move."

"Oh, no, Kerstin, I know him. In that case, he wouldn't make a move at all." Like most people seeking advice, she had determined before she asked on the course she meant to take. "I think I'll ring the pub around midday and say it's Tamara. He'll know it's me because he'll know it can't be Winifred."

I said there was no doubt about that.

"Thanks, anyway. For your advice, I mean. You've helped me clear my mind. I'll phone at lunchtime. He may even be in the pub and come to the phone."

She returned in a little while to say the police wanted to speak to me but there was some difficulty as to where this interview should take place. I said that perhaps the dining room would do.

"Oh, Kerstin, I'm so sorry but Mother's in there covering all the presents up with sheets and Ida's busy in the kitchen."

This was probably the first time I knew Mrs. Cosway to do anything that could be remotely construed as housework. "Then they'd better come up here."

They came up, the same young sergeant and a different older man, a detective superintendent whose name I do remember. It was Strickland. He had been in my room no more than a minute before he, like Ella, picked up the diary but, unlike her, asked what it was. I told him.

"Look if you like," I said.

He looked, smiled, closed it and made no comment. I had to say it, though I was hoarse with fear and a kind of shyness.

"John didn't kill her."

Strickland said, very gently, "You weren't there, were you, Miss Kvist?"

I had to say I wasn't. I was asked a lot of questions about where in fact I had been when the attack happened, what had been said, and how much I had seen. I answered as best I could, but all the time I was wondering what was in store for me when I finally went downstairs. At some point I had to eat. It seemed that I was not welcome in the dining room or the kitchen. Strickland and the other man left and I sat in the window, watching them get into their car and drive away. I wanted very much to phone Mark. By this time he would know what had happened at Lydstep Old Hall, he would have heard it on the radio or read about it in the paper.

If all this were happening today, I would have a cell phone and access to the Internet and the means to send e-mails. Eating would not be a problem. The White Rose probably has a restaurant now as well as serving bar meals and there would be at least one other place to eat in Windrose. Every inhabitant of Lydstep would be offered counseling, for good or ill. The police would have sent a family liaison officer to be with us all. None of this was the case thirty-five years ago.

Eventually, because I could hardly stay in my room indefinitely, I went slowly downstairs. The sound of a furious argument reached me as I came down into the hall. The gist of it seemed to be that Ella was insisting on her right to use the phone while Mrs. Cosway was equally adamantly shouting at her that it was the wrong time of day and lunch was ready. I approached the dining room, anxious to appear neither timid nor assertive and finding it hard to strike the middle way. Ida was serving meat loaf, mashed potatoes, and very bright green peas. She looked at her mother; Mrs. Cosway met her eyes and then looked at me.

"Your lunch is on the kitchen table." With the prong of a fork Ida picked up a pea she had dropped on the table.

"I don't believe this," Ella said. "You can't do this."

"My mistake was in not doing it from the start," said Mrs. Cosway. "We should never have allowed her to eat with us."

It is said that your feelings can't be hurt by someone you dislike and don't admire. I disliked Mrs. Cosway and certainly had never admired her, but I was hurt. Tears pricked my eyelids and I went quickly out so that no one should see. Two slices of meat loaf, a scoop of mashed potatoes, and a spoonful of peas awaited me on a plate on the kitchen table. Four tinned peach halves were in a bowl, covered by an inverted saucer. My appetite had entirely gone. As I was fetching my coat, hat, and snowboots from upstairs, I thought for the first time that this was to have been Winifred's wedding day.

It was very cold, but Swedes are used to cold and conditioned not to make a fuss about it. A sky like the one that day, a thick yellowish-gray as if made of some solid substance like pea soup, is often described as being full of snow. I expected it to start as I walked down the hill, but none fell. Windrose seemed emptier than usual on a Saturday, as if everyone had been driven indoors by the shock and manner of Winifred's death. But the cause may only have been the bitter cold.

Two women I didn't know were in the shop. Wordless and unsmiling, they turned to look at me. I expected the girl behind the counter to make some remark about the events at Lydstep Old Hall, but she said nothing beyond an offhand "thanks" when I paid her for the brown loaf, piece of cheese, and chocolate bars I bought. In the phone box outside the post office I phoned Mark, but I hadn't enough change to talk to him for long and—foolishly, perhaps—I said nothing about being sent to

Coventry (a phrase I learned from Ella that day) or banished to eat in the kitchen. We were still constrained with each other and a little awkward, our frankness gone. Once I would have said to him that when the police would let me, I would come to him in London and stay, but those words were no longer possible.

In spite of the cold, I was reluctant to go back to Lydstep before I had to. The White Rose was about to close and I was afraid that unless I quickly got away I might encounter Felix Dunsford leaving the saloon bar. There, though, I later found out I did him an injustice, for he had stayed away from the pub that day. I walked across the Memorial Green. The architect and his wife had thrown out their Christmas tree, but no one had collected it and it lay, brown and forlorn, on their garage drive. On the rectory gate was the painted sign Felix had made for Winifred, frost still clinging to it. Eric's car stood on the curved drive outside the front door. I was sure there must be some etiquette laying down the correct procedure for behaving toward someone whose bride-to-be has been murdered, but I had no idea what this might be. I rang the bell, expecting a friend or relative to answer it, but Eric came himself.

We notice such absurd and trivial details in people. The first thing I saw wasn't his wretched tear-stained face or his haunted eyes but the fact that he hadn't shaved. The stubble was white and it aged him by ten years. He stood there and I stood there, wishing I hadn't come.

"It's going to snow," he said.

"Yes." I was cold, shivering with cold. "Can I come in?"

"Of course. I'm so sorry."

In his living room, over the mantelpiece, Winifred looked down at me, joy and triumph in her face. I wondered why I had once thought the portrait a poor likeness. It was her to the life. It was enormously better than my own drawing. She looked as if at any minute she might spring from the canvas and run to meet the painter with outstretched arms. Poor Eric. How could he bear to have it there?

He seemed scarcely aware of it. "Can I get you anything?"

"No, thanks. Of course not."

"Some guests arrived for the wedding. They didn't know. We forgot to let people know. Bill Cusp told me. He sent them away." Briefly he closed his eyes. "How are they all up there?"

"As you'd expect," I said. Or as I would have.

"We were going to Majorca," he said.

I looked inquiring.

"On our honeymoon." He was silent. Then he said, "I won't be able to take her funeral service, you know. I'm afraid I might break down. Will you tell them?"

I said of course I would and then that I must go. He shook hands with me very formally, as he had in the church porch on the day we first met.

"I suppose they'll put him in an asylum," he said.

The word, old-fashioned even then, was new to me. In the thirty-five years gone by it has utterly changed its meaning, a mental hospital in those days, a place of safety for refugees now. I looked it up in **Esselte** when I was back at Lydstep, having some difficulty because I didn't know how to spell it. After that I went into the library and looked for it in the massive **Shorter Oxford Dictionary** which I had once found John reading. **"1. a sanctuary,"** it said, **"for criminals and debtors, from which they cannot be forcibly taken without sacrilege. 2. a secure place of refuge or shelter."** And, finally, after other definitions, **"a lunatic asylum."**

So John was a criminal or a lunatic or both. This place had been his sanctuary, I thought, books surrounding me in the dimness, and he had been forcibly taken from it. That was the sacrilege.

26

SEVERAL TIMES DURING THAT EVENING THE phone rang. With nothing to do but read and nothing to read but third-class Victorian novels, I wrote an account of the day in the diary. Who had made those calls? Eric, perhaps. Felix, if Ella had phoned him first. The police? They had left at about six but they might easily have called back. Jane Trintowel for me? If Mrs. Cosway or Ida had answered I thought it unlikely they would have told me.

Ella tapped on my door just after nine and came in carrying a bottle of rosé.

She glanced at the remains of my meal, crumbs and chocolate bar wrappers. "You should have come down for dinner."

"I'd have been banished to the kitchen," I said.

"Mother will get over all that, you know. It's just that she's in a state."

"Is she, Ella? Is anyone in a state except John? I'm sure he is. I don't like to think of the kind of state he's in."

"Oh, nor do I, nor do I. It's dreadful. Come on,

let me give you a drink. I've brought wineglasses. It's not the same drinking it out of a cup, is it?" Ella drank her first glassful as if it were water. "That's better. I phoned the White Rose like I said. That girl who works the bar answered. I didn't much like that, but I thought, in for a penny, in for a pound. I said, 'It's Tamara' and she didn't wait for me to say I wanted Felix, she just said, 'He hasn't been in today' and put the phone down."

Another of his women, I thought. This seemed not to have occurred to Ella. "I suppose he stayed away out of respect," she said. "Unlike him, but you never know how this sort of thing is going to affect people."

"No, you don't."

"I'll try again tomorrow and if he still doesn't phone I think I'll go down to The Studio. I miss him so terribly, Kerstin. You asked if anyone was in a state. I am, I really am. Sometimes I think I'm going mad. Of course there's madness in our family. Look at John." She picked up the diary but put it down again, saying, "Fancy you writing it in Swedish. It's like a code, isn't it? I suppose you do it so that no one but you can read it."

"Other Swedes could."

"Well, of course. But there aren't any here, are there? Zorah phoned. Imagine, no one had bothered to tell her. She had to read it in the paper. She's coming down. Oh, and a man called Mark phoned, asking for you. I heard Mother tell him she couldn't take phone calls at this time of night. I'm afraid I didn't take much notice because it wasn't Felix, you see."

The snow which had loaded the skies began to fall that night and much more heavily than last time. Lydstep Old Hall was filled with the peculiar white glow which radiates from snow, lighting hall and rooms and even passages more than the sun ever did. Sick of being in my bedroom, I came down early and found the table laid with four pieces and no one in the dining room but Ida. In overall and carpet slippers, a lock of hair at her forehead twisted into a curl with a clip, she looked up from her bread and butter to say a cold "Good morning," as icy as the weather. Her hands were bandaged from forearm to fingertips like a mummy's.

I poured my coffee, almost elated to find that it had been made, for no one but me ever drank it. I thanked her and she said, "I always do make it," in the sort of voice that implied my ingratitude, her own stoicism, and the enormous effort making coffee took. I tentatively took a seat at the table, wondering if I was to be banished to the kitchen today. Just as I had cracked the shell on my egg and was lifting my first piece of toast to my lips, Mrs. Cosway appeared. She had taken once more to the stick she had discarded a month before and was leaning on it, her body bent and her face grim. I wondered why the stick. She didn't need it and had always cursed it when using it was essential. The hand which grasped its hooked top was bandaged like Ida's but the other one had no more than an adhesive strip around the thumb. Neither Ida nor I had a word from her. Breakfast was eaten in silence until Ella came in, wanting to know if anyone intended to go to church.

"One of us should. Winifred would have wished it."

"Don't be ridiculous," said Mrs. Cosway, her voice creaky from lack of use.

That morning I had the curious feeling that everything would continue at Lydstep Old Hall just as it was at that moment. Ella would go back to school, of course, I would leave as soon as the police would let me, but Ida and Mrs. Cosway would continue to live here in this cold calm, Mrs. Lilly coming in twice a week, the gardener gardening, the phone ringing only at prescribed times. The promise Zorah had made would be carried out and she would never be seen again. Nor would John. He would be incarcerated for the rest of his life in a high-security mental hospital or, as Eric called it, an asylum. And this state of affairs was what Mrs. Cosway wanted, had wanted for years.

Ella and I went to church. She asked me to go with her. It suddenly seemed dreadful to me that she should have to go alone when she had previously always been accompanied by Winifred, even though the terms they had been on were seldom friendly and often hostile.

"You'll say I'm only going because Felix might be there," she said as we drove down the hill.

Even if I had thought such a thing I wouldn't have said it, but I was accustomed to this usage of hers and this was no time for arguing. Tiny flakes of snow, pinhead size, pattered lightly against the windscreen. The sky was leaden, the color it is before a summer storm. There was an umbrella in the car and I held it over both of us as we ran into the church porch.

A few regulars came to the service, but most of the people I knew stayed away, whether because of the snow or the fear of awkwardness if a Cosway came, I couldn't tell. Mr. Trewith, he who heard confessions, took the service, and the architect's wife was there, fetching in a Russian fur hat, but Felix didn't come. Ella watched for him, turning her head from the pew he had once or twice sat in to the door and back again several times until Mr. Trewith came down the chancel steps and began telling us that the Scripture moved us in sundry places. Alone of the congregation, Mrs. Waltham and the architect's wife came up to Ella afterward and said how sorry they were. After they had gone I asked Ella what she was called.

"The architect's wife? I don't know. I don't think anyone knows. I used to be so jealous because

Felix admired her. Well, I still am. I can't bear him even looking at another woman."

And then he was upon us.

A meeting was unavoidable. He had been to see Eric and was coming down the rectory drive to the gate. We were leaving the churchyard by the gate which was next to it, as near as the entrances to two semi-detached houses.

"Good morning, ladies," he said.

We might have been any two women from the village, June Prothero's mother perhaps and Mrs. Cusp. His tone was polite, indifferent, cheerful. In spite of the cold, he wore no coat over his check flannel shirt and jeans. Something about his appearance made me think of the leading actor in one of those western films, and I felt I should be looking about me for his horse. What Ella felt showed plainly in her face. She had gone very white and suddenly she looked much older than she was. She lifted her eyes to Felix's face and, to my alarm, took hold of him by his upper arms, clutching the stuff of his shirt.

"Oh, Felix, how can you speak to me like that?"

He appealed to me. "What have I done?" I think he genuinely didn't know. "I'm sorry if I've put my foot in it. Believe me, I'm pretty upset myself about what happened to Winifred."

He was one of the few people I have ever known with no feeling of empathy whatsoever. He simply seemed to believe that other people felt the same about things, **everything,** as he did. In this, curiously, he was behaving like a high-functioning autistic. Ella was near to tears and when she spoke her voice rose. Mr. Trewith, coming down the path with Bill Cusp, turned his head sharply away, as did his companion.

"Winifred's dead but I'm alive," Ella said. "Have you forgotten what we've been to each other?" Her voice rose. She held on to his shirt, shaking it and shaking him. "Have you, Felix? I love you. I want to be with you again. You said you loved me. Didn't you? Didn't you?"

"I never did," he said. "I'm sure I never did."

He seemed to stop in midsentence. "I never do say it," was what I am sure he was holding back. He was not in the least embarrassed. I suspect he had been through this kind of thing too many times for awkwardness. Slightly shaking his head, he tried to prise apart the fingers that clutched his shirt.

"Let go," he said. "Now, come on. Let go of me."

"I will never let you go!"

Incredibly, he began to laugh. It sounded real. It sounded as if he found the situation hilarious. I turned away then, I walked away, unwilling to do a Cosway and tell Ella to keep her voice down. It would anyway have been too late. She was beyond control, his laughter touching the switch that released her screaming and loosened her hands. She began to beat them against his chest, but he ducked and ran away from her across the Memorial Green.

"As if all the devils in hell were after him," Mrs. Cusp remarked to me. She had been part of the little crowd who gathered to watch the scene. I took Ella by the arm and put her into the passenger seat of the car, where she rocked herself back and forward, sobbing and clutching handfuls of her hair. Without waiting for her to calm down—something which might have taken a long time—I drove us back to Lydstep Old Hall.

The drawing room, which had been out of bounds for three days, by Monday morning was once again made accessible to the family. Ida had made a fire in the grate, logs piled precariously high but the fender securely in place. The police had performed all their tasks and tests and cleaned up, the sergeant recommending Ida to have the place redecorated if she wanted all the stains eradicated. The spots and stains and splashes could still be seen, though bleached to a yellowish-brown so that, if you didn't know, you wouldn't have identified them as made by flying blood. At first I thought that all remains of the Roman vase had gone too, that priceless object I had seen John stroking reverently, but crossing to the window, I spotted a green shard winking in the snow-light. It was half embedded in the carpet, its sharp point sticking up out of the faded pile.

That is how I happen to have it still, not from souvenir-hunting but because I picked it up for fear someone would tread on it. I put it in the pocket of my skirt. By the time I found it again Mrs. Cosway had turned me out of Lydstep Old Hall.

The police came back just as she and Ida were returning to the drawing room, Ida with new knitting wool and needles, the bloodstained gray discarded. This time it was Strickland and the sergeant. A calm and tragic Ella, a kind of **Mourning Becomes Electra** figure, brought them in. Strickland said, "I'd like a few words with Miss Kvist."

Without saying so, he indicated by not taking a seat and holding the door open, that the interview was to be in private.

"You can talk to her here," said Mrs. Cosway. "She has nothing to say that she can't say in front of us."

"I won't keep you more than a minute or two, Miss Kvist," Strickland said. "The purpose of my visit is to ask you if we might borrow your diary."

Mrs. Cosway's face was frightening. I got up and Strickland followed me out of the room, leaving the sergeant behind. The request had shaken me, as I think it would most people. Unless we are the sort of people who keep diaries for future publication, we think of this record as more private than our thoughts and more secret than the most awkward moments of our pasts.

"Will it help John Cosway?" I said as we went upstairs.

"Does he need help?"

I said I didn't know. Could he tell me where John was and what had become of him?

"He hasn't been charged," Strickland said. "I don't know yet if he will be. At present he is in the hospital." The sight of my stricken face must have made him say quickly, "As a voluntary patient."

"Does Mrs. Cosway know all this?"

"Of course. I'm surprised no one has told you."

I wasn't surprised. We went into my bedroom. Bright sunshine streamed through my windows, melting the long icicles which hung, dripping, from the eaves. I took the diary out of the drawer where I kept it and handed it to him.

"We have a translator lined up," he said.

Dreading his answer, I asked him if it would be produced as evidence in court at John's trial; to my immense relief he shook his head, saying it was for the eyes of the investigating officers only and for counsel. My knowledge of English law was almost nil. If Strickland thought my ignorance profound when I asked him if John could be executed, he gave no sign of it. He seemed unaffected by my drawings.

"The death penalty for murder came to an end three years ago," he said, leafing through the diary with its incomprehensible language. "It was suspended under the Abolition of Death Penalty Act of 1965."

I asked him what the punishment now was.

"Imprisonment for life."

He moved toward the door. "A beautiful day for the time of year," he said. "Now that your duties here have ended, for the time being at least, you may be tempted to leave. Please remember we would like you to remain for the present or let us know at once if you—well, change your place of residence."

It was as if he knew what was coming, though this was impossible. "I'll see myself out, Miss Kvist. We shall take good care of your diary."

I felt strangely bereft without it. Since then I have been told this is a common reaction of diarists to being deprived, through losing it, having it stolen, or simply coming to the end of the volume, of the physical thing itself, the book, in which the words have been written. A substitute will be adequate but only just. That which is remembered flows less smoothly when it is applied to different paper between alien covers. Much worse would be to stop writing altogether, so I found a notebook I had bought for some forgotten purpose and wrote down, faithfully but with less than my usual enthusiasm, the events of the evening before and that morning.

I felt a strong reluctance to go downstairs. The sun was as high in the sky as it ever gets at that time of the year and the icicles had shrunk to half their length. I saw how they might themselves be regarded as a sort of clock, the rate at which they dissolved depending on their length, their thickness, and the heat of the sun. These, for instance, had diminished by four or five inches in an hour and a half. Somehow I was sure that all this would have interested John very much, that I could have told him about it, talking to him in a way, alas, I never had while he was here. I wrote all these reflections down and then I went downstairs.

Mrs. Cosway and Ella were in the drawing room and I could hear them arguing about whether Ella should return to school or wait another week. In keeping with her usual attitude of getting her children out of the way as much as possible and then growing resentful at their absence, Mrs. Cosway was telling Ella it was her duty to go back while Ella was responding that she was too sad and too wretched even to consider it. Was I her only hearer who knew the real cause of her misery? I went into the kitchen, from where I could see Ida pegging washing out on the line. It reminded me of my first day at Lydstep Old Hall when she had been doing the same thing on a fine summer's evening with John to help her.

I looked in the fridge to see what was for lunch and set about peeling potatoes and cleaning a cauliflower. Her hands in cotton gloves, Ida came back with her empty washing basket and my whole body tensed as I waited for a curt nod from her or a shrug. But she was as affable as she ever was—not very, that is, but it was a great improvement on her breakfast greeting.

"You've started on the vegetables, I see."

I agreed, the point being beyond doubt.

"That's just as well. I shouldn't get my poor hands wet. They're cut to pieces. It made things very awkward doing the washing. With Winifred gone, I suppose I shall have to do all the ironing."

Once, this remark would have shocked me, but by now I was used to it and comments like it and what we would now perhaps call "Cosway-speak."

"Do you want any shopping done?" I asked. "I could go down to the village this afternoon, if you like."

"No, thanks. I can do it."

"It's no trouble, Ida." I was placating her and, by association, her mother; I knew it and despised myself for it, but that was the demoralizing effect they had on me. I had reached a stage when any scrap of kindness, when a word which wasn't actually rude, made me absurdly grateful. "I can go after lunch."

She didn't bother to answer. "Mother is furious about your diary," she said. "She thinks you had no business to keep a diary while you were working for us."

I picked up a handful of silver, the cloth, and the napkins and went into the dining room to lay the table. Ella was there, apparently talking to some member of the staff at the White Rose. I heard her say, "You **are** giving him my messages, aren't you?" The reply must have been short and sharp for she had flushed when she put down the receiver.

I had to say something. "No luck?"

"That girl is very impertinent. I think I shall go out of my mind, Kerstin. You needn't lay a place for me. I couldn't eat a thing. Have you noticed what a lot of weight I've lost?"

I hadn't, but I said I had and added humbly that did she think it would be all right for me to make a phone call to London?

"Well, as far as I'm concerned, Kerstin, it's fine. Better do it before Mother comes in here. Oh, and don't be too long, will you, in case Felix is trying to get through to me? I know he will. He'll want to say sorry for the way he behaved yesterday."

There was no reply from Mark and no way of letting him know what was going on, in those days before answering machines and faxes and text messaging and e-mails. A sudden darkening in the dining room drew me to the window and I saw that the brightness of the day was past. Great ponderous snow clouds, black and streaked with livid light, were gathering overhead.

Lunch was a horrible English dish which at the present day, thank God, seems to have disappeared entirely from cooks' repertoires: toad-in-the-hole, pork sausages in a Yorkshire pudding–like batter. In spite of what she had said, Ella sat down at the table with us. She had brought a bottle of rosé—I was beginning to wonder if she had a running order with a Sudbury wine merchant—and offered it to everyone, this being the only way, I suppose, of being able to drink it herself. The bottle might have contained arsenic from the look Mrs. Cosway gave it.

"No one used to drink wine at luncheon," she said. "It is a nasty habit we've picked up from the French."

"Ida?" said Ella. "Kerstin?"

My nervous state was such that I wasn't able to resist. Under her mother's horrified eyes, Ella poured me a large glassful. It was a poisoned chalice and I knew it. No good could come of it. But I was both so relieved that I had been allowed to sit down to eat with the family and so afraid of what might be said at any moment about my presence there, the diary, my phone calls, and my talking to Strickland in private, that my hands shook and my mouth was dry. Six months before I had thought myself a confident, intrepid girl, but all that was gone, driven out of me by this frowning old woman with her pinched, grim face.

As it happened, nothing was said, at least on the subjects of phone calls, the diary, and my interview with the police, for the duration of the meal. A good deal of comment was made on the weather, for the storm clouds had begun to shed their load of snow. Big fluffy flakes of it were flying at the window panes and quickly covering paving and grass and tree branches. Ella drank her glass of rosé, then a second. Mine was welcome, yet nauseating. I began to realize that Mrs. Cosway, though addressing both her daughters, hadn't said a word to me. She was making it plain that she excluded me by calling them by their Christian names each time she spoke.

Normally, she would have made her statement to the assembled company, but at that lunchtime, she singled out both sisters. "Zorah should be here by three, Ida and Ella. I do hope this snow doesn't hold her up."

It was childish, it was grotesque, it was the kind of thing adolescent girls do, and I was a fool to be affected by it. Yet I don't think that anything which had been said in my presence before then or much afterward made me feel so alone and so utterly rejected as Mrs. Cosway's remark about Zorah. Ida smiled slightly—she hardly ever did smile more than slightly—but Ella, wrapped up as she was in her own woes, reached for my hand under the tablecloth and squeezed it. It made me like her. Perhaps it was this which, all those years later, made me bother to ask her to meet me for a drink that evening in Riga.

I drank my wine, though I'd have been wiser not to. The meal was over. I was getting up from the table to help Ida clear away when Mrs. Cosway expelled me or gave me the order of release, depending how you look at it. She said to me, without using my name, "When you've taken those things out you can go. Now, I mean, this afternoon. Pack your bags and what you can't carry we shall have sent on."

In Cosway fashion, Ella screamed, "You can't do this, Mother. You're crazy."

"And you are not to give her a lift anywhere, Ella. Not if you want to come back into this house."

Ella began to say something, incomprehensible to me, about having things she could say if she chose to the "authorities," but the rest of it I didn't hear. Nausea overcame me and with my napkin over my mouth I ran to the downstairs lavatory, getting there just in time. I was very sick, throwing up again and again. Afterward, drinking water with my mouth held under the cold tap, I felt so weak I had to sit down in there and rest, gasping. John and his sojourns in that very place came back to me, and how he had locked himself in.

About ten minutes went by before I came out and went upstairs. There was no sign of any of them. The smell of sausages in batter and overcooked cauliflower pervaded the place. In my bedroom I threw things into my cases, keeping back a second sweater to wear on top of the one I had on in case I had to be outdoors a long time. It was the way characters in films pack, folding nothing, tossing clothes and shoes in haphazardly on top of each other. I was putting my toothbrush and toothpaste into my sponge bag when Ella came in to promise to send on the bags I couldn't carry.

"You do see I can't drive you anywhere, don't you, Kerstin? Mother and Ida really wouldn't let me back in. All the outer doors can be bolted, you know."

I said I did see.

"Please don't lose touch. You must write to me as soon as you're settled somewhere or I shall be so dreadfully worried. Besides, you'll want to know what's happening with me and Felix. I've got a sort of feeling he'll ring before the day is out and I'm determined not to stray far from the phone. That's actually another reason why I can't take you to the station."

Promising to write to her, I put the diary-notebook in on top of the clothes in my overnight bag, closed it, and picked it up along with the smaller of the other two. But I had to set them down again as Ella threw her arms around me. She covered my face with kisses in an almost amorous way, explaining herself when she released me.

"That's what I'd do if you were Felix, you see. You don't mind, do you?"

27

I walked out of Lydstep Old Hall at three-thirty in the afternoon. It would have been dark by then in Göteburg and it was growing dark here, the snow still falling but lightly, as a fine powder. Wearing my padded boots and my thick coat with its hood, I felt better and more myself, my old self, than I had for weeks, so fast was the effect of the Cosways shed once I was out of the house. This return to an old, once habitual feeling restored what I thought I had once had in abundance, a sense of well-being. Exercising it, I looked at what the Cosways had done and began to laugh at the whole concept, so dear to the hearts of those Victorian novelists, of the young woman, whatever she might be, some dependant or governess, turned out into the snow. The cold, cold snow.

I was laughing like this when Zorah's Lotus passed me. Whether she recognized me or not, she very likely didn't want to stop for a madwoman who was prancing down the road laughing. It was hysterical, of course, and the happiness I felt was illusory. Still, I had left. I had shaken the dust of

Lydstep Old Hall off my feet forever. At once I asked myself why I hadn't done so weeks before, when I first thought of it. But for a few minutes I was happy and then, when I thought of John, I became somber again. At least I knew that he was in a hospital as a voluntary patient. I need no longer have those visions I had been experiencing, especially in the night, of him in a prison cell, insufficiently heated and with nowhere to hide. I wondered then if I would ever see him again and as I remembered him, the things he liked doing and the things they stopped him doing, I realized that I loved him. Not as I had once or twice loved a lover or would love my husband, but nearer to the feeling I had for my brother. Coupled with that was a tenderness which had begun, I believe, from his asking me to marry him. Many would have said that his proposal was all nonsense, that he had no idea of what marriage was, but I knew that he would only have made his offer because he liked me enough to want me to be with him, because he knew that I, of all the people in that household, to some extent understood the strange workings of his mind. I make an exception there for Zorah. She was fond of him and "on his side," but I think she had been made too egotistical by the way life and her family had treated her to care very much for anyone else at all. So I thought then, walking down the hill into Windrose.

I had decided to seek refuge with Eric. For a

night or two. The rectory was huge and it seemed to me that he would hardly notice I was there. If he wanted me to do things for him, I could cook and clean and wash. While I was there I would decide where to go and what to do next. First of all I had to find out from the police if I was expected to stay in the immediate neighborhood. I would keep trying Mark until I got hold of him. I would phone my parents from Eric's and pay for the call. I had plenty of money, having had nothing much but train fares on which to spend my wages while at Lydstep.

Lights were on in The Studio as I passed it. In fact, I didn't immediately pass it, but stood by the gate for a moment, looking into the half-lit, disordered sitting room, but then I thought that if Felix saw me and came out he would certainly invite me to stay with him, a situation to be avoided. The White Rose was shut, as it was bound to be at this hour, but the general store was open. I went in to buy myself a bar of chocolate. Jane Trintowel was standing at the counter, being served with a tin of coffee and twenty cigarettes.

I remember these things because I stood staring at them for perhaps a whole minute before she must have become aware of my gaze and turned around. She said hello, then saw my big suitcase, which I had rested on the floor.

"You've left!"

"Yes."

"Yes, just like that? What else?"

"They threw me out." The whole shop could hear, but I cared very little about that. Jane didn't ask me why but paid for her groceries and moved across into a corner. I went with her. "I'm going to Eric," I said. "Just for a couple of nights."

"No, you aren't. He's staying with his sister. Mr. Moxon is taking the services. You're coming to us."

Of course, I did. I made deprecating noises at first, I couldn't possibly, it would be an imposition, that sort of thing.

"If you don't," Jane said. "Charles will never forgive me."

Mr. Waltham, the grocer, said he would look after my cases until Gerald Trintowel brought the car and fetched them up to White Lodge. Jane was very hospitable and fond of company and, not to underrate her kindness, I think she was quite excited at doing something which, as she put it, was "one in the eye for the Cosways."

A tremendous gossip, she wanted to know everything. Had John done it? If he had, why? Was it something to do with "both those women carrying on with Felix Dunsford"? Ignorant of village life, I was amazed that she knew, but I soon understood that the whole of Windrose did.

"Even Eric?" I said.

"Oh, well, probably not, but they always say the husband, or in this case, the fiancé, is the last to know, don't they?"

She wanted to know if it was true the Cosways possessed a solid gold Roman figurine and that this was the murder weapon. I disappointed her by telling her it was a glass vase and it was broken, though it had been Roman.

"And he hit her with it in front of everyone, those three girls—well, they're not girls anymore, are they?—and their mother and you?"

"Not Zorah and not me," I said. "I wasn't there and Ella wasn't."

As I said it I knew I wished I had been. I wished I had seen what had happened so that I could have helped John, but then Gerald came into the room with my two cases and gave us drinks, a strong vodka and orange for me which he said I must need after being turned out into the snow.

After I'd been up to the guest bedroom, I asked Jane if I could make a phone call to London. It would be nothing these days, a call one made as casually and easily as phoning the people next door or in the flat upstairs. Things were different then. This was "long distance," almost a serious undertaking. Of course she said I could but again I failed to get an answer and I felt I couldn't ask again without saying I would pay, an offer which I knew she would refuse. Of an inveterately inquiring turn of mind—nosy, according to Gerald—she wanted to know if it was "some very close friend you wanted to ring."

I had to tell her, though as I did so I remembered what she had said about Charles never forgiving her. "He's my boyfriend, but I don't think he is anymore. Still, I ought to let him know what's happened."

"Try again in the morning," she said.

I had slept as soundly as usual since Winifred's death, but that night I couldn't get to sleep, although there was no doubt White Lodge was a far warmer and more comfortable house than Lydstep Old Hall. Perhaps my wakefulness had something to do with the fact that, taking off my skirt, I felt in one of the pockets and found the triangular piece of green glass I had picked up off the drawing-room floor. Though I handled it with care, I still cut my finger on its razor-sharp edge.

Next day Mark came to Lydstep to look for me. He came on the train and walked to Windrose from Marks Tey. While I was trying to phone him he was half a mile away down the hill, inquiring for me in the White Rose and in the shop. If Mrs. Waltham had been serving there when Jane and I met the day before, a piece of gossip as juicy as the foreign girl being turned out of Lydstep Old Hall would have been all over the village before nightfall. But her husband was rather a taciturn man and the shop assistant from Sudbury had no interest in me, the Cosways, or the Trintowels. All that concerned her was knocking off and going home as soon as possible. So she had no information on my whereabouts to offer him. The landlord of the White Rose had no idea who I was. I had never been in there and he had never heard my name.

By then Mark had already been to Lydstep Old Hall. Apparently—according to Ella later—he had been very worried about me. Being Mark, interested in people the way I believe few men are, he must have remembered all the things I had told him about the Cosways' eccentricities and decided I was in some sort of danger. He hadn't seen Mrs. Cosway, only Ida, who told him I had left the day before, saying I would like my luggage sent on. I had gone to London, she supposed. Mark had phoned his brother, Isabel's husband, but they knew nothing of my whereabouts.

Circumstances seemed to conspire against him finding me. Eric, from whom he might have inquired and who would have made an intelligent guess that I was with the Trintowels, was away, staying with his sister. Mark went to various houses in the village, ringing doorbells at random, but by chance not to June Prothero's or Bridget Mills's parents. At last he came to White Lodge, but it was a fine day and Gerald was playing golf while Jane and I had driven in to Sudbury to visit the market.

He told me all this weeks later, not by then, for another reason, regretting any of it. My failure to get in touch with him when I was in what was, after all, a dire situation, showed him that our relationship was over. If I had loved him as he loved me, I would have gone straight to him and all the invitations from country neighbors would have meant nothing to me. So, very dispirited and low, he went back to London.

The train had come from Ipswich and there was already someone in the carriage he got into, a girl of about my own age. She was hunting through her bags, looking more and more distraught. He asked her what was wrong and she told him she had lost her wallet or it had been stolen. Few people had credit cards then, but twenty pounds had been in that wallet and her ticket. Of course, it was the oldest con trick in the world, but Mark didn't think it was a con trick and he was right. He explained to the ticket collector and was obliged to buy her a new ticket. He lent her five pounds—it went quite a long way in those days—bought her a cup of tea at Liverpool Street Station, and escorted her on the subway to the flat she shared with four others in Islington. She told him her name was Anna and he, sore from what he thought of as my rejection of him, asked when he could see her again.

She has been his wife for as long as I have been married to Charles. So failing to find me was good for him and for Anna too.

Charles came down for the weekend and we met again.

But before that, two visitors came to see me at White Lodge. Strickland was the first of them. My diary, he said, had been "infinitely helpful," though he didn't say in what way. It must have had something to do with the characters of the people involved and, notably, of John's.

I asked about him. When he came out of the hospital, they would release him, wouldn't they?

He didn't answer. Disappointment and a kind of fear descended on me but I managed quite a comprehensive answer when Strickland asked me about the Roman vase.

"You said in your diary that John Cosway loved it," he said. "What did you mean by that?"

"It wasn't his in the way the objects were that he carried in his dressing-gown pockets," I said. "I suppose it didn't really belong to any of them. It should have been public property, in a museum somewhere. But I think it was the only thing he truly loved, the way he isn't really able to love people. He used to touch it—well, caress it." I was proud of that word, which I had just learned, though I feared misusing it. "I didn't think of this before," I said. "It suddenly came into my head. But I think he was lying on the ground after it happened, not because he'd done what was done to Winifred but because the vase that was so precious to him was broken."

Strickland looked strangely at me, but he thanked me for what I'd said. I held up my hand with the bandage around my left forefinger. "I cut myself on a piece of it," I said. "That happened much later. It was a piece I picked up from the carpet. Apart from Ella, John was the only one who didn't have cut hands after . . . it happened. He couldn't have picked up that vase and struck Winifred with it without cutting his hands. I know he couldn't."

"I know," he said. "You put that in your diary."

After he had gone I reflected on it, quite astonished at the discovery I had made and voiced without any prior consideration or even realizing I had made it. But I was convinced of its truth. The whole essence of John, of what he was, seemed contained in his grief over a broken object, the whole truth in the evidence of the cut and the intact hands.

If Strickland had looked at my drawings he said nothing about them. They, at least, needed no translation.

"Now, I know you won't want to see her," said Jane, who was taking me over with a kind of motherly bossiness unknown in my own family. She made me her daughter long before I became her daughter-in-law. "What shall I tell her? I don't in the least mind being rude."

I laughed. "Of course I'll see her. I rather like her."

Jane wasn't too pleased. "On your own head be it."

Ella threw herself on me. Not exactly into my

arms because they weren't outstretched. To say she put me into her arms would be more accurate. "Oh, I do love this house, don't you, Kerstin? I haven't been here for years and there have been lots of changes. I think that's lovely, don't you? That's the trouble with the Hall." The Cosways always referred to their home as "the Hall." "It never changes. I don't think Mrs. Trintowel was very pleased to see me but I can't help that. I came to see you. How are you?"

"I'm fine."

"A man came looking for you." It was then that she told me about Mark's visit and how he had called on the Cosways. "It just made me think how lucky you were to have your man want to find you. Felix hasn't given the slightest sign he wants to find me. I've phoned the pub over and over but I've given up now, it got humiliating. I've been to The Studio too, but he doesn't answer the door. You'll tell me I ought to go into the pub because I'll find him there, won't you?"

Knowing it would do no good, I assured her this was the last thing I would tell her. But I lacked the heart to say he couldn't have made it plainer that all was over between them.

"I've cried so much I don't think I've any water left in my eyes." This was a line from a recent film I had seen with Mark and I knew Ella had seen with Bridget Mills. "I shall never get over him," she said. "I shall never marry now. I shall never have children. What goes on in the head of someone like him who goes about ruining women's lives? Do you know, Kerstin?"

I said truthfully that I did not.

"Now, I have to ask you something. You may say no, but I do hope you won't. Mother wants to see you. She's very sorry for the way she behaved and she knows it's too late to make all that right, but it would be a great favor on your part if you'd just come and see her for half an hour. I'll actually fetch you if you like."

The proffered lift I wouldn't need. I said I would come. At any rate, I thought, I could make my own time and said I would be with Mrs. Cosway on Sunday morning.

"You're mad," said Jane when she had shown Ella out. "Letting that woman walk all over you."

"I don't think she'll do that," I said, while having no idea what she would do or why she wanted to see me. I was accepting the invitation for the sake of finding out about John.

I had several telephone conversations with Mark. I felt grateful to him for coming to look for me and even more grateful to him for not finding me. Perhaps I knew that if he had and I had gone back to London with him, our relationship would have moved on to a permanent footing. He thought that too. He was cold with me, or rather he was cool. But that word has taken on such an over-used new meaning that it can hardly any longer be applied in its old sense. It was only when I said that I was determined to stay friends with him, and communicating attentive friends, that he warmed to me and told me about Anna. I agreed to meet him in London, and meet her too, before he left for America.

I hadn't gone down to the village once since I went to stay at White Lodge. Fear of meeting a Cosway kept me away, but once I had agreed to the invitation to Lydstep Old Hall, I felt that encountering one of them would no longer be an ordeal but only a preliminary step toward Sunday morning. In any event, I met none of them.

It was a bright blue-skied day, the low-hanging sun making the kind of long shadows that seem uncanny at eleven in the morning. The greengrocer's was crowded, but nothing to Walthams' shop which brimmed with people, and at first it looked as if everyone I knew except the Cosways were in there: Eric, Bridget Mills, June Prothero, Bill Cusp and his son George, and the architect's wife Felix had walked home from church that day. He wasn't there and nor was Serena Lombard, who had moved into her father's house. I had no shopping to do, for, except when she ran out of essentials, Jane did all hers for the household in the Sudbury shops, and I was turning away when Eric came out with two carrier bags of food.

"I mustn't be a minute," he said. "I have a bride to marry in half an hour."

I wasn't aware at that time of that particular usage, that a vicar or rector "marries" a couple just as they "marry" each other, and I must have looked at him aghast, thinking he must be deranged or that he had really already found a substitute for Winifred.

"A wedding," he said, realizing I hadn't understood. "Diane Waltham and her fiancé from Duke's Colne." His bags on the ground on either side of him, he took off his glasses, rubbed them on his sleeve and put them on again. "Life must go on."

This I recognized as a reference to his loss.

"I have been spending a lot of time at the Hall since I came back from my sister's," he said. "We find each other's company mutually comforting. I gather you have left them. May I hope to see you in church on Sunday?"

I told him Mrs. Cosway had invited me to come and see her on Sunday morning.

"Some other time, then." He made church attendance sound like a purely social duty. "I must get off. This wedding, you know." I thought then that in all the time I knew him I had never heard Eric make a single reference to God or the Christian faith or heaven or hell except when he was conducting a service.

Guests started arriving at the church about two minutes after he had closed the rectory door behind him. Felix's signboard can't have been very securely fixed to the gate for it was already hanging off at an angle. The bridegroom and his best man (I supposed), both in gray morning suits and carrying gray top hats, arrived in a battered old car, its rear license plate tied on with string. Standing about, I was beginning to feel cold and I continued with my walk, taking the long road around back to White Lodge.

A section of that road passed through woodland, where branches of trees on either side come close to meeting in the middle. I heard a car behind me and stepped on to the grass verge, close to the trunks of those trees, as Zorah's Lotus went past me, not fast enough to prevent my seeing Felix sitting next to her, his arm resting lightly along the back of the driver's seat.

28

CHARLES OFFERED TO WAIT FOR ME, PARKED ON the forecourt, but I told him I had no idea how long I would be and I would walk back. Yet when I saw his car disappear down the drive, I felt a great sense of isolation, very different from my feelings when I had first come there seven months before. The house had been hidden under its quivering mantle of green leaves while now it was veiled in a dark web. I wondered why nothing was ever planted in those two red earthenware pots and why, kept empty, they were there at all, and then I rang the doorbell.

As that first time, Ida came. For once she was without her apron and she had shoes on instead of slippers. It looked as if they were going out or, more likely, some guest, deemed special, was expected for lunch. The drawing room was diminished by the absence of the Roman vase, its gloom not much alleviated by an alabaster lamp and a set of watercolors, restored by Zorah. Ella, in bright pink wool, got up and kissed me, an action I saw as showing defiance to her mother. But Mrs. Cosway was as affable as she ever could be, asking me to sit down close to the fireplace.

"We were just about to have coffee," said Ida. "Can I offer you some?"

I had had my fill of Ida's coffee every morning for seven months, but I accepted for the sake of being polite. This time, when she came back with the tray, she had resumed her apron but the pins in her hair were gone. The cotton gloves were no longer on her hands. They had been replaced by bandages which were soon streaked with black when she had made up the fire with pieces of coal to supplement the logs. Mrs. Cosway too had patched hands. She was as usual in her unrelieved black, a tall, crow-like figure, folded up on the sofa, her legs too long for the distance between seat cushions and floor. On the console table behind her, the geode had replaced the Roman vase. But the worst thing about that room was that the bloodstains, splashes and drops, were still there; paler, yellower, but resistant as blood is to soap and water and cleansers. Only redecorating and a replacement carpet would serve, as the police had advised. If I knew the Cosways, and I believe I did, those dull yellow-brown spots and streaks would be there as long as they were.

In spite of what Ella had said, I knew Mrs. Cosway wouldn't apologize to me. I wouldn't have known how to react if she had, saying sorry would be such a departure from the norm for her. She went as far to compensate by asking me how I was, an inquiry to which I am certain she wanted no reply, so I only smiled and took my cup of coffee from Ida.

"I don't know how much you have heard about what's happening to my son," Mrs. Cosway said. "Of course there's so much tittle-tattle in this village that one can't keep anything dark for a moment."

I hadn't heard any gossip, I said, but the police had told me he was in the hospital.

"He has probably appeared in the magistrates' court by now. Of course, nobody tells me anything. They haven't the courtesy for that. His trial proper may not be for a long time." Mrs. Cosway looked hard at me, then from one daughter to the other, as if expecting a chorus of support. "If it takes place at all."

"Don't be so cryptic, Mother," said Ella.

"I was merely leading up to what must be a very shocking disclosure, Ella. I never have believed it necessary to call a spade a bloody shovel without preamble." There could be no mistaking from the way Mrs. Cosway leaned toward me, lifting her head, that I was being particularly addressed. "It is most probable, indeed a foregone conclusion, that John will be found unfit to plead."

The triumph in her face was chilling. "I don't know what that means," I said.

"It's no good asking me." Mrs. Cosway's assumed graciousness was quickly giving place to her usual manner. "I don't know the ins and outs of these things. All it means to me is that since John is in an advanced state of schizophrenia, in other words, he's stark mad, he won't be able to understand the charge or say whether he's guilty or not guilty or, probably, even remember what he's done. The trial will stop and he'll be sent to a prison for the criminally insane. There you are."

I think that even Ida and Ella were shocked. This, after all, was John's mother talking. She seemed to read our faces.

"Dr. Lombard told me his trouble was brought on by a severe emotional shock. He always knew what he was talking about, he was a wonderful man. Possibly the birth of Ella. John wasn't the precious baby anymore, you see. That was Dr. Lombard's view and he was always right."

Perhaps my "Really?" sounded doubtful.

"Please don't start arguing with me again, Kerstin. Dr. Lombard was sure and that was quite enough for me. It should be enough for you."

"Why did you want me to come?" I could easily have asked her this back in June. Seven months later it took a great deal of screwing up my courage. "Was it just to tell me this?"

"Isn't it enough?" It was a week since I had heard the Cosway laugh, the coughing bark, as often as not uttered with the mouth closed. Mrs. Cosway laughed like this for a long while, shaking her head. "My purpose was principally to tell you that John will be unfit to plead. This will be something for you to tell all your new friends. And if you want an explanation I should ask that son of the house who brought you here. Oh, yes, Ida saw him from the hall window. He's a lawyer. Ask him."

I did ask him. But first, of course, I said goodbye and thank you for the coffee, before escaping from that drawing room. I had been in there less than half an hour and wished very much I had asked Charles to wait or at least come back for me. A little way down the drive, Ella caught up with me. She had put on a pink parka with white fur or faux fur around hood and hem, a garment more suitable for skiing than the Essex countryside on a damp gray day. The tree branches hung quite still and thin shreds of mist wove themselves around their trunks. Gray and white toadstools like hats with frilled brims grew along the wet grass verge.

"You can eat them, you know," Ella said, picking one and holding it up to my face. "They're quite harmless but people are such cowards, aren't they? Felix cooks fungus for himself. It doesn't cost anything, you see. Have you seen anything of him?"

The last thing I would have mentioned was my sighting of him and Zorah in the Lotus. "Have you?"

"I think he's gone away. Not for good, I don't mean that. He'll be back. I don't think he's capable of love. What do you think?"

"I don't know, Ella. I suppose everyone is capable of it."

"When John is sent to Broadmoor or wherever it is, I mean a place for the criminally insane, the house reverts to Mother for her life and the money comes to us. Well, it was never right that John had it."

"Wasn't it?"

"If Felix knew I was going to have money of my own, do you think he'd come back to me?"

The morning had brought too many shocks. This last one had almost struck me dumb. I don't know how I would have answered her for, at that moment, Eric's car came up the hill and drew up beside us.

"Goodness, I quite forgot he was coming to lunch," Ella said, but she got into the passenger seat beside him and waved good-bye to me.

Alone and thankful to be, I considered what she had said and thought it quite possible that Felix might return to her when he knew about the money. Of course, whatever she got from the estate would be very little compared with what Zorah had, but Zorah would never marry him. If he was a playboy or would have liked to be, then she was a playgirl and successful at it.

Charles told me a lot about an accused's fitness to plead. He said that the issue could be raised by the trial judge on his own initiative or at the request of the prosecution or the defense. If neither party does so, the judge should do so himself if he has doubts about the accused's fitness. If the issue is raised by either party, or the judge has doubts, the issue must be tried by a jury specially empaneled for the purpose. If it were decided that John was unfit to plead, an order would be made committing him to a hospital for the criminally insane.

"Prison, really," said Charles. "His life in there would be hell on earth."

"How long for?" I asked.

"During Her Majesty's pleasure, is how they put it. For life, is what it probably means."

Those words stayed in my mind and whenever I was alone they surfaced. I fretted miserably about John, fearing I would have to go home to Sweden without knowing what his fate was to be. Then he came home. I heard the news no more than a few hours after he was brought back to Lydstep Old Hall, Jane running into the house to tell me.

I will never know if it was the diary or what I said to Strickland, John's love for the Roman vase, his unwounded hands, or the cut hands of Ida and her mother that released him. But at home he was, the police apparently having insufficient evidence to charge him with anything.

Once at Lydstep Old Hall, he seemed to me to be in danger from those two, though I wasn't able to formulate what they might realistically do to him. But Ella, at least, was in the house, for what that was worth. I had had dreadful misgivings about her, sometimes thinking she was losing her mind. Like some operatic heroine, a Lucia di Lammermoor perhaps, she was distraught and wandering, saying things that seemed scarcely sane, that she would camp on Felix's doorstep, she would kill him and herself.

She wanted to spend part of every day with me. Telling me repeatedly that I was her only friend and no one else cared about her, she still had some diffidence about invading White Lodge. Charles had gone back to London, James was up at his university, and Gerald mostly out somewhere, but Jane was usually at home, and Ella, insensitive as she was, couldn't fail to notice that she wasn't welcome. I too was made very aware of the difficulties attendant on being a guest, even a very kindly received and wonderfully treated guest, in someone else's house. Not that I particularly wanted to see Ella, but I longed to be free to see her. Jane made it very clear how deeply she disliked the Cosways. Also she had heard all about the scene at the rectory gate, as had everyone else in the village, churchgoers or not.

"Even Julia herself wouldn't have behaved like that," was her comment.

So Ella and I arranged to meet on neutral ground. There was a teashop in Windrose, the front part of it selling handicrafts and souvenirs no one ever seemed to buy, so depressing and shabby had they become over the years, and the back part a café with four sets of tables and chairs and a counter where the cakes under a glass dome looked as old as the souvenirs. There Ella and I had begun meeting either for morning coffee or afternoon tea. Ella wanted to vary our venue to take in the White Rose, but there I was adamant, fearing another encounter with Felix.

"I know he and I will never be together again, Kerstin," she said sadly. "It's just that I thought if we went to the pub I could look at him across the bar. I could just look at him and remember. He'll never see me in my bridesmaid's dress now, will he?"

"How is John?" I said. He was my concern and I wished passionately I could see him, though I knew the chances were that, like Felix and the pink silk dress, I never would.

"I don't know," Ella said. She sounded impatient. "I hardly see him. He's in the library all the time."

That pleased me. He was happier in there than I had ever seen him. I could imagine him trying to discover the square root of minus one, doing the theorems which soothed him, moving the hated Bible from Longinus's hands and replacing it with the works of one of those writers of classical antiquity. Who would replace it now Winifred was gone?

"No one had been in there," said Ella, "since they came and took him away. Mother said there was a trail of blood leading into the middle bit but there wasn't. I looked. And there couldn't have been, you know, because John's hands weren't cut. She must know that now, though she's never said."

"Is he all right?"

"I said I don't know." Ella was growing irritable as she always did when the conversation wandered too far from her own troubles. "He's never exactly all right, is he? Ida takes him food in there on a tray, otherwise he wouldn't eat. She says he seems afraid of her. He's very afraid of Mother. You can't wonder really, can you? After all, he may be mad but he's not stupid."

"No," I said. "No."

"I think he remembers they both accused him of killing Winifred and he does understand cause and effect. He thinks it's because of what they said that the police took him away."

"Can you wonder?"

"Well, perhaps not. But do we have to be always talking about John? He's really very boring, you know. You'll say the mad are and it's not their fault but one doesn't have to be always discussing them. This coffee is awful, isn't it? It's worse than the stuff Ida makes. I dreamed last night that Felix came to the Hall and said he'd really loved me all along and we'd get married and he'd take me to Morocco on our honeymoon."

I asked why Morocco.

"I don't know, it sounds so romantic. Anyway, it was nothing to do with me, it was in the dream. I believed it, you know, I thought it was all true. But it wasn't. I woke up and I was crying as if my heart would break—only it's broken already. Do you want a cake?"

"Not one of those," I said.

She hadn't mentioned Zorah and I didn't ask. The next day was Winifred's funeral.

"You won't go to that," Jane said to me later that day.

It was more of a statement of fact than an inquiry. I was growing fretful and fidgety under her increasing habit of directing my life. I liked her—I was always to like her—and I could see that she had singled me out to be her son's wife, something that I too was soon to desire, though her selection had more to do with her own taste than with Charles's or my preferences. But I was determined to tread that fine line between resisting her commands and being a good guest, even if it rather wore me down, for I had so recently come from another and much more savage domination.

"I think I'll go," I said. "She was always pleasant to me. I had no quarrel with her."

"I hope you won't regret it," Jane said in the grim tone she used when thwarted.

It was hard to see how I could feel much regret, even though there should be scenes among the

Cosways and hysterical outbursts. In the event, nothing like that took place. Mrs. Cosway wasn't there. For the very good reason, I found out later, that she was at home being closely questioned by the police. Ida turned up, wearing the big hat I had last seen on Winifred's head and on which Eric had complimented her. Ella came to sit next to me and chatted away through the solemn voluntaries.

"Have you seen the papers this morning? There's a group photograph of us all and one of those Ida took of you and me and Winifred. Mrs. Lilly sneaked them out and gave them to the paper. Well, sold them, more likely. I don't absolutely know it was her, but it's an intelligent guess, don't you think? Mother said it was you, but I told her she shouldn't make accusations like that."

Someone had had the idea of bringing the coffin up the aisle to the Dead March in Handel's **Saul.** It was only the fact that we had to rise which stemmed the tide of Ella's chatter. Even so, as Mr. Trewith began to say the words, something about man born of woman being full of misery—the women, presumably, were as happy as the day is long—she managed to whisper in my ear that she knew she looked awful in black and hoped Felix wouldn't be there to see her.

He wasn't but Eric was, looking thinner and even more gaunt than usual. Instead of joining us, he sat alone in the pew several times occupied by Felix. What do people think about at funerals? If they were close to the dead, no doubt they think of what they have lost, their past with them and their future without them. As for the rest of us, I suppose our thoughts wander as mine did that day, returning always from these journeys through the associative process to John, then to Felix and Zorah. When did they meet? How did they come together? Where were they now? And then, as the coffin was carried out again to begin its journey to the crematorium, I thought of something else.

It seems strange that this hadn't really come into my mind before. It entered now, driving away everything else. If John hadn't killed Winifred, who had? I said it aloud to Ella on the dreadful drive back after Winifred was ashes. Ida had gone home, driven by Eric. Ella looked blankly at me, as if she hadn't heard. I repeated it. I had a horrible feeling of being doomed to say this over and over, but unheard.

"I don't want to think about it," she said.

I found myself coming out with the absurd usage I hated so much from her. "You'll say it's no business of mine."

"Oh, no, Kerstin. No, I won't. It's just that it's so awful, one's mother and one's sister . . ."

"Which one?" I said, my voice a breath or a whisper.

She pulled the car into a lay-by and switched off the engine. Her face was full of woe, like a hurt child's, her eyes glistening with tears. "I don't know." Hope—a ridiculous hope—sent the color into her white cheeks. "Does it have to be either of them?"

"What else?"

"I thought someone might have got in from outside. By the French windows. No, they couldn't, could they? That's impossible. And Winifred couldn't have—well, done it herself. No. No, she couldn't have."

We sat silent in the car, starting to shiver. Our breath steamed up the windows. "I'd better tell you."

I had reached the point of dreading revelations. I wished I hadn't asked which one, but I had asked. It was too late.

"The police came yesterday. They asked a lot of questions and then they took Mother and Ida away to a police station somewhere. When they brought them back it was very late. They were questioned separately and—well, I'll have to tell you now I've begun. Ida said Mother did it and Mother said Ida did."

"Would you like me to drive?" I said.

"I can't be always letting you take over," she said, but she was half out of the car by then.

I moved into the driver's seat. It wasn't yet four but already dark and I put the lights on. The road we were on was a narrow lane, which was why it had lay-bys, and tree branches met above our head, creating a dark winding tunnel. Much as I wanted to know, I resolved not to ask Ella any more. She was crying by then. All those five or six miles back to Windrose no cars passed us and we met only one, its headlights' beam full on, blinding me. Still crying quietly, Ella had laid her head back against the seat. When I saw the dark bulk of All Saints' tower loom up ahead, I stopped the car and asked her if she was all right.

Instead of replying, she said, "They both told me and that's what they said. Ida blamed Mother and Mother blamed Ida. Both had cut hands, you see. Each one of them described what had happened and it was—I don't quite know how to put this—it was as if the roles were reversed in their accounts. I mean Mother described Ida as doing it exactly as Ida described Mother as doing it. Mother said Ida did it because she couldn't bear Winifred doing what she was doing to Eric, and Ida said Mother did it when Ella came in and told her Winifred was going to Felix. But I think one of them did it to put the blame on John. To get rid of him, you see, and get the house the only way they could."

As if it was all in the day's work, the kind of thing that might happen in any family. "What happens now?" I asked.

"They said they'd want to question them again.

I mean, I think they let Mother go home on account of her age. And someone had to be there to look after John."

I had nothing to say about any of it. "I'll take you home," I said, forgetting it was her car.

"The police were there again when I came out. They tried asking John which one of them it was. They had to go into the library after him. Of course he wouldn't say anything at all, let alone answer them." We were on the drive by then and again I stopped when the house came into sight. Light streamed not very brightly out of the front doorway as Strickland and another man came out and got into their car. "They've been there all this time," Ella said wonderingly.

As the car passed us, Strickland turned his eyes in our direction and nodded. It was just a nod, cold and formal. I drove up onto the gravel as an unseen hand closed the door.

"I can't go in there, Kerstin."

"All right," I said. "Wait a minute. Try to keep calm."

"I can't go into a house where those two are. One of them is a murderer, Kerstin. Or both of them. Both of them could have done it. It might be me next. I can't go in. I should never sleep, never again. Oh, what shall I do?"

We had been out for hours. I had told Jane I would be back by four, for I had never meant to go to the crematorium but had only done so at Ella's insistence. Sitting there beside her, I thought ungratefully how hopeless it was to be obliged to tell someone of your comings and goings, your whereabouts and the time of your return, and resolved I would never be in that trap again. Of course I was in it because I got married but somehow that was different.

"Did you mean that about not going back?" I said.

"I can't go in there ever again."

"You'll have to go in to get your things. Phone Bridget and ask her if you can stay, pack a bag, and I'll drive you to the Millses'."

After a good deal of arguing she did. She was in the house a very short time and when she came back she was breathless. "Bridget was very nice about it, said I could stay as long as I wanted, but we know what that means, don't we? I saw Ida. She looked terrible, I mean more terrible than usual, all gray in the face. Strickland had been what she called cross-examining her for hours."

I asked her if she had seen John.

"Oh, no. He was in the library. He lives there now apart from when he's out for a walk. Could they have Mother and Ida both up in court for murder?"

"I don't know," I said.

I took her to the cottage where Bridget Mills lived with her elderly parents. Where they would put her I couldn't guess.

"I shall go and see Felix tomorrow," were her parting words, "and he'll have to take me in even if he doesn't want to."

Jane I found in a panic because, in her own words, I had disappeared. The police had been and returned my diary. I took it up to my bedroom and wrote down the events of the day. That evening I discussed with Jane and Gerald—discreetly, I hope—what was to be done about Ella. Saying nothing about the relentless questioning of Mrs. Cosway and Ida, I told them of her fear of going back into Lydstep Old Hall, something they both seemed to understand without further explanation.

"The Millses won't want her for long," Jane said. "They've only got two bedrooms and Ronald Mills is bedbound."

I said nothing about Felix. "Perhaps she could get a flat somewhere with Bridget."

"Bridget Mills is needed at home."

There seemed no solution except for Ella to give in and return home. To have nowhere to go, nowhere to lay one's head but with grudging friends, is dreadful to think of. I felt a little like that myself, though the Trintowels were far from grudging. I thought that night of phoning Isabel and asking her to put me up, but I remembered she was Mark's sister-in-law and very fond of Mark. Next morning I phoned Strickland and then I went into Colchester and booked my passage back to Göteborg for a week ahead.

I told Jane at lunchtime and she put up a good many objections. But I had already spoken to Charles on the phone and arranged to meet him in London in two days' time. He had promised to find me a cheap hotel.

Meeting Ella next day was unavoidable, but I refused tea and cakes at the souvenir shop and we drove into Sudbury. It was a pleasant, pretty little town then, with a market square and water meadows by the Stour. Morning rain had been blown away by a sharp little wind and by the time we were in Friar Street, looking for a tea place, the sky was pale winter blue with streaks of gray and yellowish cloud.

Ella, of course, seethed with complaints about the hospitality of Bridget Mills and her parents. In Bridget's place she would have given up her bed to the guest and slept on the sofa herself, but in fact the roles had been reversed. She didn't know how long she could stand it. She had called at The Studio at nine, knowing Felix wasn't an early riser and believing she could catch him before he went out, but he wasn't there. The neighbors in that row of cottages were all consulted before she gave up. No one knew where Felix was and the retired colonel next door said he had never spoken to him.

My decision to go to London and come back this way only to Harwich and the Göteborg boat dismayed her.

"But you can't! The police won't let you."

"I've asked them," I said. "They don't mind."

"I wonder what that means," she said. "Does it mean they're going to arrest Mother or Ida? Surely not Mother, not at her age. Maybe the police think they're only saying one of them killed Winifred to protect John."

I said that if this were so, it was a pity they blamed him in the first place. As for me, I had spoken to Strickland and he said I could go. That was all. She asked me why I was going to London first.

Perhaps it was rude, what I said. "Because I want to."

It was almost impossible to repulse Ella. "Where are you going in London? Are you going to stay with Isabel Croft? I wonder if I could come too. I really don't see why not."

I said I wouldn't be staying with Isabel but in an hotel. "What about your work?"

From her position, after Winifred's death, of longing to be back, she had since used her loss as an excuse for not returning. She hadn't, up till then, done an hour's teaching at her Sudbury school, the playground and outbuildings of which we could see from the tea-shop window. "Of course I'll have to go back," she said. "But not quite yet. D'you know, I haven't been to London for ages, literally years."

I couldn't encourage her. The sad fact was that I didn't want her. There are words for people like

Ella today and perhaps there were then, only I hadn't heard of them: "clingy" and "needy" were among them. I could almost, but never quite, sympathize with Felix Dunsford. She plainly wanted to stay out, keep away from Windrose as long as she could, and after we had talked exhaustively about the Millses, her mother, how Eric was coping, and when she and Felix would next meet, she suggested we have lunch in one of Sudbury's hotels.

I didn't care for the idea. Before I went the next day I wanted to see John for the last time and there was a half-formed plan in my mind of catching him on his walk—if he went for a walk. He didn't always, but he often did when the day was fine and when he did he took one of two routes. I would have to take my chance. I knew the chances of his speaking to me were slight, but he might just say, "Hello, Shashtin," giving my name its proper pronunciation, the way he invariably did. But I was feeling guilty over Ella, irrationally guilty no doubt, but most guilt is irrational. I felt I owed her something because I had refused her the chance of an innocent and harmless trip to London, so I said yes to her lunch invitation. Perhaps I could still be back in time to see John.

In the intervening years, the world has utterly changed. We could park the car anywhere we liked and where we liked was right outside the hotel. Lunch in English country hotels then was quite different from pub lunches today with the menus chalked on blackboards and help-yourself paper napkins. It was all rather grand, the white damask tablecloth, starched stiff, the heavy silver, the waiters; somewhat less pleasant was their attitude, slightly contemptuous, faintly amused, that two women should be eating in a restaurant alone together.

We ate and I clock-watched. Would I be in time for John? If not, could I manage to see him tomorrow before I went to London? Ella smoked between courses, wreathing the air above us with gray plumes, but no one minded in those days, no one even looked disapproving. Most people were doing the same. We weren't back in the car until nearly three and I knew we would be too late. Plainly, Ella didn't know what to do, where to go. Bridget was at work till five. Her parents slept most of the afternoon away and they hadn't given her a key. Did I think she could come to White Lodge with me?

"You'll say Jane Trintowel won't like it."

For once she was right but I couldn't bring myself to say so. "Ella, couldn't you go home? You're going to have to sometime. What else can you do?"

An explosive "No!"

Not if I came with her? I suggested this most reluctantly, though I did think that this way at least I could contrive to see John. An argument ensued, Ella insisting that she would never set foot in Lydstep Old Hall again and I telling her to be realistic and ask what options she had. All the time this was going on she drove erratically, sometimes mounting the grass verge, and I could see what Zorah had meant when she told her to improve her driving. In spite of all this, we came safely into Windrose just before half past three, the question of where Ella was to go not resolved.

The sun was setting in the distance behind Lydstep Old Hall, a crimson and orange sunset showing under the hem of a black cloud curtain. I got out of the car outside the church and stared at it, seeing something wrong, off-key, the red glare just in the wrong place, not due west where it should have been, where sunsets always were. And then I saw a man walking toward me, down the village street, past the White Rose, past the general store and the butcher's, and he too was in the wrong place. John never came into Windrose. Years had passed since he had walked this way and the locals had laughed at him. He wore his winter coat with the Black Watch tartan blanket over it and he was holding his sleeping bag unzipped around his shoulders.

I began to move slowly to meet him, hoping in vain that he would smile.

29

UNLIKE THORNFIELD, UNLIKE MANDERLEY, those mansions of fiction, most of the house survived the fire. The local fire brigade, composed of volunteers, got to Lydstep Old Hall before it reached the south side of the house, but the drawing room and those rooms along the passage I had never been in and the library, all those were burnt out. The ten thousand books in the library resisted the volunteers' hoses for a long while and nothing that had been in there was left but the statue of Longinus, which was found next day, lying on the lawn.

It was Cox the gardener who phoned for help. The first time he ever went into Lydstep Old Hall was to pick up the telephone and do the only thing he could to lessen its destruction. Next day he went into the pub and told everyone prepared to listen, and that I am sure was most people, that he had found "Miss Ida" sitting at the kitchen table with a knife in her hand and a bowl of water in front of her, peeling potatoes. He got no answer from her when he asked her where her mother and her brother were. The phone, of course, was in the dining room, and although he hadn't a phone of his own, he knew how to dial Emergency. The drawing room was impenetrable because of the flames and smoke. Later on he heard that Mrs. Cosway had been in there, asleep on the sofa, and as for her son, "the one that's off his rocker," there was no sign of him either.

What had happened to John? He did talk to me a little but most of this I pieced together from what I knew of the place and his habits. He had been out for his walk, came back and saw the flames, and did the kind of thing he would always do: he walked away from something alien and different and which frightened him. It was lucky for me, and I hope for him, that we met where we did. At that moment, when we met in the village street, I wanted more than anything in the world to take him in my arms and hold him. It was the one thing I could never, must never, do.

Ida was taken to the hospital, though I don't think anything was wrong with her—not physically wrong, that is. Mrs. Cosway was dead. She had been overcome by smoke and fumes and at her age didn't stand a chance. Dr. Barker told Ella she would have known nothing of what happened to her. Ella wouldn't go back to what remained of the house. Eric gave her one of the bedrooms at the rectory and offered another to John. Kind though it was, I knew he wouldn't do it but stood shaking his head and refusing to step over the rectory threshold.

He and I went back together to the near-ruin of Lydstep Old Hall because he wouldn't go anywhere else. It was late evening by then. The fire brigade and the police had left after telling us the house was unsafe even to set foot in. We were forbidden to go there. But we did go, making our way up the hill close by the hedge. People who have no experience of living in the English countryside thirty-five years ago have no idea how dark it was by night. Those were the days before what is now called light pollution, when the sky wasn't dark red from the lights of the nearest towns but impenetrable, sometimes starry, black. There were no stars visible that night. Without the flashlight I borrowed from Eric, getting to Lydstep Old Hall would have been impossible.

John's bedroom had gone when the drawing room went and the library too was a blackened ruin. Everything was covered up with tarpaulins and battens had been nailed up to shut off the drawing room but there was nothing to stop us standing at the end of what had been the passage and looking at where the library and the labyrinth had been. Is there any sadder sight than a burnt-out library? The moon rose slowly and eerily, shedding a pale cold light over the ruins. We stood outside and looked. The temperature was normal for a January night but for once John seemed not to feel the cold. His face showed no emotion, it never did, and perhaps he felt none to show. I don't know, but he addressed to me the longest sentence I ever heard him utter.

"I am thinking of Ptolemy's great library at Alexandria. That was burnt too."

I found candles in the kitchen and an oil lamp—a real oil lamp, not one of those paraffin heaters—and we had a little light. John had decided to spend the night in the dining room. His ritual objects were gone, his dressing gown and all his quilts were gone. If this distressed him he gave no sign of it. I found pillows and quilts for him in the undamaged bedrooms and made a bed out of them for him on the dining-room floor. Zorah's rooms had been so badly damaged as to be unusable and Ella's suffered more from the water and chemical sprays the fire brigade had used than from the fire itself, but my bedroom was untouched. Ida or Mrs. Lilly had stripped the bed once I was gone and I didn't bother to make it up but lay down on a blanket on the mattress with a quilt and a bedspread over me. I slept very little. Worrying about what would happen to John kept me awake, that and the cold. I dared not leave the candles burning. Although so much of the house still stood, the electricity supply was gone and the water in the taps was cold. The phone no longer worked.

I got up at five, lit more candles and the three oil stoves. By the time John was up, silent and expressionless, the kitchen was quite warm. I fried eggs and bacon on top of one of the stoves and boiled a kettle on the other, a slow process. It was all right for one night and one morning, but I knew we couldn't stay here after today. The police wouldn't have let us do what we had done even for the ten hours or so that we had been in the house. I thought of the mental hospital where John had been when he was suspected of killing Winifred and a chill ran through me at the idea of his going back there because there was nowhere else for him to be.

Surely the trust would provide somewhere for him? Would Ella look after him? Somehow I doubted it. There was Ida, of course, but I had no faith in her. I couldn't imagine her returning to the world of the sane and balanced. I don't know now why there was one person, one obvious person, I never thought of.

I washed the dishes as best I could in cold water mixed with the kettle dregs. John had gone. I wasn't worried, I knew where he would be. The passage of locked doors was open now to a flat gray sky, cross-hatched by burnt blackened beams. John stood where he and I had stood the night before. We hadn't been able to see much then. Now it was like looking at some kind of geological phenomenon, a beach or plain of wet black rocks, only these stones were spongy and when you touched them, they made a soggy squelch. Once they had been books. Not one of them was recognizable, not Homer or Euclid or **Mrs. Halliburton's Troubles** or the Bible. All were made one, an undifferentiated amorphous black pulp.

John stood with his sleeping bag around his shoulders, simply staring at it. Impossible to tell if he was upset or angry or afraid. He turned his head when he heard me and he spoke.

"Shashtin."

I loved him then. Again I would have liked to take him in my arms and hold him, protect him forever, save him from the world. Of course I could do nothing. He would have screamed and hidden himself if I had touched him. Suddenly I thought, for the first time really, that his mother was dead. Did he mind? Did he **know?** Whether she had loved him or he had loved her, I didn't know. She alone had been allowed to give him his drug and that must have meant something.

I will try to get him to the rectory, I thought. His sister is there. Eric is there. Surely they won't desert him, abandon him. I walked back to the dining room. Winifred's wedding presents were still there, still covered in sheets, miraculously dry, untouched by fire or water. I heard a key in the front-door lock and I turned around, expecting to see Ella. Zorah was in the hall. In trenchcoat and boots, she looked like a forties star in a war film.

"Hello," she said. "Do you know what's become of my brother?"

I told her.

"How did it happen?"

"Apparently, a log fell out of the fireplace on to the rug. That's what they think. Your mother was asleep and Ida was . . ."

"In the kitchen," she said. "Ella phoned me at six. I'd have come last night if I'd known." We went to look for John. "The man I took him to says he's never to have drugs again. His walking will get better without them and his hands will stop shaking. There's nothing much to be done for what he's got."

John was still standing where I had left him.

"Hello, you," said Zorah.

I didn't know what she meant to do. If she intended to take him away, take him to London or some hotel, I thought it likely, probable, he would simply refuse to go. He smiled a little when he saw her. I am ashamed to admit it but I was jealous. That smile should have been for me. For all that, I was happy to see him follow her out of the front door to where her car was.

"His things?" I said. "He'll need clothes, I don't know if there are any."

"We'll buy new," she said. "We'll buy books. Would you like to go to Italy, John? When we were kids we said we'd go to Venice. We'd go to Florence. Remember? We can go now."

He said nothing but the smile was still there.

"Good-bye, John," I said.

Quite gravely he said, "Good-bye, Shashtin," and with that I had to be content.

Zorah wound down the driver's window. "Lift to White Lodge?"

"No, thanks," I said, "I'd like the walk."

"Whatever happened to that bloody geode?" she said but she didn't wait for an answer.

I spent my last night in Windrose with the Trintowels, staying one night longer than I had meant to. Nothing was talked about but the fire and its consequences and Mrs. Cosway's death. I said very little about John, only that Zorah had taken him away. Jane was mystified by my decision to stay overnight with John in a cold, wet, half-burnt-out house after those supposed to know had told me it was unsafe. She kept asking me why, but I didn't know the answer. In the afternoon I went down to the rectory. Eric's daily woman let me in and I found Eric in the living room with Ella—and Felix.

They were all behaving in a subdued and controlled fashion, talking of course about the fire. I was able to tell Ella what had survived and that I thought the things in her room would be very little damaged.

"Your clothes are all right," I said, "and the dolls are only a bit damp."

"Dolls?" Felix obviously knew nothing of Ella's hobby. "What do you do? Play with them?"

"I'll make a cup of tea," Ella said coldly.

I followed her to the kitchen, that grim high-ceilinged chamber. The only efficient modern thing in it was Winifred's wedding present.

"Thank God," said Ella, "they sent Zorah's fridge here and not to the Hall. Ida would have got her hooks into it."

I drank my tea. I told them I would be leaving the next morning and returning to Sweden in five days' time. Ella said nothing this time about coming to London with me, nothing about her mother's death. She was sitting next to Felix on the sofa, her right hand lying beside his knee, not quite touching it. I kissed her when I left. Thirty-five years were to pass before I saw her again. The two men I never saw, though I occasionally heard of Felix, who became quite a famous artist and at the age of sixty-nine was nominated for some quite important prize.

I walked back to White Lodge, thinking of seeing Charles the next day, thinking of him in a romantic, ardent way, very different from how I had thought of Mark. The feeling I had had for John was of course separate and unique.

Zorah had asked me what started the fire and I gave her the accepted theory: a log had fallen out of the fireplace onto the rug while Mrs. Cosway slept. This was impossible, as anyone acquainted with that room knew well. But the room was destroyed and the fireplace with it, Mrs. Cosway was dead,

John seldom spoke and certainly never about things like that, and Ella had no interest in the fate of the house or the cause of its destruction. That her clothes and dolls were safe was all that concerned her. Ida would certainly never deny the official version.

A log falling from the fire would have toppled onto the brown glazed tiles of the hearth and been stopped from rolling onto the rug by the fender. To prevent such a thing was its function. Ever since the first fire of the winter had been lit, the fender had been in place. I remembered, very distinctly, Ida bringing it from the boot room, placing it around the hearth and telling me—astonished that I didn't know—what it was and what it was called.

No log falling from the fire could have rolled past it. Logs don't have wings, nor are they fired from catapults. So what had really happened?

I believe I know that answer. It has to be. Ida went into the drawing room, clearing up, emptying an ashtray, plumping a seat cushion, performing one of the myriad tasks she set herself every day. The fire had reached that red glowing stage of maximum heat when it can either be left to burn out in ten minutes or fed with more logs, in which case it will lose heat for a moment or two. I think Ida seized her chance, moved away the fender with the toe of her shoe, and again with the toe of her shoe dislodged the topmost log from the fire. Perhaps she watched it and the sparks it scattered catch the tufts of the rug and a little flame flicker, take hold, and strengthen. Or perhaps she went straight back to the kitchen, filled a bowl with water, sat at the table, and began to peel potatoes. It will never be known, I thought, because she will never say.

Why? Because her mother had killed Winifred and burning alive was fit punishment for her? Or because Ida herself had killed Winifred and to lose her home and perhaps her life was fit punishment for **her?** I don't think so. I don't think either of these dramatic solutions is true. I remembered what she said to me that day when Dr. Barker had refused her the prescription.

"Sometimes I think I'd do anything for a change."

Now

SHE CAME. THE WORDS SHE HAD CALLED BACK TO me were "Love to." She had brought Daisy with her, having left Zoë behind with some people of her own age she had met. Charles and Mark and Anna were in the far corner of the bar, but I had decided to make no introductions yet. We sat at a little table, the child quiet and staring, her hands folded in her lap.

Ella looked less like her mother. She had put on a red jacket and shoes with high heels. Her face was discreetly made up and her hair had been done in one of Riga's many hairdressers. That day, it appeared, we had both been to see the art nouveau in Alberta Street, that place of bad dreams for some and fantasies for others, which she had hated and I had loved, anything between the two being impossible. Though nothing like it, though belonging to a different period, it had reminded me of the library at Lydstep Old Hall.

"I was so glad to hear about John," I said.

"Yes," she said rather doubtfully, as if hearing her brother was in a mental hospital or had come to some other bad end would have been better options.

The same old Ella, I thought. I asked Daisy if she would like orange juice or a Coke. "I don't mind," she said meekly, and then, "What can I do, Grandma?"

Inspiration came to me. "I'll make you a Dog Growing," I said, taking the drinks menu off the table and beginning to fold it. "Would you like a glass of rosé, Ella?"

"Rosé?"

"It used to be your favorite."

"Did it? Goodness, I haven't touched the stuff since I married. Still, why not?"

I thought then that she would say who she had married and I waited expectantly. Not Felix, surely. I tried to remember a profile I had read of him in some paper. No wife had been mentioned. Daisy, a serious child, watched me beginning to draw the dog's outline.

"I'm a widow now," Ella said. "Have been for ten years." She sipped the wine and then went on, "You live in Sweden, do you?"

"I live in London. I've lived in London since before I married. You remember my husband, Charles Trintowel? That's him over there. I'll introduce you in a minute."

"Oh, yes." She sounded bored.

Daisy moved to sit beside me and started giggling as I drew the dog's nose and floppy ears. "Is Ida still alive?"

Ella peered into her glass as if into a crystal ball. "She's in an old people's home. After the fire she stayed with us for a while, but we never really got on. Mr. Trewith's wife died—do you remember Mr. Trewith?—and he offered her a job as his housekeeper." I remembered Mr. Trewith. He heard confessions, had perhaps heard Winifred's. "That's what really always suited Ida, housework, waiting on others, that sort of thing. Would never have done for me but of course I was a professional woman."

I had to know. "Felix Dunsford did well for himself. I saw the other day that one of his paintings fetched fifty thousand pounds."

Not a flicker of memory or reminiscence, still less of pain, showed in her face. "Oh, yes. We sold his portrait of Winifred for quite a tidy sum. Not fifty thousand, I may add, but not far off. It's been a godsend to me. Talking of Felix, when we saw you'd become a cartoonist we couldn't understand you never said anything to him about it. You having that in common, I mean." She peered at the now recognizable dog without enthusiasm. "He might have given you some tips."

She laughed, so I laughed and Daisy burst into a peal of laughter. "Who are 'we,' Ella?"

"We?"

"Who did you marry?"

"Oh, didn't I say? Eric, of course."

Eric.

"I wore Winifred's wedding dress, so it wasn't wasted. But you know, Kerstin, the Church of England are so mean-spirited. When Eric died they made me get out of the rectory in three months. Three months to find another place and move out. I ask you."

I pulled open the folds and the spaniel became a dachshund. Once more serious, Daisy put out her hand for the drawing. She folded it, pulled it out, and smiled. "Can I keep it?"

"Of course," I said. "Come and say hello to Charles."

And they did, Daisy with the Dog Growing in her hand.

ABOUT THE AUTHOR

Barbara Vine is the pen name of Ruth Rendell. Her books include the award-winning **A Dark-Adapted Eye, King Solomon's Carpet,** and, most recently, **The Blood Doctor.** Ruth Rendell sits in the House of Lords as a Labour peer. She lives in Maida Vale, London.